Georg Ebers, Clara Bell

Per Aspera - A Thorny Path

Vol. II

Georg Ebers, Clara Bell

Per Aspera - A Thorny Path
Vol. II

ISBN/EAN: 9783337280512

Printed in Europe, USA, Canada, Australia, Japan

Cover: Foto ©Andreas Hilbeck / pixelio.de

More available books at **www.hansebooks.com**

PER ASPERA.

[A THORNY PATH].

BY

GEORG EBERS,

AUTHOR OF "AN EGYPTIAN PRINCESS," "UARDA," ETC.

FROM THE GERMAN BY

CLARA BELL.

IN TWO VOLUMES.—VOL. II.

Copyright Edition.

LEIPZIG 1892

BERNHARD TAUCHNITZ.

LONDON: SAMPSON LOW, MARSTON & COMPANY, LIMITED.
ST. DUNSTAN'S HOUSE, FETTER LANE, FLEET STREET, E.C.
PARIS; C. REINWALD & CIE, 15, RUE DES SAINTS-PÈRES; THE GALIGNANI
LIBRARY, 224, RUE DE RIVOLI.

PER ASPERA.

———

CHAPTER I.

The high-priest of Serapis presided over the sacrifices to be offered this morning. Cæsar had given beasts in abundance to do honor to the god; still, the priest had gone but ill-disposed to fulfil his part; for the imperial command that the citizens' houses should be filled with the troops, who were also authorized to make unheard-of demands on their hosts, had roused his ire against the tyrant, who, in the morning, after his bath, had appeared to him unhappy indeed, but at the same time a gifted and conscientious ruler, capable of the highest and grandest enterprise.

Melissa, in obedience to the lady Euryale, had taken an hour's rest, and then refreshed herself by bathing. She now was breakfasting with her venerated friend, and Philostratus had joined them. He was able to tell them that a swift State galley was already on its way to overtake and release her father and brother; and when he saw how glad she was to hear it, how beautiful, fresh, and pure she was, he thought to himself with anxiety that it would be a wonder if the imperial slave to his own passions should not desire to possess this lovely creature.

Euryale also feared this, and Melissa realized what filled them with anxiety; yet she by no means shared the feeling, and the happy confidence with which she tried to comfort her old friends, at the same time pacified and alarmed them. It seemed to her quite foolish and vain to suppose that the emperor, the mighty ruler of the world, should fall in love with her, the humble, obscure gem-cutter's child, who aspired to one suitor alone. It was merely as a patient wishes for the physician, she assured herself, that the emperor wished for her presence —Philostratus had also understood that. During the night she had certainly been seized with great fears, but, as she now thought, without any cause. What she really had to dread was that she might be falsely judged by his followers; still, she cared nothing about all these Romans. However, she would beg Euryale to see Diodoros, and to tell him what forced her to obey the emperor's summons, if he should send for her. It was highly probable that the sick man had been informed of her interview with Caracalla, and, as her betrothed, he must be told how she felt toward Cæsar; for this was his right, and jealous agitation might injure him.

Her face so expressed the hope and confidence of a pure heart that when, after a little time, she withdrew, Euryale said to the philosopher:

"We must not alarm her more! Her trustful innocence perhaps may protect her better than anxious precautions."

And Philostratus agreed, and assured her that in any case he expected good results for Melissa, for she was one of those who were the elect of the gods and whom they chose to be their instruments. And then he related what wonderful influence she had over Cæsar's sufferings, and praised her with his usual enthusiastic warmth.

When Melissa returned, Philostratus had left the matron. She was again alone with Euryale, who reminded her of the lesson conveyed in the Christian words that she had explained to her yesterday. Every deed, every thought, had some influence on the way in which the fulfilment of time would come for each one; and when the hour of death was over, no regrets, repentance, or efforts could then alter the past. A single moment, as her own young experience had taught her, was often sufficient to brand the name of an estimable man. Till now, her way through life had led along level paths, through meadows and gardens, and others had kept their eyes open for her; now she was drawing near to the edge of a precipice, and at every turning, even at the smallest step, she must never forget the threatening danger. The best will and the greatest prudence could not save her if she did not trust to a higher guidance; and then she asked the girl to whom she raised her heart when she prayed; and Melissa named Isis and other gods, and lastly the Manes of her dead mother.

During this confession, old Adventus appeared, to summon the girl to his sovereign. Melissa promised to follow him immediately: and, when the old man had gone, the matron said:

"Few here pray to the same gods, and he whose worship my husband leads is not mine. I, with several others, know that there is a Father in heaven who loves us men, his creatures, and guards us as his children. You do not yet know him, and therefore you can not hope for anything from him; but if you will follow the advice of a friend, who was also once young, think in the future that your right hand is held firmly by the invisible, beloved hand of your mother. Persuade yourself that she is by you, and take care that every word, yes, every glance, meets with her approval. Then she will be there, and will protect you whenever you require her aid."

Melissa sank on the breast of her kind friend, embracing her as closely and kissing her as sincerely as if she had been the beloved mother to whose care Euryale had commended her.

The counsels of this true friend agreed with those of her own heart, and so they must be right.

When at last they had to part, Euryale wished to send for one of the gentlemen of the court, whom she knew, that he might escort her through the troops of Cæsar's attendants and friends who were waiting, and of the visitors and petitioners; but Melissa felt so happy and so well protected by Adventus, that she followed him without further delay. In fact, the old man had a friendly feeling for her, since she had covered his feet so carefully the day before; she knew it by the tone of his voice and by the troubled look in his dim eyes.

Even now she did not believe in the dangers at which her friends trembled for her, and she walked calmly across the lofty marble halls, the ante-room, and the other vast rooms of the imperial dwelling. The attendants accompanied her respectfully from door to door, in obedience to the emperor's commands, and she went on with a firm step, looking straight in front of her, without noticing the inquisitive, approving, or scornful glances which were aimed at her.

In the first rooms she needed an escort, for they

were crowded with Romans and Alexandrians who were waiting for a sign from Cæsar to appeal for his pardon or his verdict, or perhaps only wishing to see his countenance. The emperor's "friends" sat at breakfast, of which Caracalla did not partake. The generals, and the members of his court not immediately attached to his person, stood together in the various rooms, while the principal people of Alexandria—several senators and rich and important citizens of the town—as well as the envoys of the Egyptian provinces, in magnificent garments and rich gold ornaments, held aloof from the Romans, and waited in groups for the call of the usher.

Melissa saw no one, nor did she observe the costly woven hangings on the walls, the friezes decorated with rare works of art and high reliefs, nor the mosaic floors over which she passed. She did not notice the hum and murmur of the numerous voices which surrounded her; nor could she indeed have understood a single coherent sentence; for, excepting the ushers and the emperor's immediate attendants, at the reception-hour no one was allowed to raise his voice. Expectancy and servility seemed here to stifle every lively impulse; and when, now and then, the loud call of one of the ushers rang above the murmur, one of those who were waiting spontaneously bowed low, or another started up, as if ready to obey any command. The sensation, shared by many, of waiting in the vicinity of a high, almost godlike power, in whose hands lay their well-being or misery, gave rise to a sense of solemnity. Every movement was subdued; anxious, nay, fearful expectation was written on many faces, and on others impatience and disappointment. After a little while it was whispered from ear to ear that the emperor would only grant a few more audiences: and how many had already waited in vain yesterday, for hours, in the same place!

Without delay Melissa went on till she had reached the heavy curtain which, as she already knew, shut off Cæsar's inner apartments.

The usher obligingly drew it back, even before she had mentioned her name, and while a deputation of the town senators, who had been received by Caracalla, passed out, she was followed by Alexandrian citizens, the chiefs of great merchant-houses, whose request for an audience he had sanctioned. They were for the most part elderly men, and Melissa recognized among them Seleukus, Berenike's husband.

Melissa bowed to him, but he did not notice her, and passed by without a word. Perhaps he was considering the enormous sum to be expended on the show at night which he, with a few friends, intended to arrange at the circus in Cæsar's honor.

All was quite still in the large hall which separated the emperor's reception-room from the ante-room. Melissa observed only two soldiers, who were looking out of the window, and whose bodies were shaking as though they were convulsed with profound merriment.

It happened that she had to wait here some time; for the usher begged her to have patience until the merchants' audience was over. They were the last who would be received that day. He invited her to rest on the couch on which was spread a bright giraffe's skin, but she preferred to walk up and down, for her heart was beating violently. While the usher vanished from the room, one of the warriors turned his head to look about him, and directly he caught sight of Melissa he gave his comrade a push, and said to him, loud enough for Melissa to hear:

"A wonder! Apollonaris, by Eros and all the Erotes, a precious wonder!"

The next moment they both stepped back from the window and stared at the girl, who stood blushing and embarrassed, and gazed at the floor when she found with whom she had been left alone.

They were two tribunes of the prætorians, but, notwithstanding their high grade, they were only young men of about twenty. Twin brothers of the honorable house of the Aurelia, they had entered the army as centurions, but had soon been placed at the head of a thousand men, and appointed tribunes in Cæsar's body-guard. They resembled one another exactly; and this likeness, which procured them much amusement, they greatly enhanced by arranging their coal-black beards and hair in exactly the same way, and by dressing alike down to the rings on their fingers. One was called Apollonaris, the other Nemesianus Aurelius. They were of the same height, and equally well grown, and no one could say which had the finest black eyes, which mouth the haughtiest smile, or to which of them the thick short beard and the artistically shaved spot between the under lip and chin was most becoming. The beautifully embossed ornaments on their breast-plates and shirts of mail, and on the belt of the short sword, showed that they grudged no expense; in fact, they thought only of enjoyment, and it was merely for the honor of it that they were serving for a few years in the imperial guard. By and by they would rest, after all the hardships of the campaign, in their palace at Rome, or in the villas on the various estates that they had inherited from their father and mother, and then, for a change, hold honorary positions in the public service. Their friends knew that they also contemplated being married on the same day, when the game of war should be a thing of the past.

In the mean time they desired nothing in the world but honor and pleasure; and such pleasure as well-bred, healthy, and genial youths, with amiability, strength, and money to spend, can always command, they enjoyed to the full, without carrying it to reckless extravagance. Two merrier, happier, more popular comrades probably did not exist in the whole army. They did their duty in the field bravely; during peace, and in a town like Alexandria, they appeared, on the contrary, like mere effeminate men of fashion. At least, they spent a large part of their time in having their black hair crimped; they gave ridiculous sums to have it anointed with the most delicate perfumes; and it was difficult to imagine how effectively their carefully kept hands could draw a sword, and, if necessary, handle the hatchet or spade.

To-day Nemesianus was in the emperor's ante-room by command, and Apollonaris, of his own free-will, had taken the place of another tribune, that he might bear his brother company. They had caroused through half the night, and had begun the new day by a visit to the flower market, for love of the pretty saleswomen. Each had a half-opened rose stuck in between his cuirass and shirt of mail on the left breast, plucked, as the charming Daphnion had assured them, from a bush which had been introduced from Persia only the year before. The brothers, at any rate, had never seen any like them.

While they were looking out of the window they had passed the time by examining every girl or woman who went by, intending to fling one rose at the first whose perfect beauty should claim it, and the other flower at the second; but during the half-hour none had appeared who was worthy of such a gift. All the beauties in Alexandria were walking in the streets in the cool hour before sunset, and really there was no lack of handsome girls. The brothers had even heard that Cæsar, who seemed to have renounced the pleasures of love, had yielded to the charms of a lovely Greek.

Directly they saw Melissa they were convinced that they had met the beautiful plaything of the imperial fancy, and each with the same action offered her his rose, as if moved by the same invisible power.

Apollonaris, who had come into the world a little sooner than his brother, and who, by right of birth, had therefore a more audacious manner, stepped boldly up to Melissa and presented his, while Nemesianus at the same instant bowed to her, and begged her to give his the preference.

Though their speeches were flattering and well-worded, Melissa repulsed them by remarking sharply that she did not want their flowers.

"We can easily believe that," answered Apollonaris, "for are you not yourself a lovely, blooming rose?"

"Vain flattery," replied Melissa; "and I certainly do not bloom for you."

"That is both cruel and unjust," sighed Nemesianus, "for that which you refuse to us poor fellows you grant to another, who can obtain everything that other mortals yearn for."

"But we," interrupted his brother, "are modest, nay, and pious warriors. We had intended offering up these roses to Aphrodite, but lo! the goddess has met us ir. person."

"Her image at any rate," added the other.

"And you should thank the foam-born goddess," continued Apollonaris; "for she has lent you, in spite of the danger of seeing herself eclipsed, her own divine charms. Do you think she will be displeased if we withdraw the flowers and offer them to you?"

"I think nothing," anwered Melissa, "excepting that your honeyed remarks annoy me. Do what you like with your roses, I will not accept them."

"How dare you," asked Apollonaris, approaching her —"you, to whom the mother of love has given such wonderfully fresh lips—misuse them by refusing so sternly the humble petition of her faithful worshippers? If you would not have Aphrodite enraged with you, hasten to atone for this transgression. One kiss, my beauty, for her votary, and she will forgive you."

Here Apollonaris stretched out his hand toward the girl to draw her to him, but she motioned him back indignantly, declaring that it would be reprehensible and cowardly in a soldier to use violence toward a modest maid.

At this the two brothers laughed heartily, and Nemesianus exclaimed, "You do not belong to the Temple of Vesta, most lovely of roses, and yet you are well protected by such sharp thorns that it requires a great deal of courage to venture to attack you."

"More," added Apollonaris, "than to storm a fortress. But what camp or stronghold contains booty so well worth capturing?"

Thereupon he threw his arm round Melissa and drew her to him.

Neither he nor his brother had ever conducted themselves badly towards an honorable woman; and if Melissa had been but the daughter of a simple craftsman, her reproachful remarks would have sufficed to keep them at a distance. But such immunity was not to be granted to the emperor's sweetheart, who could so audaciously reject two brothers who were accustomed to easy conquests; her demure severity could hardly be meant seriously. Apollonaris therefore took no notice of her violent resistance, but held her hands forcibly, and, though he could not succeed in kissing her for her struggling, he pressed his lips to her cheek, while she endeavored to free herself and pushed him off, breathless with real indignation.

Till now, the brothers had taken the matter as a joke; but when Apollonaris seized the girl again, and she, beside herself with fear, cried for help, he at once set her free.

It was too late; for the curtains of the audience-room were already withdrawn, and Caracalla approached. His countenance was red and distorted; he trembled with rage, and his angry glance fell like a flash of lightning on the luckless brothers. Close by his side was the prefect Macrinus, who feared lest he should be attacked by a fresh fit; and Melissa shared his fears, as Caracalla cried to Apollonaris in an angry voice, "Scoundrel that you are, you shall repent of this!"

Still, Aurelius had, by various wanton jokes, incurred the emperor's wrath before now, and he was accustomed to disarm it by some insinuating confession, so he answered him with a roguish smile, while raising his eyes to him humbly:

"Forgive me, great Cæsar! Our poor strength, as you well know, is easily defeated in conflicts against over·powering beauty. Dainties are sweet, not only for children. Long ago Mars was drawn to Venus; and if I—"

He had spoken these words in Latin, which Melissa

did not understand; but the color left the emperor's face, and, pale with excitement, he stammered out laboriously:

"You have—you have dared—"

"For this rose," began the youth again, "I begged a hasty kiss from the beauty, which certainly blooms for all, and she—" He raised his hands and eyes imploringly to the despot; but Caracalla had already snatched Macrinus's sword from its sheath, and before Aurelius could defend himself he was struck first on the head with the flat of the blade, and then received a series of sharp cuts on his brow and face.

Streaming with blood from the gaping wounds which the victim, trembling with fear and rage, covered with his hands, he surrendered himself to the care of his startled brother, while Cæsar overwhelmed them both with a flood of furious reproaches.

When Nemesianus began to bind up his wounded brother's head with a handkerchief handed to him by Melissa, and Caracalla saw the gaping wounds he had inflicted, he became quieter, and said:

"I think those lips will not try to steal kisses again for some time from honorable maidens. You and Nemesianus have forfeited your lives; however, the beseeching look of those all-powerful eyes has saved you—you are spared. Take your brother away, Nemesianus. You are not to leave your quarters until further orders."

With this he turned his back on the twins, but on the threshold he again addressed them and said:

"You were mistaken about this maiden. She is not less pure and noble than your own sister."

The merchants were dismissed from the tablinum more hastily than was due to the importance of their business, in which, until this interruption, the sovereign had shown a sympathetic interest and intelligence which surprised them; and they left Cæsar's presence disappointed, but with the promise that they should be received again in the evening.

As soon as they had retired, Caracalla threw himself again on the couch.

The bath had done him good. Still somewhat exhausted, though his head was clear, he would not be hindered from receiving the deputation for which he had important matters to decide; but this fresh attack of rage revenged itself by a painful headache. Pale, and with slightly quivering limbs, he dismissed the prefect and his other friends, and desired Epagathos to call Melissa.

He needed rest, and again the girl's little hand, which had yesterday done him good, proved its healing power. The throbbing in his head yielded to her gentle touch, and by degrees exhaustion gave way to the comfortable languor of convalescence.

To-day, as yesterday, he expressed his thanks to Melissa, but he found her changed. She looked timidly and anxiously down into her lap, excepting when she replied to a direct question; and yet he had done everything to please her. Her relations would soon be free and in Alexandria once more, and Zminis was in prison, chained hand and foot. This he told her; and, though she was glad, it was not enough to restore the calm cheerfulness he had loved to see in her.

He urged her, with warm insistence, to tell him what it was that weighed on her, and at last, with eyes full of tears, she forced herself to say:

"You yourself have seen what they take me for."

"And you have seen," he quickly replied, "how I punish those who forget the respect they owe to you."

"But you are so dreadful in your wrath!" The words broke from her lips. "Where others blame, you can destroy; and you do it, too, when passion carries you away. I am bound to obey your call, and here I am. But I fancy myself like the little dog—you may see him any day—which in the beast-garden of the Panæum, shares a cage with a royal tiger. The huge brute puts up with a great deal from his small companion, but woe betide the dog if the tiger once pats him with his heavy, murderous paw—and he might, out of sheer forgetfulness!"

"But this hand," Cæsar broke in, raising his delicate hand covered with rings, "will never forget, any more than my heart, how much it owes to you."

"Until I, in some unforeseen way—perhaps quite unconsciously—excite your anger," sighed Melissa. "Then you will be carried away by passion, and I shall share the common fate."

Caracalla was about to reply indignantly, but just then Adventus entered the room, announcing the chief astrologer of the Temple of Serapis. Caracalla refused to receive him just then, but he anxiously asked whether he had any signs to report. The reply was in the affirmative, and in a few minutes Cæsar had in his hand a wax tablet covered with words and figures. He studied it eagerly, and his countenance cleared; still holding the tablets, he exclaimed to Melissa:

"You, daughter of Heron, have nothing to fear from me, you of all the world! In some quiet hour I will explain to you how my planet yearns to yours, and yours —that is, yourself—to mine. The gods have created us for each other, child; I am already under your influence, but your heart still hesitates, and I know why; it is because you distrust me."

Melissa raised her large eyes to his face in astonishment, and he went on, pensively:

"The past must stand; it is like a scar which no water will wash out. What have you not heard of my past? What did they feel, in their self-conscious virtue, when they talked of my crimes? Did it ever occur to any one, I wonder, that with the purple I assumed the sword, to protect my empire and throne? And when I have used the blade, how eagerly have fingers pointed at me, how gladly slanderous tongues have wagged! Who has ever thought of asking what compulsion led me to shed blood, or how much it cost me to do it? You, fair child—and the stars confirm it—you were sent by Fate to share the burden that oppresses me, and to you I will ease my heart, to you I will confide all, unasked, because my heart prompts me to do so. But first you must tell me with what tales they taught you to hate the man to whom, as you yourself confessed, you nevertheless felt drawn."

At this Melissa raised her hands in entreaty and remonstrance, and Cæsar went on:

"I will spare you the pains. They say that I am ever athirst for fresh bloodshed if only some one is rash enough to suggest it to me. You were told that Cæsar murdered his brother Geta, with many more who did but speak his victim's name. My father-in-law, and his daughter Plautilla, my wife, were, it is said, the victims of my fury. I killed Papinian, the lawyer and prefect, and Cilo—whom you saw yesterday—nearly shared the same fate. What did they conceal? Nothing! Your nod confesses it—well, and why should they, since speaking ill of others is their greatest delight? It is all true, and I should never think of denying it. But did it ever occur to you, or did any one ever suggest to you, to inquire how it came to pass that I perpetrated such horrors; I—who was brought up in the fear of the gods and the law, like you and other people?"

"No, my lord, never," replied Melissa, in distress. "But I beg you, I beseech you, say no more about such dreadful things. I know full well that you are not wicked; that you are much better than people think."

"And for that very reason," cried Cæsar, whose cheeks were flushed with pleasure in the hard task he had set himself, "you must hear me. I am Cæsar. There is no judge over me; I need give account to none for my actions. Nor do I. Who, besides yourself, is more to me than the flies on that cup?"

"And your conscience?" she timidly put in.

"It raises hideous questions from time to time," he replied, gloomily. "It can be obtrusive, but we can teach ourselves not to answer—besides, what you call conscience knows the motives for every action, and, remembering them, judges leniently. You, child, should do the same; for you—"

"O my lord, what can my poor judgment matter?" Melissa panted out; but Caracalla exclaimed, as if the question pained him:

"Must I explain all that? The stars, as you know, proclaim to you, as to me, that a higher power has joined us as light and warmth are joined. Have you forgotten how we both felt only yesterday? Or am I mistaken? Has not Roxana's soul entered into that divinely lovely form because it longed for its lost companion spirit?"

He spoke vehemently, with a quivering of his eyelids; but feeling her hand tremble in his own, he collected himself, and went on in a lower tone, but with urgent emphasis:

"I will let you glance into this bosom, closed to every other eye; for my desolate heart is inspired by you to fresh energy and life; I am as grateful to you as a drowning man to his deliverer. I shall suffocate and die if I repress the impulse to open my heart to you!"

What change was this that had come over this mysterious being? Melissa felt as though she was gazing on the face of a stranger, for, though his eyelids still quivered, his eyes were bright with ecstatic fire and his features looked more youthful. On that noble brow the laurel wreath he wore looked well. Also, as she now observed, he was magnificently attired; he wore a close-fitting tunic, or breast-plate made of thick woollen stuff, and over it a purple mantle, while from his bare throat hung a precious medallion, shield-shaped, and set in gold and gems, the centre formed by a large head of Medusa, with beautiful though terrible features. The lion-heads of gold attached to each corner of the short cloak he wore over the sham coat of mail, were exquisite works of art, and sandals embroidered with gold and gems covered his feet and ankles. He was dressed to-day like the heir of a lordly house, anxious to charm; nay, indeed, like an emperor, as he was; and with what care had his body-slave arranged his thin curls!

He passed his hand over his brow and cast a glance at a silver mirror on the low table at the head of his couch. When he turned to her again his amorous eyes met Melissa's.

She looked down in startled alarm. Was it for her sake that Cæsar had thus decked himself and looked in the mirror? It seemed scarcely possible, and yet it flattered and pleased her. But in the next instant she longed more fervently than she ever had before for a magic charm by which she might vanish and be borne far, far away from this dreadful man. In fancy she saw the vessel which the lady Berenike had in readiness. She would, she must fly hence, even if it should part her for a time from Diodoros.

Did Caracalla read her thought? Nay, he could not see through her, so she endured his gaze, tempting him to speak; and his heart beat high with hope as he fancied he saw that she was beginning to be infected by his intense agitation. At this moment he felt convinced, as he often had been, that the most atrocious of his crimes had been necessary and inevitable. There was something grand and vast in his deeds of blood, and that—for he flattered himself he knew the female heart—must win her admiration, besides the awe and love she already felt.

During the night, at his waking, and in his bath, he had felt that she was as necessary to him as the breath of life and hope. What he experienced was love as the poets had sung it. How often had he laughed it to scorn, and boasted that he was armed against the arrows of Eros! Now, for the first time, he was aware of the anxious rapture, the ardent longing of which he had read in so many songs. There stood the object of his passion. She must hear him, must be his—not by compulsion, not by imperial command, but of the free impulse of her heart.

His confession would help to this end.

With a swift gesture, as if to throw off the last trace of fatigue, he sat up and began in a firm voice, with a light in his eyes:

"Yes, I killed my brother Geta. You shudder. And yet, if at this day, when I know all the results of the deed, the state of affairs were the same as then, I would do it again! That shocks you. But only listen, and then you will say with me that it was Fate which compelled me to act so, and not otherwise."

He paused, and then mistaking the anxiety which was visible in Melissa's face for sympathetic attention, he began his story, confident of her interest:

"When I was born, my father had not yet assumed the purple, but he already aimed at the sovereignty. Augury had promised it to him; my mother knew this, and shared his ambition. While I was still at my nurse's breast he was made consul; four years later he seized the throne. Pertinax was killed, the wretched Didius Julianus bought the empire, and this brought my father to Rome from Pannonia. Meanwhile he had sent us children, my brother Geta and me, away from the city; nor was it till he had quelled the last resistance on the Tiber that he recalled us.

"I was then but a child of five, and yet one day of that time I remember vividly. My father was going through Rome in solemn procession. His first object was to do due honor to the corpse of Pertinax. Rich hangings floated from every window and balcony in the city. Garlands of flowers and laurel wreaths adorned the houses, and pleasant odors were wafted to us as we went. The jubilation of the people was mixed with the trumpet-call of the soldiers; handkerchiefs were waved and acclamations rang out. This was in honor of my father, and of me also, the future Cæsar. My little heart was almost bursting with pride; it seemed to me that I had grown several heads taller, not only than other boys, but than the people that surrounded me.

"When the funeral procession began, my mother wished me to go with her into the arcade where seats had been placed for the ladies, but I refused to follow her. My father became angry. But when he heard me declare that I was a man and the future Emperor, that I would rather see nothing than show myself to the people among the women, he smiled. He ordered Cilo, who was then the prefect of Rome, to lead me to the seats of the past consuls and the old senators. I was delighted at this; but when he allowed my younger brother Geta to follow me, my pleasure was entirely spoiled."

"And you were then five years old?" asked Melissa, astonished.

"That surprises you!" smiled Caracalla. "But I had already travelled through half the empire, and had experienced more than other boys of twice my age. I was, at any rate, still child enough to forget everything else in the brilliant spectacle that unfolded before my eyes. I remember to this day the colored wax statue which represented Pertinax so exactly that it might have been himself risen from the grave. And the procession! It seemed to have no end; one new thing followed another. All walked past in mourning robes, even the choir of singing boys and men. Cilo explained to me who had made the statues of the Romans who had served their country, who the artists and scholars were, whose statues and busts were carried by. Then came bronze groups of the people of every nation in the empire, in their costumes. Cilo told me what they were called, and where they lived; he then added that one day they would all belong to me; that I must learn the art of fighting, in case they resisted me, and should require suppressing. Also, when they carried the flags of the guilds past, when the horse and foot soldiers, the race-horses from the circus and several other things came by, he continued to explain them. I only remember it now because it made me so happy. The old man spoke to me alone; he regarded me alone as the future sovereign. He left Geta to eat the sweets which his aunts had given him, and when I too wanted some my brother refused to let me have any. Then Cilo stroked my hair, and said: 'Leave him his toys. When you are a man you shall have the whole Roman Empire for your own, and all the nations I told you of.' Geta meanwhile had thought better of it, and pushed some of the sweetmeats toward me. I would not have them, and, when he tried to make me take them, I threw them into the road."

"And you remember all that?" said Melissa.

"More things than these are indelibly stamped on my mind from that day," said Cæsar. "I can see before me now the pile on which Pertinax was to be burned. It was splendidly decorated, and on the top stood the gilt chariot in which he had loved to ride. Before the consuls fired the logs of Indian wood, my father led us to the image of Pertinax, that we might kiss it. He held me by the hand. Wherever we went, the senate and people hailed us with acclamations. My mother carried Geta in her arms. This delighted the populace. They shouted for her and my brother as enthusiastically as for us, and I recollect to this day how that went to my heart. He might have the sweets and welcome, but what the people had to offer was due only to my father and me, not to my brother. At that moment I first fully understood that Severus was the present and I the future Cæsar. Geta had only to obey, like every one else.

"After kissing the image, I stood, still holding my father's hand, to watch the flames. I can see them now, crackling and writhing as they gained on the wood, licking it and fawning, as it were, till it caught and sent up a rush of sparks and fire. At last the whole pile was one huge blaze. Then, suddenly, out of the heart of the flames an eagle rose. The creature flapped its broad wings in the air, which was golden with sunshine and quivering with heat, soaring above the smoke and fire, this way and that. But it soon took flight, away from the furnace beneath. I shouted with delight, and cried to my father: 'Look at the bird! Where is he flying?' And he eagerly answered: 'Well done! If you desire to preserve the power I have conquered for you always undiminished, you must keep your eyes open. Let no sign pass unnoticed, no opportunity neglected.'

"He himself acted on this rule. To him obstacles existed only to be removed, and he taught me, too, to give myself neither peace nor rest, and not to spare the life of a foe.—That festival secured my father the suffrages of the Romans. Meanwhile Pescennius Niger rose up in the East with a large army and took the field against Severus. But my father was not the man to hesitate. Within a few months of the obsequies of Pertinax his opponent was a headless corpse.

"There was yet another obstacle to be removed. You have heard of Clodius Albinus. My father had adopted him and raised him to share his throne. But Severus could not divide the rule with any man. When I was nine years old I saw, after the battle of Lugdunum, the dead face of Albinus's head; it was set up in front of the Curia on a lance.

"I now was the second personage in the empire, next to my father; the first among the youth of the whole world, and the future emperor. When I was eleven the soldiers hailed me as Augustus; that was in the war against the Parthians, before Ktesiphon. But they did the same to Geta. This was like wormwood in the sweet draught; and if then— But what can a girl care about the state, and the fate of rulers and nations?"

"Yes, go on," said Melissa. "I see already what you are coming to. You disliked the idea of sharing your power with another."

"Nay," cried Caracalla, vehemently, "I not only disliked it, it was intolerable, impossible! What I want you to see is that I did not grudge my brother his share of my father's inheritance, like any petty trader. The world —that is the point—the world itself was too small for two of us. It was not I, but Fate, which had doomed Geta to die. I am certain of this, and so must you be. Yes, it was Fate. Fate prompted the child's little hand to attempt its brother's life. And that was long before my brain could form a thought or my baby lips could stammer his hated name."

"Then you tried to kill your brother even in infancy?" asked Melissa, and her large eyes dilated with horror as she gazed at the terrible narrator. But Caracalla went on, in an apologetic tone:

"I was then but two years old. It was at Mediolanum, soon after Geta's birth. An egg was found in the court of the palace; a hen had laid it close to a pillar. It was of a purple hue—red all over like the imperial mantle, and this indicated that the newly born infant was destined to sovereignty. Great was the rejoicing. The purple marvel was shown even to me who could but just walk. I, like a naughty boy, flung it down; the shell cracked, and the contents poured out on the pavement. My mother saw it, and her exclamation, 'Wicked child, you have murdered your brother!' was often repeated to me in after-years. It never struck me as particularly motherly."

Here he paused, gazing meditatively into vacancy, and then asked the girl, who had listened intently:

"Were you never haunted by a word so that you could not be rid of it?"

"Oh, yes," cried Melissa; "a striking rhythm in a song, or a line of poetry—"

Caracalla nodded agreement, and went on more vehemently: "That is what I experienced at the words, 'You have murdered your brother!' I not only heard them now and then with my inward ear, but incessantly, like the dreary hum of the flies in my camp-tent, for hours at a time, by day and by night. No fanning could drive these away. The diabolical voice whispered loudest when Geta had done anything to vex me; or if things had been given him which I did not wish him to have. And how often that happened! For I—I was only Bassianus to my mother; but her youngest was her dear little Geta.

"So the years passed. We had, while still quite young, our own teams in the circus. One day, when we were driving for a wager—we were still boys, and I was ahead of the other lads—the horses of my chariot shied to one side. I was thrown some distance on the course. Geta saw this. He turned his horses to the right where I lay. He drove over his brother as he would over straw and apple-parings in the dust; and his wheel broke my thigh. Who knows what else it crushed in me? One thing is certain—from that date the most painful of my sufferings originated. And he, the mean scoundrel, had done it intentionally. He had sharp eyes. He knew how to guide his steeds. He had never driven his wheel over a hazelnut in the sand of the arena against his will; and I was lying some distance from the driving course."

Cæsar's eyelids blinked spasmodically as he uttered this accusation, and his very glance revealed the raging fire that was burning in his soul.

Melissa's sad cry of—

"What terrible suspicion!" he answered with a short, scornful laugh and the furious assertion:

"Oh, there were friends enough who informed me what hope Geta had founded on this act of treachery. The disappointment made him irritable and listless, when Galenus had succeeded in curing me so far that I was able to throw away my crutch; and my limp—at least so they tell me—is hardly perceptible."

"Not at all, most certainly not at all," Melissa sympathetically assured him. He, however, went on:

"Yet what I endured meanwhile!—and while I passed so many long weeks of pain and impatience on a couch, the words my mother had said about the brother whom I murdered rang constantly in my ears as though a reciter were engaged by day and night to reiterate them.

"But even this passed away. With the pain, which had spoiled many good hours for me, the quiet had brought me something more to the purpose—thoughts and plans. Yes, during those peaceful weeks the things my father and tutor had taught me became clear and real for the first time. I realized that I must become energetic if I meant ever to be a thorough sovereign. As soon as I could use my foot again I became an industrious and docile pupil under Cilo. From a child up to the time of this cruel experience, my youthful heart had clung to my nurse. She—a Christian from my father's African home—She—I knew loved me best on earth. My mother knew of no higher destiny than that of being the Domna,* the lady of the soldiers, the mother of the camp, and the lady philosopher among the sages. What she gave me in the way of love was but copper alms. She threw golden solidi of love into Geta's lap in lavish abundance. And her sister and her nieces, who often lived with us, treated me exactly as she did. They were distantly civil, or they shunned me, but my brother was their spoiled plaything. I was as incapable as Geta was master of the art of stealing hearts; but in my childhood I needed none of them; for, if I wished for a kind word, a sweet kiss, or the love of a woman, my nurse's arms were open to me. Nor was she an ordinary woman. As the widow of a tribune who had fallen in my father's service, she had undertaken to attend on me. She loved me as no one else ever did. She was also the only person whom I would willingly obey. I came into the world full of wild instincts, but she knew how to tame them kindly. My aversion to my brother was the one thing she checked but feebly, for he was a thorn in her side too. I learned this when she, who was so gentle, explained to me, with asperity in her tone, that there was but one God in heaven, and on earth but one emperor, who should govern the world in his name. She also imparted these convictions to others, and this turned to her disadvantage. My mother parted us, and sent her back to her African home. She died soon after."

He was silent, and gazed pensively into vacancy; soon, however, he collected his thoughts and said, lightly:

"Well, I became Cilo's diligent pupil."

* Domina, lady or mistress, in corrupt Latin. Hence her name of Julia Domna.

"But," asked Melissa, "did you not say that at one time you attempted his life?"

"I did so," replied Caracalla darkly; "for a moment arrived when I cursed his teaching, and yet it was certainly wise and well meant. You see, child, all of you who go through life humbly and without power are trained to submit obediently to the will of Heaven. Cilo taught me to place my own power, and the greatness of the realm which it would be incumbent on me to reign over, above everything, even above the gods. It was impressed upon you and yours to hold the life of another sacred; to us, our duty as the sovereign transcends this law. Even the blood of a brother must flow if it is for the good of the state intrusted to us. My nurse had taught me that being good meant doing unto others as we would be done by; Cilo cried to me: 'Strike down, that you may not be struck down. Away with mercy, if the welfare of the state is threatened!' And how many hands are raised against Rome, the universal empire, which I rule over! It needs a strong hand to keep its antagonistic parts together. Otherwise it would fall apart like a bundle of arrows when the string that bound them is broken. And I, even as a boy, had sworn to my father, by the Terminus stone in the Capitol, never to abandon a single inch of his ground without fighting for it. He, Severus, was the wisest of the rulers. Only the blind love for his second son, encouraged by the women, caused him to forget his moderation and prudence. My brother Geta was to reign together with me over the empire, which ought to have been mine alone as the first-born. Every year festivals were kept, with prayers and sacrifices, to the 'love of the brothers.' You have perhaps seen the coins, which show us hand in hand, and have on them the inscription, 'Eternal union'!

"I in union—I hand in hand with the man I most hated under the sun! It almost maddened me only to hear his voice. I would have liked best of all to spring at his throat when I saw him with his learned fellows squandering their time. Do you know what they did? They invented the names by which the voices of different animals were to be known. Once I snatched the pencil out of the hand of the freedman as he was writing the sentences, 'The horse neighs, the pig grunts, the goat bleats, the cow lows, the sheep baas.' 'He, himself,' I added, 'croaks like a hoarse jay.'

"That I should share the government with this miserable, faint-hearted, poisonous nobody could never be,—this enemy, who, when I said 'Yes,' cried 'No!' who frustrated all my measures,—it was impossible! It would have caused the destruction of the state, as certainly as it was the unfairest and unwisest of the deeds of Severus, to place the younger brother as co-regent with the first-born, the rightful heir to the throne. I, whom my father had taught to watch for signs, was reminded every hour that this unbearable position must come to an end.

"After the death of Severus, we lived at first close to one another in separate parts of the same palace, like two lions in a cage across which a partition has been erected, so that they may not reciprocally mangle each other.

"We used to meet at my mother's.

"That morning my mastiff had bitten Geta's wolf-hound and killed him, and they had found a black liver in the beast he had sent for sacrifice. I had been informed of this. Destiny was on my side. This indolent inactivity must be brought to a close. I myself do not know how I felt as I mounted the steps to my mother's rooms. I only remember distinctly that a demon cried continually in my ear, 'You have murdered your brother!' Then I suddenly found myself face to face with him. It was in the empress's reception-room. And when I saw the hated flat-shaped head so close to me, when his beardless mouth with its thick underlip smiled at me so sweetly and at the same time so falsely, I felt as if I again heard the cry with which he had cheered on his horse. And I felt . . . I even felt the pain—as if he broke my thigh again with his wheel. And at the same time a fiend whispered in my ear: 'Destroy him, or he will kill you, and through him Rome will perish!'

"Then I seized my sword. In his odious, peevish voice he said something—I forget what nonsense—to me. Then it appeared to me as if all the sheep and goats over which he had squandered his time were bleating at me. The blood rushed to my head. The room spun round me in a circle. Black spots on a red ground danced before my eyes. And then— What flashed in my right hand was my own naked sword! I neither heard nor said anything further. Nor had I planned, nor ever thought of, what then occurred. . . . But suddenly I felt as if a mountain of oppressive lead had fallen from my breast. How easily I could breathe again! All that had just before turned round me in a mad, whirling dance stood still. The sun shone brightly in the large room; a shaft of light, showing dancing dust, fell on Geta. He sank on his knees close to me, with my sword in his breast. My mother made a fruitless effort to shield him. His blood trickled over her hand. I can still see every ring on those slender, white fingers. I also remember distinctly how, when I raised my sword against him, my mother rushed in between us to protect her favorite. The sharp blade, as she tried to seize it, accidentally grazed her hand—I know not how—only the skin was slightly cut. Yet what a scream she gave over the wound which the son had given his mother! Julia Maesa, her daughter Mammæa, and the other women, rushed in. How they exaggerated! They made a river out of every drop of blood.

"So the dreadful deed was done; and yet, had I let the wretch live, I should have been a traitor to Rome, to myself, and to my father's life's work. That day, for the first time, I was ruler of the world. Those who accuse me of fratricide no doubt believe themselves to be right. But they certainly are not. I know better. You also know now with me that destiny, and not I, struck Geta out from among the living."

Here he for some time sat in breathless silence. Then he asked Melissa:

"You understand now how I came to shed my brother's blood?"

She started, and repeated gently after him:

"Yes, I understand it."

Deep compassion filled her heart, and yet she felt she dare not sanction what she had heard and deplored. Torn by deep and conflicting feelings she threw back her head, brushed her hair off her face, and cried; "Let me go now; I can bear it no longer!"

"So soft-hearted?" asked he, and shook his head disapprovingly. "Life rages more wildly round the throne than in an artist's home. You will have to learn to swim through the roaring torrent with me. Believe me, even enormities can become quite commonplace. And, besides, why does it still shock you when you yourself know that it was indispensable?"

"I am only a weak girl, and I feel as if I had witnessed these fearful deeds, and had to bear the terrible blood-guiltiness with you!" broke from her lips.

"That is what you must and shall do! It is to that end that I have confided to you what no one else has ever heard from my mouth!" cried Caracalla, his eyes flashing more brightly. She felt as though this cry called her from her slumbers and revealed the precipice to which she had strayed in her sleep-walking.

When Caracalla had begun telling her of his youth, she had only listened with half an ear; for she could not forget Berenike's rescuing ship. But soon his confessions completely attracted her attention, and the lament of this powerful man on whom so many injuries and wrongs had fallen, who even in childhood had been deprived of the happiness of a mother's love, had touched her tender heart. That which was afterwards told to her she had identified with her own humble life; she heard with a shudder that it was to the malice of his brother that this unhappy being owed the injury which, like a poisonous blight, had marred for him all the joys of existence, while she owed all that was loveliest and best in her young life to a brother's love.

The grounds on which Caracalla had based the assertion that destiny had compelled him to murder Geta appeared to her young and inexperienced mind as indisputable. He was only the pitiable victim of his birth and of a cruel fate. Besides, the humblest and most sober-minded can not resist the charm of majesty; and this hapless man, who had honored Melissa with his confidence, and who had assured her so earnestly that she was of such importance to him and could do so much for him, was the ruler of the universe.

She had also felt, after Cæsar's confession, that she had a right to be proud, since he had thought her worthy to take an interest in the tragedy in the imperial palace, as if she had been a member of the court. In her lively imagination she had witnessed the ghastly act to which he—as she had certainly believed it, even when she had replied to his question—had been forced by fate.

But the demand which had followed her answer now recurred to her. The picture of Diodoros, which had completely vanished from her thoughts while she had been listening, suddenly appeared to her, and, as she fancied, he looked at her reproachfully.

Had she, then, transgressed against her betrothed?

No, no, indeed she had not!

She loved him, and only him; and for that very reason, her upright judgment told her now, that it would be sinning against her lover to carry out Caracalla's wish, as if she had become his fellow-culprit, or certainly the advocate of the bloody outrage. She could think of no answer to his "That is what you must and shall do!" that would not awaken his wrath. Cautiously, and with sincere thanks for his confidence in her, she begged him once more to allow her to leave him, because she needed rest after such a shock to her mind. And it would also do him good to grant himself a short rest. But he assured her he knew that he could only rest when he had fulfilled his duty as a sovereign. His father had said, a few minutes before he drew his last breath:

"If there is anything more to be done, give it me to do," and he, the son, would do likewise.

"Moreover," he concluded, "it has done me good to

bring to light that which I had for so long kept sealed within me. To gaze in your face at the same time was, perhaps, even better physic."

At this he rose and, seizing the startled girl by both hands, he cried:

"You, child, can satisfy the insatiable! The love which I offer you resembles a full bunch of grapes, and yet I am quite content if you will give me back but one berry."

At the very commencement, this declaration was drowned by a loud shout which rang through the room in waves of sound.

Caracalla started, but, before he could reach the window, old Adventus rushed in breathless; and he was followed, though in a more dignified manner, with a not less hasty step and every sign of excitement, by Macrinus, the prefect of the prætorians, with his handsome young son and a few of Cæsar's friends.

"This is how I rest!" exclaimed Caracalla, bitterly, as he released Melissa's hand and turned inquiringly to the intruders.

The news had spread among the prætorians and the Macedonian legions, that the emperor, who, contrary to his custom, had not shown himself for two days, was seriously ill, and at the point of death. Feeling extremely anxious about one who had showered gold on them, and given them such a degree of freedom as no other im-perator had ever allowed them, they had collected before the Serapeum and demanded to see Cæsar. Caracalla's eyes lighted up at this information, and, excitedly pleased, he cried:

"They only are really faithful!"

He asked for his sword and helmet, and sent for the

paludamentum, the general's cloak of purple, embroidered with gold, which he never otherwise wore except in the field. The soldiers should see that he intended leading in future battles.

While they waited, he conversed quietly with Macrinus and the others; when, however, the costly garment covered his shoulders, and when his favorite, Theocritus, who had known best how to support him during his illness, offered him an arm, he answered imperiously that he required no assistance.

"Nevertheless, you should, after so serious an attack—" the physician in ordinary ventured to exhort him; but he interrupted him scornfully, and, glancing toward Melissa, exclaimed:

"Those little hands there contain more healing power than yours and the great Galenus's put together."

Thereupon he beckoned to the young girl, and when she once more besought his permission to go, he left the room with the commanding cry, "You are to wait!"

He had rather far to go and some steps to mount in order to reach the balcony which ran round the base of the cupola of the Pantheon which his father had joined to the Serapeum, yet he undertook this willingly, as thence he could best be seen and heard.

A few hours earlier it would have been impossible for him to reach this point, and Epagathos had arranged that a sedan-chair and strong bearers should be waiting at the foot of the steps; but he refused it, for he felt entirely restored, and the shouts of his warriors intoxicated him like sparkling wine.

Meanwhile Melissa remained behind in the audience-chamber. She must obey Cæsar's command. Yet it frightened her; and, besides, she was woman enough to feel it as an offence that the man who had assured her so sincerely of his gratitude, and who even feigned to love her, should have refused so harshly her desire to rest. She foresaw that, as long as he remained in Alexandria, she would have to be his constant companion. She trembled at the idea; yet, if she tried to fly from him, all she loved would be lost. No, this must not be thought of! She must remain.

She threw herself on a divan, lost in thought, and as she realized the confidence of which the unapproachable, proud emperor had thought her worthy, a secret voice whispered to her that it was certainly a delightful thing to share the overwhelming agitations of the highest and greatest. And was he then really bad, he who felt the necessity of vindicating himself before a simple girl, and to whom it appeared so intolerable to be misjudged and condemned even by her? Besides being the emperor and a suffering man, Caracalla had also become her wooer. It never once entered her mind to accept him; but still it flattered her extremely that the greatest of men should declare his love for her. Why, then, need she fear him? She was so important to him, she could do so much for him, that he would surely take care not to insult or offend her. This modest child, who till quite lately had trembled before her own father's temper, now, in the consciousness of Cæsar's favor, felt herself strong to triumph over the wrath and passions of the most powerful and most terrible of men. In the mean time she dared not risk confessing to him that she was another's bride, for that might determine him to let Diodoros feel his power. The thought that the emperor could care about her good opinion greatly pleased her; it even had the effect of raising the hope in her inexperienced mind that Caracalla would moderate his passion for her sake—when old Adventus came into the room.

He was in a hurry; for preparations had to be made in the dining-hall for the reception of the ambassadors. But when at his appearance Melissa rose from the divan he begged her good-naturally to continue resting. No one could tell what humor Caracalla might be in when he returned. She had often seen how rapidly that chameleon could change color. Who that had seen him just now, going to meet his soldiers, would believe that he had a few hours before sent away, with hard words, the widow of the Egyptian governor, who had come to beg mercy for her husband?

"So that wretch, Theocritus, has really carried out his intention of ruining the honest Titianus?" asked Melissa, horrified.

"Not only of ruining him," answered the chamberlain; "Titianus is by this time beheaded."

The old man bowed and left the room; but Melissa remained behind, feeling as if the floor had opened in front of her. He, whose ardent assurance she had just now believed, that he had been forced to shed the blood of an impious wretch, in obedience to an overpowering fate, was capable of allowing the noblest of men to be beheaded, unjudged, merely to please a mercenary favorite! His confession, then, had been nothing but a revolting piece of acting! He had endeavored to vanquish the disgust she felt for him merely to ensnare her and her healing hand more surely—as his plaything, his physic, his sleeping draught. And she had entered the trap, and acquitted him of the most horrible blood-guiltiness.

He had that very day rejected, without pity, a noble

Roman lady who petitioned for her husband's life, and with the same breath he had afterwards befooled her!

She started up, indignant and deeply wounded.

Was it not ignominious even to wait here like a prisoner in obedience to the command of this wretch?

And she had dared for one moment to compare this monster with Diodoros, the handsomest, the best, and most amiable of youths!

It seemed to her inconceivable. If only he had not the power to destroy all that was dearest to her heart, what pleasure it would have been to shout in his face:

"I detest you, murderer, and I am the betrothed of another, who is as good and beautiful as you are vile and odious!"

Then the question occurred to her whether it was only for the sake of her healing hands that he had felt attracted to her, and had made her an avowal as if she were his equal.

The blood mounted to her face at this thought, and with a burning brow she walked to the open window.

A crowd of presentiments rushed into her innocent and, till then, unsuspecting heart, and they were all so alarming that it was a relief to her when a shout of joy from the panoplied breasts of several thousand armed men rent the air. Mingling with this overpowering demonstration of united rejoicing from such huge masses, came the blare of the trumpets and horns of the assembled legions. What a maddening noise!

Before her lay the square, filled with many legions of warriors who surrounded the Serapeum in their shining armor, with their eagles and vexilla. The prætorians stood by the picked men of the Macedonian phalanx, and with these were all the troops who had escorted the imperial general hither, and the garrisons of the city of Alexander who hoped to be called out in the next war.

On the balcony decorated with statues, which surrounded the colonnade of the Pantheon on which the cupola rested, she saw Caracalla, and at a respectful distance a superb escort of his friends, in red and white togas, bordered with purple stripes, and wearing armor. Having taken off his gold helmet, the imperial general bowed to his people, and at every nod of his head, and each more vigorous movement, the enthusiastic cheers were renewed more loudly than ever.

Macrinus then stepped up to Cæsar's side, and the lictors who followed him, by lowering their fasces, signalled to the warriors to keep silence.

Instantly the ear-splitting din changed to a speechless lull.

At first she still heard the lances and shields, which several of the warriors had waved in enthusiastic joy, ringing against the ground, and the clatter of the swords being put back in their sheaths; then this also ceased, and finally, although only the superior officers had arrived on horseback, the stamping of hoofs, the snorting of the horses, and the rattle of the chains at their bits, were the only sounds.

Melissa listened breathlessly, looking first at the square and the soldiers below, then at the balcony where the emperor stood. In spite of the aversion she felt, her heart beat quicker. It was as if this immeasurable army had only one voice; as if an irresistible force drew all these thousands of eyes toward one point—the one little man up there on the Pantheon.

Directly he began to speak, Melissa's glance was also fixed on Caracalla.

She only heard the closing sentence, as, with raised voice, he shouted to the soldiers; and from it she gathered that he thanked his companions in arms for their anxiety, but that he still felt strong enough to share all their difficulties with them. Severe exertions lay behind them. The rest in this luxurious city would do them all good. There was still much to be conquered in the rich East, and to add to what they had already won, before they could return to Rome to celebrate a well-earned triumph. The weary should make themselves comfortable here. The wealthy merchants in whose houses he had quartered them had been told to attend to their wants, and if they neglected to do so every single warrior was man enough to show them what a soldier needed for his comfort. The people here looked askance at him and his soldiers, but too much moderation would be misplaced. There certainly were some things even here which the host was not bound to supply to his military; he, Cæsar, would provide them with these, and for that purpose he had put aside two million denarii out of his own poverty to distribute among them.

This speech had several times been interrupted by applause, but now such a tremendous shout of joy went up that it would have drowned the loudest thunder. The number of voices as well as their power seemed to have doubled.

Caracalla had added another link to the golden chain which already bound him to these faithful people; and, as he smiled and nodded to the delighted crowd from the balcony, he looked like a happy, light-hearted youth who had prepared a great treat for himself and several beloved friends.

What he said further was lost in the confusion of

voices in the square. The ranks were broken up, and the cuirasses, helmets, and arms of the moving warriors caught the sun and sent bright beams of light crossing one another over the wide space surrounded with dazzling white marble statues.

When Caracalla left the balcony, Melissa drew back from the window.

The compassionate impulse to lighten the lot of a sufferer, which had before drawn her so strongly to Caracalla, had now lost its sense and meaning for this healthy, high-spirited man. She considered herself cheated, as if she had been fooled by sham suffering into giving excessively large alms to an artful beggar.

Besides, she loved her native town, and Caracalla's advice to the soldiers to force the citizens to provide luxurious living for them, had made her considerably more rebellious. If he ever put her again in a position to speak her mind freely to him, she would tell him all undisguisedly; but instantly it again rushed into her mind that she must keep guard over her tongue before the easily unchained wrath of this despot, until her father and brothers were in safety once more.

Before the emperor returned, the room was filled with people, of whom she knew none, excepting her old friend the white-haired, learned Samonicus. She was the aim and centre of all eyes, and when even the kindly old man greeted her from a distance, and so contemptuously that the blood rushed to her face, she begged Adventus to take her into the next room.

The chamberlain did as she wished, but before he left her he whispered to her: "Innocence is trusting; but it is not of much avail here. Take care, child! They say there are sand-banks in the Nile which, like soft pillows, entice one to rest. But if you use them they become alive, and a crocodile creeps out, with open jaws. I am talking already in metaphor like an Alexandrian, but you will understand me."

Melissa bowed acknowledgment to him, and the old man went on:

"He may perhaps forget you; for many things had accumulated during his illness. If the mass of business, as it comes in, is not settled for twenty-four hours, it swells like a mill-stream that has the sluice down. But when work is begun, it quite carries him away. He forgets then to eat and drink. Ambassadors have arrived also from the Empress-mother, from Armenia, and Parthia. If he does not ask for you in half an hour, it will be supper-time, and I will let you out through that door."

"Do so at once," begged Melissa, with raised, petitioning hands; but the old man replied: "I should then reward you but ill for having warmed my feet for me. Remember the crocodile under the sand! Patience, child! There is Cæsar's zithern. If you can play, amuse yourself with that. The door shuts closely and the curtains are thick. My old ears just now were listening to no purpose."

But Caracalla was so far from forgetting Melissa that although he had attended to the communication brought to him by the ambassadors, and the various despatches from the senate, he asked for her even at the door of the tablinum. He had seen her from the balcony looking out on the square; so she had witnessed the reception his soldiers had given him. The magnificent spectacle must have impressed her and filled her with joy. He was anxious to hear all this from her own lips, before he settled down to work.

Adventus whispered to him where he had taken her,

to avoid the persecuting glances of the numerous strangers, and Caracalla nodded to him approvingly and went into the next room.

She sat there with the zithern, letting her fingers glide gently over the strings.

On his entering, she drew back hastily; but he cried to her brightly: "Do not disturb yourself. I love that instrument. I am having a statue erected to Mesomedes, the great zithern-player—you perhaps know his songs. This evening, when the feast and the press of work are over, I will hear how you play. I will also play a few airs to you."

Melissa then plucked up courage and said, decidedly: "No, my lord; I am about to bid you farewell for to-day."

"That sounds very determined," he answered, half surprised and half amused. "But may I be allowed to know what has made you decide on this step?"

"There is a great deal of work waiting for you," she replied, quietly.

"That is my affair, not yours," was the crushing answer.

"It is also mine," she said, endeavoring to keep calm; "for you have not yet completely recovered, and, should you require my help again this evening, I could not attend to your call."

"No?" he asked, wrathfully, and his eyelids began to twitch.

"No, my lord; for it would not be seemly in a maiden to visit you by night, unless you were ill and needed nursing. As it is, I shall meet your friends—my heart stands still only to think of it—"

"I will teach them what is due to you!" Caracalla bellowed out, and his brow was knit once more.

"But you cannot compel me," she replied, firmly, "to

change my mind as to what is seemly," and the courage
which failed her if she met a spider, but which stood by
her in serious danger as a faithful ally, made her perfectly
steadfast as she eagerly added: "Not an hour since you
promised me that so long as I remained with you I should
need no other protector, and might count on your
gratitude. But those were mere words, for, when I besought you to grant me some repose, you scorned my
very reasonable request, and roughly ordered me to remain and attend on you."

At this Cæsar laughed aloud.

"Just so! You are a woman, and like all the rest.
You are sweet and gentle only so long as you have your
own way."

"No, indeed," cried Melissa, and her eyes filled with
tears. "I only look further than from one hour to the
next. If I should sacrifice what I think right, merely to
come and go at my own will, I should soon be not only
miserable myself, but the object of your contempt."

Overcome by irresistible distress, she broke into loud
sobs; but Caracalla, with a furious stamp of his foot, exclaimed:

"No tears! I can not, I will not see you weep. Can
any harm come to you? Nothing but good; nothing but
the best of happiness do I propose for you. By Apollo
and Zeus, that is the truth! Till now you have been unlike other women, but when you behave like them, you
shall—I swear it—you shall feel which of us two is the
stronger!"

He roughly snatched her hand away from her face
and thereby achieved his end, for her indignation at being
thus touched by a man's brutal hand gave Melissa strength
to suppress her sobs. Only her wet cheeks showed what

a flood of tears she had shed, as, almost beside herself
with anger, she exclaimed:

"Let my hand go! Shame on the man who insults
a defenceless girl! You swear! Then I, too, may take
an oath, and, by the head of my mother, you shall never
see me again excepting as a corpse, if you ever attempt
violence! You are Cæsar—you are the stronger. Who
ever doubted it? But you will never compel me to a
vile action, not if you could inflict a thousand deaths on
me instead of one!"

Caracalla, without a word, had released her hand and
was staring at her in amazement.

A woman, and so gentle a woman, defying him as no
man would have dared to do!

She stood before him, her hand raised, her bosom
heaving; a flame of anger sparkled in her eyes through
their tears, and he had never before thought her so fair.
What majesty there was in this girl, whose simple grace
had made him more than once address her as "child!"
She was like a queen, an empress; perhaps she might
become one. The idea struck him for the first time. And
that little hand which now fell—what soothing power it
had, how much he owed to it! How fervently he had
wished but just now to be understood by her, and to be
thought better of by her than by the rest! And this
wish still possessed him. Nay, he was more strongly
attracted than ever to this creature, worthy as she was
of the highest in the land, and made doubly bewitching
by her proud wilfulness. That he should see her for the
last time seemed to him as impossible as that he should
never again see daylight; and yet her whole aspect announced that her threat was serious.

His aggrieved pride and offended sense of absolute

power struggled with his love, repentance, and fear of losing her healing presence; but the struggle was brief, especially as a mass of business to be attended to lay before him like a steep hill to climb, and haste was imperative. ·

He went up to her, shaking his head, and said in the superior tone of a sage rebuking thoughtlessness:

"Like all the rest of them—I repeat it. My demands had no object in view but to make you happy and derive comfort from you. How hot must be the blood which boils and foams at the contact of a spark! Only too like my own; and, since I understand you, I find it easy to forgive you. Indeed, I must finally express myself grateful; for I was in danger of neglecting my duties as a sovereign for the sake of pleasing my heart. Go, then, and rest, while I devote myself to business."

At this, Melissa forced herself to smile, and said, still somewhat tearfully: "How grateful I am! And you will not again require me to remain, will you, when I assure you that it is not fitting?"

"Unluckily, I am not in the habit of yielding to a girl's whims."

"I have no whims," she eagerly declared. "But you will keep your word now and allow me to withdraw? I implore you to let me go!"

With a deep sigh and an amount of self-control of which he would yesterday have thought himself incapable, he let go her hand, and she with a shudder thought that she had found the answer to the question he had asked her. His eyes, not his words, had betrayed it; for a woman can see in a suitor's look what color his wishes take, while a woman's eyes only tell her lover whether or no she reciprocates his feelings.

"I am going," she said, but he remarked the deadly paleness which overspread her features, and her colourless cheeks encouraged him in the belief that, after a sleepless night and the agitations of the last few hours, it was only physical exhaustion which made Melissa so suddenly anxious to escape from him. So, saying kindly—

"Till to-morrow, then," he dismissed her.

But when she had almost left the room, he added: "One thing more! To-morrow we will try our zitherns together. After my bath is the time I like best for such pleasant things; Adventus will fetch you. I am curious to hear you play and sing. Of all sounds, that of the human voice is the sweetest. Even the shouting of my legions is pleasing to the ear and heart. Do you not think so, and does not the acclamation of so many thousands stir your soul?"

"Certainly," she replied, hastily, and she longed to reproach him for the injustice he was doing the populace of Alexandria to benefit his warriors, but she felt that the time was ill chosen, and everything gave way to her longing to be gone out of the dreadful man's sight.

In the next room she met Philostratus, and begged him to conduct her to the lady Euryale; for all the ante-rooms were now thronged, and she had lost the calm confidence in which she had come thither.

CHAPTER II.

As Melissa made her way with the philosopher through the crowd, Philostratus said to her: "It is for your sake, child, that these hundreds have had so long to wait to-day, and many hopes will be disappointed. To satisfy all is a giant's task. But Caracalla must do it, well or ill."

"Then he will forget me!" replied Melissa, with a sigh of relief.

"Hardly," answered the philosopher. He was sorry for the terrified girl, and in his wish to lighten her woes as far as he could, he said, gravely: "You called him terrible, and he can be more terrible than any man living. But he has been kind to you so far, and, if you take my advice, you will always seem to expect nothing from him that is not good and noble."

"Then I must be a hypocrite," replied Melissa. "Only to-day, he has murdered the noble Titianus."

"That is an affair of state which does not concern you," replied Philostratus. "Read my description of Achilles. I represent him among other heroes such as Caracalla might be. Try, on your part, to see him in that light. I know that it is sometimes a pleasure to him to justify the good opinion of others. Encourage your imagination to think the best of him. I shall tell him that you regard him as magnanimous and noble."

"No, no!" cried Melissa; "that would make everything worse."

But the philosopher interrupted her.

"Trust my riper experience. I know him. If you let him know your true opinion of him, I will answer for nothing. My Achilles reveals the good qualities with which he came into the world, and if you look closely you may still find sparks among the ashes."

He here took his leave, for they had reached the vestibule leading to the high-priest's lodgings, and a few minutes later Melissa found herself with Euryale, to whom she related all that she had seen and felt. When she told her older friend what Philostratus had advised, the lady stroked her hair, and said: "Try to follow the advice of so experienced a man. It can not be very difficult. When a woman's heart has once been attached to a man—and pity is one of the strongest of human ties—the bond may be strained and worn, but a few threads must always remain."

But Melissa hastily broke in:

"There is not a spider's thread left which blinds me to that cruel man. The murder of Titianus has snapped them all."

"Not so," replied the lady, confidently. "Pity is the only form of love which even the worst crime can not eradicate from a kind heart. You prayed for Cæsar before you knew him, and that was out of pure human charity. Exercise now a wider compassion, and reflect that Fate has called you to take care of a hapless creature raving in fever and hard to deal with. How many Christian women, especially such as call themselves deaconesses, voluntarily assume such duties! and good is good, right is right for all, whether they pray to one God or to several. If you keep your heart pure, and constantly think of the time which shall be fulfilled for each of us, to our ruin or to our salvation, you will pass unharmed through this great peril. I know it, I feel it."

"But you do not know him," exclaimed Melissa, "and how terrible he can be! And Diodoros! When he is well again, if he hears that I am with Cæsar, in obedience to his call whenever he sends for me, and if evil tongues tell him dreadful things about me, he, too, will condemn me!"

"No, no," the matron declared, kissing her brow and eyes. "If he loves you truly, he will trust you."

"He loves me," sobbed Melissa; "but, even if he does

not desert me when I am thus branded, his father will come between us."

"God forbid!" cried Euryale. "Remain what you are, and I will always be the same to you, come what may; and those who love you will not refuse to listen to an old woman who has grown gray in honor."

And Melissa believed her motherly, kind, worthy friend; and, with the new confidence which revived in her, her longing for her lover began to stir irresistibly. She wanted a fond glance from the eyes of the youth who loved her, and to whom, for another man's sake, she could not give all his due, nay, who had perhaps a right to complain of her. This she frankly confessed, and the matron herself conducted the impatient girl to see Diodoros.

Melissa again found Andreas in attendance on the sufferer, and she was surprised at the warmth with which the high-priest's wife greeted the Christian.

Diodoros was already able to be dressed and to sit up. He was pale and weak, and his head was still bound up, but he welcomed the girl affectionately, though with a mild reproach as to the rarity of her visits.

Andreas had already informed him that Melissa was kept away by her mediation for the prisoners, and so he was comforted by her assurance that if her duty would allow of it she would never leave him again. And the joy of having her there, the delight of gazing into her sweet, lovely face, and the youthful gift of forgetting the past in favor of the present, silenced every bitter reflection. He was soon blissfully listening to her with a fresh color in his cheeks, and never had he seen her so tender, so devoted, so anxious to show him the fullness of her great love. The quiet, reserved girl was to-day the wooer, and with the zeal called forth by her ardent wish to do him good, she expressed all the tenderness of her warm heart so frankly and gladly that to him it seemed as though Eros had never till now pierced her with the right shaft.

As soon as Euryale was absorbed in conversation with Andreas, she offered him her lips with gay audacity, as though in defiance of some stern dragon of virtue, and he, drunk with rapture, enjoyed what she granted him. And soon it was he who became daring, declaring that there would be time enough to talk another day; that for the present her rosy mouth had nothing to do but to cure him with kisses. And during this sweet give and take, she implored him with pathetic fervor never, never to doubt her love, whatever he might hear of her. Their older friends, who had turned their backs on the couple and were talking busily by a window, paid no heed to them, and the blissful conviction of being loved as ardently as she loved flooded her whole being.

Only now and then did the thought of Cæsar trouble for a moment the rapture of that hour, like a hideous form appearing out of distant clouds. She felt prompted indeed to tell her lover everything, but it seemed so difficult to make him understand exactly how everything had happened, and Diodoros must not be distressed. And, indeed, intoxicated as he was with heated passion, he made the attempt impossible.

When he spoke it was only to assure her of his love; and when the lady Euryale at last called her to go, and looked in the girl's glowing face, Melissa felt as though she were snatched from a rapturous dream.

In the ante-room they were stopped by Andreas.

Euryale had indeed relieved his worst fears, still he

was anxious to lay before the girl the question whether
she would not be wise to take advantage of this very
night to make her escape. She, however, her eyes still
beaming with happiness, laid her little hand coaxingly on
his bearded mouth, and begged him not to sadden her
high spirits and hopes of a better time by warnings and
dismal forecasts. Even the lady Euryale had advised
her to trust fearlessly to herself, and sitting with her lover
she had acquired the certainty that it was best so. The
freedman could not bear to disturb this happy confidence,
and only impressed on Melissa that she should send for
him if ever she needed him. He would find her a hiding place, and the lady Euryale had undertaken to provide
a messenger. He then bade them god-speed, and they
returned to the high-priest's dwelling.

In the vestibule they found a servant from the lady
Berenike; in his mistress's name he desired Euryale to
send Melissa to spend the night with her. This invitation,
which would remove Melissa from the Serapeum, was
welcome to them both, and the matron herself accompanied
the young girl down a private staircase leading to a small
side-door. Argutis, who had come to inquire for his
young mistress, was to be her escort and to bring her
back early next morning to the same entrance.

The old slave had much to tell her. He had been
on his feet all day. He had been to the harbor to inquire
as to the return of the vessel with the prisoners on board;
to the Serapeum to inquire for her; to Dido, to give her
the news. He had met Alexander in the forenoon on
the quay where the imperial galleys were moored. When
the young man learned that the trireme could not come
in before next morning at the soonest, he had set out to
cross the lake and see Zeno and his daughter. He had

charged Argutis to let Melissa know that his longing for the fair Agatha gave him no peace.

He and old Dido disapproved of their young master's feather-brain, which had not been made more steady and patient even by the serious events of this day and his sister's peril; however, he did not allow a word of blame to escape him. He was happy only to be allowed to walk behind Melissa, and to hear from her own lips that all was well with her, and that Cæsar was gracious.

Alexander, indeed, had also told the old man that he and Cæsar were "good friends"; and now the slave was thinking of Pandion, Theocritus, and the other favorites of whom he had heard; and he assured Melissa that, as soon as her father should be free, Caracalla would be certain to raise him to the rank of knight, to give him lands and wealth, perhaps one of the imperial residences on the Bruchium. Then he, Argutis, would be house steward, and show that he knew other things besides keeping the work-room and garden in order, splitting wood, and buying cheaply at market.

Melissa laughed and said he should be no worse off if only the first wish of her heart were fulfilled, and she were wife to Diodoros; and Argutis declared he would be amply content if only she allowed him to remain with her.

But she only half listened und answered absently, for she breathed faster as she pictured to herself how she would show Cæsar, on whom she had already proved her power, that she had ceased to tremble before him.

Thus they came to the house of Seleukus.

A large force had taken up their quarters there.

In the pillared hall beyond the vestibule bearded soldiers were sitting on benches or squatting in groups on the ground, drinking noisily and singing, or laughing and squabbling as they threw the dice on the costly mosaic pavement. A riotous party were toping and reveling in the beautiful garden of the impluvium round a fire which they had lighted on the velvet turf. A dozen or so of officers had stretched themselves on cushions under one of the colonnades, and, without attempting to check the wild behavior of their men, were watching the dancing of some Egyptian girls who had been brought into the house of their involuntary host. Although Melissa was closely veiled and accompanied by a servant, she did not escape rude words and insolent glances. Indeed, an audacious young prætorian had put out his hand to pull away her veil, but an older officer stopped him.

The lady Berenike's rooms had so far not been intruded on; for Macrinus, the prætorian prefect, who knew Berenike through her brother-in-law the senator Cœranus, had given orders that the women's apartments were to be exempt from the encroachments of the quartermaster of the body-guard. Breathing rapidly and with a heightened color, Melissa at last entered the room of Seleukus's wife.

The matron's voice was full of bitterness as she greeted her young visitor with the exclamation: "You look as if you had fled to escape persecution! And in my house, too! Or"—and her large eyes flashed brightly—"or is the blood-hound on the track of his prey? My boat is quite ready—"

Wen Melissa denied this, and related what had happened, Berenike exclaimed: "But you know that the panther lies still and gathers himself up before he springs; or, if you do not, you may see it to-morrow at the Circus. There is to be a performance in Cæsar's honor, the like of which not even Nero ever saw. My husband bears the chief part of the cost, and can think of nothing else. He has even forgotten his only child, and all to please the man who insults us, robs and humiliates us! Now that men kiss the hands which maltreat them, it is the part of women to defy them. You must fly, child! The harbor is now closed, but it will be open again to-morrow morning, and, if your folks are set free in the course of the day, then away with you at once! Or do you really hope for any good from the tyrant who has made this house what you now see it?"

"I know him," replied Melissa, "and I look for nothing but the worst."

At this the elder woman warmly grasped the girl's hand, but she was interrupted by the waiting-woman Johanna, who said that a Roman officer of rank, a tribune, craved to be admitted.

When Berenike refused to receive him, the maid assured her that he was a young man, and had expressed his wish to bring an urgent request to the lady's notice, in a becoming and modest manner.

On this the matron allowed him to be shown in to her, and Melissa hastily obeyed her instructions to withdraw into the adjoining room.

Only a half-drawn curtain divided it from the room where Berenike received the soldier, and without listening she could hear the loud voice which riveted her attention as soon as she had recognized it.

The young tribune, in a tone of courteous entreaty, begged his hostess to provide a room for his brother, who was severely wounded. The sufferer was in a high fever, and the physician said that the noise and rattle of vehicles in the street, on which the room where he now lay looked out, and the perpetual coming and going of the men, might endanger his life. He had just been told that on

the side of the women's apartments there was a row of
rooms looking out on the impluvium, and he ventured to
entreat her to spare one of them for the injured man. If
she had a brother or a child, she would forgive the boldness of his request.

So far she listened in silence; then she suddenly
raised her head and measured the petitioner's tall figure
with a lurid fire in her eye. Then she replied, while she
looked into his handsome young face with a half-scornful,
half-indignant air: "Oh, yes! I know what it is to see
one we love suffer. I had an only child; she was the joy
of my heart. Death—death snatched her from me, and
a few days later the sovereign whom you serve commanded us to prepare a feast for him. It seemed to him
something new and delightful to hold a revel in a house
of mourning. At the last moment—all the guests were
assembled—he sent us word that he himself did not intend to appear. But his friends laughed and revelled
wildly enough! They enjoyed themselves, and no doubt
praised our cook and our wine. And now—another
honor we can duly appreciate!—he sends his prætorians
to turn this house of mourning into a tavern, a wine-shop,
where they call creatures in from the street to dance and
sing. The rank to which you have risen while yet so
young shows that you are of good family, so you can
imagine how highly we esteem the honor of seeing your
men trampling, destroying, and burning in their campfires everything which years of labor and care had produced to make our little garden a thing of beauty. Only
look down on them! Macrinus, who commands you promised me, moreover, that the women's apartments should
be respected. No prætorian, whether common soldier or
commander," and here she raised her voice, "shall set

foot within them! Here is his writing. The prefect set the seal beneath it in Cæsar's name."

"I know of the order, noble lady," interrupted Nemesianus, "and should be the last to wish to act against it. I do not demand, I only appeal humbly to the heart of a woman and a mother."

"A mother!" broke in Berenike, scornfully; "yes! and one whose soul your lord has pierced with daggers—a woman whose home has been dishonored and made hateful to her. I have enjoyed sufficient honor now, and shall stand firmly on my rights."

"Hear but one thing more," began the youth, timidly; but the lady Berenike had already turned her back upon him, and returned with a proud and stately carriage to Melissa in the adjoining apartment.

Breathing hard, as if stunned by her words, the tribune remained standing on the threshold where the terrible lady had vanished from his sight, and then, striving to regain his composure, pushed back the curling locks from his brow. But scarcely had Berenike entered the other room than Melissa whispered to her, "The wounded man is the unfortunate Aurelius, whose face Caracalla wounded for my sake."

At this the lady's eyes suddenly flashed and blazed so strangely that the girl's blood ran cold. But she had no time to ask the reason of this emotion, for the next moment the queenly woman grasped the weaker one by the wrist with her strong right hand, and with a commanding "Come with me," drew her back into the room they had just quitted. She called to the tribune, whose hand was already on the door, to come back.

The young man stood still, surprised and startled to see Melissa; but the lady Berenike said, calmly:

"Now that I have learned the honor that has been accorded to you, too, by the master whom you so faithfully serve, the poor injured man whom you call your brother shall be made welcome within these walls. He is my companion in suffering. A quiet, airy chamber shall be set apart for him, and he shall not lack careful attention, nor anything which even his own mother could offer him. Only two things I desire of you in return: that you admit no one of your companions-in-arms, nor any man whatever, into this dwelling, save only the physician whom I shall send to you. Furthermore, that you do not betray, even to your nearest friend, whom you found here besides myself."

Under the mortification that had wounded his brotherly heart, Aurelius Nemesianus had lost countenance; but now he replied with a soldier's ready presence of mind: "It is difficult for me to find a proper answer to you, noble lady. I know right well that I owe you my warmest thanks, and equally so that he whom you call our master has inflicted as deep a wrong on us as on you; but Cæsar is still my military chief."

"Still!" broke in Berenike. "But you are too youthful a tribune for me to believe that you took up the sword as a means of livelihood."

"We are sons of the Aurelia," answered Nemesianus, haughtily, "and it is very possible that this day's work may be the cause of our deserting the eagles we have followed in order to win glory and taste the delights of warfare. But all that is for the future to decide. Meanwhile, I thank you, noble lady, and also in the name of my brother, who is my second self. On behalf of Apollonaris, too, I beg you to pardon the rudeness which we offered to this maiden—"

"I am not angry with you any more," cried Melissa, eagerly and frankly, and the tribune thanked her in his own and his brother's name.

He began trying to explain the unfortunate occurrence, but Berenike admonished him to lose no time. The soldier withdrew, and the lady Berenike ordered her handmaiden to call the housekeeper and other serving-women. Then she repaired quickly to the room she had destined for the wounded man and his brother. But neither Melissa nor the other women could succeed in really lending her any help, for she herself put forth all her cleverness and power of head and hand, forgetting nothing that might be useful or agreeable in the nursing of the sick. In that wealthy, well-ordered house everything stood ready to hand; and in less than a quarter of an hour the tribune Nemesianus was informed that the chamber was ready for the reception of his brother.

The lady then returned with Melissa to her own sleeping-apartment, and took various little bottles and jars from a small medicine-chest, begging the girl at the same time to excuse her, as she intended to undertake the nursing of the wounded man herself. Here were books, and there Korinna's lute. Johanna would attend to the evening meal. To-morrow morning they could consult further as to what was necessary to be done; then she kissed her guest and left the room.

Left to herself, Melissa gave herself up to varying thoughts, till Johanna brought her repast. While she hardly nibbled at it, the Christian told her that matters looked ill with the tribune, and that the wound in the forehead especially caused the physician much anxiety. Many questions were needed to draw this much from the freedwoman, for she spoke but little. When she did speak, however, it was with great kindliness, and there lay something so simple and gentle in her whole manner that it awakened confidence. Having satisfied her appetite, Melissa returned to the lady Berenike's apartment; but there her heart grew heavy at the thought of what awaited her on the morrow. When, at the moment of leaving, Johanna inquired whether she desired anything further, she asked her if she knew a saying of her fellow-believers which ran, "The fullness of time was come."

"Yes, surely," returned the other; "our Lord himself spoke them, and Paul wrote them to the Galatians."

"Who is this Paul?" Melissa asked; and the Christian replied that of all the teachers of her faith he was the one she most dearly loved. Then, hesitating a little, she asked if Melissa, being a heathen, had inquired the meaning of this saying.

"Andrew, the freedman of Polybius and the lady Euryale, explained it to me. Did the moment ever come to you in which you felt assured that for you the time was fulfilled?"

"Yes," replied Johanna, with decision; "and, in every life, sooner or later that moment comes."

"You are a maiden like myself," began Melissa, simply. "A heavy task lies before me, and if you would confide to me—"

But the Christian broke in: "My life has moved in other paths than yours, and what has happened to me, the freedwoman and the Christian, can have no interest for you. But the saying which has stirred your soul refers to the coming of One who is all in all to us Christians. Did Andrew tell you nothing of His life?"

"Only a little," answered the girl, "but I would gladly hear more of Him."

Then the Christian seated herself at Melissa's side, and, clasping the maiden's hand in hers, told her of the birth of the Saviour, of His loving heart, and His willing death as a sacrifice for the sins of the whole world. The girl listened with attentive ear. With no word did she interrupt the narrative, and the image of the Crucified One rose before her mind's eye, pure and noble, and worthy of all love. A thousand questions rose to her lips, but, before she could ask one, the Christian was called away to attend the lady Berenike, and Melissa was again alone.

What she had already heard of the teaching of the Christians occurred to her once more, and above all that first saying from the sacred Scriptures which had attracted her attention, and about which she had just asked Johanna. Perhaps for her, too, the time was already fulfilled, when she had taken courage to defy the emperor's commands.

She rejoiced at this action, for she felt that the strength would never fail her now to set her will against his. She felt as though she bore a charm against his power since she had parted from her lover, and since the murder of the governor had opened her eyes to the true character of him on whom she had all too willingly expended her pity. And yet she shuddered at the thought of meeting the emperor again, and of having to show him that she felt safe with him because she trusted to his generosity.

Lost in deep thought, she waited for the return of the lady and the Christian waiting-woman, but in vain.

At last her eye fell upon the scrolls which the lady Berenike had pointed out to her. They lay in beautiful alabaster caskets on an ebony stand. If they had only been the writings of the Christians telling of the life and death of their Saviour! But how should writings such as those come here? The casket only held the works of Philostratus, and she took from it the roll containing the story of the hero of which he had himself spoken to her. Full of curiosity, she smoothed out the papyrus with the ivory stick, and her attention was soon engaged by the lively conversation between the vintner and his Phœnician guest. She passed rapidly over the beginning, but soon reached the part of which Philostratus had told her. Under the form of Achilles he had striven to represent Caracalla as he appeared to the author's indulgent imagination. But it was no true portrait; it described the original at most as his mother would have wished him to be. There it was written that the vehemence flashing from the hero's bright eyes, even when peacefully inclined, showed how easily his wrath could break forth. But to those who loved him he was even more endearing during these outbursts than before. The Athenians felt toward him as they did toward a lion; for, if the king of beasts pleased them when he was at rest, he charmed them infinitely more when, foaming with bloodthirsty rage, he fell upon a bull, a wild boar, or some such ferocious animal.

Yes, indeed! Caracalla, too, fell mercilessly upon his prey! Had she not seen him hewing down Apollonaris a few hours ago?

Furthermore, Achilles was said to have declared that he could drive away care by fearlessly encountering the greatest dangers for the sake of his friends. But where were Caracalla's friends?

At best, the allusion could only refer to the Roman state, for whose sake the emperor certainly did endure many a hardship and many a wearisome task, and he was not the only person who had told her so.

Then she turned back a little and found the words: "But because he was easily inclined to anger, Chiron instructed him in music; for is it not inherent in this art to soothe violence and wrath? And Achilles acquired without trouble the laws of harmony and sang to the lyre."

This all corresponded with the truth, and to-morrow she was to discover what had suggested to Philostratus the story that when Achilles begged Calliope to endow him with the gifts of music and poetry she had given him so much of both as he required to enliven the feast and banish sadness. He was also said to be a poet, and devote himself most ardently to verse when resting from the toils of war. To hear that man unjustly blamed on whom her heart is set, only increases a woman's love; but unmerited praise makes her criticise him more sharply, and is apt to transform a fond smile into a scornful one. Thus the picture that raised Caracalla to the level of an Achilles made Melissa shrug her shoulders over the man she dreaded; and while she even doubted Cæsar's musical capacities, Diodoros's young, fresh, bell-like voice rose doubly beautiful and true upon her memory's ear. The image of her lover finally drove out that of the emperor, and, while she seemed to hear the wedding song which the youths and maidens were so soon to sing for them both, she fell asleep.

It was late when Johanna came to admonish her to retire to rest. Shortly before sunrise she was awakened by Berenike, who wished to take some rest, and who told her, before seeking her couch, that Apollonaris was doing well. The lady was still sleeping when Johanna came to inform Melissa that the slave Argutis was waiting to see her.

The Christian undertook to convey the maiden's farewell greetings to her mistress.

As they entered the living-room, the gardener had just brought in fresh flowers, among them three rose-bushes covered with full-blown flowers and half-opened, dewy buds. Melissa asked Johanna timidly if the lady Berenike would permit her to pluck one—there were so many; to which the Christian replied that it would depend on the use it was to be put to.

"Only for the sick tribune," answered Melissa, reddening. So Johanna plucked two of the fairest blooms and gave them to the maiden—one for the man who had injured her and one for her betrothed. Melissa kissed her, gratefully, and begged her to present the flower to the sick man in her name.

Johanna carried out her wish at once; but the wounded man gazing mournfully at the rose, murmured to himself: "Poor, lovely, gentle child! She will be ruined or dead before Caracalla leaves Alexandria!"

CHAPTER III.

The slave Argutis was waiting for Melissa in the antechamber. It was evident that he brought good news, for he beamed with joy as she came toward him; and before she left the house she knew that her father and Philip had returned and had regained their freedom.

The slave had not allowed these joyful tidings to

reach his beloved mistress's ear, that he might have the undivided pleasure of bringing them himself, and the delight she expressed was fully as great as he had anticipated. Melissa even hurried back to Johanna to impart to her the joyful intelligence that she might tell it to her mistress.

When they were in the street the slave told her that, at break of day, the ship had cast anchor which brought back father and son. The prisoners had received their freedom while they were still at sea, and had been permitted to return home at once. All was well, only—he added, hesitatingly and with tears in his eyes—things were not as they used to be, and now the old were stronger than the young. Her father had taken no harm from the heavy work at the oars, but Philip had returned from the galleys very ill, and they had carried him forthwith to the bedchamber, where Dido was now nursing him. It was a good thing that she had not been there to hear how the master had stormed and cursed over the infamy they had had to endure; but the meeting with his birds had calmed him down quickly enough.

Melissa and her attendant were walking in the direction of the Serapeum, but now she declared that she must first see the liberated prisoners. And she insisted upon it, although Argutis assured her of her father's intention of seeking her at the house of the high-priest, as soon as he had removed all traces of his captivity and his shameful work at the galleys in the bath. Philip she would, of course, find at home, he being too weak to leave the house. The old man had some difficulty in following his young mistress, and she soon stepped lightly over the "Welcome" on the threshold of her father's house. Never had the red mosaic inscription seemed to shine so bright and friendly, and she heard her name called in delighted tones from the kitchen.

This joyful greeting from Dido was not to be returned from the door only. In a moment Melissa was standing by the hearth; but the slave, speechless with happiness, could only point with fork and spoon, first to the pot in which a large piece of meat was being boiled down into a strengthening soup for Philip, then to a spit on which two young chickens were browning before the fire, and then to the pan where she was frying the little fish of which the returned wanderer was so fond.

But the old woman's struggle between the duty that kept her near the fire and the love that drew her away from it, was not of long duration. In a few minutes Melissa, her hands clasping the slave's withered arm, was listening to the tender words of welcome that Dido had ready for her. The slave woman declared that she scarcely dared to let her eyes rest upon her mistress, much less touch her with the fingers that had just been cleaning fish; for the girl was dressed as grandly as the daughter of the high-priest. Melissa laughed at this; but the slave went on to say that they had not been able to detain her master. His longing to see his daughter and the desire to speak with Cæsar had driven him out of the house, and Alexander had, of course, accompanied him. Only Philip, poor, crushed worm, was at home, and the sight of her would put more strength into him than the strong soup and the old wine which his father had fetched for him from the store-room, although he generally reserved it for libations on her mother's grave.

Melissa soon stood beside her brother's couch, and the sight of him cast a dark shadow over the brightness of this happy morn. As he recognized her, a fleeting smile crossed the pale, spiritualized face, which seemed to her to have grown ten years older in this short time; but it vanished as quickly as it had come. Then the great eyes gazed blankly again from the shadows that surrounded them, and a spasm of pain quivered from time to time round the thin, tightly closed lips. Melissa could hardly restrain her tears. Was this what he had been brought to—the youth who only a few days ago had made them all feel conscious of the superiority of his brilliant mind!

Her warm heart made her feel more lovingly toward her sick brother than she had ever done when he was in health, and surely he was conscious of the tenderness with which she strove to comfort him.

The unaccustomed, hard, and degrading work at the oars, she assured him, would have worn out a stronger man than he; but he would soon be able to visit the Museum again and argue as bravely as ever. With this, she bent over him to kiss his brow, but he raised himself a little, and said, with a contemptuous smile:

"Apathy — ataraxy — complete indifference — is the highest aim after which the soul of the skeptic strives. That at least"—and here his eyes flashed for a moment —"I have attained to in these cursed days. That a thinking being could become so utterly callous to everything —everything, be it what it may—even I could never have believed!" He sank into silence, but his sister urged him to take courage—surely many a glad day was before him yet.

At this he raised himself more energetically, and exclaimed:

"Glad days?—for me, and with you? That you should still be of such good cheer would please or else astonish me if I were still capable of those sentiments. If things were different, I should ask you now, what have you given the imperial bloodhound in return for our freedom?"

Here Melissa exclaimed indignantly, but he continued unabashed:

"Alexander says you have found favor with our imperial master. He calls, and you come. Naturally, it is for him to command. See how much can be made of the child of a gem-cutter! But what says handsome Diodoros to all this? Why turn so pale? These, truly, are questions which I would fling in your face were things as they used to be. *Now* I say in all unconcern, do what you will!"

The blood had ebbed from Melissa's cheeks during this attack of her brother's. His injurious and false accusations roused her indignation to the utmost, but one glance at his weary, suffering face showed her how great was the pain he endured, and in her compassionate heart pity strove against righteous anger. The struggle was sharp, but pity prevailed; and, instead of punishing him by a sharp retort, she forced herself to explain to him in a few gentle words what had happened, in order to dispel the unworthy suspicion that must surely hurt him as much as it did her. She felt convinced that the sufferer would be cheered by her words; but he made no attempt to show that he appreciated her kindly moderation, nor to express any satisfaction. On the contrary, when he spoke it was in the same tone as before.

"If that be the case," he said, "so much the better; but were it otherwise, it would have to be endured just the same. I can think of nothing that could affect me now, and it is well. Only my body troubles me still. It weighs upon me like lead, and grow heavier with every word I utter. Therefore, I pray you, leave me to myself!"

But his sister would not obey. "No, Philip," she cried, eagerly, "this may not be. Let your strong spirit arise and burst asunder the bonds that fetter and cripple it."

At this a groan of pain escaped the philosopher, and, turning again to the girl, he answered, with a mournful smile:

"Bid the cushion in that arm-chair do so. It will succeed better than I." Then crying out impatiently and as loudly as he could, "Now go—you know not how you torture me!" he turned away from her and buried his face in the pillows.

But Melissa, as if beside herself, laid her hands upon his shoulder, and, shaking him gently, exclaimed: "And even if it vexes you, I will not be driven away thus. The misfortunes that have befallen you in these days will end by destroying you, if you will not pull yourself together. We must have patience, and it can only come about slowly, but you must make an effort. The least thing that pains you hurts us too, and you, in return, may not remain indifferent to what we feel. See, Philip, our mother and Andreas taught us often not to think only of ourselves, but of others. We ask so little of you; but if you—"

At this the philosopher shook himself free of her hand, and cried in a voice of anguish:

"Away, I say! Leave me alone! One word more, and I die!" With this he hid his head in the coverlet, and Melissa could see how his limbs quivered convulsively as if shaken by an ague.

To see a being so dear to her thus utterly broken down cut her to the heart. Oh, that she could help him! If she did not succeed, or if he never found strength to rouse himself, he too, would be one of Cæsar's victims. Corrupted and ruined lives marked the path of this terrible being, and, with a shudder, she asked herself when her turn would come.

Her hair had become disordered, and as she smoothed it she looked in the mirror, and could not but observe that in the simple but costly white robe of the dead Korinna she looked like a maiden of noble birth rather than the lowly daughter of an artist. She would have liked to tear it off and replace it by another, but her one modest festival robe had been left behind at the house of the lady Berenike. To appear in broad daylight before the neighbors or to walk in the streets clad in this fashion seemed to her impossible after her brother's unjust suspicion, and she bade Argutis fetch her a litter.

When they parted, Dido could see distinctly that Philip had wounded her. And she could guess how, so she withheld any questions that she might not hurt her. Over the fire, however, she stabbed fiercely into the fowl destined for the philosopher, but cooked it, nevertheless, with all possible care.

On the way to the Serapeum, Melissa's anxiety increased. Till now, eagerness for the fray, fear, hope, and the joyful consciousness of right-doing, had alternated in her mind. Now, for the first time, she was seized with a premonition of misfortune. Fate itself had turned against her. Even should she succeed in escaping, she could not hope to regain her lost peace of mind.

Philip's biting words had shown her what most of them must think of her; and, though the ship should bear her far away, would it be right to bring Diodoros away from his old father to follow her? She must see her lover, and if possible tell him all. The rose, too, which the Christian had given her for him, and which lay in her lap, she wished so much to carry to him herself. She could not go alone to the chamber of the convalescent, and the attendance of a slave counted for nothing in the eyes of other people. It was even doubtful if a bondsman might be admitted into the inner apartments of the sanctuary. However, she would, she must see Diodoros and speak to him; and thus planning ways and means by which to accomplish this, looking forward joyfully to the meeting with her father, and wondering how Agatha, the Christian, had received Alexander, she lost the feeling of deep depression which had weighed on her when she had left the house.

- The litter stopped, and Argutis helped her to descend. He was breathless, for it had been most difficult to open a way for her through the dense crowds that were already thronging to the Circus, where the grand evening performance in honor of the emperor was to begin as soon as it was dark.

Just as she was entering the house, she perceived Andreas coming toward them along the street of Hermes, and she at once bade the slave call him. He was soon at her side, and declared himself willing to accompany her to Diodoros.

This time, however, she did not find her lover alone in the sick-room. Two physicians were with him, and she grew pale as she recognized in one of them the emperor's Roman body-physician.

But it was too late to escape detection; so she only hastened to her lover's side, whispered warm words of love in his ear, and, while she gave him the rose, conjured him ever and always to have faith in her and in her love, whatever reports he might hear.

Diodoros was up and had fully recovered. His face lighted up with joy as he saw her; but, when she repeated the old, disquieting request, he anxiously begged to know what she meant by it. She assured him, however, that she had already delayed too long, and referred him to Andreas and the lady Euryale, who would relate to him what had befallen her and spoiled every happy hour she had. Then, thinking herself unobserved by those present, she breathed a kiss upon his lips. But he would not let her go, urging with passionate tenderness his rights as her betrothed, till she tore herself away from him and hurried from the room.

As she left, she heard a ringing laugh, followed by loud, sprightly talking. It was not her lover's voice, and endeavoring, while she waited for Andreas, to catch what was being said on the other side of the door, she distinctly heard the body-physician (for no other pronounced the Greek language in that curious, halting manner) exclaim, gaily: "By Cerberus, young man, you are to be envied! The beauty my sovereign lord is limping after flies unbidden into your arms!"

Then came loud laughter as before, but this time interrupted by Diodoros's indignant question as to what this all meant. At last Melissa heard Andreas's deep voice promising the young man to tell him everything later on; and when the convalescent impatiently asked for an immediate explanation, the Christian exhorted him to be calm, and finally requested the physician to grant him a few moments' conversation.

Then there was quiet for a time in the room, only broken by Diodoros's angry questions and the pacifying exclamations of the freedman. She felt as if she must return to her lover and tell him herself what she had been forced to do in these last days, but maidenly shyness restrained her, till at last Andreas came out. The freedman's honest face expressed the deepest solicitude, and his voice sounded rough and hasty as he exclaimed, "You must fly—fly this day!"

"And my father and brother, and Diodoros?" she asked, anxiously. But he answered, urgently:

"Let them get away as they may. There is no hole or corner obscure enough to keep you hidden. Therefore take advantage of the ship that waits for you. Follow Argutis at once to the lady Berenike. I can not accompany you, for it lies with me to occupy for the next few hours the attention of the body-physician, from whom you have the most to fear. He has consented to go with me to my garden across the water. There I promised him a delicious, real Alexandrian feast, and you know how gladly Polybius will seize the opportunity to share it with him. No doubt, too, some golden means may be found to bind his tongue; for woe to you if Caracalla discovers prematurely that you are promised to another, and woe then to your betrothed! After sundown, when every one here has gone to the Circus, I will take Diodoros to a place of safety. Farewell, child, and may our heavenly Father defend you!"

He laid his right hand upon her head as if in blessing; but Melissa cried, wringing her hands: "Oh, let me go to him once more! How can I leave him and go far away without one word of farewell or of forgiveness?"

But Andreas interrupted her, saying: "You can not. His life is at stake as well as your own. I shall make it my business to look after his safety. The wife of Seleukus will assist you in your flight."

"And you will persuade him to trust me?" urged Melissa, clinging convulsively to his arm.

"I will try," answered the freedman, gloomily. Melissa dropped his arm, for loud, manly voices were approaching down the stairs near which they stood.

It was Heron and Alexander, returning from their audience with the emperor. Instantly the Christian went to meet them, and dismissed the temple servant who accompanied them.

In the half-darkness of the corridor, Melissa threw herself weeping into her father's arms. But he stroked her hair lovingly, and kissed her more tenderly on brow and eyes than he had ever done before, whispering gaily to her: "Dry your tears, my darling. You have been a brave maiden, and now comes your reward. Fear and sorrow will now be changed into happiness and power, and all the glories of the world. I have not even told Alexander yet what promises to make our fortunes, for I know my duty." Then, raising his voice, he said to the freedman, "If I have been rightly informed, we shall find the son of Polybius in one of the apartments close at hand."

"Quite right," answered the freedman, gravely, and then went on to explain to the gem-cutter that he could not see Diodoros just now, but must instantly leave the country with his son and daughter on Berenike's ship. Not a moment was to be lost. Melissa would tell him all on the way.

But Heron laughed scornfully: "That would be a pretty business! We have plenty of time, and, with the greatness that lies before us, everything must be done openly and in the right way. My first thought, you see, was to come here, for I had promised the girl to Diodoros, and he must be informed before I can consent to her betrothal to another."

"Father!" cried Melissa, scarcely able to command her voice. But Heron took no notice of her, and continued, composedly: "Diodoros would have been dear to me as a son-in-law. I shall certainly tell him so. But when Cæsar, the ruler of the world, condescends to ask a plain man for his daughter, every other consideration must naturally be put aside. Diodoros is sensible, and is sure to see it in the right light. We all know how Cæsar treats those who are in his way; but I wish the son of Polybius no ill, so I forbore to betray to Cæsar what tie had once bound you, my child, to the gallant youth."

Heron had never liked the freedman. The man's firm character had always gone against the gem-cutter's surly, capricious nature; and it was no little satisfaction to him to let him feel his superiority, and boast before him of the apparent good luck that had befallen the artist's family.

But Andreas had already heard from the physician that Caracalla had informed his mother's envoys of his intended marriage with an Alexandrian, the daughter of an artist of Macedonian extraction. This could only refer to Melissa, and it was this news which had caused him to urge the maiden to instant flight.

Pale, incapable of uttering a word, Melissa stood before her father; but the freedman grasped her hand, looked Heron reproachfully in the face, and asked, quietly, "And you would really have the heart to join this dear child's life to that of a bloody tyrant?"

"Certainly I have," returned Heron with decision, and he drew his daughter's hand out of that of Andreas, who turned his back upon the artist with a meaning shrug of the shoulders. But Melissa ran after him, and, clinging to him, cried as she turned first to him and then to her father:

"I am promised to Diodoros, and shall hold fast to him and my love; tell him that, Andreas! Come what may, I will be his and his alone! Cæsar—"

"Swear not!" broke in Heron, angrily, "for by great Serapis—"

But Alexander interposed between them, and begged his father to consider what he was asking of the girl. Cæsar's proposals could scarcely have been very pleasing to him, or why had he concealed till now what Caracalla was whispering to him in the adjoining room? He might imagine for himself what fate awaited the helpless child at the side of a husband at whose name even men trembled. He should remember her mother, and what she would have said to such a union. There was little time to escape from this terrible wooer.

Then Melissa turned to her brother and begged him earnestly: "Then *you* take me to the ship, Alexander; take charge of me yourself!"

"And I?" asked Heron, his eye cast gloomily on the ground.

"You must come with us!" implored the girl, clasping her hands.—"O Andreas! say something! Tell him what I have to expect!"

"He knows that without my telling him," replied the freedman.—"I must go now, for two lives are at stake, Heron. If I can not keep the physician away from Cæsar, your daughter, too, will be in danger. If you desire to see your daughter forever in fear of death, give her in marriage to Caracalla. If you have her happiness at heart, then escape with her into a far country."

He nodded to the brother and sister, and returned to the sick-room.

"Fly!—escape!" repeated the old man, and he waived his hand angrily. "This Andreas—the freedman, the Christian—always in extremes. Why run one's head against the wall? First consider, then act; that was what she taught us whose sacred memory you have but now invoked, Alexander."

With this he walked out of the half-dark corridor into the open court-yard, in front of his children. Here he looked at his daughter, who was breathing fast, and evidently prepared to resist to the last. And as he beheld her in Korinna's white and costly robes, like a noble priestess, it occurred to him that even before his captivity she had ceased to be the humble, unquestioning instrument of his capricious temper. Into what a haughty beauty the quiet embroideress had been transformed!

By all the gods! Caracalla had no cause to be ashamed of such an empress.

And, unaccustomed as he was to keep back anything whatever from his children, he began to express these sentiments. But he did not get far, for the hour for the morning meal being just over, the court-yard began to fill from all sides with officials and servants of the temple. So, father and son silently followed the maiden through the crowded galleries and apartments, into the house of the high-priest.

Here they were received by Philostratus, who hardly gave Melissa time to greet the lady Euryale before he informed her, but with unwonted hurry and excitement, that the emperor was awaiting her with impatience.

The philosopher motioned to her to follow him, but she clung, as if seeking help, to her brother, and cried: "I will not go again to Caracalla! You are the kindest and best of them all, Philostratus, and you will understand me. Evil will come of it if I follow you—I can not go again to Cæsar."

But it was impossible for the courtier to yield to her, in the face of his monarch's direct commands; therefore, hard as it was to him, he said, resolutely: "I well understand what holds you back; still, if you would not ruin yourself and your family, you must submit. Besides which, you know not what Cæsar is about to offer you— fortunate, unhappy child!"

"I know—oh, I know it!" sobbed Melissa; "but it is just that . . . I have served the emperor willingly, but before I consent to become the wife of such a monster—"

"She is right," broke in Euryale, and drew Melissa toward her. But the philosopher took the girl's hand and said, kindly: "You must come with me now, my child, and pretend that you know nothing of Cæsar's intentions toward you. It is the only way to save you. But while you are with the emperor, who, in any case, can devote but a short time to you to-day, I will return here and consult with your people. There is much to be decided, of the greatest moment, and not to you alone."

Melissa turned with tearful eyes to Euryale, and questioned her with a look; whereupon the lady drew the girl's hand out of that of the philosopher, and saying to him, "She shall be with you directly," took her away to her own apartment.

Here she begged Melissa to dry her eyes, and arranging the girl's hair and robe with her own hands, she promised to do all in her power to facilitate her flight. She must do her part now by going into Cæsar's presence as frankly as she had done yesterday and the day before. She might be quite easy; her interests were being faithfully watched over.

Taking a short leave of her father, who was looking very sulky because nobody seemed to care for his opinion, and of Alexander, who lovingly promised her his help, she took the philosopher's hand and walked with him through one crowded apartment after another. They often had difficulty in pressing through the throng of people who were waiting for an audience, and in the ante-chamber, where the Aurelians had had to pay so bitterly for their insolence yesterday, they were detained by the blonde and red-haired giants of the Germanic body-guard, whose leader, Sabinus, a Thracian of exceptional height and strength, was acquainted with the philosopher.

Caracalla had given orders that no one was to be admitted till the negotiations with the Parthian ambassadors, which had begun an hour ago, were brought to a conclusion. Philostratus well knew that the emperor would interrupt the most important business if Melissa were announced, but there was much that he would have the maiden lay to heart before he led her to the monarch; while she wished for nothing so earnestly as that the door which separated her from her terrible wooer might remain closed to the end of time. When the chamberlain Adventus looked out from the imperial apartments, she begged him to give her a little time before announcing her.

The old man blinked consent with his dim eyes, but the philosopher took care that Melissa should not be left to herself and the terrors of her heart. He employed all the eloquence at his command to make her comprehend what it meant to be an empress and the consort of the ruler of the world. In flaming colors he painted to her the good she might do in such a position, and the tears she might wipe away. Then he reminded her of the healing and soothing influence she had over Caracalla, and that this influence came doubtless from the gods, since it passed the bounds of nature and acted so beneficently. No one might reject such a gift from the immortals merely to gratify an ordinary passion. The youth whose love she must give up would be able to comfort himself with the thought that many others had had much worse to bear, and he would find no difficulty in getting a substitute, though not so beautiful a one. On the other hand, she was the only one among millions whose heart, obedient to a heaven-sent impulse, had turned in pity toward Caracalla. If she fled, she would deprive the emperor of the only being on whose love he felt he had some claim. If she listened to the wooing of her noble lover, she would be able to tame this ungovernable being and soothe his fury and would gain in return for a sacrifice such as, many had made before her, the blissful consciousness of having rendered an inestimable service to the whole world. For by her means and her love, the imperial tyrant would be transformed into a beneficent ruler. The blessing of the thousands whom she could protect and save would make the hardest task sweet and endurable.

Here Philostratus paused, and gazed inquiringly at her; but she only shook her head gently, and answered:

"My brain is so confused that I can scarcely hear even, but I feel that your words are well meant and wise. What you put before me would certainly be worth considering if there were anything left for me to consider about. I have promised myself to another, who is more to me than all the world—more than the gratitude and blessings of endangered lives of which I know nothing. I am but a poor girl who only asks to be happy. Neither gods nor men expect more of me than that I should do my duty toward those whom I love. And, then, who can say for certain that I should succeed in persuading Cæsar to carry out my desires, whatever they might be?"

"We were witnessess of the power you exercised over him," replied the philosopher; but Melissa shook her head, and continued eagerly: "No, no! he only values in me the hand that eases his pain and want of sleep. The love which he may feel for me makes him neither gentler nor better. Only an hour or two before he declared that his heart was inclined to me, he had Titianus murdered!"

"One word from you," the philosopher assured her, "and it would never have happened. As empress, they will obey you as much as him. Truly, child, it is no small thing to sit, like the gods, far above the rest of mankind."

"No, no!" cried Melissa, shuddering. "Those heights! Only to think of them makes everything spin round me. Only one who is free from such giddiness dare to occupy such a place. Every one must desire to do what he can best. I could be a good housewife to Diodoros, but I should be a bad empress. I was not born to greatness. And, besides—what is happiness? I only felt happy when I did what was my duty, in peace and quiet. Were I empress, fear would never leave me for a moment. Oh, I know enough of the hideous terror which this awful being creates around him; before I would consent to let it torture me to death by day and by night—morning, noon, and evening—far rather would I die this very day.

Therefore, I have no choice. I must flee from Cæsar's sight—away from hence—far, far, away!"

Tears nearly choked her voice, but she struggled bravely against them. Philostratus, however, did not fail to observe it, and gazed, first mournfully into her face and then thoughtfully on the ground. At length he spoke with a slight sigh:

"We gather experience in life, and yet, however old we may be, we act contrary to it. Now I have to pay for it. And yet it still lies in your hands to make me bless the day on which I spoke on your behalf. Could you but succeed in rising to real greatness of soul, girl—through you, I swear it, the subjects of this mighty kingdom would be saved from great tribulations!"

"But, my lord," Melissa broke in, "who would ask such lofty things of a lowly maiden? My mother taught me to be kind and helpful to others in the house, to friends, and fellow-citizens; my own heart tells me to be faithful to my betrothed. But I care not greatly for the Romans, and what to me are Gauls, Dacians, or whatever else these barbarians may be called?"

"And yet," said Philostratus, "you offered a sacrifice for the foreign tyrant."

"Because his pain excited my compassion," rejoined Melissa, blushing.

"And would you have done the same for any masterless black slave, covered with pitiably deep wounds?" asked the philosopher.

"No," she answered, quickly; "him I would have helped with my own hand. When I can do without their aid, I do not appeal to the gods. And then—I said before, his trouble seemed doubly great because it contrasted so sharply with all the splendor and joy that surrounded him."

"Aye," said the philosopher, earnestly, "and a small thing that affects the ruler recoils tenfold—a thousand-fold —on his subjects. Look at one tree through a cut glass with many facets, and it becomes a forest. Thus the merest trifle, when it affects the emperor, becomes important for the millions over whom he rules. Caracalla's vexation entails evil on thousands—his anger is death and ruin. I fear me, girl, your flight will bring down heavy misfortune on those who surround Cæsar, and first of all upon the Alexandrians, to whom you belong, and against whom he already bears a grudge. You once said your native city was dear to you."

"So it is," returned Melissa, who, at his last words had grown first red and then pale; "but Cæsar can not surely be so narrow-minded as to punish a whole great city for what the poor daughter of a gem-cutter has done."

"You are thinking of my Achilles," answered the philosopher. "But I only transferred what I saw of good in Caracalla to the figure of my hero. Besides, you know that Cæsar is not himself when he is in wrath. Has not experience taught me that no reasons are strong enough to convince a loving woman's heart? Once more I entreat you, stay here! Reject not the splendid gift which the gods offer you, that trouble may not come upon your city as it did on hapless Troy, all for a woman's sake. What says the proverb? 'Zeus hearkens not to lovers' vows', but I say that to renounce love in order to make others happy, is greater and harder than to hold fast to it when it is menaced."

These words reminded her of many a lesson of Andreas, and went to her heart. In her mind's eye she saw Caracalla, after hearing of her flight, set his lions on Philostratus, and then, foaming with rage, give orders to drag her father and brothers, Polybius and his son, to the place of execution, like Titianus. And Philostratus perceived what was going on in her mind, and with the exhortation, "Remember how many persons' weal or woe lies in your hands!" he rose and began a conversation with the Thracian commander of the Germanic guard.

Melissa remained alone upon the divan. The picture changed before her, and she saw herself in costly purple raiment, glittering with jewels, and seated by the emperor's side in a golden chariot. A thousand voices shouted to her, and beside her stood a horn of plenty, running over with golden solidi and crimson roses, and it never grew empty, however much she took from it. Her heart was moved; and when, in the crowd which her lively imagination had conjured up before her, she caught sight of the wife of the blacksmith Herophilus, who had been thrown into prison through an accusation from Zminis, she turned to Caracalla whom she still imagined seated beside her, and cried, "Pardon!" and Caracalla nodded a gracious consent, and the next moment Herophilus's wife lay on her liberated husband's breast, while the broken fetters still clanked upon his wrists. Their children were there, too, and stretched up their arms to their parents, offering their happy lips first to them and then to Melissa.

How beautiful it all was, and how it cheered her compassionate heart!

And this, said the newly awakened, meditative spirit within her, need be no dream; no, it lay in her power to impart this happiness to herself and many others, day by day, until the end.

Then she felt that she must arise and cry to her friend, "I will follow your counsel and remain!"

But her imagination had already begun to work again, and showed her the widow of Titianus, as she entreated Cæsar to spare her noble, innocent husband, while he mercilessly repulsed her. And it flashed through her mind that her petitions might share the same fate, when at that moment the emperor's threatening voice sounded from the adjoining room.

How hateful its strident tones were to her ear! She dropped her eyes and caught sight of a dark stain on the snow-white plumage of the doves in the mosaic pavement at her feet.

That was a last trace of the blood of the young tribune, which the attendants had been unable to remove. And this indelible mark of the crime which she had witnessed brought the image of the wounded Apollonaris before her: just as he now lay, shaken with fever, so had she seen her lover a few days before. His pale face rose before her inward sight; would it not be to him a worse blow than that from the stone, when he should learn that she had broken her faith to him in order to gain power and greatness, and to protect others, who were strangers to her, from the fury of the tyrant?

His heart had been hers from childhood's hour, and it would bleed and break if she were false to the vows in which he placed his faith. And even if he succeeded at last in recovering from the wound she must deal him, his peace and happiness would be destroyed for many a long day. How could she have doubted for a moment where her real duty lay?

If she followed Philostratus's advice—if she acceded
to Caracalla's wishes—Diodoros would have every right
to condemn and curse her.   And could she then feel so
entirely blameless? A voice within her instantly said no;
for there had been moments in which her pity had grown
so strong that she felt more warmly toward the sick Cæsar
than was justifiable. She could not deny it, for she could
not without a blush have described to her lover what she
felt when that mysterious, inexplicable power had drawn
her to the emperor.

And now the conviction rapidly grew strong in her
that she must not only preserve her lover from further
trouble, but strive to make good to him her past errors.
The idea of renouncing her love in order to intercede for
others, most likely in vain, and lighten their lot by sacrificing herself for strangers, rendering her own and her
lover's life miserable, now seemed to her unnatural, criminal, impossible; and with a sigh of relief she remembered her promise to Andreas. Now she could once more
look freely into the grave and earnest face of him who
had ever guided her in the right way.

This alone was right—this she would do!

But after the first quick step toward Philostratus, she
stood still, once more hesitating. The saying about the
fulfilling of the time recurred to her as she thought of
the Christian, and she said to herself that the critical
moment which comes in every life was before her now.
The weal or woe of her whole future depended on the
answer she should give to Philostratus. The thought
struck terror to her heart, but only for a moment. Then
she drew herself up proudly, and, as she approached her
friend, felt with joy that she had chosen the better part;

yea, that it would cost her but little to lay down her life for it.

Though apparently absorbed in his conversation with the Thracian, Philostratus had not ceased to observe the girl, and his knowledge of human nature showed him quickly to what decision she had come. Firmly persuaded that he had won her over to Caracalla's side, he had left her to her own reflections. He was certain that the seed he had sown in her mind would take root; she could now clearly picture to herself what pleasures she would enjoy as empress, and from what she could preserve others. For she was shrewd and capable of reasoning, and above all—and from this he hoped the most—she was but a woman. But just because she was a woman he could not be surprised at her disappointing him in his expectations. For the sake of Caracalla and those who surrounded him he would have wished it to be otherwise; but he had become too fond of her, and had too good a heart, not to be distressed at the thought of seeing her fettered to the unbridled young tyrant.

Before she could address him, he took his leave of the Thracian. Then, as he led her back to the divan, he whispered: "Well, I have gained one more experience. The next time I leave a woman to come to a decision, I shall anticipate from the first that she will come to an opposite conclusion to that which, as a philosopher and logical thinker, I should expect of her. You are determined to keep faith with your betrothed and stab the heart of this highest of all wooers—after death he will be raised among the gods—for such will be the effect of your flight."

Melissa nodded gaily, and rejoined, "The blunt weapon

that I carry would surely not cost Cæsar his life, even if he were no future immortal."

"Scarcely," answered Philostratus; "but what he may suffer through you will drive him to turn his own all-too-sharp sword against others. Caracalla being a man, my calculations regarding him have generally proved right. You will see how firmly I believe in them in this case, when I tell you that I have already taken advantage of a letter brought by the messengers of the empress-mother to take my leave of the emperor. For, I reasoned, if Melissa listens to the emperor, she will need no other confederate than the boy Eros; if, however, she takes flight—then woe betide those who are within range of the tyrant's arm, and ten times woe to me who brought the fugitive before his notice! Early to-morrow, before Caracalla leaves his couch, I shall return with the messengers to Julia; my place in the ship—"

"O my lord," interrupted Melissa, in consternation, "if you, my kind protector, forsake me, to whom shall I look for help?"

"You will not require it if you carry out your intentions," said the philosopher. "Throughout this day you will doubtless need me; and let me impress upon you once more to behave before Caracalla in such a manner that even his suspicious mind may not guess what you intend to do. To-day you will still find me ready to help you. But, hark! That is Cæsar raging again. It is thus he loves to dismiss ambassadors, when he wishes they should clearly understand that their conditions are not agreeable to him. And one word more: When a man has grown gray, it is doubly soothing to his heart that a lovely maiden should so frankly regret the parting. I was ever a friend of your amiable sex, and even to this day Eros is sometimes not unfavorably inclined to me. But you, the more charming you are, the more deeply do I regret that I may not be more to you than an old and friendly mentor. But pity at first kept love from speaking, and then the old truth that every woman's heart may be won save that which already belongs to another."

The elderly admirer of the fair sex spoke these words in such a pleasant, regretful tone that Melissa gave him an affectionate glance from her large, bright eyes, and answered, archly: "Had Eros shown Philostratus the way to Melissa instead of Diodoros, Philostratus might now be occupying the place in this heart which belongs to the son of Polybius, and which must always be his in spite of Cæsar!"

CHAPTER IV.

THE door of the tablinum flew open, and through it streamed the Parthian ambassadors, seven stately personages, wearing the gorgeous costume of their country, and followed by an interpreter and several scribes. Melissa noticed how one of them, a young warrior with a fair beard framing his finely moulded, heroic face, and thick, curling locks escaping from beneath his tiara, grasped the hilt of his sword in his sinewy hand, and how his neighbor, a cautious, elderly man, was endeavoring to calm him.

Scarcely had they left the ante-chamber than Adventus called Melissa and Philostratus to the emperor. Caracalla was seated on a raised throue of gold and ivory, with bright scarlet cushions. As on the preceding day, he was magnificently dressed, and wore a laurel wreath on his head. The lion, who lay chained beside the throne, stirred as he caught sight of the new-comers, which caused Caracalla to exclaim to Melissa: "You have stayed away from me so long that my 'Sword of Persia' fails to recognize you. Were it not more to my taste to show you how dear you are to me, I could be angry with you, coy bird that you are!"

As Melissa bent respectfully before him, he gazed delighted into her glowing face, saying, as he turned half to her and half to Philostratus: "How she blushes! She is ashamed that, though I could get no sleep during the night, and was tortured by an indescribable restlessness, she refused to obey my call, although she very well knows that the one remedy for her sleepless friend lies in her beautiful little hand. Hush, hush! The high-priest has told me that you did not sleep beneath the same roof as I. But that only turned my thoughts in the right direction. Child, child!—See now, Philostratus—the red rose has become a white one. And how timid she is! Not that it offends me, far from it—it delights me.—Those flowers, Philostratus!—Take them, Melissa; they add less to your beauty than you to theirs." He seized the splendid roses he had ordered for her early that morning and fastened the finest in her girdle himself. She did not forbid him, and stammered a few low words of thanks.

How his face glowed! His eyes rested in ecstatic delight upon his chosen one. In this past night, after he had called for her and waited in vain with feverish longing for her coming, it had dawned on him with convincing force that this gentle child had awakened a new, intense passion in him. He loved her and was glad of it —he who till now had taken but a passing pleasure in beautiful women. Longing for her till it became torture, he swore to himself to make her his, and share his all with her, even to the purple.

It was not his habit to hesitate, and at day-break he had sent for his mother's messengers that they might inform her of his resolve. No one dared to gainsay him, and he expected it least of all from her whom he designed to raise so high. But she felt utterly estranged from him, and would gladly have told him to his face what she felt.

Still, it was absolutely necessary that she should restrain herself and endure his insufferable endearments, and even force herself to speak. And yet her tongue seemed tied, and it was only by the utmost effort of her will that she could bring herself to express her astonishment at his rapid return to health.

"It is like magic," she concluded, and he heartily agreed. Attacks of that kind generally left their effects for four days or more. But the most astonishing thing was that in spite of being in the best of health, he was suffering from the gravest illness in the world. "I have fallen a victim to the fever of love, my Philostratus," he cried, with a tender glance at Melissa.

"Nay, Cæsar," interrupted the philosopher, "love is not a disease, but rather not loving."

"Prove this new assertion," laughed the emperor; and the philosopher rejoined, with a meaning look at the maiden, "If love is born in the eyes, then those who do not love are blind."

"But," answered Caracalla, gaily, "they say that love comes not only from what delights the eye, but the soul and the mind as well."

"And have not the mind and the spirit eyes also?" was the reply, to which the emperor heartily assented.

Then he turned to Melissa, and asked with gentle reproach why she, who had proved herself so ready of wit yesterday, should be so reserved to-day; but she excused her taciturnity on the score of violent emotions that had stormed in upon her since the morning.

Her voice broke at the end of this explanation, and Caracalla, concluding that it was the thought of the grandeur that awaited her through his favor which confused her and brought the delicate color to her cheeks, seized her hand, and, obedient to an impulse of his better nature, said:

"I understand you, child. Things are befalling you that would make a stouter heart tremble. You have only heard hints of what must effect such a decisive change in your future life. You know how I feel toward you. I acknowledged to you yesterday what you already knew without words. We both feel the mysterious power that draws us to one another. We belong to each other. In the future, neither time nor space nor any other thing may part us. Where I am there you must be also. You shall be my equal in every respect. Every honor paid to me shall be offered to you likewise. I have shown the malcontents what they have to expect. The fate which awaits the consul Claudius Vindex and his nephew, who by their want of respect to you offended me, will teach the others to have a care."

"O my lord, that aged man!" cried Melissa, clasping her hands, imploringly.

"He shall die, and his nephew," was the inexorable answer. "During my conference with my mother's messengers they had the presumption to raise objections against you and the ardent desire of my heart in a manner which came very near to being treason. And they must suffer for it."

"You would punish them for my sake?" exclaimed Melissa. "But I forgive them willingly. Grant them pardon! I beg, I entreat you."

"Impossible! Unless I make an example, it will be long before the slanderous tongues would hold their peace. Their sentence stands."

But Melissa would not be appeased. With passionate eagerness she entreated the emperor to grant a pardon, but he cut her short with the request not to interfere in matters which he alone had to decide and answer for.

"I owe it to you as well as to myself," he continued, "to remove every obstacle from the path. Were I to spare Vindex, they would never again believe in my strength of purpose. He shall die, and his nephew with him! To raise a structure without first securing a solid foundation would be an act of rashness and folly. Besides, I undertake nothing without consulting the omens. The horoscope which the priest of this temple has drawn up for you only confirms me in my purpose. The examination of the sacrifices this morning was favorable. It now only remains to be seen what the stars say to my resolve. I had not yet taken it when I last questioned the fortune-tellers of the sky. This night we shall learn what future the planets promise to our union. From the signs on yonder tablet it is scarcely possible that their answer should be otherwise than favorable. But even should they warn me of misfortune at your side, I could not let you go now. It is too late for that. I should merely take advantage of the warning, and continue with redoubled severity to sweep away every obstacle that threatens our union. And one thing more—"

But he did not finish, for Epagathos here reminded him of the deputation of Alexandrian citizens who had come to speak about the games in the Circus. They had been waiting several hours, and had still many arrangements to make.

"Did they send you to me?" inquired Caracalla, with irritation, and the freedman answering in the affirmative, he cried: "The princes who wait in my ante-chamber do not stir until their turn comes. These tradesmen's senses are confused by the dazzle of their gold! Tell them they shall be called when we find time to attend to them."

"The head of the night-watch too is waiting," said the freedman; and to the emperor's question whether he had seen him, and if he had anything of consequence to report, the other replied that the man was much disquieted, but seemed to be exercising proper severity. He ventured to remind his master of the saying that the Alexandrians must have *Panem et circenses;* they did not trouble themselves much about anything else. In these days, when there had been neither games, nor pageants, nor distribution of corn, the Romans and Cæsar had been their sole subjects of conversation. However, there was to be something quite unusually grand in the Circus to-night. That would distract the attention of the impudent slanderers. The night-watchman greatly desired to speak to the emperor himself, to prepare him for the fact that excitement ran higher in the Circus here than even in Rome. In spite of every precaution, he would not be able to keep the rabble in the upper rows quiet.

"Nor need they be," broke in the emperor; "the louder they shout the better; and I fancy they will see things which will be worth shouting for. I have no time to see the man. Let him thoroughly realize that he is answerable for any real breach of order."

He signed to Epagathos to retire, but Melissa went nearer to Cæsar and begged him gently not to let the worthy citizens wait any longer on her account.

At this Caracalla frowned ominously, and cried:

"For the second time, let me ask you not to interfere in matters that do not concern you! If anyone dares to order me——" Here he stopped short, for, as Melissa drew back from him frightened, he was conscious of having betrayed that even love was not strong enough to make him control himself. He was angry with himself, and with a great effort he went on, more quietly:

"When I give an order, my child, there often lies much behind it of which I alone know. Those who force themselves upon Cæsar, as these citizens do, must learn to have patience. And you—if you would fill the position to which I intend to raise you—must first take care to leave all paltry considerations and doubts behind you. However, all that will come of itself. Softness and mercy melt on the throne like ice before the sun. You will soon learn to scorn this tribe of beggars who come whining round us. If I flew in a passion just now, it was partly your fault. I had a right to expect that you would be more eager to hear me out than to shorten the time of waiting for these miserable merchants."

With this his voice grew rough again, but as she raised her eyes to him and cried beseechingly, "O, my lord!" he continued, more gently:

"There was not much more to be said. You shall be mine. Should the stars confirm their first revelations, I shall raise you to-morrow to my side, here in the city of Alexandria, and make the people do homage to you as their empress. The priest of Alexandria is ready to conduct the marriage ceremonial. Philostratus will inform my mother of my determination."

Melissa had listened to these arrangements with growing distress; her breath came fast, and she was incapable of uttering a word; but Cæsar was delighted at the lovely confusion painted on her features, and cried, in joyful excitement:

"How I have looked forward to this moment—and I have succeeded in surprising her! This is what makes imperial power divine; by one wave of the hand it can raise the lowest to the highest place!"

With this he drew Melissa toward him, kissed the trembling girl upon the brow, and continued, in delighted tones:

"Time does not stand still, and only a few hours separate us from the accomplishment of our desires. Let us lend them wings. We resolved yesterday to show one another what we could do as singers and lute-players. There lies my lyre—give it me, Philostratus. I know what I shall begin with."

The philosopher brought and tuned the instrument; but Melissa had some difficulty in keeping back her tears. Caracalla's kiss burned like a brand of infamy on her brow. A nameless, torturing restlessness had come over her, and she wished she could dash the lyre to the ground, when Caracalla began to play, and called out to Philostratus:

"As you are leaving us to-morrow, I will sing the song which you honored with a place in your heroic tale."

He turned to Melissa, and, as she owned to having read the work of the philosopher, he went on: "You know, then, that I was the model for his Achilles. The departed spirit of the hero is enjoying in the island of Leuke, in the Pontus, the rest which he so richly deserves, after a life full of heroic deeds. Now he finds time to sing to the lyre, and Philostratus put the following verses—but they are mine—into his mouth.—I am about to play, Adventus! Open the door!"

The freedman obeyed, and the emperor peered into the ante-chamber to see for himself who was waiting there.

He required an audience when he sang. The Circus had accustomed him to louder applause than his beloved and one skilled musician could award him. At last he swept the strings, and began singing in a well-trained tenor, whose sharp, hard quality, however, offended the girl's critical ear, the song to the echo on the shores of Pontus:

> Echo, by the rolling waters
> Bathing Pontus' rocky shore,
> Wake, and answer to the lyre
> Swept by my inspired hand!
>
> Wake, and raise thy voice in numbers;
> Sing to Homer, to the bard
> Who has given life immortal
> To the heroes of his lay.
>
> He it was from death who snatched me;
> He who gave Patroclus life;
> Rescued, in perennial glory,
> Godlike Ajax from the dead!—
>
> His the lute to whose sweet accents
> Ilion owes undying fame,
> And the triumph and the praises
> Which surround her deathless name. '

The "Sword of Persia" seemed peculiarly affected by his master's song, which he accompanied by a long-drawn howl of woe; and, before the imperial *virtuoso* had concluded, a discordant cry sounded for a short time from the street, in imitation of the squeaking of young pigs. It arose from the crowd who were waiting round the Serapeum to see Cæsar drive to the Circus; and Caracalla must have noticed it, for, when it waxed louder, he gave a sidelong glance toward the place from which it came, and an ominous frown gathered upon his brow.

But it soon vanished, for scarcely had he finished when stormy shouts of applause rose from the ante-chamber. They proceeded from the friends of Cæsar, and the deep voices of the Germanic body-guard, who, joining in with the cries they had learned in the Circus, lent such impetuous force to the applause, as even to satisfy this artist in the purple.

Therefore, when Philostratus spoke words of praise, and Melissa thanked him with a blush, he answered with a smile: "There is something frank and untrammelled in their manner of expressing their feelings outside. Forced applause sounds differently. There must be something in my singing that carries the hearers away. My Alexandrian hosts, however, are over-ready to show me what they think. It did not escape me, and I shall add it to the rest."

Then he invited Melissa to make a return for his song by singing Sappho's Ode to Aphrodite.

Pale, and as if obeying some strange compulsion, she seated herself at the instrument, and the prelude sounded clear and tuneful from her skilful fingers.

"Beautiful! Worthy of Mesomedes!" cried Caracalla, but Melissa could not sing, for at the first note her voice was broken by stormy sobs. "The power of the goddess whom she meant to extol!" said Philostratus, pointing to her; and the tearful, beseeching look with which she met

the emperor's gaze while she begged him in low tones—
"Not now! I can not do it to-day!"—confirmed Caracalla
in his opinion that the passion he had awakened in the
maiden was in no way inferior to his own—perhaps even
greater. He relieved his full heart by whispering to Melissa a passionate, "I love you," and, desiring to show her
by a favor how kindly he felt toward her, added: "I will
not let your fellow-citizens wait outside any longer—Adventus! The deputation from the Circus!"

The chamberlain withdrew at once, and the emperor
throwing himself back on the throne, continued, with a
sigh:

"I wonder how any of these rich tradesmen would
like to undertake what I have already gone through this
day. First, the bath; then, while I rested, Macrinus's
report; after that, the inspection of the sacrifices; then a
review of the troops, with a gracious word to every one.
Scarcely returned, I had to receive the ambassadors from
my mother, and then came the troublesome affair with
Vindex. Then the despatches from Rome arrived, the
letters to be examined, and each one to be decided on
and signed. Finally the settling of accounts with the
idiologos, who, as high-priest of my choosing, has to collect the tribute from all the temples in Egypt. . . . Next
I gave audience to several people—to your father among
the rest. He is strange, but a thorough man, and a true
Macedonian of the old stock. He repelled both greeting
and presents, but he longed to be revenged—heavily and
bloodily—on Zminis, who denounced him and brought
him to the galleys. . . . How the old fellow must have
raged and stormed when he was a prisoner! I treated
the droll old gray-beard like my father. The giant pleases
me, and what skilful fingers he has on his powerful

hands! He gave me that ring with the portraits of Castor and Pollux."

"My brothers were the models," remarked Melissa, glad to find something to say without dissembling.

Caracalla examined the stone in the gold ring more closely, and exclaimed in admiration: "How delicate the little heads are! At the first glance one recognizes the hand of the happily gifted artist. Your father's is one of the noblest and most refined of the arts. If I can raise a statue to a lute-player, I can do so to a gem-cutter."

Here the deputation for the arrangement of the festival was announced, but the emperor, calling out once more, "Let them wait," continued:

"You are a handsome race—the men powerful, the women as lovely as Aphrodite. That is as it should be! My father before me took the wisest and fairest woman to wife. You are the fairest,—the wisest?—well, that too perhaps. Time will show. But Aphrodite never has a high forehead, and, according to Philostratus, beauty and wisdom are hostile sisters with you women."

"Exceptions," interposed the philosopher, as he pointed to Melissa, "prove the rule."

"Describe her in that manner to my mother," said Caracalla. "I would not let you go from me, were you not the only person who knows Melissa. I may trust in your eloquence to represent her as she deserves. And now," he continued, hurriedly, "one thing more. As soon as the deputation is dismissed and I have received a few other persons, the feast is to begin. You would perhaps be entertained at it. However, it will be better to intro-duce you to my 'friends' after the marriage ceremony,

After dark, to make up for it, there is the Circus, to which you will, of course, accompany me."

"Oh, my lord!" exclaimed the maiden, frightened and unwilling. But Caracalla cried, decisively: "No refusal, I must beg! I imagine that I have proved sufficiently that I know how to shield you from what is not fitting for a maiden. What I ask of you now is but the first step on the new path of honor that awaits you as future empress."

Melissa raised both voice and hands in entreaty, but in vain. Caracalla cut her short, saying in authoritative tones:

"I have arranged everything. You will go to the Circus. Not alone with me—that would give welcome work to slanderous tongues. Your father shall accompany you—your brothers, too, if you wish it. I shall not join you till after the performance has begun. Your fellow citizens will divine the meaning of this visit. Besides, Theocritus and the rest have orders to acquaint the people with the distinction that awaits you and the Alexandrians. But why so pale? Your cheeks will regain their color in the Circus. I know I am right—you will leave it delighted and enthralled. You have only to learn for the first time how the acclamations of tens of thousands take hold upon the heart and intoxicate the senses. Courage, courage, Macedonian maiden! Everything grand and unexpected, even unforeseen happiness, is alarming and confusing. But we become accustomed even to the impossible. A strong spirit like yours soon gets over anything of the kind. But the time is running on. One word more: You must be in the Circus by sunset. In any case, you must be in your place before I come. Adventus will see that you have a chariot or a litter, whichever you please.

Theocritus will be waiting at the entrance to lead you to your seats."

Melissa could restrain herself no longer, and, carried away by the wild conflict of passions in her breast, she threw control and prudence to the winds, and cried:

"I will not!" Then throwing back her head as if to call the heavens to witness, she raised her great, wide-open eyes and gazed above.

But not for long. Her bold defiance had roused Cæsar's utmost fury, and he broke out with a growl of rage:

"You will not, you say? And you think, unreasoning fool, that this settles the matter?"

He uttered a wild laugh, pressed his hand firmly on his left eyelid, which began to twitch convulsively, and went on in a lower but defiantly contemptuous tone:

"I know better! You shall! And you will not only go to the Circus, but you will do it willingly, or at least with smiling lips. You will start at sunset! At the time appointed I shall find you in your place. If not!—Must I begin so soon to teach you that I can be serious? Have a care, girl! You are dear to me; yet—by the head of my father!—if you defy me, my Numidian lion-keepers shall drag you to the place you belong to!"

Thus far Melissa had listened to the emperor's raging with panting bosom and quivering nostrils, as at a performance which must sooner or later come to an end, and now she broke in regardless of the consequences:

"Send for them," she cried, "and order them to throw me to the wild beasts! It will doubtless be a welcome surprise to the lookers-on. Which of them can say they have ever seen the daughter of a free Roman citizen who never yet came before the law, torn to pieces in the sand of the arena? They delight in anything new! Yes, murder me, as you did Plautilla, although I never offended either you or your mother! Better die a hundred deaths than parade my dishonor before the eyes of the multitude in the open Circus!"

She ceased, incapable of further resistance, threw herself weeping on the divan, and buried her face in the cushions.

Confounded and bewildered by such audacity, the emperor had heard her out. The soul of a hero dwelt in the frail body of this maiden! Majestic as all-conquering Venus she had resisted him for the second time, and now how touching did she appear in her tears and weakness! He loved her, and his heart yearned to raise her in his arms, to beg her forgiveness, and fulfill her every wish. But he was a man and a monarch, and his desire to show Melissa to the people in the Circus as his chosen bride had become a fixed resolve during the past sleepless night. And indeed he was incapable of renouncing any wish or a plan, even if he felt inclined to do so. Yet he heartily regretted having stormed at the gentle Greek girl like some wild barbarian, and thus himself thrown obstacles in the way of attaining his desire. His hot blood had carried him away again. Surely some demon led him so often into excesses which he afterward repented of. This time the fiend had been strong in him, and he must use every gentle persuasion he knew of to bend the deeply offended maiden to his will.

He was relieved not to meet her intense gaze as he advanced toward her and took Philostratus's place, who whispered to her to control herself and not bring death and ruin upon them all.

"Truly I meant well toward you, dearest," he began,

in altered tones. "But we are both like over-full vessels —one drop will make them over-flow. You—confess now that you forgot yourself. And I— On the throne we grow unaccustomed to opposition. It is fortunate that the flame of my anger dies out so quickly. But it lies with you to prevent it from ever breaking out; for I should always endeavor to fulfill a kindly expressed wish, if it were possible. This time, however, I must insist—"

Melissa turned toward the emperor, and stretching out beseeching hands, she cried:

"Bid me do anything, however hard, and it shall be done, but do not force me to go with you to the Circus. If my mother were only alive! Wherever I could go with her was right. But my father, not to speak of my mad-cap brother Alexander, do not know what befits a maiden, nor does anybody expect it of them."

"And rightly," interposed Caracalla. "Now I understand your opposition, and thank you for it. But it fortunately lies in my power to remove your objection. The women have to obey me, too. I shall at once issue the necessary orders. You shall appear in the Circus surrounded by the noblest matrons of the city. The wives of these citizens shall accompany you. Even my mother will be sure to approve of this arrangement. Farewell, then, till we meet again in the Circus!"

He spoke the last words with proud satisfaction, and with the grave demeanor that Cilo had taught him to adopt in the curia.

He then gave the order to admit the Alexandrian citizens, and the words of entreaty died upon the lips of the unfortunate imperial bride, for the folding doors were thrown open and the deputation advanced through them.

Old Adventus signed to Melissa, and with drooping

head she followed him through the rooms and corridors that led to the apartments of the high-priest.

CHAPTER V.

MELISSA had wept her fill on the breast of the lady Euryale, who listened to her woes with motherly sympathy, and yet she felt as if a biting frost had broken and destroyed the blossoms which only yesterday had so richly and hopefully decked her young heart. Diodoros's love had been to her like the fair and sunny summer days that turn the sour, hard fruit into sweet and juicy grapes. And now the frost had nipped them. The whole future, and everything around her, now looked gray, colorless, and flat. Only two thoughts held possession of her mind: on the one hand, that of her betrothed, from whom this visit to the Circus threatened to separate her forever; and on the other, that of her imperial lover, to escape whom she would have flown anywhere, even to the grave.

Euryale remarked with concern how weary and broken Melissa looked—so different from her usual bright self, while she listened to her father and Alexander as they consulted with the lady as to the future. Philostratus, who had promised his advice, did not appear; and to the gem-cutter, no proposal could seem so unwelcome as that of leaving his native city and his sick favorite, Philip.

He considered it senseless, and a result of the thoroughly wrong-headed views of sentimental women, to reject the monarch of the world when he made honorable proposals to an unpretending girl. But the lady Euryale —of whom his late wife had always spoken with the highest respect—and, supported by her, his son Alexander, had both represented to him so forcibly that a union with the emperor would render Melissa most unhappy, if it did not lead to death, that he had been reduced to silence. Only, when they spoke of the necessity of flight, he burst out again, declaring that the time had not yet come for such extreme measures.

When Melissa now rejoined them, he spoke of the emperor's behavior toward her as being worthy of a man of honor, and endeavored to touch her heart by representing what an old man must feel who should be forced to leave the house where his father and grandfather had lived before him, and even the town whose earth held all that was dearest to him.

Here the tears which so easily rose to his eyes began to flow, and, seeing that Melissa's tender heart was moved by his sorrow, he gained confidence, and reproached his daughter for having kindled Caracalla's love, by her radiant eyes—so like her mother's! Honestly believing that his affection was returned, Cæsar was offering her the highest honor in his power; if she fled from him, he would have every right to complain of having been basely deceived, and to call her a heartless wanton.

Alexander now came to his sister's aid, and reminded him how Melissa had hazarded life and liberty to save him and her brothers. She had been forced to look so kindly into the tyrant's face if only to sue for their pardon, and it became him ill to make this a reproach to his daughter.

Melissa nodded gratefully to her brother, but Heron remained firm in his assertion that to think of flight would be foolish, or at least premature.

At this, Alexander repeated to him that Melissa had whispered in his ear that she would rather die at once than live in splendor but in perpetual fear of death by the side of an unloved husband; whereupon Heron began to breathe hard, as he always did before an outburst of anger.

But a message, calling him to the emperor's presence, soon calmed him.

At parting, he kissed Melissa, and murmured:

"Would you really drive your old father out of our dear home, away from his work, and his birds—from his garden, and your mother's grave? Is it then so terrible to live as empress, in splendor and honor? I am going to Cæsar—you can not hinder me from greeting him kindly from you."

Without waiting for an answer, he left the room; but when he was outside he took care to glance at himself in the mirror, arrange his beard and hair, and place his gigantic form in a few of the dignified attitudes he intended to adopt in the presence of the emperor.

Meanwhile Melissa had thrown off the indifference into which she had fallen, and her old doubts raised their warning heads with renewed force.

Alexander swore to be her faithful ally; Euryale once more assured her of her assistance; and yet, more especially when she was moved with pity for her father, who was to leave all he loved for her sake, she felt as if she were being driven hither and thither, in some frail bark, at the mercy of the waves.

Suddenly a new idea flashed through her mind. She rose quickly.

"I will go to Diodoros," she cried, "and tell him all! He shall decide."

"Just now?" asked Euryale, startled. "You would certainly not find your betrothed alone, and since all the world knows of Caracalla's intentions, and gazes curiously after you, your visit would instantly be reported to Cæsar. Nor is it advisable for you to present yourself before your offended lover, when you have neither Andreas nor any one else to speak for you and take your part."

Melissa burst into tears, but the matron drew her to her and continued tenderly:

"You must give that up—but, Alexander, do you go to your friend, and be your sister's mouth-piece!"

The artist consented with all the ardor of brotherly affection, and having received from Melissa, whose courage began to rise again, strict injunctions as to what he was to say to her lover, he departed on his errand.

Wholly absorbed by the stormy emotions of her heart, the maiden had forgotten time and every external consideration; but the lady Euryale was thoughtful for her, and now led her to her chamber to have her hair dressed for the Circus. The matron carefully avoided, for the present, all mention of her young friend's flight, though her mind was constantly occupied with it—and not in vain.

The skilful waiting-woman, whom she had bought from the house of the priest of Alexander, who was a Roman knight, loosened the girl's abundant brown hair, and, with loud cries of admiration, declared it would be easy to dress such locks in the most approved style of fashion. She then laid the curling-irons on the dish of coals which stood on a slender tripod, and was about to twist it into ringlets; but Melissa, who had never resorted to such arts, refused to permit it. The slave assured her, however, as earnestly as if it were a matter of the highest importance, that it was impossible to arrange the curls of a lady of distinction without the irons. Euryale, too, begged Melissa to allow it, as nothing would make her so conspicuous in her overdressed surroundings as excessive simplicity. That was quite true, but it made the girl realize so vividly what was before her, that she covered her face with her hands and sobbed out:

"To be exposed to the gaze of the whole city—to its envy and its scorn!"

The matron's warning inquiry, what had become of her favorite's high-minded calm, and her advice to restrain her weeping, lest she should appear before the public in the Amphitheatre with tear-stained eyes, helped her to compose herself.

The tire-woman had not finished her work when Alexander returned, and Melissa dared not turn her head for fear of disturbing her in her task. But when Alexander began his report with the exclamation, "Who knows what foolish gossip has driven him to this?" she sprang up, regardless of the slave's warning cry. And as her brother went on to relate how Diodoros had left the Serapeum, in spite of the physician's entreaty to wait at least until next morning, but that Melissa need not take it greatly to heart, it was too much for the girl who had already that day gone through such severe and varied experiences. The ground seemed to heave beneath her feet, and sick and giddy she put out her hand to find some support, that she might not sink on her knees; in so doing, she caught the tall tripod which held the dish of coals. It swayed and fell clattering to the ground, bringing the irons with it. Its burning contents fell partly on the floor and partly on the festal robe which Melissa had thrown over a chair before loosening her hair. Alexander caught her just in time to prevent her falling.

With her healthy nature, Melissa soon regained consciousness, and during the first few moments her distress over the spoiled garment threw every other thought into the background. Shaking her head gravely over the black-edged holes which the coals had burned in the peplos and the under-robes, Euryale secretly rejoiced at the accident. She remembered that when her heart was torn and bleeding, after the death of her only child, her thoughts were taken off herself by the necessary duty of providing mourning garments for herself, her husband, and the slaves. This trivial task had at least helped her to forget for a few hours the bitterness of her grief.

Only anxious to lighten in some sort the fate of the sweet young creature whom she had learned to love, she made much of the difficulty of procuring a fresh dress for Melissa, though she was perfectly aware that her sister-in-law possessed many such. Alexander was commissioned to take one of the emperor's chariots—which always stood ready for the use of the courtiers between the Serapeum and the springs—on the east and to hasten to the lady Berenike. The lady begged that he, as an artist, would assist in choosing the robe; and the less conspicuous and costly it was the better.

In this Melissa heartily agreed, and, after Alexander had gone, Euryale bore off her pale young charge to the eating-room, where she forced her to take some old wine and a little food, which she would not touch before. As the attendant filled the wine-cup, the high-priest himself joined them, greeted Melissa briefly and with measured courtesy, and begged his wife to follow him for a moment into the tablinum.

The attendant, a slave who had grown gray in the service of Timotheus, now begged the young guest, as though he represented his mistress, to take a little food, and not to sip so timidly from the wine-cup. But the lonely repast was soon ended, and Melissa, strengthened and refreshed, withdrew to the sleeping-apartment. Only light curtains hung at the doors of the high-priest's hurriedly furnished rooms, and no one noticed Melissa's entrance into the adjoining chamber.

She had never played the eavesdropper, but she had neither the presence of mind to withdraw, nor could she avoid hearing that her own name was mentioned.

It was the lady who spoke, and her husband answered in excited tones:

"As to your Christianity, and whatever there may be in it that is offensive to me as high-priest of a heathen god, we will speak of that later. It is not a question now of a difference of opinion, but of a serious danger which you with your easily moved heart will bring down upon yourself and me. The gem-cutter's daughter is a lovely creature—I will not deny it—and worthy of your sympathy; besides which, you, as a woman, can not bear to see her most sacred feelings wounded."

"And would you let your hands lie idle in your lap," interposed his wife, "if you saw a lovable, innocent child on the edge of a precipice, and felt yourself strong enough to save her from falling? You can not have asked yourself what would be the fate of a girl like Melissa if she were Caracalla's wife."

"Indeed I have," Timotheus assured her gravely, "and nothing would please me better than that the maiden should succeed in escaping that fate. But—the time is short, and I must be brief—the emperor is our guest, and honors me with boundless confidence. Just now he disclosed to me his determination to make Melissa his wife, and I was forced to approve it. Thus he looks to me to carry out his wishes; and if the maiden escapes, and there falls on you, or, through you, on me, the shadow of a suspicion of having assisted in her flight, he will have every right to regard me as a traitor and to treat me as such. To others my life is made sacred by my high office, but the man to whom a human life—no matter whose—is no more than that of a sacrificial animal is to you or me, that man would shed the blood of us both without a quiver of the eyelid."

"Then let him!" cried Euryale, hotly. "My bereaved and worn-out life is but a small price to pay for that of an innocent, blameless creature, glowing with youth and all the happiness of requited love, and with a right to the highest joys that life can offer."

"And I?" exclaimed Timotheus, angrily. "What am I to you since the death of our child? For the sake of the first person that came to you as a poor substitute for our lost daughter, you are ready to go to your death, and to drag me with you into the gloom of Hades. There speaks the Christian! Even that gentle philosopher on the throne, Marcus Aurelius, was disgusted at your fellow-believers' hideous mania for death. The Christian expects in the next world all that is denied to him in this. But we think of this life, in which the Deity has placed us. To me life is the highest blessing, and yours is dearer to me than my own. Therefore I say, firmly and decidedly: Melissa must not make her escape from this house. If she is determined to fly this night, let her do so—I shall not hinder her. If your counsel is of service to her, I am glad; but she must not enter this house again after the performance in the Circus, unless she be firmly resolved to become Cæsar's wife. If she can not bring herself to this, the apartments which belong to us must be closed against her, as against a dangerous foe."

"And whither can she go?" asked Euryale, sadly and with tearful eyes, for there was no gainsaying so definite an order from her lord and master. "The moment she is missed, they will search her father's house; and, if she takes advantage of Berenike's ship, it will soon be discovered that it was your brother's wife who helped her to escape from Caracalla."

"Berenike will know what to do," answered Timotheus, composedly. "She if any one knows how to take care of herself. She has the protection of her influential brother-in-law, Cœranus; and just now there is nothing she would not do to strike a blow at her hated enemy."

"How sorrow and revenge have worked upon that strange woman!" exclaimed the lady, sadly. "Caracalla has injured her, it is true—"

"He has, and to-day he has added a further, deeper insult, for he forces her to appear in the Circus, with the wives of the other citizens who bear the cost of this performance. I was there, and heard him say to Seleukus, who was acting as spokesman, that he counted on seeing his wife, of whom he had heard so much, in her appointed place this evening. This will add fuel to the fire of her hatred. If she only does not allow her anger to carry her away, and to show it in a manner that she will afterward regret! But my time is short.—I have to walk before the sacred images in full ceremonial vestments, and accompanied by the priest of Alexander. You, unfortunately, take no pleasure in such spectacles. Once more, then—if the girl is determined to fly, she must not return here. I repeat, if any one can help her to get away, it is Berenike. Our sister-in-law must take the consequences. Cæsar can not accuse her of treason, at any rate, and her interference in the matter will clear us of all suspicion of complicity."

No word of this conversation had escaped Melissa. She learned nothing new from it, but it affected her deeply.

Warm-hearted as she was, she fully realized the debt of gratitude she owed to the lady Euryale; and she could not blame the high-priest, whom prudence certainly compelled to close his doors against her. And yet she was wounded by his words. She had struggled so hard in these last days to banish all thought of her own happiness, and shield her dear ones from harm, that such selfishness appeared doubly cruel to her. Did it not seem as if this priest of the great Deity to whom she had been taught to pray, cared little what became of his nearest relatives, so long as he and his wife were unmolested? That was the opposite of what Andreas had praised as the highest duty, the last time she had walked with him to the ferry; and since then Johanna had told her the story of Christ's sufferings, and she understood the fervor with which the freedman had spoken of the crucified Son of God—the great example of all unselfishness.

In the enthusiasm of her warm young heart she felt that what she had heard of the Christian's teacher was beautiful, and that she too would not find it hard to die for those she loved.

With drooping head Euryale re-entered the room, and gazed with kind, anxious eyes into the girl's face, as if asking her forgiveness. Following the impulse of her candid heart, Melissa threw her fair young arms round the aged lady, and, to her great surprise, after kissing her warmly on brow and mouth and eyes, cried in tones of tender entreaty:

"Forgive me. I did not want to listen, and yet I could

not choose but hear. No word of your discourse escaped me. I know now that I must not fly, and that I must bear whatever fate the gods may send me. I used often to say to myself, 'Of how little importance is my life or my happiness!' And now that I must give up my lover, whatever happens, I care not what the future has in store for me. I can never forget Diodoros; and, when I think that everything is at an end between us, it is as if my heart were torn in pieces. But I have found out, in these last days, what heavy troubles one may bear without breaking down. If my flight is to bring danger to so many good people, if not death and ruin, I had better stay. The man who lusts after me—it is true, when I think of his caresses, my blood runs cold! But perhaps I shall be able to endure them. And then—if I crush my heart into silence, and renounce Diodoros forever and give myself up to Cæsar—as I must—tell me—you will not then close your doors against me, and I may stay with you till the horrid hour comes when Caracalla calls me?"

The matron had listened with deep emotion to Melissa's victory over her desires and her aversion. This heathen maiden, brought up in the right way by a good mother, and to whom life had taught many a hard lesson, was she not already treading in the footsteps of the Saviour? This child was offering up the great and pure love of her heart to preserve others from sorrow and danger; and what a different course of action she herself to pursue in obedience to her husband's counsel—her husband, whose duty it was to offer a shining example to the whole heathen world!

She thought of Abraham's sacrifice, and wondered if the Lord might not perhaps be satisfied with Melissa's willi ess to lay her love upon the altar. In any case, what r she, Euryale, could do to save her from the wors te that could befall a woman, that should be done, and t's time it was she who drew the other toward her and sed her.

H heart was full to overflowing, and yet she did not forge o warn Melissa to be careful, when she was about to la her head with its artificially arranged curls upon the lay's breast.

" , no," she said, tenderly warding off the maiden's embrœe. Then, laying her hands on the girl's shoulders, she l ked her straight in the face, and continued: "Here you wl ever find a resting-place. When your hair lies smootly round your sweet face as it did yesterday, then lay it n my breast as often as you will. Aye, and it can and tall be here in the Serapeum; though not in these room. which my lord and master closes against you. I told yu of the time being fulfilled for each one of us, and wen yours came you proved yourself to be the good tree o which our Lord speaks as bearing good fruit. You look . me inquiringly; how indeed should you understand ie words of a Christian? But I shall find time enoug in the next few days to explain them to you; for —I sv it again—you shall remain near me while the emper searches the city and half the world over for you. eep that firmly in your mind and let it help to give yu courage in the Circus."

"ht my father?" cried Melissa, pointing to the curtain, throug which Heron's loud voice now became audible.

"Lpend on me," whispered the lady, hurriedly; "and rest aured that he will be warned in time. Do not betray n promise. If we were to take him into our confidece now, he would spoil all. As soon as he is gone, and your brother has returned, you two shall hear—"

They were interrupted by the steward, who, with a peculiar smile upon his clean-shaven lips, came to announce Heron's visit.

The communicative gem-cutter had already confided to the servant what it was that agitated him so greatly, but Melissa was astonished at the change in her father's manner.

The shuffling gait of the gigantic, unwieldy man, who had grown gray stooping over his work, had gained a certain majestic dignity. His cheeks glowed, and the gray eyes, which had long since acquired a fixed look from straining over the gem-cutting, now beamed with a blissful radiance. Something wonderful must have happened to him, and, without waiting to be questioned by the lady, he poured out to her the news that he would have been overjoyed to have shouted in the market-place for all to hear.

The reception accorded to him at Cæsar's table, he declared, had been flattering beyond all words. The godlike monarch had treated him more considerately, nay, sometimes with more reverence, than his own sons. The best dishes had been put before him, and Caracalla had asked all sorts of questions about his future consort, and, on hearing that Melissa had sent him greetings, he had raised himself and drunk to him as if he were a friend.

His table-companions, too, had treated Heron with every distinction. Immediately on his arrival the monarch had desired them to honor him as the father of the future empress. They had all agreed with him in demanding that Zminis the Egyptian should be punished with death, and had even encouraged him to give the reins to his righteous anger. He, if any one, was in the habit of being moderate in all things, if only as a good example to his sons; and he had proved in many a Dionysiac feast that the god could not easily overpower him. The amount of wine he had drunk to-day would generally have had no more effect upon him than water, and yet he had felt now and then as if he were drunken, and the whole festal hall turned round with him. Even now he would be quite incapable of walking forward in a given straight line.

With the exclamation, "Such is life!—a few hours ago on the rowing-bench, and fighting with the brander of the galleys for trying to brand me with the slave-mark, and now one of the greatest among the great!" he closed his tale, for a glance through the window showed him that time pressed.

With strange bashfulness he then gazed at a ring upon his right hand, and said hesitatingly that his own modesty made the avowal difficult to him; but the fact was, he was not the same man as when he last left the ladies. By the grace of the emperor he had been made a prætorian. Cæsar had at first wanted to make him a knight; but he esteemed his Macedonian descent higher than that class, to which too many freed slaves belonged for his taste. This he had frankly acknowledged, and the emperor must have considered his objections valid, for he immediately spoke a few words to the prefect Macrinus, and then told the others to greet him as senator with the rank of prætorian.

Then indeed he felt as if the seat beneath him were transformed into a wild steed carrying him away through sea and sky—wherever it pleased. He had had to hold tightly to the arm of the couch, and only remembered that some one—who it was he did not know—had whispered to him to thank Cæsar.

"This," continued the gem-cutter, "restored me so far to myself that I could express my gratitude to your future husband, my child. I am only the second Egyptian who has entered the senate. Cœranus was the only one before me. What favor! And how can I describe what followed? All the distinguished members of the senate and the past consuls offered me a brotherly embrace as their new colleague. When Cæsar commanded me to appear at your side in the Circus, wearing the white toga with the broad purple stripe, and I remarked that the shops of the better clothes-sellers would be shut by this time on account of the performance, and that such a toga was not to be obtained, there was a great laugh over the Alexandrian love of amusement. From all sides they offered me what I required; but I gave the preference to Theocritus, on account of his height. What is long enough for him will not be too short for me.—And now one of the emperor's chariots is waiting for me. If only Alexander were at home! The house ought to have been illuminated and hung with garlands for my arrival, and a crowd of slaves waiting to kiss my hands. There will soon be more than our two. I hope Argutis may understand how to fasten on the shoes with the straps and the crescent! Philip knows even less of these things than I do myself, besides which the poor boy is laid low. It is lucky that I remembered him. I had nearly forgotten his existence. Ah!—if your mother were still alive! She had clever fingers! She— Ah, lady Euryale, Melissa has perhaps told you about her. Olympias she was called, like the mother of the great Alexander, and, like her, she bore good children. You yourself were praising my boys just now. And the girl! . . . Only a few days ago, it was a pretty, shy thing that no one would ever have expected to do anything great; and now, what have we not to thank that gentle child for? The little one was always her mother's darling. Eternal gods! I dare not think of it! If only she who is gone might have had the joy of hearing me called senator and prætor! O child! if she could have sat with us to-day in the emperor's seats, and we two could have seen you there—you, our pride, honored by the whole city, Cæsar's future bride—"

Here the strong man with the soft heart broke down, and, clasping his hands over his face, sobbed aloud, while Melissa clung to him and stroked his bearded cheeks.

Under her loving words of consolation he soon regained his composure, and, still struggling against the rising tears, he cried:

"Thank Heaven, there can be no more foolish talk of flight! I shall stay here; I shall never take advantage of the ivory chair that belongs to me in the curia in Rome. Your husband, my child, and the state, would scarcely expect it of me. If, however, Cæsar presents me, as his father, with estates and treasures, my first thought shall be to raise a monument to your mother. You shall see! A monument, I tell you, without a rival. It shall represent the strength of man submissive to womanly charm."

He bent down to kiss his daughter's brow, and whispered in her ear:

"Gaze confidently into the future, my girl. A father's eye is not easily deceived, and so I tell you—that the emperor has been forced to shed blood to insure the safety of the throne; but, in personal intercourse with him, I learned to know your future husband as a noble-hearted

man. Indeed, I am not rich enough to thank the gods
for such a son-in-law!"

Melissa gazed after her father, incapable of speaking.
It went to her heart that all these hopes should be
changed to sorrow and disappointment through her. And
so she said, with tearful eyes, and shook her head when
the lady assured her that with her it was a question of a
cruelly spoiled life, whereas her father would only have to
renounce some idle vanities which he would forget as
easily as he had seized upon them,

"You do not know him," answered the maiden, sadly.
"If I fly, then he too must hide himself in a far country.
He will never be happy again if they take him from the
little house—his birds—our mother's grave. It was for her
sake alone that he took no thought for the ivory seat in
the curia. If you only knew how he clings to everything
that reminds him of our mother, and she never left our
city."

· Here she was interrupted by the entrance of Philostratus. He was not alone; an imperial slave accompanied
him, bringing a graceful basket with gifts from the
emperor to Melissa.

First came a wreath of roses and lotos-flowers, looking
as if they had been plucked just before sunrise, for among
the blossoms and leaves there flashed and sparkled a
glittering dew of diamonds, lightly fastened on delicate
silver wires. Next came a bunch of flowers, round whose
stems a supple golden snake was twined, covered with
rubies and diamonds and destined to coil itself round a
woman's arm. The third was a necklace of extremely
costly Persian pearls, which had once belonged—so the
merchant had declared—to great Cleopatra's treasure.

Melissa loved flowers, and the costly gifts that accompanied them could not fail to rejoice a woman's heart. And yet she only gave them a passing glance, reddening painfully as she did so.

What the bearer had to say to her was of more importance to her than the gifts he brought, and in fact the troubled manner of the usually composed philosopher betrayed that he had something more serious to deliver than the gifts of his love-sick lord.

The lady Euryale, perceiving that he meant once more to persuade Melissa to yield, hastened to declare that she had found ways and means to help the maiden to escape; but he shook his head with a sigh, and said, thoughtfully:

"Well—well—I shall go on board the ship while the wild beasts are doing their part in the Circus. May we meet again happily, either here or elsewhere! My way leads me first to Cæsar's mother, to inform her of his choice of a wife. Not that he needs her consent: whose consent or disapproval does Caracalla care for? But I am to win Julia's heart for you. Possibly I may succeed; but you—you scorn it, and fly from her son. And yet —believe me, child—the heart of that woman is a treasure that has no equal, and, if she should open her arms to you, there would be little that you could not endure. When I left you, just now, I put myself in your place, and approved of your resolve; but it would be wrong not to remind you once more of what you must expect if you follow your own will, and if Cæsar considers himself scorned, ill-treated, and deceived by you."

"In the name of all the gods, what has happened?" broke in Melissa, pallid with fear. Philostratus pressed his hand to his brow, and his voice was hoarse with suppressed emotion as he continued: "Nothing new—only things are taking their old course. You know that Caracalla threatened old Claudius Vindex and his nephew with death because of their opposition to his union with you. We all hoped, however, that he would be moved to exercise mercy. He is in love—he was so gracious at the feast! I myself was foremost among those who did their utmost to dispose Cæsar to clemency. But he would not be moved, and, before the sun goes down upon this day, the old man and the young one—the chiefest among the nobles of Rome—will be no more. And it is Caracella's love for you, child, that sheds this blood. Ask yourself after this how many lives will be sacrificed when your flight causes hatred and fury to reign supreme in the soul of the cheated monarch!"

With quickened breath Euryale had listened to the philosopher, without regarding the girl; but scarcely had Philostratus uttered his last words than Melissa ran to her, and, clasping her hands passionately on the matron's arm, she cried, "Ought I to obey you, Euryale, and the terrors of my own heart, and flee?"

Then releasing the lady, she turned again to the philosopher, and burst out: "Or are you in the right, Philostratus? Must I stay, to prevent the misery that threatens to overtake others?"

Beside herself, torn by the storm that raged in her soul, she clasped her hands upon her brow and continued, wildly: "You are both of you so wise, and surely wish the best. How can you give me such opposite advice? And my own heart?—why have the gods struck it dumb? Time was when it spoke loudly enough if ever I was in doubt. One thing I know for certain: if by the sacrifice of my life I could undo it all, I would joyfully cast myself before the lions and panthers, like the Christian maiden whom my mother saw smiling radiantly as she was led into the arena. Splendor and power are as hateful to me as the flowers yonder with their false dew. I was ever taught to close my ear to the voice of selfishness. If I have any wish for myself, it is that I may keep my faith with him to whom it was promised. But for love of my father, and if I could be certain of saving many from death and misery, I would stay, though I should despise myself and be separated forever from my beloved!"

"Submit to the inevitable," interposed the philosopher, with eager entreaty, "The immortal gods will reward you with the blessings of hundreds whom a word from you will have saved from ruin and destruction."

"And what say you?" asked the maiden, gazing with anxious expectancy into the matron's face.

"Follow your own heart!" replied the lady, deeply moved.

Melissa had hearkened to both counsellors with eager ear, and both hung anxiously on her lips, while, as if taken out of herself, she gazed with panting bosom into the empty air. They had not long to wait. Suddenly the maiden approached Philostratus and said with a firmness and decision that astonished her friend:

"This will I do—this—I feel it here—this is the right. I remain, I renounce the love of my heart, and accept what Fate has laid upon me. It will be hard, and the sacrifice that I offer is great. But I must first have the certainty that it shall not be in vain."

"But, child," cried Philostratus, "who can look into the future, and answer for what is still to come?"

"Who?" asked Melissa, undaunted. "He alone in whose hand lies my future. To Cæsar himself I leave the decision. Go you to him now and speak for me.

Bring him greeting from me, and tell him that I, whom he honors with his love, dare to entreat him modestly but earnestly not to punish the aged Claudius Vindex and his nephew for the fault they were guilty of on my account. For my sake would he deign to grant them life and liberty? Add to this that it is the first proof I have asked of his magnanimity, and clothe it all in such winning words as Peitho can lay upon your eloquent lips. If he grants pardon to these unfortunate ones, it shall be a sign to me that I may be permitted to shield others from his wrath. If he refuses, and they are put to death, then will he himself have decided our fate otherwise, and he sees me for the last time alive in the Circus. Thus shall it be—I have spoken."

The last words came like a stern order, and Philostratus seemed to have some hopes of the emperor's clemency, for his love's sake, and the philosopher's own eloquence. The moment Melissa ceased, he seized her hand and cried, eagerly:

"I will try it; and, if he grant your request, you remain?"

"Yes," answered the maiden, firmly. "Pray Cæsar to have mercy, soften his heart as much as you are able. I expect an answer before going to the Circus."

She hurried back into the sleeping-room without regarding Philostratus's answer. Once there, she threw herself upon her knees and prayed, now to the Manes of her mother, now—it was for the first time—to the crucified Saviour of the Christians, who had taken upon himself a painful death to bring happiness to others. First she prayed for strength to keep her vow, come what might; and then she prayed for Diodoros, that he might not be made wretched if she found herself compelled to

break her troth with him. Her father and brothers, too,
were not forgotten, as she commended their lives to a
higher power.

When Euryale looked into the room, she found Melissa
still upon her knees, her young frame shaken as with fever.
So she withdrew softly, and in the Temple of Serapis,
where her husband served as high-priest, she prayed to
Jesus Christ that he who suffered little children to come
unto him would lead this wandering lamb into the right
path.

CHAPTER VI.

THE lady Euryale's silent prayer was interrupted by
the return of Alexander. He brought the clothes which
Seleukus's wife had given him for Melissa. He was
already dressed in his best, and crowned like all those
who occupied the first seats in the Circus; but his festal
garb accorded ill with the pained look on his features,
from which every trace had vanished of the overflowing
joy in life which had embellished them only this morning.

He had seen and heard things which made him feel
that it would no longer be a sacrifice to give his life to
save his sister.

Sad thoughts had flitted across his cheerful spirit like
dark bats, even while he was talking with Melissa and
her protectress, for he knew well how infinitely hard his
father would find it to have to quit Alexandria; and if
he himself fled with Melissa he would be obliged to give
up the winning of fair Agatha. The girl's Christian
father had indeed received him kindly, but had given
him to understand plainly enough that he would never
allow a professed heathen to sue for his daughter's hand.

Besides this, he had met with other humiliations which placed themselves like a wall between him and his beloved, the only child of a rich and respected man. He had forfeited the right of appearing before Zeno as a suitor; for indeed he was no longer such as he had been only yesterday.

The news that Caracalla proposed to marry Melissa had been echoed by insolent tongues, with the addition that he, Alexander, had ingratiated himself with Cæsar by serving him as a spy. No one had expressly said this to him; but, while he was hurrying through the city in Cæsar's chariot on the ladies' message, it had been made very plain to his apprehension. Honest men had avoided him—him to whom hitherto every one for whose regard he cared had held out a friendly hand; and much else that he had experienced in the course of this drive had been unpleasant enough to give rise to a change of his whole inner being.

The feeling that every one was pointing at him the finger of scorn, or of wrath, had never ceased to pursue him. And he had been under no illusion; for when he met the old sculptor Lysander, who only yesterday had so kindly told him and Melissa about Cæsar's mother, as he nodded from the chariot, his greeting was not returned; and the honest artist had waved his hand with a gesture which no Alexandrian could fail to understand as meaning, "I no longer know you, and do not wish to be recognized by you."

He had from his childhood loved Diodoros as a brother, and in one of the side streets, down which the chariot had turned to avoid the tumult in the Kanopic way, Alexander had seen his old friend. He had desired the charioteer to stop, and had leaped out on the road to speak to Diodoros and give him at once Melissa's message; but the young man had turned his back with evident displeasure, and to the painter's pathetic appeal, "But, at any rate, hear me!" he answered, sharply: "The less I hear of you and yours the better for me. Go on—go on, in Cæsar's chariot!"

With this he had turned away and knocked at the door of an architect who was known to them both; and Alexander, tortured with painful feelings, had gone on, and for the first time the idea had taken possession of him that he had indeed descended to the part of spy when he had betrayed to Cæsar what Alexandrian wit had to say about him. He could, of course, tell himself that he would rather have faced death or imprisonment than have betrayed to Caracalla the name of one of the gibers; still, he had to admit to himself that, but for the hope of saving his father and brother from death and imprisonment, he would hardly have done Cæsar such service. The mercy shown to them was certainly too like payment, and his own part in the matter struck him as hateful and base. His fellow-townsmen had a right to bear him a grudge, and his friends to keep out of his way. A feeling came over him of bitter self-contempt, hitherto strange to him; and he understood for the first time how Philip could regard life as a burden and call it a malicious Danaos-gift of the gods. When, finally, in the Kanopic way, close in front of Seleukus's house, a youth unknown to him cried, scornfully, as the chariot was slowly making its way through the throng, "The brother-in-law of Tarautas!" he had great difficulty in restraining himself from leaping down and letting the rascal feel the weight of his fists. He knew, too, that Tarautas was the name of a hateful and bloodthirsty

gladiator which had been given as a nickname to Cæsar
in Rome; and when he heard the insolent fellow's cry
taken up by the mob, who shouted after him, "Tarautas's
brother-in-law!" wherever he went, he felt as though he
were being pelted with mire and stones.

It would have been a real comfort to him if the earth
would have opened to swallow him with the chariot, to
hide him from the sight of men. He could have burst
out crying like a child that has been beaten. When at
last he was safe inside Seleukus's house, he was easier;
for here he was known; here he would be understood.
Berenike must know what he thought of Cæsar's suit,
and seeing her wholesome and honest hatred, he had
sworn to himself that he would snatch his sister from
the hands of the tyrant, if it were to lead him to the
most agonizing death.

While she was engaged in selecting a dress for her
protégée, he related to the lady Euryale what had happened to him in the street and in the house of Seleukus.
He had been conducted past the soldiers in the vestibule
and impluvium to the lady's private rooms, and there he
had been witness to a violent matrimonial dispute. Seleukus had previously delivered to his wife Cæsar's command that she should appear in the Amphitheatre with
the other noble dames of the city. Her answer was a
bitter laugh, and a declaration that she would mingle
with the spectators in none but mourning robes. Thereupon her husband, pointing out to her the danger to
which such conduct would expose them, had raised objections, and she at last had seemed to yield. When
Alexander joined her he had found her in a splendid
dress of shining purple brocade, her black hair crowned
with a wreath of roses, and a splendid diadem; a garland

of roses hung across her bosom, and precious stones sparkled round her throat and arms. In short, she was arrayed like a happy mother for her daughter's wedding-day.

Soon after Alexander's arrival Seleukus had come in, and this conspicuously handsome dress, so unbecoming to the matron's age, and so unlike her usual attire—chosen, evidently, to put the monstrosity of Cæsar's demand in the strongest light—had roused her husband's wrath. He had expressed his dissatisfaction in strong terms, and again pointed out to her the danger in which such a daring demonstration might involve them; but this time there was no moving the lady; she would not despoil herself of a single rose. After she had solemnly declared that she would appear in the Circus either as she thought fit or not at all, her husband had left her in anger.

"What a fool she is!" Euryale exclaimed.

Then she showed him a white robe of beautiful bombyx, woven in the isle of Kos, which she had decided on for Melissa, and a peplos with a border of tender sea-green; and Alexander approved of the choice.

Time pressed, and Euryale went at once to Melissa with the new festal raiment. Once more she nodded kindly to the girl, and begged her, as she herself had something to discuss with Alexander, to allow the waiting-woman to dress her. She felt as if she were bringing the robe to a condemned creature, in which she was to be led to execution, and Melissa felt the same.

Euryale then returned to the painter, and bade him end his narrative.

The lady Berenike had forthwith desired Johanna to pack together all the dead Korinna's festal dresses.

Alexander had then followed her guidance, accompanying her to a court in the slaves' quarters, where a number of men were awaiting her. These were the captains of Seleukus's ships, which were now in port, and the superintendents of his granaries and offices, altogether above a hundred freedmen in the merchant's service. Each one seemed to know what he was here for.

The matron responded to their hearty greetings with a word of thanks, and added, bitterly:

"You see before you a mourning mother whom a ruthless tyrant compels to go to a festival thus—thus—only look at me—bedizened like a peacock!"

At this the bearded assembly gave loud expression to their dissatisfaction, but Berenike went on: "Melapompus has taken care to secure good places; but he has wisely not taken them all together. You are all free men; I have no orders to give you. But, if you are indeed indignant at the scorn and heart-ache inflicted on your lord's wife, make it known in the Circus to him who has brought them on her. You are all past your first youth, and will carefully avoid any rashness which may involve you in ruin. May the avenging god aid and protect you!"

With this she had turned her back on the multitude; but Johannes, the Christian lawyer, the chief freedman of the household, had hurried into the court-yard, just in time to entreat her to give up this ill-starred demonstration, and to extinguish the fire she had tried to kindle. So long as Cæsar wore the purple, rebellion against him, to whom the Divinity had intrusted the sovereignty, was a sin. The scheme she was plotting was meant to punish him who had pained her; but she forgot that it might cost these brave men, husbands and fathers, their life or liberty. The vengeance she called on them to take might be balm to the wounds of her own heart; but if Cæsar in his wrath brought destruction down on these, her innocent instruments, that balm would turn to burning poison.

These words, whispered to her with entire conviction, had not been without their effect. For some minutes Berenike had stared gloomily at the ground; but then she had again approached the assembly, to repeat the warning given her by the Christian, whom all respected, and by whom some indeed had been persuaded to be baptized.

"Johannes is right," she ended. "This ill-used heart did wrong when it sent up its cry of anguish before you. Rather will I be trodden under foot by the enemy, as is the manner of the Christians, than bring such misfortune on innocent men, who are so faithful to our house. Be cautious, then. Give no overt expression to your feelings. Let each one who feels too weak to control his wrath, avoid the Circus; and those who go, keep still if they feel moved to act in my behalf. One thing only you may do. Tell every one, far and wide, what I had purposed. What others may do, they themselves must answer for."

The Christian had strongly disapproved of this last clause; but Berenike had paid no heed, and had left the court-yard, followed by Alexander.

The shouts of the indignant multitude had rung in their ears, and, in spite of her warning, they had sounded like a terrible threat. Johannes, to be sure, had remained, to move them to moderation by further remonstrances.

"What were the mad creatures plotting?" Euryale anxiously broke in; and he hastily went on: "They call

Cæsar by no name but Tarautas; every mouth is full of gibes and rage at the new and monstrous taxes, the billeting of the troops, and the intolerable insolence of the soldiery, which Caracalla wickedly encourages. His contemptuous indifference has deeply offended the heads of the town. And then his suit to my sister! Young and old are wagging their tongues over it."

"It would be more like them to triumph in it," said the matron, interrupting him. "An Alexandrian in the purple, on the throne of the Cæsars!"

"I too had hoped that," cried Alexander, "and it seemed so likely. But who can understand the populace? Every woman in the place, I should have thought, would hold her head higher, at the thought that an Alexandrian girl was empress; but it was from the women that I heard the most vindictive and shameless abuse. I heard more than enough; for, as we got closer to the Serapeum, the more slowly was the chariot obliged to proceed, to make its way through the crowd. And the things I heard! I clinch my fists now as I only think of them.—And what will it be in the Circus? What will not Melissa have to endure?"

"It is envy," the matron murmured to herself; but she was immediately silent, for the young girl came toward them, out of the bedroom. Her toilet was complete; the beautiful white dress became her well. The wreath of roses, with diamond dewdrops, lay lightly on her hair, the snake-shaped bracelet which her imperial suitor had sent. her clasped her white arm, and her small head, somewhat bent, her pale, sweet face, and large, bashful, inquiring, drooping eyes formed such an engaging, modest, and unspeakably touching picture, that Euryale dared to hope that even in the Circus none but hardened hearts could harbor a hostile feeling against this gentle, pure blossom, slightly drooping with silent sorrow. She could not resist the impulse to kiss Melissa, and the half-formed purpose ripened within her to venture the utmost for the child's protection. The pity in her heart had turned to love; and when she saw that to this sweet creature, at the mere sight of whom her heart went forth, the most splendid jewels, in which any other girl would have been glad to deck herself, were as a heavy burden to be borne but sadly, she felt it a sacred duty to comfort her and lighten this trial, and shelter Melissa, so far as was in her power, from insult and humiliation.

It was many years since she had visited the Circus, where the horrible butchery was an abomination to her; but to-day her heart bade her conquer her old aversion, and accompany the girl to the Circus.

Had not Melissa taken the place in her heart of her lost daughter? Was not she, Euryale, the only person who, by showing herself with Melissa and declaring herself her friend, could give the people assurance that the girl, who was exposed to misapprehension and odium by the favor she had met with from the ruthless and hated sovereign, was in truth pure and lovable? Under her guardianship, by her side, the girl, as she knew, would be protected from misapprehension and insult; and she, an old woman and a Christian, should she evade the first opportunity of taking up a cross in imitation of the Divine Master, among whose followers she joyfully counted herself—though secretly, for fear of men? All this flashed through her mind with the swiftness of lightning, and her call, "Doris!" addressed to her waiting-woman, was so clear and unexpected that Melissa's over-strung nerves startled. She looked up at the lady in amazement, as, without a word of explanation, she said to the woman who had hurried in:

"The blue robe I wore at the festival of Adonis, my mother's diadem, and a large gem with the head of Serapis for my shoulder. My hair—oh, a veil will cover it! What does it matter for an old woman?—You, child, why do you look at me in such amazement? What mother would allow a pretty young daughter to appear alone in the Circus? Besides, I may surely hope that it will confirm your courage to feel that I am at your side. Perhaps the populace may be moved a little in your favor if the wife of the high-priest of their greatest god is your companion."

But she could scarcely end her speech, for Melissa had flown into her arms, exclaiming, "And you will do this for me?" while Alexander, deeply touched by gratitude and joy, kissed her thin arm and the hem of her peplos.

While Melissa helped the matron to change her dress —in the next room—Alexander paced to and fro in great unrest. He knew the Alexandrians, and there was not the slightest doubt but that the presence of the universally revered lady would make them look with kindlier eyes on his sister. Nothing else could so effectually impress them with the entire propriety of her appearance in the Circus. The more seriously he had feared that Melissa might be deeply insulted and offended by the rough demonstrations of the mob, the more gratefully did his heart beat; nay, his facile nature saw in this kind act the first smile of returning good fortune.

He only longed to be hopeful once more, to enjoy the present—as so many philosophers and poets advised—

and especially the show in the Circus, his last pleasure, perhaps; to forget the imminent future.

The old bright look came back to his face; but it soon vanished, for even while he pictured himself in the amphitheatre, he remembered that there, too, his former acquaintances might refuse to speak to him; that the odious names of "Tarautas' brother-in-law" or of "traitor" might be shouted after him on the road. A cold chill came over him, and the image of pretty Ino rose up before him—Ino, who had trusted in his love; and to whom, of all others, he had given cause to accuse him of false-heartedness. An unpleasant sense came over him of dis·satisfaction with himself, such as he, who always regarded self-accusation, repentance, and atonement as a foolish waste of life, had never before experienced.

The fine, sunny autumn day had turned to a sultry, dull evening, and Alexander went to the window to let the sea-breeze fan his dewy brow; but he soon heard voices behind him, for Euryale and Melissa had re-entered the room, followed by the house-steward, who presented to his mistress a sealed tablet which a slave had just brought from Philostratus. The women had been talking of Melissa's vow; and Euryale had promised her that, if Fate should decide against Cæsar, she would convey the girl to a place of safety, where she could certainly not be discovered, and might look forward in peace to the future. Then she had impressed on her that, if things should be otherwise ordered, she must endure even the unendurable with patience, as an obedient wife, as em-press, but still ever conscious of the solemn and beneficent power she might wield in her new position.

The tablets would settle the question; and side by side the two women hastily read the missive which

Philostratus had written in the wax, in his fine, legible hand.   It was as follows:

"The condemned have ceased to live.   Your efforts had no effect but to hasten their end.   Cæsar's desire was to rid you of adversaries, even against your will. Vindex and his nephew are no more; but I embarked soon enough to escape the rage of him who might have attained the highest favors of fortune if he had but known how to be merciful."

"God be praised!—but alas, poor Vindex!" cried Euryale, as she laid down the tablets.   But Melissa kissed her, and then exclaimed to her brother:

"Now all doubts are at an end.   I may fly.   He himself has settled the matter!"

Then she added, more gently, but still urgently: "Do you take care of my father, and Philip, and of yourself. The lady Euryale will protect me.   Oh, how thankful am I!"

She looked up to heaven with fervent devotion. Euryale whispered to them: "My plan is laid.   As soon as the performance is over, Alexander shall take you home, child, to your father's house; you must go in one of Cæsar's chariots.   Afterward come back here with your brother; I will wait for you below.   But now we will go together to the Circus, and can discuss the details on our way.   You, my young friend, go now and order away the imperial litter; bid my steward to have the horses put to my covered harmamaxa.   There is room in it for us all three."

By the time Alexander returned the daylight was waning, and the clatter of the chariots began to be audible, which conveyed Cæsar's court to the Circus.

CHAPTER VII.

THE great Amphitheatre of Dionysos was in the Bruchium, the splendid palatial quarter of the city, close to the large harbor between the Choma and the peninsula of Lochias. Hard by the spacious and lofty rotunda, in which ten thousand spectators could be seated, stood the most fashionable gymnasia and riding-schools. These buildings, which had been founded long since by the Ptolemaic kings, and had been repeatedly extended and beautified, formed, with the adjoining schools for gladiators and beast-fighters, and the stables for wild beasts from every part of the world, a little town by themselves.

At this moment the amphitheatre looked like a bee-hive, of which every cell seems to be full, but in which a whole swarm expects yet to find room. The upper places, mere standing-room for the common people, and the cheaper seats, had been full early in the day. By the afternoon the better class of citizens had come in, if their places were not reserved; and now, at sunset, those who were arriving in litters and chariots, just before the beginning of the show, were for the most part in Cæsar's train, court officials, senators, or the rich magnates of the city.

The strains of music were by this time mingling with the shouting and loud talk of the spectators, or of the thousands who were crowding round the building without hoping to obtain admission. But even for them there was plenty to be seen. How delightful to watch the well-dressed women, and the men of rank and wealth, crowned with wreaths, as they dismounted; to see the learned men and artists arrive—more or less eagerly applauded, according to the esteem in which they were held by the populace! The most splendid sight of all was the procession of priests, with Timotheus, the high-priest of Serapis, at their head, and by his side the priest of Alexander, both marching with dignity under a canopy. They were followed by the animals to be slaughtered for sacrifice, and the images of the gods and the deified Cæsars, which were to be placed in the arena, as the most worshipful of all the spectators. Timotheus wore the splendid insignia of his office; the priest of Alexander was in purple, as being the idiologos and head of all the temples of Egypt, and representative of Cæsar.

The advent of the images of the Cæsars gave rise to a sort of judgment of the dead: for the mob hailed that of Julius Cæsar with enthusiasm, that of Augustus, with murmurs of disapproval; when Caligula appeared, he was hissed; while the statues of Vespasian, Titus, Hadrian, and Antonine, met with loud acclamations. That of Septimius Severus, Caracalla's father, to whom the town owed many benefits, was very well received. The images of the gods, too, had very various fates. Serapis, and Alexander, the divine hero of the town, were enthusiastically welcomed, while scarcely a voice was heard on the approach of Zeus-Jupiter and Ares-Mars. They were regarded as the gods of the hated Romans.

The companies of the imperial body-guard, who were placed about the amphitheatre, found no great difference, so long as it was daylight, between the crowd round the Circus of Alexandria and that by the Tiber. What chiefly struck them was the larger number of dusky faces, and the fanciful garb of the Magians. The almost naked rabble, too, with nothing on but a loin-cloth, who wriggled in and out of the throng, ready for any service or errand, formed a feature unknown at Rome. But, as it grew darker the Romans began to perceive that it was not for nothing that they had come hither.

At Rome, when some great show was promised, of beast-fighting, gladiators, and the like, there were, no doubt, barbarian princes to be seen, and envoys from the remotest ends of the earth in strange and gorgeous array; and there, too, small wares of every kind were for sale. By the Tiber, again, night shows were given, with grand illuminations, especially for the feast of Flora; but here, as soon as the sun had set, and the sports were about to begin, the scene was one never to be forgotten. Some of the ladies who descended from the litters, wore garments of indescribable splendor; the men even displayed strange and handsome costumes as they were helped out of their gilt and plated chariots by their servants. What untold wealth must these men have at their command, to be able to dress their slaves in gold and silver brocade; and the runners, who kept up with the swiftest horses, must have lungs of iron! The prætorians, who had not for many a day seen anything to cause them to forget the motto of the greatest philosopher among their poets— never to be astonished at anything—repeatedly pushed each other with surprise and admiration; nay, the centurion Julius Martialis, who had just now had a visit in camp from his wife and children, in defiance of orders, while Cæsar himself was looking on, struck his fist on his greaves, and, exclaiming loudly, "Look out!" pointed to Seleukus's chariot, for which four runnners, in tunics with long sleeves, made of sea-green bombyx, richly embroidered with silver, were making a way through the crowd.

The barefooted lads, with their nimble, gazelle-like legs, were all well looking and might have been cast all in one mould. But what struck the centurion and his comrades as most remarkable in their appearance were the flash and sparkle from their slender ankles, as the setting sun suddenly shot a fleeting ray through a rift in the heavy clouds. Each of these fellows wore on his legs gold bands set with precious stones, and the rubies which glittered on the harness of Seleukus's horse were of far greater value.

He, as master of the festival, had come betimes, and this was the first of many such displays of wealth which followed each other in quick succession, as soon as the brief twilight of Egypt had given way to darkness, and the lighting up of the Circus was begun.

Here came a beautifully dressed woman in a roomy litter, over which waved a canopy entirely of white ostrich-plumes, which the evening breeze swayed like a thicket of fern-leaves. This throne was borne by ten black and ten white slave-girls, and before it two fair children rode on tame ostriches. The tall heir of a noble house, who, like Cæsar at Rome, belonged to the "Blues," drove his own team of four splendid white horses; and he himself was covered with turquoises, while the harness was set with cut sapphires.

The centurion shook his head in silent admiration. His face had been tanned in many wars, both in the East and West, and he had fought even in distant Caledonia, but the low forehead, loose under lip, and dull eye spoke of small gifts of intellect. Nevertheless, he was not lacking in strength of will, and was regarded by his comrades as a good beast of burden who would submit to a great deal before it became too much for him. But then he would break out like a mad bull, and he might long ago have risen to higher rank, had he not once in such a fit

of passion nearly throttled a fellow-soldier. For this crime
he had been severely punished, and condemned to begin
again at the bottom of the ladder. He owed it chiefly
to the young tribune Aurelius Apollinaris that he had
very soon regained the centurion's staff, in spite of his
humble birth; he had saved that officer's life in the war
with the Armenians—to be here, in Alexandria, cruelly
mutilated by the hand of his sovereign.

The centurion had a faithful heart. He was as much
attached to the two noble brothers as to his wife and
children, for indeed he owed them much; and if the
service had allowed it he would long since have made his
way to the house of Seleukus to learn how the wounded
tribune was faring. But he had not time even to see his
own family, for his younger and richer comrades, who
wanted to enjoy the pleasures of the city, had put upon
him no small share of their own duties. Only this morning a young soldier of high birth, who had begun his
career at the same time as Martialis, had promised him
some tickets of admission to the evening's performance
in the Circus if he would take his duty on guard outside
the amphitheatre. And this offer had been very welcome
to the centurion, for he thus found it possible to give
those he loved best, his wife and his mother, the greatest
treat which could be offered to any Alexandrian. And
now, when anything noteworthy was to be seen outside,
he only regretted that he had already some time since
conducted them to their seats in one of the upper rows.
He would have liked that they, too, should have seen the
horses and the chariots and the "Blue" charioteer's turquoises and sapphires; although a decurion observed, as
he saw them, that a Roman patrician would scorn to
dress out his person with such barbaric splendor, and an

Alexandrian of the prætorian guard declared that his fellow-citizens of Greek extraction thought more of a graceful fold than of whole strings of precious stones.

"But why, then, was this 'Blue' so vehemently hailed by the mob!" asked a Pannonian in the guard.

"The mob!" retorted the Alexandrian, scornfully. "Only the Syrians and other Asiatics. Look at the Greeks. The great merchant Seleukus is the richest of them all, but splendid as his horses, his chariots, and his slaves are, he himself wears only the simple Macedonian mantle. Though it is of costly material, who would suspect it? If you see a man swaggering in such a blaze of gems you may wager your house—if you have one—that his birth-place lies not very far from Syria."

"Now, that one, in a mother-of-pearl shell on two wheels, is the Jew Poseidonius," the Pannonian put in. "I am quartered on his father. But he is dressed like a Greek."

At this the centurion, in his delight at knowing something, opened his mouth with a broad grin: "I am a native here," said he, "and I can tell you the Jew would make you answer for it if you took him for anything but a Greek."

"And quite right," added another soldier, from Antioch. "The Jews here are many, but they have little in common with those in Palestine. They wish to pass for Greeks; they speak Greek, assume Greek names, and even cease to believe in the great God their father; they study Greek philosophy, and I know one who worships in the Temple of Serapis."

"Many do the same in Rome," said a man of Ostia. "I know an epigram which ridicules them for it."

At this point they were interrupted, for Martialis

pointed to a tall man who was coming toward them, and whom his sharp eye had recognized as Macrinus, the prefect of the prætorians. In an instant the soldiers were erect and rigid, but still many a helmeted head was turned toward the spot where their chief stood talking in an undertone to the Magian Serapion.

Macrinus had persuaded Cæsar to send for the exorciser, to test his arts. Immediately after the performance, however late it might be, the Magian was to be admitted to his presence.

Serapion thanked the prefect, and then whispered to him, "I have had a second revelation."

"Not here!" exclaimed Macrinus, uneasily, and, leading away his handsome little son, he turned toward the entrance.

Dusk, meanwhile, had given way to darkness, and several slaves stood ready to light the innumerable little lamps which were to illuminate the outside of the Circus. They edged the high arches which surrounded the two lower stories, and supported the upper ranks of the enormous circular structure. Separated only by narrow intervals, the rows of lights formed a glittering series of frames which outlined the noble building and rendered it visible from afar.

The arches on the ground-floor led to the cells from which the men and beasts were let out into the arena; but some, too, were fitted with shops, where flowers and wreaths, refreshments, drinks, handkerchiefs, fans, and other articles in request, were sold. On the footway between the building and the row of pitch torches which surrounded it, men and women in thousands were walking to and fro. Smart, inquisitive girls were pushing their way singly or in groups, and their laughter drowned the deep, tragical voices of the soothsayers and Magians who announced their magic powers to the passers by. Some of these even made their way into the waiting-rooms of the gladiators and wrestlers, who to-day so greatly needed their support that, in spite of severe and newly enforced prohibitions, many a one stole out into the crowd to buy some effectual charm or protecting amulet.

Where the illuminations were completed, attempts of another kind were being made to work upon the mood of the people; nimble-tongued fellows—some in the service of Macrinus and some in that of the anxious senate—were distributing handkerchiefs to wave on Cæsar's approach, or flowers to strew in his path. More than one, who was known for a malcontent, found a gold coin in his hand, with the image of the monarch he was expected to hail; and on the way by which Cæsar was to come many of those who awaited him wore the *caracalla*. These were for the most part bribed, and their acclamations were to mollify the tyrant's mood.

As soon as the prefect had disappeared within the building, the prætorian ranks fell out again. It was lucky that among them were several Alexandrians, besides the centurion Martialis, who had not long been absent from their native town; for without them much would have remained incomprehensible. The strangest thing to foreign eyes was a stately though undecorated harmamaxa, out of which stepped first a handsome wreathed youth, then a matron of middle age, and at last an elegantly dressed girl, whose rare beauty made even Martialis—who rarely noticed women—exclaim, "Now, she is to my taste the sweetest thing of all."

But there must have been something very remarkable about these three; for where they appeared the crowd broke out at first in loud shouts and outcries, which soon turned to acclamations and welcome, though through it all shrill whistles and hisses were heard.

"Cæsar's new mistress, the daughter of a gem-cutter!" the Alexandrian muttered to his comrades. "That handsome boy is her brother, no doubt. He is said to be a mean sycophant, a spy paid by Cæsar."

"He?" said an older centurion, shaking his scarred head. "Sooner would I believe that the shouts of the populace were intended for the old woman and not for the young one."

"Then a sycophant he is and will remain," said the Alexandrian with a laugh. "For, as a matter of fact, it is the elder lady they are greeting, and, by Heracles, she deserves it! She is the wife of the high-priest of Serapis. There are few poor in this city to whom she has not done a kindness. She is well able, no doubt, for her husband is the brother of Seleukus, and her father, too, sat over his ears in gold."

"Yes, she is able," interrupted Martialis, with a tone of pride, as though it were some credit to himself. "But how many have even more, and keep their purse-strings tight! I have known her since she was a child, and she is the best of all that is good. What does not the town owe to her! She risked her life to move Cæsar's father to mercy toward the citizens, after they had openly declared against him and in favor of his rival Pescennius Niger. And she succeeded, too."

"Why, then, are they whistling?" asked the older centurion.

"Because her companion is a spy," repeated the Alexandrian. "And the girl— In Cæsar's favor! But, after all, which of you all would not gladly see his sister or his niece Cæsar's light of love?"

"Not I!" cried Martialis. "But the man who speaks ill of that girl only does so because he likes blue eyes best. The maiden who comes in the lady Euryale's chariot is spotless, you may swear."

"Nay, nay," said the younger Alexandrian soothingly. "That black-haired fellow and his companions would whistle another tune if they knew any evil of her, and she would not be in the lady Euryale's company—that is the chief point.—But, look there! The shameless dogs are stopping their way!—'Green' to a man—But here come the lictors."

"Attention!" shouted Martialis, firmly resolved to uphold the guardians of the peace, and not to suffer any harm to the matron and her fair companion; for Euryale's husband was the brother of Seleukus, whom his father-in-law had served years ago, while in the villa at Kanopus his mother and wife were left in charge to keep it in order. He felt that he was bound in duty to the merchant, and that all who were of that household had a right to count on his protection. But no active measures were needed; a number of "Blues" had driven off the "Greens" who had tried to bar Alexander's way, and the lictors came to their assistance.

A young man in festal array, who had pushed into the front rank of the bystanders, had looked on with panting breath. He was very pale, and the thick wreath he wore was scarcely sufficient to hide the bandage under it. This was Diodoros, Melissa's lover. After resting awhile at his friend's house he had been carried in a litter to the amphitheatre, for he could yet hardly walk. His father being one of the senators of the town, his family had a row of seats in the lowest and best tier; but this, on this occasion, was entirely given up to Cæsar and his court. Consequently the different members of the senate could have only half the usual number of seats. Still, the son of Polybius might in any case claim two in his father's name; and his friend Timon—who had also provided him with suitable clothing—had gone to procure the tickets from the curia. They were to meet at the entrance leading to their places, and it would be some little time yet before Timon could return.

Diodoros had thought he would behold his imperial rival; however, instead of Caracalla he had seen the contemptuous reception which awaited Alexander and Melissa from some at least of the populace. Still, how fair and desirable had she seemed in his eyes, whom, only that morning, he had been blessed in calling his! As he now moved away from the main entrance, he asked himself why it was such torture to him to witness the humiliation of a being who had done him such a wrong, and whom he thought he hated and scorned so utterly. Hardly an hour since he had declared to Timon that he had rooted his love for Melissa out of his heart. He himself would feel the better for using the whistle he wore, in derision of her, and for seeing her faithlessness punished by the crowd. But now? When the insolent uproar went up from the "Greens," whose color he himself wore, he had found it difficult to refrain from rushing on the cowardly crew and knocking some of them down.

He now made his way with feeble steps to the entrance where he was to meet his friend. The blood throbbed in his temples, his mouth was parched, and, as a fruit-seller cried her wares from one of the archways, he took a few apples from her basket to refresh himself with their juice. His hand trembled, and the experienced old woman observing the bandage under his wreath, supposed him to be one of the excited malcontents who had perhaps already fallen into the hands of the lictors. So, with a significant grin, she pointed under the table on which her fruit-baskets stood, and said: "I have plenty of rotten ones. Six in a wrapper, quite easy to hide under your cloak. For whom you will. Cæsar has given the golden apple of Paris to a goddess of this town. I should best like to see these flung at her brother, the sycophant."

"Do you know them?" asked Diodoros, hoarsely.

"No," replied the old woman. "No need for that. I have plenty of customers and good ears. The slut broke her word with a handsome youth of the town for the sake of the Roman, and they who do such things are repaid by the avenging gods."

Diodoros felt his knees failing under him, and a wrathful answer was on his lips, when the huckster suddenly shouted like mad: "Cæsar, Cæsar! He is coming."

The shouts of the crowd hailing their emperor had already become audible through the heavy evening air, at first low and distant, and louder by degrees. They now suddenly rose to a deafening uproar, and while the sound rolled on like approaching thunder, broken by shrill whistles suggesting lightning, the sturdy old apple-seller clambered unaided on to her table, and shouted with all her might:

"Cæsar! Here he is!—Hail, hail, hail to great Cæsar!"

At the imminent risk of tumbling off her platform, she bent low down to reach under the table for the blue cloth which covered her store of rotten apples, snatched it off, and waved it with frantic enthusiasm, as though her elderly heart had suddenly gone forth to the very man for whom a moment ago she had been ready to sell her disgusting missiles. And still she shouted in ringing tones, "Hail, hail, Cæsar!" again and again, with all her might, till there was no breath left in her over-buxom, panting breast, and her round face was purple with the effort. Nay, her emotion was so vehement that the bright tears streamed down her fat cheeks.

And every one near was shrieking like the apple-woman, "Hail, Cæsar!" and it was only where the crowd was densest that a sharp whistle now and then rent the roar of acclamations.

Diodoros, meanwhile, had turned to look at the main entrance, and, carried away by the universal desire to see, had perched himself on an unopened case of dried figs. His tall figure now towered far above the throng, and he tet his teeth as he heard the old woman, almost speechless with delight, gasp out:

"Lovely! wonderful! He would never have found the like in Rome. Here, among us——"

But the cheers of the multitude now drowned every other sound. Fathers or mothers who had children with them lifted them up as high as they could; where a small man stood behind a tall one, way was willingly made, for it would have been a shame to hinder his view of such a spectacle. Many had already seen the great monarch in his shining, golden chariot, drawn by four splendid horses; but such an array of torch-bearers as now preceded Caracalla was a thing never seen within the memory of the oldest or most travelled man. Three elephants marched before him and three came behind, and all six carried in their trunks blazing torches, which they held now low and now aloft to light his road. To think that beasts could be trained to such a service! And that here, in Alexandria, such a display could be made before the haughty and pampered Romans!

The chariot stood still, and the black Ethiopians who guided the huge four-footed torch-bearers took the three leaders to join their fellows behind the chariot. This really was a fine sight; this could not but fill the heart of every one who loved his native town, with pride and delight. For what should a man ever shout himself hoarse, if not for such a splendid and unique show? Diodoros himself could not take his eyes off the elephants. At first he was delighted with them, but presently the sight annoyed him even more than it had pleased him; for he reflected that the tyrant, the villain, his deadly enemy, would certainly take to himself the applause bestowed on the clever beasts. With this, he grasped the reed pipe in the breast of his tunic. He had been on the point of using it before now, to retaliate on Melissa for some portion of the pain she had inflicted on him. At this thought, however, the paltriness of such revenge struck him with horror, and with a hasty impulse he snapped the pipe in two, and flung the pieces on the ground in front of the apple-stall. The old woman observed it and exclaimed:

"Ay, ay, such a sight makes one forgive a great deal;" but he turned his back on her in silence, and joined his friend at the appointed spot.

They made their way without difficulty to the seats reserved for the senators' families, and when they had taken their places, the young man replied but briefly to the sympathetic inquiries as to his health which were addressed to him by his acquaintances. His friend Timon gazed anxiously into his handsome but pale, sad face, as Diodoros sat crushed and absorbed in thought. He would have liked to urge him to quit the scene at once, for the

seats just opposite were those destined to Cæsar and his
court—among them, no doubt, Melissa. In the dim light
which still prevailed in the vast amphitheatre it was impossible to recognize faces. But there would soon be a
blaze of light, and what misery must await the hapless
victim of her faithlessness, still so far from perfect health!
After the glare of light outside, which was almost blinding, the twilight within was for the moment a relief to
Diodoros. His weary limbs were resting, a pleasant smell
came up from the perfumed fountains in the arena, and
his eyes, which could not here rest on anything to gratify
him, were fixed on vacancy.

And yet it was a comfort to him to think that he had
broken his pipe. It would have disgraced him to whistle
it; and, moreover, the tone would have reached the ear
of the noble lady who had accompanied Melissa, and whom
he himself had, only yesterday, revered as a second mother.

Loud music now struck up, he heard shouts and
cheers, and just above him—for it could only proceed
from the uppermost tiers—there was an extraordinary
tumult. Still he paid no heed, and as he thought of that
matron the question suddenly arose in his mind, whether
she would have consented to be seen with Melissa if she
thought that the girl was indeed capable of ruthless falsehood or any other unworthy act. He, who never missed
a show in the arena, had never seen the lady Euryale
here. She could hardly have come to-day for her own
pleasure; she had come, then, for Melissa's sake; and yet
she knew that the girl was betrothed to him. Unless
Cæsar had commanded the matron's presence, Melissa
must still be worthy of the esteem and affection of this
best of women; and at this reflection Hope once more
raised her head in his tortured soul.

He now suddenly wished that brighter light might dispel the gloom which just now he had found so restful; for the lady Euryale's demeanor would show him whether Melissa were still a virtuous maiden. If the matron were as friendly with her as ever, her heart was perhaps still his; it was not the splendor of the purple that had led her astray, but the coercion of the tyrant.

His silent reflections were here interrupted by the loud sounding of trumpets, battle-cries, and, immediately after, the fall of some heavy body, followed by repeated acclamations, noisy outcries, and the applause of those about him. Not till then had he been aware that the performances had begun. Below him, indeed, on the arena from which he had not once raised his eyes, nothing was to be seen on the yellow sand but the scented fountain and a shapeless body, by which a second and a third were soon lying; but overhead something was astir, and, from the right hand side, bright rays flashed across the wide space. Above the vast circle of seats, arranged on seven tiers, suns and huge, strangely shaped stars were seen, which shed a subdued, many-tinted radiance; and what the youth saw over his head was not the vault of heaven, which to-night bent over his native city darkened by clouds, but a velarium of immense size on which the nocturnal firmament was depicted. This covered in the whole of the open space. Every constellation which rose over Alexandria was plainly recognizable. Jupiter and Mars, Cæsar's favourites, outdid the other planets in size and brightness; and in the centre of this picture of the sky, which slowly revolved round it, stars were set to form the letters of Caracalla's names, Bassianus and Antoninus. But their light, too, was dim, and veiled as it were with clouds. Soft music was heard from these artificial heavens, and in the stratum of air immediately beneath, the blare of war-trumpets and battle-cries were heard. Thus all eyes were directed upward, and Diodoros's with the rest.

He perceived, with amazement, that the givers of the entertainment, in their anxiety to set something absolutely new before their imperial guest, had arranged that the first games should take place in the air. A battle was being fought overhead, on a level with the highest places, in a way that must surely be a surprise even to the pampered Romans. Black and gold barks were jostling each other in mid-air, and their crews were fighting with the energy of despair. The Egyptian myth of the gods of the great lights who sail the celestial ocean in golden barks, and of the sun-god who each morning conquers the demons of darkness, had suggested the subject of this performance.

The battle between the Spirits of Darkness and of Light was to be fought out high above the best rows of seats occupied by Cæsar and his court; and the combatants were living men, for the most part such as had been condemned to death or to the hardest forced labor. The black vessels were manned by negroes, the golden by fair-haired criminals, and they had embarked readily enough; for some of them would escape from the fray with only a few wounds and some quite unhurt, and each one was resolved to use his weapons so as to bring the frightful combat to a speedy end.

The woolly-haired blacks did not indeed know that they had been provided with loosely made swords which would go to pieces at the first shock, and with shields which could not resist a serious blow; while the fair-haired representatives of the light were supplied with sharp and strong weapons of offence and defence. At any cost the spirits of Darkness must not be allowed to triumph over those of Light. Of what value was a negro's life, especially when it was already forfeited?

While Euryale and Melissa sat with eyes averted from the horrible scene going on above them, and the matron, holding her young companion's hand, whispered to her:

"O child, child! to think that I should be compelled to bring you here!" loud applause and uproarious clapping surrounded them on every side.

The gem-cutter Heron, occupying one of the foremost cushioned seats, radiant with pride and delight in the red-bordered toga of his new dignity, clapped his big hands with such vehemence that his immediate neighbors were almost deafened. He, too, had been badly received, on his arrival, with shrill whistling, but he had been far from troubling himself about that. But when a troop of "Greens" had met him, just in front of the imperial dais, shouting brutal abuse in his face, he had paused, chucked the nearest man under the chin with his powerful fist, and fired a storm of violent epithets at the rest. Thanks to the lictors, he had got off without any harm, and as soon as he found himself among friends and men of rank, on whom he looked in speechless respect, he had recovered his spirits. He was looking forward with intense satisfaction to the moment when he might ask Cæsar what he now thought of Alexandria.

Like his father, Alexander was intent on the bloody struggle—gazing upward with breathless interest as the combatants tried to fling each other into the yawning depth below them. But at the same time he never for an instant forgot the insults he had endured outside. How deeply he felt them was legible in his clouded face.

Only once did a smile pass over it—when, toward the end of this first fight, the place was made lighter, he perceived in the row of seats next above him the daughter of his neighbor Skopas, pretty Ino, whom but a few days since he had vowed to love. He was conscious of having treated her badly, and given her the right to call him faithless. Toward her, indeed, he had been guilty of treachery, and it had really weighed on his soul. Their eyes met, and she gave him to understand in the plainest way that she had heard him stigmatized as Cæsar's spy, and had believed the calumny. The mere sight of him seemed to fill her with anger, and she did her utmost to show him that she had quickly found a substitute for him; and it was to Alexander, no doubt, that Ktesias, her young kinsman, who had long paid her his addresses, owed the kindliness with which Ino now gazed into his eyes. This was some comfort to the luckless, banished lover. On her account, at any rate, he need reproach himself no longer.

Diodoros was sitting opposite to him, and his attention, too, was frequently interrupted.

The flashing swords and torches in the hands of the Spirits of Light, and the dimly gleaming stars above their heads, had not so far dispelled the darkness that the two young people could identify each other. Diodoros, indeed, even throughout this absorbing fight, had frequently glanced at the imperial seats, but had failed to distinguish his beloved from the other women in Caracalla's immediate vicinity. But it now grew lighter, for, while the battle was as yet undecided, a fresh bark, full of Spirits of Light, flourishing their torches, was unexpectedly launched to support their comrades, and Heaven seemed to have sent them forth to win the fight, which had already lasted longer than the masters of the ceremonies had thought possible.

The wild shouts of the combatants and the yells of the wounded had long since drowned the soft music of the spheres above their heads. The call of tubas and bugles rang without ceasing through the great building, to the frequent accompaniment of the most horrible sound of all in this hideous spectacle—the heavy fall of a dead man dropping from above into the gulf.

But this dreadful thud was what gave rise to the loudest applause among the spectators, falling on their satiated ears as a new sound. This frenzied fight in the air, such as had never before been seen, gave rise to the wildest delight, for it led the eye, which was wont in this place to gaze downward, in a direction in which it had never yet been attracted. And what a glorious spectacle it was when black and white wrestled together! How well the contrast of color distinguished the individual combatants, even when they clung together in close embrace! And when, toward the end of the struggle, a bark was overturned bodily, and some of the antagonists would not be parted, even as they fell, trying to kill each other in their rage and hatred, the very walls of the great structure shook with the wild clamor and applause of thousands of every degree.

Only once did the roar of approval reach a higher pitch, and that was after the battle was ended, at what succeeded. Hardly had the victorious Spirits of Light been seen to stand up in their barks, waving their torches, to receive from fluttering genii wreaths of laurel which they flung down to where Cæsar sat, than a perfumed vapor, emanating from the place where the painted sky met the wall of the circular building, hid the whole of the upper part of it from the sight of the spectators. The music stopped, and from above there came a strange and ominous growling, hissing, rustling, and crackling. A dull light, dimmer even than before, filled the place, and anxious suspicions took possession of the ten thousand spectators.

What was happening? Was the velarium on fire; had the machinery for lighting up refused to work; and must they remain in this uncomfortable twilight?

Here and there a shout of indignation was heard, or a shrill whistle from the capricious mob. But the mist had already gradually vanished, and those who gazed upward could see that the velarium with the sun and stars had made way for a black surface. No one knew whether this was the real cloudy sky, or whether another, colorless awning closed them in. But suddenly the woven roof parted; invisible hands drew away the two halves. Quick, soft music began as if at a signal from a magician, and at the same time such a flood of light burst down into the theatre that every one covered his eyes with his hand to avoid being blinded. The full glory of sunshine followed on the footsteps of night, like a triumphant chorus on a dismal mourning chant.

The machinists of Alexandria had done wonders. The Romans, who, even at the night performances of the festival of Flora, had never seen the like, hailed the effect with a storm of applause which showed no signs of ceasing, for, when they had sufficiently admired the source of the light which flooded the theatre, reflected from numberless mirrors, and glanced round the auditorium, they began again to applaud with hands and voices. At a given signal thousands of lights appeared round the tiers of seats, and, if the splendor of the entertain-

ment answered at all to that of the Alexandrian spectators, something fine indeed was to be expected.

It was now possible to see the beauty of the women
and the costliness of their attire; not till now had the
precious stones shown their flashing and changeful
radiance. How many gardens and lotus-pools must have
been plundered, how many laurel-groves stripped to
supply the wreaths which graced every head in the upper
rows! And to look round those ranks and note the
handsome raiment in which men and women alike were
arrayed, suggested a belief that all the inhabitants of
Alexandria must be rich. Wherever the eye turned, something beautiful or magnificent was to be seen; and the
numerous delightful pictures which crowded on the sight
were framed with massive garlands of lotos and mallow,
lilies and roses, olive and laurel, tall papyrus and waving
palm, branches of pine and willow—here hanging in thick
festoons, there twining round the columns or wreathing
the pilasters and backs of seats.

Of all the couples in this incomparable amphitheatre
one alone neither saw nor heard all that was going on.
Scarcely had the darkness given way to light, when
Melissa's eyes met those of her lover, and recognition was
immediately followed by a swift inquiry and reply which
filled the unhappy pair with revived hopes. Melissa's eyes
told Diodoros that she loved him and him alone, and she
read in his that he could never give her up. Still, his
also expressed the doubt and anxiety of his tortured soul,
and sent question after question across to Melissa.

And she understood the mute appeal as well as
though looks were words. Without heeding the curious
crowd about her, or considering the danger of such
audacity, she took up her nosegay and waved it toward

him as though to refresh him with its fragrance, and then pressed a hasty kiss on the finest of the half-opened buds. His responsive gesture showed that she had been understood, for her lover's expressive eyes beamed with unqualified love and gratitude. Never, she thought, had he gazed more frequently in her face, and again she bent over the bunch of roses.

But even in the midst of her newly found happiness her cheeks tingled with maidenly modesty at her own boldness. Too happy to regret what she had done, but still anxious lest the friend whose opinion was all in all to her should disapprove, she forgot time and place, and, laying her head on Euryale's shoulder, looked up at her in inquiry with her large eyes as though imploring forgiveness. The matron understood, for she had followed the girl's glance and felt what it was that stirred her heart; and, little thinking of the joy she was giving to a third person, she clasped her closely and kissed her on the temple, regardless of the people about them.

At this Diodoros felt as though he had won the prize in a race; and his friend Timon, whose artistic eye was feasting on the magnificent scene, started at the vehement and ardent pressure which Diodoros bestowed on his hand.

What had come over the poor, suffering youth whom he, Timon, had escorted to the Circus out of sheer compassion? His eyes sparkled, and he held his head as high as ever. What was the meaning of his declaring that everything would go well with him now? But it was in vain that he questioned the youth, for Diodoros could not reveal, even to his best friend, what it was that made him happy. It was enough for him to know that Melissa loved him, and that the woman to whom he looked up with enthusiastic reverence esteemed her as highly as ever. And now, for the first time, he began to feel ashamed of his doubts of Melissa. How could he, who had known her from childhood, have believed of her anything so base and foul? It must be some strong compulsion which bound her to Cæsar, and she could never have looked at him thus unless she had some scheme—in which, perhaps, the lady Euryale meant to abet her—for escaping her imperial suitor before it was too late. Yes, it must be so; and the oftener he gazed at her the more convinced he felt.

Now he rejoiced in the blaze of light about him, for it showed him his beloved. The words which Euryale had whispered in her ear must have been an admonition to prudence, for she only rarely bestowed on him a loving glance, and he acknowledged that the mute but eager exchange of signals would have been fraught with danger for both of them.

The first sudden illumination had revealed too many things to distract the attention of the spectators, including Cæsar's, for their proceedings to be observed. Now curiosity was to some extent satisfied, and even Diodoros felt that reserve was imperative.

Caracalla had not yet shown himself to the people. A golden screen, in which there were holes for him to look through without being seen, hid him from public gaze; still Diodoros could recognize those who were admitted to his presence. First came the givers of the entertainment; then the Parthian envoys, and some delegates from the municipal authorities of the town. Finally, Seleukus presented the wives of the magnates who had shared with him the cost of this display, and among these, all magnificently dressed, the lady Berenike shone supreme by the pride of her demeanor and the startling magnificence of her attire. As her large eyes met those of Cæsar with a flash of defiance, he frowned, and remarked satirically:

"It seems to be the custom here to mourn in much splendor!"

But Berenike promptly replied:

"It has nothing to do with mourning. It is in honor of the sovereign who commanded the presence of the mourner at the Circus."

Diodoros could not see the flame of rage in Cæsar's threatening eye, nor hear his reply to the audacious matron:

"This is a misapprehension of how to do me honor, but an opportunity will occur for teaching the Alexandrians better."

Even across the amphitheatre the youth could see the sudden flush and pallor of the lady's haughty face; and immediately after, Macrinus, the prætorian prefect, approached Caracalla with the master of the games, the superintendent of the school of gladiators.

At the same time Diodoros heard his next neighbor, a member of the city senate, say:

"How quietly it is going off! My proposal that Cæsar should come in to a dim light, so as to keep him and his unpopular favorites out of sight for a while, has worked capitally. Who could the mob whistle at, so long as they could not see one from another? Now they are too much delighted to be uproarious. Cæsar's bride, of all others, has reason to thank me. And she reminds me of the Persian warriors who, before going into battle, bound cats to their bucklers because they knew that the Egyptian foe would not shoot at them so long as the sacred beasts were exposed to being hit by his arrows."

"What do you mean by that?" asked another, and received the brisk reply:

"The lady Euryale is the cat who protects the damsel. Out of respect for her, and for fear of hurting her, too, her companion has hitherto been spared even by those fellows up there."

And he pointed to a party of "Greens" who were laying their heads together in one of the topmost tiers. But his friend replied:

"Something besides that keeps them within bounds. The three beardless fellows just behind them belong to the city watch, who are scattered through the general mass like raisins in dough-cakes."

"That is very judicious," replied the senator. "We might otherwise have had to quit the Circus a great deal quicker than we came in. We shall hardly get home with dry garments as it is. Look how the lights up there are flaring; you can hear the lashing of the storm, and such flashes are not produced by machinery. Zeus is preparing his bolts, and if the storm bursts—"

Here his discourse was interrupted by the sound of trumpets, mingling with the roar of distant thunder following a vivid flash. The procession now began, which was the preliminary to every such performance.

The statues of the gods had, before Cæsar's arrival, been placed on the pedestals erected for them to prevent any risk of a demonstration at the appearance of the deified emperors. The priests now first marched solemnly round these statues, and Timotheus poured a libation on the sand to Serapis, while the priest of Alexandria did the same to the tutelary hero of the town. Then the masters of the games, the gladiators, and beast-fighters came out, who were to make proof of their skill. As the priests approached Cæsar's dais, Caracalla came forward and greeted the spectators, thus showing himself for the first time.

While he was still sitting behind the screen, he had sent for Melissa, who had obeyed the command, under the protection of Euryale, and he had spoken to her graciously. He now took no further notice of her, of her father, or her brother, and by his orders their places had been separated by some little distance from his. By the advice of Timotheus he would not let her be seen at his side till the stars had once more been consulted, and he would then conduct Melissa to the Circus as his wife— the day after to-morrow, perhaps. He thanked the matron for having escorted Melissa, and added, with a braggart air of virtue, that the world should see that he, too, could sacrifice the most ardent wish of his heart to moral propriety.

The elephant torch-bearers had greatly delighted him; and in the expectation of seeing Melissa again, and of a public recognition that he had won the fairest maid there, he had come into the Circus in the best spirits. He still wore his natural expression; yet now and then his brow was knit, for he was haunted by the eyes of Seleukus's wife. The haughty woman—"that bedizened Niobe" he had contemptuously called her in speaking to Macrinus —had appeared to him as an avenging goddess; strangely enough, every time he thought of her, he remembered, too, the consul Vindex and his nephew, whose execution Melissa's intercession had only hastened, and he was vexed now that he had not lent an ear to her entreaties. The fact that the name Vindex signified an avenger disturbed him greatly, and he could no more get it out of his mind than the image of the "Niobe" with her ominous dark eyes.

He would see her no more; and in this he was helped by the gladiators, for they now approached him, and their frantic enthusiasm kept him for some time from all other thoughts. While they flourished their weapons—some the sword and buckler, and others the not less terrible net and harpoon—the time-honored cry rose from their husky throats in eager acclamation: "Hail, Cæsar! those about to die salute thee!" Then, in rows of ten men each, they crossed the arena at a rapid pace.

Between the first and second group one man swaggered past alone, as though he were something apart, and he strutted and rolled as he walked with pompous self-importance. It was his prescriptive right, and in his broad, coarse features, with a snub nose, thick lips, and white, flashing teeth like those of a beast of prey, it was easy to see that the adversary would fare but ill who should try to humble him. And yet he was not tall; but on his deep chest, his enormous square shoulders, and short, bandy legs, the muscles stood out like elastic balls, showing the connoisseur that in strength he was a giant. A loin-cloth was all he wore, for he was proud of the many scars which gleamed red and white on his fair skin. He had pushed back his little bronze helmet, so that the terrible aspect of the left side of his face might not be lost on the populace. While he was engaged in fighting three panthers and a lion, the lion had torn out his eye and with it part of his cheek. His name was Tarautas, and he was known throughout the empire as the most brutal of gladiators, for he had also earned the further privilege of never fighting but for life or death, and never under any circumstances either granting or asking quarter. Where he was engaged corpses strewed the plain.

Cæsar knew that he himself had been nicknamed

Tarautas after this man, and he was not ill pleased; for, above all things, he aimed at being thought strong and terrible, and this the gladiator was, without a peer in his own rank of life. They knew each other: Tarautas had received many a gift from his imperial patron after hard-won victories in which his blood had flowed. And now, as the scarred veteran, who, puffed up with conceit, walked singly and apart in the long train of gladiators, cast a roving and haughty glance on the ranks of spectators, he was filled out of due time with the longing to centre all eyes on himself, the one aim of his so frequently risking his life in these games. His chest swelled, he braced up the tension of his supple sinews, and as he passed the imperial seats he whirled his short sword round his head, describing a circle in the air, with such skill and such persistent rapidity, that it appeared like a disk of flashing steel. At the same time his harsh, powerful voice bellowed out, "Hail, Cæsar!" sounding above the shouts of his comrades like the roar of a lion; and Caracalla, who had not yet vouchsafed a friendly word or pleasant look to any Alexandrian, waved his hand graciously again and again to this audacious monster, whose strength and skill delighted him.

This was the instant for which the "Greens" in the third tier were waiting. No one could prohibit their applauding the man whom Cæsar himself approved, so they forthwith began shouting "Tarautas!" with all their might. They knew that this would suggest the comparison between Cæsar and the sanguinary wretch whose name had been applied to him, and all who were eager to give expression to their vexation or dissatisfaction took the hint and joined in the outcry. Thus in a moment the whole amphitheatre was ringing with the name of "Tarautas!"

At first it rose here and there; but soon, no one knew how, the whole crowd in the upper ranks joined in one huge chorus, giving free vent to their long-suppressed irritation with childish and increasing uproar, shouting the word with steady reiteration and a sort of involuntary rhythm. Before long it sounded as though the multitude must have practiced the mad chant which swelled to a perfect roar.

"Taráu—Taráu—Taráutas!" and, as is always the case when a breach has been made in the dam, one after another joined in, with here the shrill whistle of a reed pipe and there the clatter of a rattle. Mingling with these were the angry outcries of those whom the lictors or guardians of the peace had laid hands on, or their indignant companions; and the thunder outside, rolled a solemn accompaniment to the mutinous tumult within.

Cæsar's scowling brow showed that a storm threatened in that quarter also; and no sooner had he discerned the aim of the crowd than, foaming with rage, he commanded Macrinus to restore order.

Then, above the chaos of voices, trumpet-calls were sounded. The masters of the games perceived that, if only they could succeed in rivetting the attention of the mob by some exciting or interesting scene, that would surely silence the demonstration which was threatening ruin to the whole community; so the order was at once given to begin the performance with the most important and effective scene with which it had been intended that the whole should conclude.

The spectacle was to represent a camp of the Alemanni, surprised and seized by Roman warriors. In this there was a covert compliment to Cæsar, who, after a doubtful victory over that valiant people, had assumed the name of Alemannicus. Part of the gladiators, clothed in skins, represented the barbarians, and wore long flowing wigs of red or yellow hair; others played the part of Roman troops, who were to conquer them. The Alemanni were all condemned criminals, who were allowed no armor, and only blunt swords wherewith to defend themselves. But life and freedom were promised to the women if, after the camp was seized, they wounded themselves with the sharp knives with which each one was provided, at least deeply enough to draw blood. And any who succeeded in feigning death really deceptively were to earn a special reward. Among the Germans there were, too, a few gladiators of exceptional stature, armed with sharp weapons, so as to defer the decision for a while.

In a few minutes, and under the eyes of the spectators, carts, cattle, and horses were placed together in a camp, and surrounded by a wall of tree-trunks, stones, and shields. Meanwhile shouts and whistles were still heard; nay, when Tarautas came out on the arena in the highly decorated armor of a Roman legate, at the head of a troop of heavily armed men, and again greeted the emperor, the commotion began afresh. But Caracalla's patience was exhausted, and the high-priest saw by his pale cheeks and twitching eyelids what was passing in his mind; so, inspired by the fervent hope of averting some incalculable disaster from his fellow-citizens, he took his place in front of the statue of the god, and, lifting up his hands, he began:

"In the name of Serapis, O Macedonians!" His deep, ringing tones sounded above the voices of the insurgents in the upper rows, and there was silence. Not a sound was to be heard but the long-drawn howling of the wind, and now and then the flap of a strip of cloth torn from the velarium by the gale. Mingling with these might be heard the uncanny hooting of owls and daws which the illumination had brought out of their nests in the cornice, and which the storm was now driving in again.

Timotheus, in a clear and audible address, now appealed to his audience to remain quiet, not to disturb the splendid entertainment here set before them, and above all to remember that great Cæsar, the divine ruler of the world, was in their midst, an honor to each and all. As the guest of the most hospitable city on earth, their illustrious sovereign had a right to expect from every Alexandrian the most ardent endeavors to make his stay here delightful. It was his part as high-priest to uplift his warning voice in the name of the greatest of the gods, that the ill-will of a few malcontents might not give rise to an idea in the mind of their beloved guest that the natives of Alexandria were blind to the blessings for which every citizen had to thank his beneficent rule.

A shrill whistle here interrupted his discourse, and a voice shouted: "What blessings? We know of none."

But Timotheus was not to be checked, and went on more vehemently:

"All of you who, by the grace of Cæsar, have been made Roman citizens—"

But again a voice broke in—the speaker was the overseer of the granaries of Seleukus, sitting in the second tier—"And do you suppose we do not know what the honor costs us?"

This query was heartily applauded, and then suddenly, as if by magic, a perfect chorus arose, chanting a distich which one man in the crowd had first given out and then two or three had repeated, to which a fourth had given a sort of tune, till it was shouted by every one present at the very top of his voice, with marked application to him of whom it spoke. From the topmost row of places, on every side of the amphitheatre, rang out the following lines, which but a moment before no one had ever heard:

"Death to the living, to pay for burying those that are dead;
Since, what the taxes have spared, soldiers have ruthlessly seized."

And the words certainly came from the hearts of the people, for they seemed never weary of repeating them; and it was not till a tremendous clap of thunder shook the very walls that several were silent and looked up with increasing alarm. The moment's pause was seized on to begin the fight. Cæsar bit his lip in powerless fury, and his hatred of the towns-people, who had thus so plainly given him to understand their sentiments, was rising from one minute to the next. He felt it a real misfortune that he was unable to punish on the spot the insult thus offered him; swelling with rage, he remembered a speech made by Caligula, and wished the town had but one head, that he might sever it from the body. The blood throbbed so fiercely in his temples, and there was such a singing in his ears, that for some little time he neither saw nor heard what was going on. This terrible agitation might cost him yet some hours of great suffering.

But he need no longer dread them so much; for there sat the living remedy which he believed he had secured by the strongest possible ties.

How fair she was! And, as he looked round once more at Melissa, he observed that her eye was turned on him with evident anxiety. At this a light seemed to dawn in his clouded soul, and he was once more conscious of the love which had blossomed in his heart. But it would never do to make her who had wrought the miracle, so

soon the confidante of his hatred. He had seen her
angry, had seen her weep, and had seen her smile; and
within the next few days, which were to make him a
happy man instead of a tortured victim, he longed only
to see her great eyes sparkle and her lips overflow with
words of love, joy, and gratitude. His score with the
Alexandrians must be settled later, and it was in his
power to make them atone with their blood and bitterly
rue the deeds of this night.

He passed his hand over his furrowed brow, as though
to wake himself from a bad dream; nay, he even found
a smile when next his eyes met hers; and those spectators to whom his aspect seemed more absorbing than the
horrible slaughter in the arena, looked at each other in
amazement, for the indifference or the dissimulation,
whichever it might be, with which Cæsar regarded this
unequalled scene of bloodshed, seemed to them quite
incredible.

Never, since his very first visit to a circus, had Caracalla left unnoticed for so long a time the progress of
such a battle as this. However, nothing very remarkable
had so far occurred, for the actual seizure of the camp
had but just begun with the massacre of the Alemanni
and the suicide of the women.

At this moment the gladiator Tarautas; as nimble as
a cat and as bloodthirsty as a hungry wolf, sprang on to
one of the enemy's piled-up wagons, and a tall swords-
man, with a bear-skin over his shoulder, and long, reddish-
gold hair, flew to meet him.

This was no sham German! Caracalla knew the man.
He had been brought to Rome among the captive chiefs,
and, as he had proved to be a splendid horseman, he had
found employment in Cæsar's stables. His conduct had

always been blameless till, on the day when Caracalla had entered Alexandria, he had, in a drunken fit, killed first the man set over him, a hot-headed Gaul, and then the two lictors who had attempted to apprehend him. He was condemned to death, and had been placed on the German side to fight for his life in the arena.

And how he fought! How he defied the most determined of gladiators, and parried his strokes with his short sword! This was a combat really worth watching; indeed, it so captivated Caracalla that he forgot everything else. The name of the German's antagonist had been applied to him—Cæsar. Just now the many-voiced yell "Tarautas!" had been meant for him; and, accustomed as he was to read an omen in every incident, he said to himself, and called Fate to witness, that the gladiator's doom would foreshadow his own. If Tarautas fell, then Cæsar's days were numbered; if he triumphed, then a long and happy life would be his.

He could leave the decision to Tarautas with perfect confidence; he was the strongest gladiator in the empire, and he was fighting with a sharp sword against the blunt one in his antagonist's hand, who probably had forgotten in the stable how to wield the sword as he had done of yore. But the German was the son of a chief, and had followed arms from his earliest youth. Here it was defence for dear life, however glorious it might be to die under the eyes of the man whom he had learned to honor as the conqueror and tyrant of many nations, among them his own. So the strong and practiced athlete did his best.

He, like his opponent, felt that the eyes of ten thousand were on him, and he also longed to purge himself of the dishonor which, by actual murder, he had brought on himself and on the race of which he was still a son.

Every muscle of his powerful frame gained more rigid tension at the thought, and when he was presently hit by the sword of his hitherto unconquered foe, and felt the warm blood flow over his breast and left arm, he collected all his strength. With the battle-cry of his tribe, he flung his huge body on the gladiator. Heedless of the furious sword-thrust with which Tarautas returned the assault, he threw himself off the top of the packed wagon on to the stones of the camp inclosure, and the combatants rolled, locked together like one man, from the wall into the sand of the arena.

Caracalla started as though he himself had been the injured victim, and watched, but in vain, to see the supple Tarautas, who had escaped such perils before now, free himself from the weight of the German's body.

But the struggle continued to rage round the pair, and neither stirred a finger. At this Cæsar, greatly disturbed, started to his feet, and desired Theocritus to make inquiry as to whether Tarautas were wounded or dead; and while the favorite was gone he could not sit still. Agitated by distressing fears, he rose to speak first to one and then to another of his suite, only to drop on his seat again and glance once more at the butchery below. He was fully persuaded that his own end must be near, if indeed Tarautas were dead. At last he heard Theocritus's voice, and, as he turned to ask him the news, he met a look from the lady Berenike, who had risen to quit the theatre.

He shuddered!—the image of Vindex and his nephew rose once more before his mind's eye; at the same moment, however, Theocritus hailed him with the exclamation:

"That fellow, Tarautas, is not a man at all! I should call him an eel if he were not so broad-shouldered. The rascal is alive, and the physician says that in three weeks he will be ready again to fight four bears or two Alemanni!"

A light as of sudden sunshine broke on Cæsar's face, and he was perfectly cheerful again, though a fearful clap of thunder rattled through the building, and one of those deluges of rain which are known only in the south came pouring down into the open theatre, extinguishing the fires and lights, and tearing the velarium from its fastenings till it hung flapping in the wind and lashing the upper tiers of places, so as to drive the spectators to a hasty retreat.

Men were flying, women screaming and sobbing, and the heralds loudly proclaimed that the performance was suspended, and would be resumed on the next day but one.

CHAPTER VII.

THE amphitheatre was soon emptied, amid the flare of lightning and the crash and roll of thunder. Caracalla, thinking only of the happy omen of Tarautas's wonderful escape, called out to Melissa, with affectionate anxiety, to fly to shelter as quickly as possible; a chariot was in waiting to convey her to the Serapeum. On this she humbly represented that she would rather be permitted to return under her brother's escort to her father's house, and Caracalla cheerfully acceded. He had business on hand this night, which made it seem desirable to him that she should not be too near him. He should expect her brother presently at the Serapeum.

With his own hand he wrapped her in the caracalla and hood which old Adventus was about to put on his master's shoulders, remarking, as he did so, that he had weathered worse storms in the field.

Melissa thanked him with a blush, and, going close up to her, he whispered: "To-morrow, if Fate grants us gracious answers to the questions I shall put to her presently after this storm—to-morrow the horn of happiness will be filled to overflowing for you and me. The thrifty goddess promises to be lavish to me through you."

Slaves were standing round with lighted lanterns; for the torches in the theatre were all extinguished, and the darkened auditorium lay like an extinct crater, in which a crowd of indistinguishable figures were moving to and fro. It reminded him of Hades and a troop of descending spirits; but he would not allow anything but what was pleasant to occupy his mind or eye. By a sudden impulse he took a lantern from one of the attendants, held it up above Melissa's head, and gazed long and earnestly into her brightly illuminated face. Then he dropped his hand with a sigh and said, as though speaking in a dream: "Yes, this is life! Now I begin to live."

He lifted the dripping laurel crown from his head, tossed it into the arena, and added to Melissa:

"Now, get under shelter at once, sweetheart. I have been able to see you this whole evening; even when the lamps were out, for lightning gives light. Thus even the storm has brought me joy. Sleep well. I shall expect you early, as soon as I have bathed."

Melissa wished him sound slumbers, and he replied, lightly:

"If only all life were a dream, and if to-morrow I might but wake up, no longer the son of Severus, but Alexander; and you, not Melissa, but Roxana, whom you so strongly resemble! To be sure I might find myself the gladiator Tarautas. But, then, who would you be? And your stalwart father, who stands there defying the rain, certainly does not look like a vision, and this storm is not favorable to philosophizing."

He kissed his hand to her, had a dry caracalla thrown over his shoulders, ordered Theocritus to take care of Tarautas and carry him a purse of gold—which he handed to the favorite—and then, pulling the hood over his head, led the way, followed by his impatient courtiers; but not till he had answered Heron, who had come forward to ask him what he thought of the mechanical arts of the Alexandrians, desiring him to postpone that matter till the morrow.

The storm had silenced the music. Only a few stanch trumpeters had remained in their places; and when they saw by the lanterns that Cæsar had left the Circus, they sounded a fanfare after him, which followed the ruler of the world with a dull, hoarse echo.

Outside, the streets were still crowded with people pouring out of the amphitheatre. Those of the commoner sort sought shelter under the archways of the building, or else hurried boldly home through the rain. Heron stood waiting at the entrance for his daughter, though the purple-hemmed toga was wet through and through. But she had, in fact, hurried out while he was pushing forward to speak to Cæsar, and in his excitement overlooked everything else. The behavior of his fellow-citizens had annoyed him, and he had an obscure impression that it would be a blunder to claim Cæsar's approval of anything they had done; still, he had not self-control enough to suppress the question which had fluttered on his lips all through the performance. At last, in high dudgeon at the inconsiderateness of young people and at the rebuff he had met with—with the prospect, too, of a cold for his pains—he made his way homeward on foot.

To Caracalla the bad weather was for once really an advantage, for it put a stop to the unpleasant demonstrations which the "Green" party had prepared for him on his way home.

Alexander soon found the closed carruca intended for Melissa, and placed her in it as soon as he had helped Euryale into her harmamaxa. He was astonished to find a man inside it, waiting for his sister. This was Diodoros, who, while Alexander was giving his directions to the charioteer, had, under cover of the darkness, sprung into the vehicle from the opposite side. An exclamation of surprise was followed by explanations and excuses, and the three young people, each with a heart full almost to bursting, drove off toward Heron's house. Their conveyance was already rolling over the pavement, while most of the magnates of the town were still waiting for their slaves to find their chariots or litters.

For the lovers this was a very different scene from the terrible one they had just witnessed in the Circus, for, in spite of the narrow space and total darkness in which they sat, and the rain rattling and splashing on the dripping black leather hood which sheltered them, in their hearts they did not lack for sunshine. Caracalla's saying that the lightning, too, was light, proved true more than once in the course of their drive, for the vivid flashes which still followed in quick succession enabled the re-united lovers to exchange many confidences with their eyes, for which it would have been hard to find words. When both parties to a quarrel are conscious of blame, it is more quickly made up than when one only needs forgiveness; and the pair in the carruca were so fully prepared to think the best of each other that there was no need for Alexander's good offices to make them ready and willing to renew their broken pledges. Besides, each had cause to fear for the other; for Diodoros was afraid that the lady Euryale's power was not far-reaching enough to conceal Melissa from Cæsar's spies, and Melissa trembled at the thought that the physician might too soon betray to Cæsar that she had been betrothed before he had ever seen her, and to whom; for, in that case, Diodoros would be the object of relentless pursuit. So she urged on her lover to embark, if possible, this very night.

Hitherto Alexander had taken no part in the conversation. He could not forget the reception he had met with outside the amphitheatre. Euryale's presence had saved his sister from evil imputations, but had not helped him; and even his gay spirits could make no head against the consciousness of being regarded by his fellow-citizens as a hired traitor. He had withdrawn to one of the back seats to see the performance; for as soon as the theatre was suddenly lighted up, he had become the object of dark looks and threatening gestures. For the first time in his life he had felt compassion for the criminals torn by wild beasts, and for the wounded gladiators, whose companion in misfortune he vaguely felt himself to be. But, what was worst of all, he could not regard himself as altogether free from the reproach of having accepted a reward for the service he had so thoughtlessly rendered.

Nor did he see the remotest possibility of ever making those whose opinion he cared for, understand how it had come to pass that he should have acceded to the desire of the villain in the purple, now that his father, by showing himself to the people in the *toga pretexta*, had set the seal to their basest suspicions. The thought that henceforth he could never hope to feel the grasp of an honest man's hand, gnawed at his heart.

The esteem of Diodoros was dear to him, and, when his young comrade spoke to him, he felt at first as though he were doing him an unexpected honor; but then he fell back into the suspicion that this was only for his sister's sake.

The deep sigh that broke from him induced Melissa to speak a few words of comfort, and now the unhappy man's bursting heart overflowed. In eloquent words he described to Diodoros and Melissa all he had felt, and the terrible consequences of his heedless folly, and as he spoke acute regret filled his eyes with tears.

He had pronounced judgment on himself, and expected nothing of his friend but a little pity. But in the darkness Diodoros sought and found his hand, and grasped it fervently; and if Alexander could but have seen his old playfellow's face, he would have perceived that his eyes glistened as he said what he could to encourage him to hope for better days.

Diodoros knew his friend well. He was incapable of falsehood; and his deed, which under a false light so easily assumed an aspect of villainy, had, in fact, been no more than an act of thoughtlessness such as he had himself often lent a hand in. Alexander, however, seemed determined not to hear the comfort offered him by his sister and his friend. A flash of lightning revealed him to them, sitting with a bent head and his hands over his brow; and this gloomy vision of one who so lately had been the gayest of the gay troubled their revived happiness even more than the thought of the danger which, as each knew, threatened the others.

As they passed the Temple of Artemis, which was brightly illuminated, reminding them that they were reaching their destination, Alexander at last looked up and begged the lovers to consider their immediate affairs. His mind had remained clear, and what he said showed that he had not lost sight of his sister's future.

As soon as Melissa should have effected her escape, Cæsar would undoubtedly seize, not only her lover, but his father as well. Diodoros must forthwith cross the lake and rouse Polybius and Praxilla, to warn them of the imminent danger, while Alexander undertook to hire a ship for the party. Argutis would await the fugitives in a tavern by the harbor, and conduct them on board the vessel which would be in readiness. Diodoros, who was not yet able to walk far, promised to avail himself of one of the litters waiting outside the Temple of Artemis.

Just before the vehicle stopped, the lovers took leave. They arranged where and how they might have news of each other, and all they said, in brief words and a fervent parting kiss, in this moment, when death or imprisonment might await them, had the solemn purport of a vow.

The swift horses stopped. Alexander hastily leaned over to his friend, kissed him on both cheeks, and whispered:

"Take good care of her; think of me kindly if we should never meet again, and tell the others that wild Alexander has played another fool's trick, but at any rate not a wicked one, however badly it may turn out for him."

For the sake of the charioteer, who, after Melissa's flight, would be certainly cross-examined, Diodoros could make no reply. The carruca rattled off by the way by which it had come; Diodoros vanished in the darkness, and Melissa clasped her hands over her face. She felt as though this were her last parting from her lover, and the sun would never shine on earth again.

It was now near midnight. The slaves had heard the

approach of the chariot, and received them as heartily as
ever, but in obedience to Heron's orders they added the
most respectful bows to their usual well-meant welcome.
Since their master had shown himself to Dido, in the
afternoon, with braggart dignity, as a Roman magnate, she
had felt as though the age of miracles had come, and
nothing was impossible. Splendid visions of future grandeur
awaiting the whole family, including herself and Argutis,
had not ceased to haunt her; but as to the empress, something seemed to have gone wrong, for why had the girl
wet eyes and so sad a face? What was all this long
whispering with Argutis? But it was no concern of hers,
after all, and she would know all in good time, no doubt.
"What the masters plot to-day the slaves hear next week,"
was a favourite saying of the Gaul's, and she had often
proved its truth.

The cool way in which Melissa received the felicita-
tions which the old woman poured out in honor of the
future empress, and her tear-reddened eyes, seemed at
any rate quite comprehensible. The child was thinking,
no doubt, of her handsome Diodoros. Among the splendors
of the palace she would soon forget. And how truly
magnificent were the dress and jewels in which the damsel
had appeared in the amphitheatre!

"How they must have hailed her!" thought the old
woman when she had helped Melissa to exchange her
dress for a simpler robe, and the girl sat down to write.
"If only the mistress had lived to see this day! And all
the other women must have been bursting with envy.
Eternal gods! But, after all, who knows whether the good
luck we envy others is great or small? Why, even in this
house, which the gods have filled to the roof with gifts
and favors, misfortune has crept in through the key-hole.

Poor Philip! Still, if all goes well with the girl— Things have befallen her such as rarely come to any one, and yet no more than her due. The fairest and best will be the greatest and wealthiest in the empire."

And she clutched the amulets and the cross which hung round her arm and throat, and muttered a hasty prayer for her darling.

Argutis, for his part, did not know what to think of it all. He, if any one, rejoiced in the good fortune of his master and Melissa; but Heron's promotion to the rank of prætor had been too sudden, and Heron demeaned himself too strangely in his purple-bordered toga. It was to be hoped that this new and unexpected honor had not turned his brain! And the state in which his master's eldest son remained caused him the greatest anxiety. Instead of rejoicing in the honors of his family, he had at his first interview with his father flown into a violent rage; and though he, Argutis, had not understood what they were saying, he perceived that they were in vehement altercation, and that Heron had turned away in great wrath. And then—he remembered it with horror, and could hardly tell what he had seen to Alexander and Melissa in a reasonable and respectful manner—Philip had sprung out of bed, had dressed himself without help, even to his shoes, and scarcely had his father set out in his litter before Philip had come into the kitchen. He looked like one risen from the grave, and his voice was hollow as he told the slaves that he meant to go to the Circus to see for himself that justice was done. But Argutis felt his heart sink within him when the philosopher desired him to fetch the pipe his father used to teach the birds to whistle, and at the same time took up the sharp kitchen knife with which Argutis slaughtered the sheep.

The young man then turned to go, but even on the threshold he had stumbled over the straps of his sandals which dragged unfastened, and Argutis had had to lead him, almost to carry him in from the garden, for a violent fit of coughing had left him quite exhausted. The effort of pulling at the heavy oars on board the galley had been too much for his weak chest. Argutis and Dido had carried him to bed, and he had soon fallen into a deep sleep, from which he had not waked since.

And now what were these two plotting? They were writing; and not on wax tablets, but with reed pens on papyrus, as though it were a matter of importance.

All this gave the slave much to think about, and the faithful soul did not know whether to weep for joy or grief when Alexander told him, with a gravity which frightened him in this light-hearted youth, that, partly as the reward of his faithful service and partly to put him in a position to aid them all in a crisis of peculiar difficulty, he gave him his freedom. His father had long since intended to do this, and the deed was already drawn out. Here was the document; and he knew that, even as a freedman, Argutis would continue to serve them as faithfully as ever. With this he gave the slave his manumission, which he was in any case to have received within a month, at the end of thirty years' service, and Argutis took it with tears of joy, not unmixed with grief and anxiety, while only a few hours since it would have been enough to make him the happiest of mortals.

While he kissed their hands and stammered out words of gratitude, his uncultured but upright spirit told him that he had been blind ever to have rejoiced for a moment at the news that Melissa had been chosen to be empress. All that he had seen during the last half-hour had convinced him, as surely as if he had been told it in words, that his beloved young mistress scorned her imperial suitor, and firmly intended to evade him—how, Argutis could not guess. And, recognizing this, a spirit of adventure and daring stirred him also. This was a struggle of the weak against the strong; and to him, who had spent his life as one of the oppressed, nothing could be more tempting than to help on the side of the weak.

Argutis now undertook with ardent zeal to get Diodoros and his parents safely on board the ship he was to engage, and to explain to Heron, as soon as he should have read the letter which Alexander was now writing, that, unless he could escape at once with Philip, he was lost. Finally, he promised that the epistle to Cæsar, which Melissa was composing, should reach his hands on the morrow.

He could now receive his letter of freedom with gladness, and consented to dress up in Heron's garments; for, as a slave, he would have been forbidden to conclude a bargain with a ship's captain or any one else.

All this was done in hot haste, for Cæsar was awaiting Alexander, and Euryale expected Melissa. The ready zeal of the old man, free for the first time to act on his own responsibility in matters which would have been too much for many a free-born man, but to which he felt quite equal, had an encouraging effect even on the oppressed hearts of the other two. They knew now that, even if death should be their lot, Argutis would be faithful to their father and sick brother, and the slave at once showed his ingenuity and shrewdness; for, while the young people were vainly trying to think of a hiding-place for Heron and Philip, he suggested a spot which would hardly be discovered even by the sharpest spies.

Glaukias, the sculptor, who had already fled, was

Heron's tenant. His work-room, a barn-like structure, stood in the little vegetable-garden which the gem-cutter had inherited from his father-in-law, and none but Heron and the slave knew that, under the flooring, instead of a cellar, there was a vast reservoir connected with the ancient aqueducts constructed by Vespasian. Many years since Argutis had helped his master to construct a trap-door to the entrance to these underground passages, of which the existence had remained unknown even to Glaukias during all the years he had inhabited the place. It was here that Heron kept his gold, not taking his children even into his confidence; and only a few months ago Argutis had been down with him and had found the old reservoir dry, airy, and quite habitable. The gem-cutter would be quite content to conceal himself where his treasure was, and the garden and work-room were only distant a few hundred paces from his own home. To get Philip there without being seen was to Argutis a mere trifle. Alexander, too, old Dido, and, if needful, Diodoros, could all be concealed there. But for Melissa, neither he nor Alexander thought it sufficiently secure.

As she took leave of him the young girl once more charged the newly freed man to greet her father from her a thousand times, to beseech his forgiveness of her for the bitter grief she must cause him, and to assure him of her affection.

"Tell him," she added, as the tears streamed down her cheeks, "that I feel as if I were going to my death. But, come what may, I am always his dutiful child, always ready to sacrifice anything—excepting only the man to whom, with my father's consent, I pledged my heart. Tell him that for love of him I might have been ready even to give my hand to the blood-stained Cæsar, but that Fate—and perhaps the Manes of her we loved, and who is dead—have ordered it otherwise."

She then went into the room where her mother had closed her eyes. After a short prayer by that bed, which still stood there, she hastened to Philip's room. He lay sleeping heavily; she bent over him and kissed the too high brow, which looked as though even in sleep the brain within were still busy over some difficult and painful question.

Her way led her once more through her father's work-room, and she had already crossed it when she hastily turned back to look once more—for the last time—at the little table where she had sat for so many years, busy with her needle, in modest contentment by the artist's side, dreaming with waking eyes, and considering what she, with her small resources and great love, could do that would be of use to those she loved, or relieve them if they were in trouble. Then, as though she knew that she was bidding a last farewell to all the pleasant companionship of her youth, she looked at the birds, long since gone to roost in their cages. In spite of his recent curule honors Heron had not forgotten them, and, before quitting the house to display himself to the populace in the *toga pretexta,* he had as usual carefully covered them up. And now, as Melissa lifted the cloth from the starling's cage, and the bird muttered more gently than usual, and perhaps in its sleep, the cry, "Olympias!" a shudder ran through her; and, as she stepped out into the road by Alexander's side, she said, dejectedly:

"Everything is coming to an end! Well, and so it may; for what has come over us all in these few days? Before Cæsar came, what were you—what was Philip? In my own heart what peace reigned! And my father?

There is one comfort, at any rate; even as prætor he has not forgotten his birds, and he will find feathered friends go where he may. But I— And it is for my sake that he must hide like a criminal!"

But here Alexander vehemently broke in: "It was not you, it was I who brought all this misery on us!" And he went on to accuse himself so bitterly that Melissa regretted having alluded to the misfortunes of their family, and did her best to inspire him with courage.

As soon as Cæsar should have left the city and she had evaded his pursuit, the citizens would be easily persuaded of his innocence. They would see then how little she had cared for the splendor and wealth of empire; why, he himself knew how quickly everything was forgotten in Alexandria. His art, too, would be a comfort to him, and if he only had the chance of making his way in his career he would have no difficulty in winning Agatha. He would have her on his side, and Diodoros, and the lady Euryale.

But to all these kind speeches the young man only sadly shook his head. How could he, despised and contemned, dare to aspire to the daughter of such a man as Zeno? He ended with a deep sigh; and Melissa, whose heart grew heavier as they approached the Serapeum through the side streets, still forced herself to express her confidence as though the lady Euryale's protection had relieved her of every anxiety. It was so difficult to appear calm and cheerful that more than once she had to wipe her eyes; still, their eager talk shortened the way, and she stood still, surprised to find herself so near her destination, when Alexander showed her the chain which was stretched across the end of the street of Hermes to close in the great square in front of the Serapeum.

The storm had passed away and the rain had ceased; the sky was clear and cloudless, and the moon poured its silvery light in lavish splendor, as though revived, on the temple and on the statues round the square. Here they must part, for they saw that it was impossible that they should cross the open space together.

It was almost deserted, for the populace were not allowed to go there. Of the hundreds of tents which till lately had covered it, only those of the seventh cohort of the prætorian guard remained; for these, having to protect the person of the emperor, had not been quartered in the town. If Alexander and Melissa had crossed this vast square, where it was now as light as day, they would certainly have been seen, and Melissa would have brought not herself only but her protectress also into the greatest danger.

She still had so much on her mind that she wanted to say to her brother, especially with regard to her father's welfare; and then—what a leave-taking was this when, as her gloomy forebodings told her, they were parting never to meet again! But Euryale must have been long and anxiously waiting for her, and Alexander, too, was very late for his appointment.

It was impossible to let the girl cross the square alone, for it was guarded by soldiers. If she could but reach the side of the sanctuary where she was expected, and where the road was in the shadow of the riding-school opposite, all would be well, and it seemed as though there was no alternative but for Alexander to lead his sister through by-ways to her destination. They had just made up their minds to this inevitable waste of time, when a young woman was seen coming toward them from one of the tents with a swift, light step, winged with gladness. Alexander suddenly released his sister's hand, and saying—

"She will escort you," he advanced to meet her.

This was the wife of Martialis, who had charge of the villa at Kanopus, and whose acquaintance the artist had made when he was studying the Galatea in the merchant's country-house for the portrait of Korinna. Alexander had made friends with the soldier's wife in his winning, lively way, and she was delighted to meet him again, and quite willing to escort his sister across the square, and hold her tongue about it. So, after a short grasp of the hand, and a fervent last appeal to her brother, "Never for a moment let us forget one another, and always remember our mother!" Melissa followed her companion.

This evening the woman had sought her husband to tell him that she and her mother had got safely out of the Circus, and to thank him for the entertainment, of which the splendor, in spite of the various disturbances and interruption, had filled their hearts and minds.

The first words she spoke to the girl led to the question as to whether she, too, had been at the Circus; and when Melissa said yes, but that she had been too frightened and horrified to see much, the chattering little woman began to describe it all. Quite the best view, she declared, had been obtained from the third tier of places. Cæsar's bride, too, had been pointed out to her. Poor thing! She would pay dearly for the splendor of the purple. No one could dispute Caracalla's taste, however, for the girl was lovely beyond description; and as she spoke she paused to look at Melissa, for she fancied she resembled Cæsar's sweetheart. But she went on again quicker than before, remarking that Melissa was not so tall, and that the other was more brilliant looking, as beseemed an emperor's bride.

At this Melissa drew her kerchief more closely over her face; but it was a comfort to her when the soldier's wife, after describing to her what she herself had worn, added that Caracalla's choice had fallen on a modest and well-conducted maiden, for, if she had not been, the high-priest's wife would never have been so kind to her. And the lady Euryale was sister-in-law to the master she herself served, and she had known her all her life.

Then, when Melissa, to change the subject, asked why the public were forbidden to approach the Serapeum, her companion told her that since his return from the Circus Cæsar had been devoting himself to astrology, soothsaying, and other abstruse matters, and that the noise of the city disturbed him. He was very learned in such things, and if she only had time she could have told Melissa wonderful things. Thus conversing, they crossed the square, and when it lay behind them and they were under the shadow of the stadium, Melissa thanked her lively companion for her escort, while she, on her part, declared that it had been a pleasure to do the friendly painter a service.

The western side of the immense temple stood quite detached from the town. There were on that side but few bronze doors, and these, which were opened only to the inhabitants of the building, had long since been locked for the night and needed no guard. As the inhabitants were forbidden to cross the space dividing the stadium from the Serapeum, all was perfectly still. Dark shadows lay on the road, and the high structures which shut it in like cliffs seemed to tower to the sky. The lonely girl's heart beat fast with fears as she stole along, close under the wall, from which a warm vapor breathed on her after the recent rain. The black circles which seemed to stare at her like dark, hollow eye-sockets from the wall of the stadium, were the windows of the stables.

If a runaway slave, an escaped wild beast, or a robber were to rush out upon her! The owls swept across over her head on silent wings, and bats flitted to and fro from one building to the other, almost touching the frightened girl. Her terrors increased at every step, and the wall which she must follow to the end was so long—so endlessly long!

Supposing, too, that the lady Euryale had been tired of waiting and had given her up! There would then be nothing for it but to make her way back to the town past the guards, or to enter the temple through the great gates—where that dreadful man was—and where she would at once be recognized! Then there could be no escape, none—and she must, yes, she must evade her dreadful suitor. Every thought of Diodoros cried, "You must!"—even at the cost of her young life, of which, indeed, she saw the imminent end nearer and nearer with every step. She knew not whither her flight might take her, but a voice within declared that it would be to an early grave.

Only a narrow strip of sky was visible between the tall buildings, but, as she looked up to the heavens, she perceived that it was two hours past midnight. She hurried on, but presently checked her pace again. From the square, three trumpet-calls, one after another, rang through the silence of the night. What could these signals mean at so unwonted an hour?

There could be but one explanation—Cæsar had again condemned some hapless wretch to death, and he was being led to execution. When Vindex and his nephew were beheaded, three trumpet-calls had sounded; her brother had told her so.

And now, before her inward eye, rose the crowd of victims to Caracalla's thirst for blood. She fancied that Plautilla, whom her imperial consort had murdered, was beckoning her to follow her to an early grave. The terrors of the night were too much for her; and, as when a child, at play with her brothers, she flew on as fast as her feet would carry her. She fled as though she were pursued, her long dress hampering her steps, along by the temple wall, till her gaze, fixed on her left, fell on the spot which had been designated to her.

Here she stopped, out of breath; and, while she was identifying the landmarks which she had impressed on her memory to guide her to the right doorway, the temple wall seemed to open before her as if by a charm, and a kind voice called her name, and then exclaimed, "At last!" and in a moment she grasped Euryale's hand and was drawn into the building.

Here, as if at the touch of a magician's wand, all fear and horror vanished; and, although she still panted for breath, she would at once have explained to her beloved protectress what it was that had prompted her to run so fast, but that Euryale interrupted her, exclaiming: "Only make haste! No one must see that block of porphyry turn on its pin. It is invisible from the outside, and closes the passage by which the mystics and adepts find their way to the mysteries after dedication. All who know of it are sworn to secrecy."

With this she led the way into a dark vestibule adjoining the temple, and in a few moments the great block of stone which had admitted them had turned into its

place again. Those who passed by, even in broad sunshine, could not distinguish it from all the other blocks
of which the ground-floor of the edifice was built.

CHAPTER VIII.

While the lady Euryale preceded her young charge
with a lamp up a narrow, dark staircase, Alexander
waited in one of the audience-rooms till the emperor
should call him. The high-priest of Serapis, several soothsayers of the temple, Aristides, the new head of the night-
watch, and other "friends" of the monarch had accompanied him thus far. But admittance to the innermost
apartments had not been permitted, for Caracalla had
ordered the magician Serapion to call up spirits before
him, and was having the future declared to him in the
presence of the prefect of the prætorians and a few other
trusty followers.

The deputation of citizens, who had come to apologize
to Cæsar for the annoying occurrences in the Circus, had
been told to wait till the exorcisms were over. Alexander
would have preferred to hold aloof from the others, but
no one here seemed to think ill of him for his thought-
less behavior. On the contrary, the courtiers pressed
round him—the brother of the future empress—with the
greatest assiduity: the high-priest inquired after his brother
Philip; and Seleukus, the merchant, who had come with
the deputation, addressed many flattering remarks to him
on his sister's beauty. Some of the Roman senators
whose advances he had received coldly enough at first,
now took up his whole attention, and described to him
the works of art and the paintings in the new baths of
Caracalla; they advised him to offer himself as a candidate

for the ornamentation of some of the unfinished rooms with frescoes, and led him to expect their support. In short, they behaved toward the young man, as if he might command their services in spite of their gray hairs. But Alexander saw through their purpose.

Their discourse ceased suddenly, for voices were audible in the emperor's apartments, and they all listened with outstretched necks and bated breath if they might catch a word or two.

Alexander only regretted not having either charcoal or tablets at hand, that he might fix their intent faces on the wood; but at last he stood up, for the door was opened and the emperor entered from the tablinum, accompanied by the magician who had shown Cæsar several spirits of the departed. In the middle of the demonstration, at Caracalla's desire, the beheaded Papinian had appeared in answer to Serapion's call. Invisible hands replaced his severed head upon his shoulders, and, having greeted his sovereign, he promised him good fortune. Last of all great Alexander had appeared, and assured the emperor in verse, and with many a flowery phrase, that the soul of Roxana had chosen the form of Melissa to dwell in. Caracalla would enjoy the greatest happiness through her, as long as she was not alienated from him by love for another man. Should this happen, Roxana would be destroyed and her whole race with her, but Cæsar's glory and greatness would reach its highest point. The monarch need have no misgivings in continuing to live out his, Alexander's, life. The spirit of his god-like father Severus watched over him, and had given him a counsellor in the person of Macrinus, in whose mortal body the soul of Scipio Africanus had awakened to a new life.

With this, the apparition, which, like the others, had

shown itself as a colored picture moving to and fro upon the darkened wall of the tablinum, vanished. The voice of the great Macedonian sounded hollow and unearthly, but what he said had interested the emperor deeply and raised his spirits.

However, his wish to see more spirits had remained unsatisfied. The magician, who remained upon his knees with uplifted hands while the apparitions were visible, declared that the forces he was obliged to employ in exercising his magic power over the spirits had exhausted him. His fine, bearded face was deathly pale, and his tall form trembled and shook. His assistants had silently disappeared. They had kept themselves and their great scrolls concealed behind a curtain. Serapion explained that they were his pupils, whose office it was to support his incantations by efficient formulas.

Caracalla dismissed him graciously, then turning to the assembled company, he gave with much affability a detailed account of the wonders he had seen and heard.

"A marvellous man, this Serapion," he exclaimed to the high-priest Timotheus—"a master in his art. What he said before proceeding to the incantations is convincing, and explains much to me. According to him, magic holds the same relation to religion as power to love, as the command to the request. Power! What magic effect it has in real life? We have seen its influence upon the spirits, and who among the children of men can resist it? To it I owe my greatest results, and hope to be still further indebted. Even reluctant love must bow to it."

He gave a self-satisfied laugh, and continued: "As the pious worshipper of the gods can move the heavenly ones by prayer and sacrifice, so—the wondrous man de-clared—the magician can force them by means of his secret lore to do his will.   Therefore, he who knows and can call the gods and spirits by the right name, him they must obey, as the slave his master.   The sages who served the Pharaohs in the gray dawn of time succeeded in fathoming the mystery of these names given to the ever-lasting ones at their birth, and their wisdom has come down to him through the generations as a priceless secret. But it is not sufficient to murmur the name to one's self, or be able to write it down.   Every syllable has its special meaning like every member of the human frame. It depends, too, on how it is pronounced and where the emphasis lies; and this true name, containing in itself the spiritual essence of the immortals, and the outward sign of their presence, is different again from the names by which they are known among men.

"Could I have any conception—and here Serapion addressed himself to me—which god he forced to obey him when he uttered the words, '*Abar Barbarie Eloce Sabaoth Pachnuphis,*' and more like it!   I have only re-membered the first few words.   But, he continued, it was not enough to be able to pronounce these words.   The heavenly spirits would submit only to those mortals who shared in some of their highest characteristics.   Before the Magian dared to call them, he must purify his soul from all sensual taint, and sanctify his body by long and severe fasting.   When the Magian succeeded, as he had done in these days, in rendering himself impervious to the allurements of the senses, and in making his soul, as far as was humanly possible, independent of the body, only then had he attained to that degree of godliness which entitled him to have intercourse with the heavenly ones and the entire spirit-world as with his equals, and to subdue them to his will.

"He exerted his power, and we saw with our bodily eyes that the spirits came to his call. But we discovered that it was not done by words alone. What a noble-looking man he is! And the mortifications that he practices—these, too, are heroic deeds! The cavillers in the Museum might take example by him. Serapion performed an action and a difficult one. *They* waste their time over words, miserable words! They will prove to you by convincing argument that yonder lion is a rabbit. The Magian waved his hands and the king of beasts cringed before him. Like the worthies of the Museum, every one in this city is merely a mouth on two legs. Where but here would the Christians—I know their doctrines—have invented that term for their sublime teacher, The Word become flesh?—I have heard nothing here," he turned to the deputation, "but words and again words—from you, who humbly assure me of your love and reverence; from those who think that their insignificant persons may slip through my fingers and escape me, paltry, would-be witty words, dipped in poison and gall. In the Circus, even, they aimed words at me. The Magian alone dared to offer me deeds, and he succeeded wonderfully; he is a marvellous man!"

"What he showed you," said the high-priest, "was no more than what the sorcerers achieved, as the old writings tell us, under the builders of the Pyramids. Our astrologers, who traced out for you the path of the stars—"

"They, too," interrupted Cæsar, bowing slightly to the astrologers, "have something better to show than words. As I owe to the Magian an agreeable hour, so I thank you, my friends, for a happy one."

This remark had reference to the information which had been brought to Cæsar, during a pause in the incantations, that the stars predicted great happiness for him in his union with Melissa, and that this prediction was well founded, was proved by the constellations which the chief astrologer showed and explained to him.

While Caracalla was receiving the thanks of the astrologers, he caught sight of Alexander, and at once graciously inquired how Melissa had got back to her father's house. He then asked, laughingly, if the wits of Alexandria were going to treat him to another offering like the one on his arrival. The youth, who had determined in the Circus to risk his life, if need be, in order to clear himself of the taint of suspicion, judged that the moment had come to make good the mistake which had robbed him of his fellow-citizens' esteem.

The presence of so many witnesses strengthened his courage; and fully expecting that, like the consul Vindex, his speech would cost him his head, he drew himself up and answered gravely, "It is true, great Cæsar, that in a weak moment and without considering the results, I repeated some of those witticisms to you—"

"I commanded, and you had to obey," retorted Cæsar, and added, coldly, "But what does this mean?"

"It means," began Alexander—who already saw the sword of execution leap from its scabbard—with pathetic dignity, which astonished the emperor as coming from him, "it means that I herewith declare before you, and my Alexandrian fellow-citizens here present, that I bitterly repent my indiscretion; nay, I curse it, since I heard from your own lips how their ready wit has set you against the sons of my beloved native city."

"Ah, indeed! Hence these tears?" interposed Cæsar, adopting a well-known Latin phrase. He nodded to the painter, and continued, in a tone of amused superiority

"Go on performing as an orator, if you like; only moderate the tragic tone, which does not become you, and make it short, for before the sun rises we all—these worthy citizens and myself—desire to be in bed."

Blushes and pallor alternated on the young man's face. Sentence of death would have been more welcome to him than this supercilious check to a hazardous attempt, which he had looked upon as daring and heroic. Among the Romans he caught sight of some laughing faces, and hurt, humiliated, confused, scarcely capable of speaking a word, and yet moved by the desire to justify himself, he stammered out: "I have— I meant to assure— No, I am no spy! May my tongue wither before I— You can of course— It is in your power to take my life!"

"Most certainly it is," interposed Caracalla, and his tone was more contemptuous than angry. He could see how deeply excited the artist was, and to save him—Melissa's brother—from committing a folly which he would be obliged to punish, he went on with gracious consideration: "But I much prefer to see you live and wield the brush for a long time to come. You are dismissed."

The young man bent his head, and then turned his back upon the emperor, for he felt that he was threatened now with what, to an Alexandrian, was the most unbearable fate—to appear ridiculous before so many.

Caracalla allowed him to go, but, as he stepped across the threshold, he called after him: "To-morrow, then, with your sister, after the bath! Tell her the stars and the spirits are propitious to our union."

Cæsar then beckoned to the chief of the night-watch, and, having laid the blame of the unpleasant occurrences in the Circus on his carelessness, cut the frightened officer short when he proposed to take every one prisoner whom the lictors had marked among the noisy.

"Not yet! On no account to-morrow," Caracalla ordered. "Mark each one carefully. Keep your eyes open at the next performance. Put down the names of the disaffected. Take care that the rope hangs about the neck of the guilty. The time to draw it tight will come presently. When they think themselves safe, the cowardly show their true faces. Wait till I give the signal—certainly not in the next few days; then seize upon them, and let none escape!"

Cæsar had given these orders with smiling lips. He wanted first to make Melissa his, and, like a shepherd, to revel with her in the sweetness of their love. No moment of this time should be darkened for him by the tears and prayers of his bride. When she should hear, later on, of her husband's bloody vengeance upon his enemies, she would have to accept it as an accomplished fact; and means, no doubt, would be found to soothe her indignation.

Those who after the insulting occurrences in the Circus had expected to see Cæsar raging and storming, were hurried from one surprise to another; for even after his conversation with the night-watch he looked cheerful and contented, and exclaimed: "It is long since you have seen me thus! My own mirror will ask itself if it has not changed owners. It is to be hoped it may have cause to accustom itself to reflect me as a happy man as often as I look in it. The two highest joys of life are before me, and I know not what would be left for me to desire if only Philostratus were here to share the coming days with me."

The grave senator Cassius Dio here stepped forward and observed that there were advantages in their amiable friend's withdrawal from the turmoil of court life. His Life of Apollonius, to which all the world was looking forward, would come all the sooner to a close.

"If only that I might talk to him of the man of Tyana," cried the emperor, "I wish his biographer were here to-day. To possess little and require nothing is the wish of the sage; and I can well imagine circumstances in which one who has enjoyed power and riches to satiety should consider himself blessed as a simple countryman following out the precept of Horace, *'procul negotiis,'* plowing his fields and gathering the fruit of his own trees. According to Apollonius, the wise man must also be poor, and, though the citizens of his state are permitted to acquire treasures, the wealthy are looked upon as dishonorable. There is some sense in this paradox, for the possessions that are to be obtained with money are but vulgar joys. I know by experience what it is that purifies the soul, that lifts it up and makes it truly blessed. It does not come of power or riches. Whoso has known it, he to whom it has been revealed—"

He stopped short, surprised at himself, then laughed as he shook his head and exclaimed, "Behold, the tragedy hero in the purple with one foot in an idyl!" and wished the assembled company pleasant slumbers for the short remains of the night.

He gave his hand to a few favored ones; but, as he clasped that of the proconsul Julius Paulinus, who, with unheard-of audacity, had put on mourning garments for his brother-in-law Vindex, beheaded that day, Cæsar's countenance grew dark, and, turning his back upon them all, he walked rapidly away. Scarcely had he disappeared when the mourning proconsul exclaimed in his dry manner, as if speaking to himself:

"The idyl is to begin. Would it might be the satyr-play that closes the bloodiest of tragedies!"

"Cæsar has not been himself to-day," said the favorite Theocritus; and the senator Cassius Dio whispered to Paulinus, "And therefore he was more bearable to look at."

Old Adventus gazed in astonishment as Arjuna, the emperor's Indian body-slave, disrobed him; for, though Caracalla had entered the apartment with a dark and threatening brow, while his sandals were being unfastened, he laughed to himself, and cried to his old servant with beaming eyes, "To-morrow!" and the chamberlain called down a blessing on the morrow, and on her who was destined to fill the coming years with sunshine for mighty Cæsar.

Caracalla, generally an early riser, slept this time longer than on other days. He had retired very late to rest, and the chamberlain therefore put off waking him, especially as he had been troubled by evil dreams, in spite of his happy frame of mind when he sought his couch. When at last he rose he first inquired about the weather, and expressed his satisfaction when he heard that the sun had risen with burning rays, but was now veiled in threatening clouds.

His first visit led him to the court of sacrifice. The offerings had fallen out most favorably, and he rejoiced at the fresh and healthy appearance of the bullocks' hearts and livers which the augurs showed him. In the stomach of one of the oxen they had found a flint arrow-head, and, on showing it to Caracalla, he laughed, and observed to the high-priest Timotheus: "A shaft from Eros's quiver! A hint from the god to offer him a sacrifice on this happy day."

After his bath he caused himself to be arrayed with peculiar care, and then gave orders for the admittance, first, of the prefect of the prætorians, and then of Melissa, for whom a mass of gorgeous flowers stood ready.

But Macrinus was not to be found, although Cæsar had commanded him yesterday to give in his report before doing anything else. He had twice come to the ante-chamber, but had gone away again shortly before, and had not yet returned.

Determined to let nothing damp his spirits, Cæsar merely shrugged his shoulders, and gave orders to admit the maiden, and—should they have accompanied her— her father and brother. But neither Melissa nor the men had appeared as yet, though Caracalla distinctly remembered having commanded all three to visit him after the bath, which he had taken several hours later than usual.

Vexed, and yet endeavoring to keep his temper, he went to the window. The sky was overcast, and a sharp wind from the sea drove the first rain-drops in his face.

In the wide square at his feet a spectacle presented itself which would have delighted him at another time, when in better spirits.

The younger men of the city—as many as were of Greek extraction—were trooping in. They were divided into companies, according to the wrestling-schools or the Circus and other societies to which they belonged. The youths marched apart from the married men, and one could see that they came gladly, and hoped for much enjoyment from the events of the day. Some of the others looked less delighted. They were unaccustomed to obey the orders of a despot, and many were ill-pleased to lose a whole day from their work or business. But no one was permitted to absent himself; for, when the chief citizens had invited the emperor to visit their wrestling-schools, he replied that he preferred to inspect the entire male youths of Alexandria on the stadium. This was situated close by his residence in the Serapeum, and in this great space a spectacle would be afforded to him at one glance, which he could otherwise only enjoy by journeying laboriously from one gymnasium to another. He loved the strong effects produced by great masses; and being on the race-course, the wrestlers and boxers, the runners and discus-throwers, could give proof of their strength, dexterity, and endurance.

It occurred to him at the moment that among these youths and men there might be some of the descendants of the warriors who, under the command of the great Alexander, had conquered the world. Here, then, was an opportunity of gathering round him—rejuvenated and, so to speak, born anew—those troops who, under the guidance of the man whose mission on earth he was destined to accomplish, had won such deathless victories. That was a pleasure he had every right to permit himself, and he wished to show to Melissa the re-created military forces of him to whom, in a former existence, as Roxana, she had been so dear.

Quick as ever to suit the deed to the word, he at once ordered the head citizens to assemble the youth of Alexandria on the morning of the day in question, and to form them into a Macedonian phalanx. He wished to inspect them in the stadium, and they were now marching thither.

He had ordered helmets, shields, and lances to be made after well-known Macedonian patterns, and to be distributed to the new Hellenic legion. Later on they might be intrusted with the guarding of the city, should there be a Parthian war; and he required the attendance of the Alexandrian garrison.

The inspection of this Greek regiment would be certain to give pleasure to Melissa. He expected, too, to see Alexander among them. When once his beloved shared the purple with him, he could raise her brother to the command of this chosen phalanx.

Troop after troop streamed on to the course, and he thought he had seldom seen anything finer than these slender youths, marching along with elastic step, and garlands in their black, brown, or golden locks.

When the young noblemen who belonged to the school of Timagetes filed past him, he took such delight in the beauty of their heads, the wonderful symmetry of their limbs strengthened by athletic games, and the supple grace of most of them, that he felt as if some magic spell had carried him back to the golden age of Greece and the days of the Olympian games in the Altis.

What could be keeping Melissa? This sight would assuredly please her, and for once he would be able to say something flattering about her people. One might easily overlook a good deal from such splendid youths.

Carried away by his admiration he waved his scarf to them, which being remarked by the gymnasiarch, who with his two assistants—herculean athletes—walked in front, was answered by him with a loud "Hail, Cæsar!"

The youths who followed him imitated his example, and the troop that came after them returned his greeting loud and heartily. The young voices could be heard from afar, and the news soon spread to the last ranks of the first division to whom these greetings were addressed. But, among the men who already were masters of households of their own, there were many who deemed

it shameful and unworthy to raise their voices in greeting
to the tyrant whose heavy hand had oppressed them more
than once; and a group of young men belonging to the
party of the "Greens," who ran their own horses, had the
fatal audacity to agree among themselves that they would
leave Cæsar's greeting unanswered. A many-headed
crowd is like a row of strings which sound together as
soon as the note is struck to which they are all attuned;
and so each one now felt sure that his acclamation would
only increase the insolence of this fratricide, this blood-
stained monster, this oppressor and enemy of the citizens.
The succeeding ranks of "Greens" followed the example,
and from the midst of a troop of young married men,
members in the gymnasium of the society of the Dioscuri,
one foolhardy spirit had the reckless temerity to blow a
shrill, far-sounding whistle between his fingers.

He found no imitators, but the insulting sound reached
the emperor's ear, and seemed to him like the signal-call
of Fate; for, before it had died away, the clouds broke,
and a stream of brilliant sunshine spread over the race-
course and the assembled multitude. The cloudy day
that was to have brought happiness to Cæsar had been
suddenly transformed by the sun of Africa into a bright
one; and the radiant light which cheered the hearts of
others seemed to him to be a message from above to
warn him that, instead of the highest bliss, this day would
bring him disappointment and misfortune. He said nothing of this, for there was no one there in whom it
would be any relief to confide, or of whose sympathy he
could be sure. But those who watched him as he retired
from the window saw plainly that the idyl, which he had
promised them should begin to-day, would assuredly not
do so for the next few hours at least, unless some miracle

should occur. No, he would have to wait awhile for the pastoral joys he had promised himself. And it seemed as if, instead of the satyr-play of which old Julius Paulinus had spoken, that fatal whistle had given the signal for another act in Caracalla's terrible life-tragedy.

The "friends" of the emperor looked at him anxiously as, with furrowed brow, he asked, impatiently:

"Macrinus not here yet?"

Theocritus and others who had looked with envy upon Melissa and her relatives, and with distrust upon her union with the emperor, now heartily wished the girl back again.

But the prefect Macrinus came not; and while the emperor, having sent messengers to fetch Melissa, turned with darkly boding brow to his station overlooking the brightly lighted race-course, still hoping the augury would prove false, and the sunny day turn yet in his favor, Macrinus was in the full belief that the gate of greatness and power was opening to him. Superstitious as the emperor himself and every one else of his time, he was to-day more firmly persuaded than ever of the existence of men whose mysterious wisdom gave them powers to which even he must bend—the hard-headed man who had raised himself from the lowest to the highest station, next to the Cæsar himself.

In past nights the Magian Serapion had caused him to see and hear much that was incomprehensible. He believed in the powers exerted by that remarkable man over spirits, and his ability to work miracles, for he had proved in the most startling manner that he had perfect control even over such a determined mind as that of the perfect. The evening before, the magician had bidden Macrinus come to him at the third hour after sunrise of

the next day, which he had unhesitatingly promised to
do. But the emperor had risen later than usual this
morning, and the prefect might expect to be called to
his master at any moment. In spite of this, and although
his absence threatened to rouse Cæsar to fury, and everything pointed to the necessity of his remaining within
call, Macrinus, drawn by an irresistible craving, had followed the invitation, which sounded more like a command. This, indeed, had seemed to him decisive; for
as the seer ruled over his stern spirit, albeit he was alive,
even so must the spirits of the departed do his bidding.
His every interest urged him now to believe in the
prophecy made to him by Serapion, to-day for the third
time, which foretold that he, the prefect, should mount
the throne of the Cæsars, clad in the purple of Caracalla.
But it was not alone to repeat this prophecy that the seer
had called Macrinus to him, but to inform him that the
future empress was betrothed to a young Alexandrian,
and that the tender intercourse between the lovers had
not been interrupted during Caracalla's courtship. This
had come to Serapion's ears yesterday afternoon, through
his adroit assistant Kastor, and he had taken advantage
of the information to prepare Cæsar during the night for
the faithlessness of his chosen bride.

The Magian assured the prefect that what the spirit
of the great Macedonian had hinted at yesterday had
since been confirmed by the demons in his service. It
would now be easy for Macrinus ·to hinder Melissa, who
might have been all-powerful, from coming between him
and the great goal which the spirits had·set before him.

Serapion then repeated the prophecy, which came
with such convincing power from the bearded lips of the
sage that the prudent statesman cast his last doubts from

him, and, exclaiming, "I believe your words, and shall press forward now in spite of every danger!" he grasped the prophet's hand in farewell.

Up to this point Macrinus, the son of a poor cobbler, who had had difficulty in rearing his children at all, had received these prophetic utterances with cool deliberation, and had ventured no step nearer to the exalted aim which had been offered to his ambition. In all good faith he had done his best to perform the duties of his office as an obedient servant to his master and the state. This had all changed now, and, firmly resolved to risk the struggle for the purple, he returned to the emperor's apartments.

Macrinus had no reason to expect a favorable reception when he entered the tablinum, but his great purpose upheld his courage. He, the upstart, was well aware that Fortune requires her favorites to keep their eyes open and their hands active. He therefore took care to obtain a full account of what had happened, from his confidential friend the senator Antigonus, a soldier of mean birth, who had gained favor with Cæsar by a daring piece of horsemanship. Antigonus closed his report with the impudent whistle of the Greek athlete; he dwelt chiefly on his astonishment at Melissa's absence. This gave food for thought to the prefect, too; but before entering the tablinum he was stopped by the freedman Epagathos, who handed over to him a scroll which had been given to him for the emperor. The messenger had disappeared directly afterward, and could not be overtaken. Might it not endanger the life of the reader by exhaling a poisonous perfume?

"Nothing is impossible here," answered the prefect. "Ours it is to watch over the safety of our godlike master."

This letter was that which Melissa had entrusted to the slave Argutis for Cæsar, and with unwarrantable boldness the prefect and Epagathos now opened it and ran rapidly over its contents. They then agreed to keep this strange missive from the emperor till Macrinus should send to ask whether the youths were assembled in their full number on the race-course. They judged it necessary to prepare Cæsar in some sort, to prevent a fresh attack of illness.

Caracalla was standing near a pillar at the window whence he might see without being seen. That whistle still shrilled in his ears. But another idea occupied him so intensely that he had not yet thought of wiping out the insult with blood.

What could be delaying Melissa and her father and brother?

The painter ought to have joined the other Macedonian youths on the race-course, and Caracalla was engaged in looking out for him, stretching forward every time he caught sight of some curly head that rose above the others.

There was a bitter taste in his mouth, and at every fresh disappointment his rebellious, tortured heart beat faster; and yet the idea that Melissa might have dared to flee from him never entered his mind.

The high-priest of Serapis had informed him that his wife had seen nothing of her as yet. Then it suddenly occurred to him that she might have been wet through by the rain yesterday and now lay shaken by fever, and that this must keep her father away, too; a supposition which cheered the egoist more than it pained him, and with a sigh of relief he turned once more to the window.

How haughtily these boys carried their heads; their

fleet, elastic feet skimmed over the ground; how daringly they showed off the strength and dexterity that almost seemed their birthright! This reminded him that, prematurely aged as he was by the wild excesses of his younger years, with his ill-set broken leg and his thin locks, he must make a lamentable contrast to these others of his own age; and he said to himself that perhaps the whistle had come from the lips of one of the strongest and handsomest, who had not considered him worth greeting.

And yet he was not weaker than any single individual down there; aye, and if he chose he could crush them all together, as he would the glow-worm creeping on that window-sill. With one quick squeeze of his fingers he put an end to the pretty little insect, and at that moment he heard voices behind him.

Had his beloved come at last?

No, it was only the prefect. He should have been there long ago, if he were obedient to his sovereign's commands. Macrinus was therefore a convenient object on which to vent his anger. How mean was the face of this long-legged upstart, with its small eyes, sharp nose, and furrowed brow! Could the beautiful Diadumenianus really be his son? No matter! The boy, the apple of his father's eye, was in his power, and was a surety for the old man's loyalty. After all, Macrinus was a capable, serviceable officer, and easier to deal with than the Romans of the old noble families.

Notwithstanding these considerations, Caracalla addressed the prefect as harshly as if he had been a disobedient slave, but Macrinus received the flood of abuse with patience and humility. When the emperor reproached him with never being at hand when he was wanted, he replied submissively that it was just because he found he could be of service to Cæsar that he had dared to absent himself. The refractory young brood down there were being kept well in hand, and it was entirely owing to his effectual measures that they had contented themselves with that one whistle. Later on it would be their duty to punish such audacity and high-treason with the utmost rigor.

The emperor gazed in astonishment at the counsellor, who till now had ever advised him to use moderation, and only yesterday had begged him to ascribe much to Alexandrian manners, which in Rome would have had to be treated with severity. Had the insolence of these unruly citizens become unbearable even to this prudent, merciful man?

Yes, that must be it; and the grudge that Macrinus now showed against the Alexandrians hastened the pardon which Cæsar silently accorded him.

Caracalla even said to himself that he had underrated the prefect's intellect hitherto, for his eyes flashed and glowed like fire, notwithstanding their smallness, and lending a force to his ignoble face which Caracalla had never noticed before. Had Cæsar no premonition that in the last few hours this man had grown to be such another as himself?—for in his unyielding mind the firm resolve had been strengthened to hesitate at nothing— not even at the death of as many as might come between him and his high aim, the throne.

Macrinus knew enough of human nature to observe the miserable disquietude that had seized upon the emperor at his bride's continued absence, but he took good care not to refer to the subject. When Caracalla, however, could no longer conceal his anxiety, and asked after her himself, the prefect gave the appointed sign to Epagathos, who then handed Melissa's freshly re-sealed letter to his master.

"Let me open it, great Cæsar," entreated Macrinus. "Even Homer called Egypt the land of poison."

But the emperor did not heed him. No one had told him, and he had never in his life received a letter in a woman's hand, except from his mother; and yet he knew that this delicate little roll had come from a woman— from Melissa.

It was closed with a silken thread, and the seal with which Epagathos had replaced the one they had broken. If Caracalla tore it open, the papyrus and the writing might be damaged. He called impatiently for a knife, and the body physician, who had just entered with other courtiers, handed him his.

"Back again?" asked Caracalla as the physician drew the blade from its sheath.

"At break of day, on somewhat unsteady legs," was the jovial answer. Caracalla took the knife from him, cut the silk, hastily broke the seal, and began to read.

Till now his hands had performed their office steadily, but suddenly they began to tremble, and while he ran his eye over Melissa's refusal—there were but a few lines —his knees shook, and a sharp, low cry burst from him, like no sound that lies by nature in the throat of man. Rent in two pieces, the strip of papyrus fluttered to the ground.

The prefect caught the despot, who, seized with giddiness, stretched out his hands as if seeking a support. The physician hurriedly brought out the drug which he always carried with him, and then, pointing to the letter, asked the prefect: "In the name of all the gods, from whom?"

"From the gem-cutter's fair daughter," replied Macrinus, with a contemptuous shrug.

"From her?" cried the physician, indignantly. "From that light Phryne, who kissed and embraced my rich host's son down there in his sick-room?"

At this the emperor, who had not lost consciousness for one moment, started as if stung by a serpent, and sprang at the physician's throat, screaming while he threatened to strangle him:

"What was that? What did you say? Cursed babbler! The truth, villain, and the whole truth, if you love your life!"

The half-choked man, ever prone to talking, had no reason for concealing from Cæsar what he had seen with his own eyes, and had subsequently heard in the Serapeum and at the table of Polybius.

When life was at stake a promise to a freedman could be of no account, so he gave free rein to his tongue, and answered the questions Caracalla put to him without reserve, and—being a man used to the ways of a court —with insinuations that were doubly welcome to a judge so eager for damning evidence.

Yesterday, the day before, and the day before that— every day on which Melissa had pretended to feel the mysterious ties that bound her heart to his, every day that she had feigned love and led him on to woo her, she had—as he now learned—granted to another what she had refused to him with such stern discretion. Her prayer for him, the sympathy she said she felt, the maidenly sensibility which had charmed him in her—all had been lies, deceit, sham, in order to attain an object. And that old man and the brothers to serve whom she had dared to approach him—they all knew the cruel game she was playing with him and his heart's love. The lips that had lured him into the vilest trap with lying words had kissed another. He seemed to hear the Alexandrians laughing at the forsaken bridegroom, to see them pointing the finger of derision at the man whom cunning woman had deceived even before marriage. What a feast for their ribald wit!

And yet—he would have willingly borne it all, and more, for the certainty that she had really loved him once; that her heart had been his, if only for one short hour.

On those shreds of papyrus scattered over the floor she confessed she was not able to accede to his wishes, because she had already given her faith to another before she ever saw Caracalla. It was true she had felt herself drawn to him as to no other but her betrothed; and had he been content to let her be near him as a faithful servant and sick-nurse, then indeed . . . In short, he was informed in so many words that every tie that bound her to him must be broken in favor of another, and the hypocritical regret with which she sought to cover up the hard facts only made him doubly indignant.

Lies, lies—even in this letter nothing but lies and heartless dissimulation!

How it stabbed his heart! But he possessed the power to wound her in return. Wild beasts should tear her fair body limb from limb, as she had torn his soul in this hour.

One wish alone filled his heart—to see her whom he had loved above all others, to whom he had revealed his inmost soul, for whose sake he had amended his actions as he had never done for his own mother—to see her lying in the dust before him, and to inflict upon her such tortures as no mortal had ever endured before. And not only she, but all whom she loved and who were her accomplices, should atone for the torment of this hour. The time of reckoning had come, and every evil instinct of his nature mingled its exulting voice with the anguished cries of his bleeding heart.

The prefect knew his master well, and watched his every expression while apparently listening to the voluble physician, but in reality absorbed in a train of thought. By the twitching of his eyelids, the sharply outlined red patches on his cheeks, the quivering nostrils, and the deep furrows between his eyes, he must be revolving some frightful plan in his mind.

Yesterday, had he found him in this condition, Macrinus would have endeavored by every means in his power to calm his wrath; but to-day, if Cæsar had set the world in flames, he would only have added fuel to the fire, for who could more surely upset the firmly established power of this emperor and son of emperors as Caracalla himself? The people of Rome had endured unimaginable sufferings at his hands; but the cup was full, and, judging from Cæsar's looks, he would cause it to overflow this day. Then the rising flood which tore the son of an idolized father from the throne, might possibly bear him, the child of lowliness and poverty, into the palace.

But Macrinus remained silent. No word from him should change the tenor of the emperor's thoughts. The plan he was thinking out must be allowed to ripen to its full horror. The lowering, uncertain glance that Caracalla cast round the tablinum at the close of the physician's narrative showed that the prefect's reticence was an unnecessary precaution.

Cæsar's mind and tongue still seemed paralyzed; but at that moment something occurred which recalled him to himself and brought firmness to his wandering gaze.

There was a sudden disturbance in the ante-chamber, with a confused sound of cries and shouting. Those friends of Cæsar who wore swords drew them, and Caracalla, who was unarmed, called to Antigonus to give him his.

"A revolt?" he asked Macrinus with flashing eyes, and as if he wished the answer to be in the affirmative; but the prefect had hastened to the door with drawn sword. Before he reached it, it was thrown open, and Julius Asper, the legate, burst into the tablinum as if beside himself, crying: "Cursed den of murderers! An attempt on your life, great Cæsar; but we have him fast!"

"Assassination!" interrupted Caracalla with furious joy. "That was the only thing left undone! Bring the murderer! But first"—and he addressed himself to Aristides —-"close the city gates and the harbor. Not a man, not a ship must be let through without being searched. The vessels that have weighed anchor since daybreak must be followed and brought back. Mounted Numidians under efficient officers must scour the high-roads as soon as the gate-keepers have been examined. Every house must be open to your men, every temple, every refuge. Seize Heron, the gem-cutter, his daughter, and his two sons. Also—Diodoros is the young villain's name?—him, his parents, and everybody connected with them! The physician knows where they are to be found. *Alive,* do you hear?—not dead! I will have them alive! I give you till midnight! Your head, if you let the jade and her brothers escape!"

With drooping head the unhappy officer departed. On the threshold he was met by Martialis, the prætorian centurion. After him, his hands bound behind his back, walked the criminal. A deep flush overspread his handsome face, his eyes glowed under the too lofty brow with the fierce light of fever, his waving locks stood out in

wild confusion round his head, while the finely cut upper
lip with its disdainful curl seemed the very seat of scorn
and bitterest contempt. Every feature wore that same expression, and not a trace of fear or regret. But his panting breast betrayed to the physician's first glance that they
had here to deal with a sick man in raging fever.

They had already torn off his mantle and discovered
beneath its folds the sharp-edged butcher's knife which
plainly betrayed his intentions. He had penetrated to
the first ante-chamber when a soldier of the Germanic
body-guard laid hold on him. Martialis had him by the
girdle now, and the emperor looked sharply and mistrust-
fully at the prætorian, as he asked if it were he who had
captured the assassin.

The centurion replied that he had not. Ingiomarus,
the German, had noticed the knife; he, Martialis, was
here only in right of his privilege as a prætorian to bring
such prisoners before great Cæsar.

Caracalla bent a searching gaze upon the soldier; for
he thought he recognized in him the man who had
aroused his envy and whose happiness he had once greatly
desired to damp, when against orders he had received his
wife and child in the camp. Recollections rose in his
mind that drove the hot blood to his cheek, and he cried,
disdainfully:

"I might have guessed it! What can be expected beyond the letter of their service from one who so neglects
his duties? Did you not disport yourself with lewd women
in the camp before my very eyes, setting at naught the
well-known rules? Hands off the prisoner! This is your
last day as prætorian and in Alexandria. As soon as the
harbor is opened—to-morrow, I expect—you go on board

the ship that carries reinforcements to Edessa. A winter on the Pontus will cool your lascivious blood."

This attack was so rapid and so unexpected to the somewhat dull-witted centurion, that he failed at first to grasp its full significance. He only understood that he was to be banished again from the loved ones he had so long been deprived of. But when he recovered sufficiently to excuse himself by declaring that it was his own wife and children who had visited him, Cæsar cut him short by commanding him to report his change of service at once to the tribune of the legion.

The centurion bowed in silence and obeyed. Caracalla then went up to the prisoner, and dragging him, weakly resisting, from the dark background of the room to the window, he asked with a sneer:

"And what are assassins like in Alexandria? Ah, ha! this is not the face of a hired cut-throat! Only thus do they look whose sharp wit I will answer with still sharper steel."

"For that answer you at least are not wont to be at a loss," came contemptuously from the lips of the prisoner.

The emperor winced as if he had been struck, and then exclaimed:

"You may thank your bound hands that I do not instantly return you the answer you seem to expect of me."

Then turning to his courtiers, he asked if any of them could give him information as to the name and history of the assassin; but no one appeared to know him. Even Timotheus, the priest of Serapis, who as head of the Museum had so often delighted in the piercing intellect of this youth, and had prophesied a great future for him, was silent, and looked at him with troubled gaze.

It was the prisoner himself who satisfied Cæsar's curiosity. Glancing round the circle of courtiers, and casting a grateful look at his priestly patron, he said:

"It would be asking too much of your Roman table-companions that they should know a philosopher. You may spare yourself the question, Cæsar. I came here that you might make my acquaintance. My name is Philippus, and I am son to Heron, the gem-cutter."

"Her brother!" screamed Caracalla, as he rushed at him, and trusting his hand into the neck of the sick youth's chiton—who already could scarcely stand upon his feet—he shook him violently, crying, with a scoffing look at the high-priest:

"And is this the ornament of the Museum, the free-thinker, the profound skeptic Philippus?"

He stopped suddenly, and his eyes flashed as if a new light had burst upon him; he dropped his hand from the prisoner's robe, and bending his head close to the other, he whispered in his ear, "You have come from Melissa?"

"Not from her," the other answered quickly, the flush deepening on his face, "but in the name of that most unhappy, most pitiable maiden, and as the representative of her noble Macedonian house, which you would defile with shame and infamy; in the name of the inhabitants of this city, whom you despoil and tread under foot; in the interests of the whole world, which you disgrace!"

Trembling with fury Caracalla broke in:

"Who would choose you for their ambassador, miserable wretch?"

To which the philosopher replied with haughty calm:

"Think not so lightly of one who looks forward with longing to that of which you have an abject fear."

"Of death, do you mean?" asked Caracalla, sneering,

for his wrath had given place to astonishment. And Philip answered. "Yes, death—with whom I have sworn friendship, and who should be ten times blessed to me if he would but atone for my clumsiness and rid the world of such a monster!"

The emperor, still spell-bound by the unheard-of audacity of the youth before him, now felt moved to keep step with the philosopher, whom few could equal in sharpness of wit; and, controling the raging fury of his blood, he cried, in a tone of superiority:

"So that is the boasted logic of the Museum? Death is your dearest desire, and yet you would give it to your enemy?"

"Quite right," replied Philip, his lip curling with scorn. "For there is something which to the philosopher stands higher than logic. It is a stranger to you, but you know it perhaps by name—it is called Justice."

These words, and the contemptuous tone in which they were spoken, burst the flood-gates of Caracalla's painfully restrained passion; his voice rose harsh and loud, till the lion growled angrily and dragged at his chain, while his master flung hasty words of fury in the face of his enemy:

"We shall soon see, my cunning fencer with words, whether I know how to follow your advice, and how sternly I can exercise that virtue denied to me by an assassin. Will any one accuse me now of injustice if I punish the accursed brood that has grown up in this den of iniquity with all the rigor that it deserves? Yes, glare at me with those great, burning eyes! Alexandrian eyes, promising all and granting nothing—persuading him who trusts in them to believe in innocence and chastity, truth and affection. But let him look closer, and he finds nothing but deep corruption, foul cunning, despicable self-seeking, and atrocious faithlessness!

"And everything else in this city is like those eyes! Where are there so many gods and priests, where do they sacrifice so often, where do they fast and apply themselves so assiduously to repentance and the cleansing of the soul? And yet, where does vice display itself so freely and so unchecked? This Alexandria, —in her youth as dissolute as she was fair—what is she now but an old hag? Now that she is toothless, now that wrinkles disfigure her face, she has turned pious, that, like the wolf in sheep's clothing, she may revenge herself by malice for the loss of joy and of the admiration of her lovers! I can find no more striking comparison than this; for, even as hags find a hideous pleasure in empty chatter and spiteful slanderings, so she, once so beautiful and renowned, has sunk deeper and deeper in the mire, and can not endure to see anything which has achieved greatness or glory without maliciously bespattering it with poison.

"Justice!—yes, I will exercise justice, oh, sublime and virtuous hero, going forth to murder—a dagger hidden in your bosom! I thank you for that lesson!

"Pride of the Museum!—you lead me to the source whence all your corruption flows. It is that famous nursery of learning where you, too, were bred up. There, yes, there they cherish the heresy that makes the gods into puppets of straw, and the majesty of the throne into an owl for pert and insignificant birds to peck at. Thence comes the doctrine that teaches men and women to laugh at virtue and to break their word. There, where in other days, noble minds protected by the overshadowing favor of princes, followed out great ideas they now teach nothing but words—empty, useless words. I saw and said that yesterday, and now I know it for certain—every poison shaft that your malice has aimed at me was forged in the Museum."

He paused for breath, and then continued, with a contemptuous laugh:

"If the justice which you rate higher than logic were to take its course, nothing would be juster than to make an end this day of this hot-bed of corruption. But your unlearned fellow-citizens shall taste of my justice, too. You yourself will be prevented by the beasts in the Circus from looking on at the effect your warning words have produced. But as yet you are alive, and you shall hear what the experiences are which make the severest measures the highest justice.

"What did I hope to find, and what have I really found? I heard the Alexandrians praised for their hospitality—for the ardor with which they pursue learning—for the great proficiency of their astronomers—for the piety which has raised so many altars and invented so many doctrines; and, lastly, for the beauty and fine wit of their women.

"And this hospitality! All that I have known of it is a flood of malicious abuse and knavish scoffings, which penetrated even to the gates of this temple, my dwelling. I came here as emperor, and treason pursued me wherever I went—even into my own apartments; for there you stand, whom a barbarian had to hinder from stabbing me with the knife of the assassin. And your learning? You have heard my opinion of the Museum. And the astrologers of this renowned observatory? The very opposite of all they promised me has come to pass. . . . Religion? The people, of whom you know as little from the musty volumes of the Museum as of *Ultima Thule*—the people

indeed practice it.   The old gods are necessary to them.
They are the bread of life to them. But instead of those
you have offered them sour, unripe fruit, with a glittering
rind—from your own garden, of your own growing. The
fruit of trees is a gift from Nature, and all that she brings
forth has some good in it; but what you offer to the world
is hollow and poisonous. Your rhetoric gives it an attrac-
tive exterior, and that too comes from the Museum. There
they are shrewd enough to create new gods, which start
up out of the earth like mushrooms. If it should occur
to them, they would raise murder to the dignity of god
of gods, and you to be his high-priest."

"That would be your office," interposed the philosopher.

"You shall see," returned the emperor, laughing shrilly,
"and the witlings of the Museum with you! You use the
knife; but hear the words of the master: The teeth of
wild beasts and their claws are weapons not to be despised.
Your father and brother, and she who taught me what to
think of the virtue and faith of Alexandrian women, shall
tell you this in Hades. Soon shall every one of those
follow you thither who forgot, even by a glance of the
eye, that I was Cæsar and a guest of this city! After the
next performance in the Circus the offenders shall tell you
in the other world how I administer justice. No later than
the day after to-morrow, I imagine, you may meet there
with several companions from the Museum. There will
be enough to clap applause at the disputation!"

Caracalla ended his vehement speech with a jeering
laugh, and looked round eagerly for applause from the
"friends," for whose benefit his last words had been
spoken; and it was offered so energetically as to drown
the philosopher's reply.

But Caracalla heard it, and when the noise subsided he asked his condemned victim:

"What did you mean by your exclamation, 'And yet I would that death might spare me'?"

"In order, if *that* should come true," returned the philosopher quickly, his voice trembling with indignation, "that I might be a witness of the grim mockery with which the all-requiting gods will destroy you, their defender."

"The gods!" laughed the emperor. "My respect for your logic grows less and less. You, the skeptic, expect the deeds of a mortal man from the gods whose existence you deny!"

Then cried Philip, and his great eyes burning with hatred and indignation sought the emperor's: "Till this hour I was sure of nothing, and therefore uncertain of the existence of a god; but now I believe firmly that Nature, by whom everything is carried out according to everlasting, immutable laws, and who casts out and destroys anything that threatens to bring discord into the harmonious workings of all her parts, would of her own accord bring forth a god, if there be not one already, who should crush you, the destroyer of life and peace, in his all-powerful hand!"

Here his wild outburst of indignation was brought to an abrupt close, for a furious blow from Caracalla's fist sent his enfeebled enemy staggering back against the wall near the window.

Mad with rage, Caracalla shrieked hoarsely:

"To the beasts with him! No, not to the beasts—to the torture! He and his sister! The punishment I have bethought me of—scum of the earth—"

But the wild despair of the other, in whose breast

hatred and fever burned with equal strength, now reached the highest pitch. Like a hunted deer which stays its flight for a moment to find an outlet or to turn upon his pursuers, he gazed wildly round him, and before the emperor could finish his threat, leaning against the pillar of the window as if prepared to receive his death-blow, he interrupted Caracalla:

"If your dull wit can invent no death to satisfy your cruelty, the blood-hound Zminis can aid you. You are a worthy couple. Curses on you! . . ."

"At him!" yelled the emperor to Macrinus and the legate, for no substitute had appeared for the centurion he had dismissed.

But while the nobles advanced warily upon the madman, and Macrinus called to the Germanic body-guard in the ante-room, Philip had turned like lightning and disappeared through the window.

The legates and Cæsar came too late to hold him back, and from below came cries of "Crushed—dead! . . . What crime has he committed? . . . They cast him down! . . . He can not have done it himself . . . Impossible! . . . His arms are bound . . . A new manner of death invented specially for the Alexandrians!"

Then another whistle sounded, and the shout, "Down with the tyrant!"

But no second cry followed. The place was too full of soldiers and lictors.

Caracalla heard it all. He turned back into the room, wiped the perspiration from his brow, and said in a voice of studied unconcern, yet with horrible harshness:

"He deserved his death—ten times over. However, I have to thank him for a good suggestion. I had forgotten the Egyptian Zminis. If he is still alive, Macrinus, take him from his dungeon and bring him here. But quickly—in a chariot! Let him come just as he is. I can make use of him now."

The prefect bowed assent, and by the rapidity with which he departed he betrayed how willingly he carried out this order of his master's.

CHAPTER IX.

Scarcely had Macrinus closed the door behind him, than Caracalla threw himself exhausted on the throne, and ordered wine to brought.

The gloomy gaze he bent upon the ground was not affected this time. The physician noted with anxiety how his master's breast heaved and his eyelids quivered; but when he offered Cæsar a soothing potion, he waved him away, and commanded him to cease from troubling him.

For all that, he listened a little later to the legate, who brought the news that the youths of the city assembled on the race-course were beginning to be impatient. They were singing and applauding boisterously, and the songs they so loudly insisted on having repeated would certainly not contain matter flattering to the Romans.

"Leave them alone," answered Cæsar, roughly. "Every line is aimed at me and no other. But the condemned are always allowed their favorite meal before the last journey. The food they love is venomous satire. Let them enjoy it to the full once more!—Is it far to Zminis's prison?"

The reply was in the negative; and as Caracalla exclaimed, "So much the better!" a significant smile played on his lips.

The high-priest of Serapis had looked on in much

distress of mind. He, as the head of the Museum, had set high hopes on the youth who had come to such a terrible end. If Cæsar should carry his threats into execution, there would be an end to that celebrated home of learning which, in his opinion, bore such noble fruits of study. And what could Caracalla mean by his dark saying that the sport and mockery of those youths below was their last meal? The worst might indeed be expected from the fearful tyrant who was at once so deeply wounded and so grievously offended; and the high-priest had already sent messengers—Greeks of good credit—to warn the insurgent youths in the stadium. But, as the chief minister of the divinity, he also esteemed it his duty, at any risk to himself, to warn the despot, whom he saw on the verge of being carried away to deeds of unparallelled horror. He thought the time had come, when Caracalla looked up from the brooding reverie into which he had again sunk, and with an ominous scowl asked Timotheus whether his wife, under whose protection Melissa had been seen the day before, had known that the false-hearted girl had given herself to another man while she feigned love for him.

The high-priest repelled the suspicion with his usual dignity, and went on to adjure Cæsar not to visit on an industrious and dutiful community the sins of a light-minded girl's base folly and falsehood.

But Caracalla would not suffer him to finish; he wrathfully inquired who had given him a right to force his advice on Cæsar.

On this Timotheus replied, with calm dignity:

"Your own noble words, great Cæsar, when, to your honor be it spoken, you reminded the misguided skeptic of the true meaning of the old gods and of what is due to them. The god whom I serve, great Cæsar, is second to none: the heavens are his head, the ocean is his body, and the earth his feet; the sunshine is the light of his all-seeing eye, and everything which stirs in the heart or brain of man is an emanation of his divine spirit. Thus he is the all-pervading soul of the universe, and a portion of that soul dwells in you, in me, in all of us. His power is greater than any power on earth, and, though a well-grounded wrath and only too just indignation urge you to exert the power lent you by him—"

"And I will exert it!" Cæsar exclaimed with haughty rage. "It reaches far. I need no help, not even that of your god!"

"That I know," replied Timotheus. "And the god will let those fall into your hands who have sinned against your sacred majesty. Any punishment, even the severest, will be pleasing in his sight which you may inflict on those guilty of high-treason, for you wear the purple as his gift and in his name; those who insult you sin also against the god. I myself, with my small power, will help to bring the criminals to justice. But when a whole population is accused, when it is beyond the power of human justice to separate the innocent from the guilty, punishment is the prerogative of the god. He will visit on this city the crimes it has committed against you; and I implore you, in the name of your noble and admirable mother—whom it has been my privilege to entertain under this roof, and who in gratitude for the favors of Serapis—"

"And have I grudged sacrifices?" Cæsar broke in. "I have done my utmost to win the graces of your god—and with what success? Everything that can most aggrieve the heart of man has befallen me here under his eyes. I have as much reason to complain of him as to accuse the reprobate natives of your city. He, no doubt, knows how to be avenged; the three-headed monster at his feet does not look like a lap-dog. Why, he would despise me if I should leave the punishment of the criminals to his tender mercies! Nay, I can do that for myself. Though you have seen me in many cases show mercy, it has always been for my mother's sake. You have done well to remind me of her. That lady—she is, I know, a votary of your god. But to me the Alexandrians have dared to violate the laws of hospitality; to her they were cordial hosts. I will remember that in their favor. And if many escape unpunished, I would have the traitors to know that they owe it to the hospitality shown to my mother by their parents, or perhaps by themselves."

He was here interrupted by the arrival of Aristides, who entered in great haste and apparently pleased excitement. His spies had seized a malefactor who had affixed an epigram of malignant purport to the statue of Julia Domna in the Cæsareum. The writer was a pupil of the Museum, and had been taken in the stadium, where he was boasting of his exploit. A spy, mingling with the crowd, had laid hands on him, and the captain of the watch had forthwith hurried to the Serapeum to boast of a success which might confirm him in his yet uncertain position. The rough sketch of the lines had been found on the culprit, and Aristides held the tablets on which they were written while Caracalla listened to his report. Aristides was breathless with eagerness, and Cæsar, snatching the tablets impatiently from his hand, read the following lines:

"Wanton, I say, is this dam of irreconcilable brothers!"
    "Mean you Jocasta?"   "Nay, worse—Julia, the wife of Severus."

"The worst of all—but the last!" Caracalla snarled, as, turning pale, he laid the tablets down. But he almost instantly took them up again, and handing the malignant and lying effusion to the high-priest, he exclaimed, with a laugh:

"This seals the warrant! Here is my mother slandered, too! Now, the man who sues for mercy condemns himself to death!" And, clinching his fist, he muttered, "And this, too, is from the Museum."

Timotheus, meanwhile, had also read the lines. Even paler than Caracalla, and fully aware that any further counsel would be thrown away and only turn the emperor's wrath against himself, he expressed his anger at this calumny directed against the noblest of women, and by a boy hardly free from school!

But Caracalla furiously broke in:

"And woe to you if your god refuses me the only thing I crave in return for so many sacrifices—revenge, complete and sanguinary; atonement from great and small alike!" But he interrupted himself with the exclamation: "He grants it! Now for the tool I need."

The tool was ready—Zminis, the Egyptian, answering in every particular to the image which Caracalla had had in his mind of the instrument who might execute his most bloodthirsty purpose.

With hair in disorder and a blue-black stubble of beard on his haggard yellow cheeks, in a dirty gray prison shirt, barefoot, and treading as silently as Fate when it creeps on a victim, the rascal approached his sovereign. He stood before Caracalla exactly as the prefect, in a swift chariot, had brought him out of prison. The white of his long, narrow eyes, which had so terrified Melissa, had turned yellow, and his glance was as restless and shifting as that of a hyena. His small head on its long neck was never for a moment still; the ruthless wretch had sat waiting day after day in expectation of death, and it was by a miracle that he found himself once more at the height of his ambition. But when at last he inquired of Caracalla, in the husky voice which had gained an added hoarseness from the damp dungeon whence he had been brought, what his commands were, looking up at him like a starving dog which hopes for a titbit from his master's hand, even the fratricide, who himself held the sword sharpened to kill, shuddered at the sight and sound.

But Cæsar at once recovered himself, and when he asked the Egyptian—

"Will you undertake to help me, as captain of the night-watch, to punish the traitors of Alexandria?" the answer was confident:

"What man can do, I can do."

"Good!" replied Caracalla. "But this is not a matter of merely capturing one or another. Every one—mark me—every one has merited death who has broken the laws of hospitality, that hospitality which this lying city offered me. Do you understand? Yes? Well, then, how are we to detect the guilty? Where are we to find spies and executioners enough? How can we punish worst those whose wickedness has involved the rest in guilt, especially the epigrammatists of the Museum? How are we to discover the ringleaders of those who insulted me yesterday in the Circus, and of those among the youths in the stadium who have dared to express their vile dis-approval by whistling in my very face? What steps will you take to hinder a single one from escaping? Consider. How is it to be done so effectually that I may lie down and say: 'They have had their deserts. I am content'?"

The Egyptian's eyes wandered round the floor, but he presently drew himself up and answered briefly and positively, as though he were issuing an order to his men:

"Kill them all!"

Caracalla started, and repeated dully, "All?"

"All!" repeated Zminis, with a hideous grin. "The young ones are all there, safe in the stadium. The men in the Museum fear nothing. Those who are in the streets can be cut down. Locked doors can be broken in."

At this, Cæsar, who had dropped on to his throne, started to his feet, flung the wine-cup he held across the room, laughed loudly, and exclaimed:

"You are the man for me! To work at once! This will be a day!—Macrinus, Theocritus, Antigonus, we need your troops. Send up the legates. Those who do not like the taste of blood, may sweeten it with plunder."

He looked young again, as if relieved from some burden on his mind, and the thought flashed through his brain whether revenge were not sweeter than love.

No one spoke. Even Theocritus, on whose lips a word of flattery or applause was always ready, looked down in his dismay; but Caracalla, in his frenzy of excitement, heeded nothing.

The hideous suggestion of Zminis seemed to him worthy of his greatness by its mere enormity. It must be carried out. Ever since he had first donned the purple he had made it his aim to be feared. If this tremendous deed were done, he need never frown again at those whom he wished to terrify.

And then, what a revenge! If Melissa should hear of it, what an effect it must have on her!

To work, then!

And he added in a gentler tone, as if he had a delightful surprise in store for some old friend:

"But silence, perfect silence—do you hear?—till all is ready.—You, Zminis, may begin on the pipers in the stadium and the chatterers in the Museum. The prize for soldiers and lictors alike lies in the merchants' chests."

Still no one spoke; and now he observed it. His scheme was too grand for these feeble spirits. He must teach them to silence their conscience and the voice of Roman rectitude; he must take on himself the whole responsibility of this deed, at which the timid quaked. So he drew himself up to his full height, and, affecting not to see the hesitancy of his companions, he said, in a tone of cheerful confidence:

"Let each man do his part. All I ask of you is to carry out the sentence I pronounce as a Judge. You know the crime of the citizens of this town, and, by virtue of the power I exercise over life and death, be it known to all that I, Cæsar, condemn—mark the word, condemn—every free male of Alexandria, of whatever age or rank, to die by the sword of a Roman warrior! This is a conquered city, which has forfeited every claim to quarter. The blood and the treasure of the inhabitants are the prize of my soldiery. Only"—and he turned to Timotheus—"this house of your god, which has given me shelter, with the priests and the treasure of great Serapis, are spared. Now it lies with each of you to show whether or no he is faithful to me. All of you"—and he addressed his friends—"all who do me service in avenging me for the audacious insults which have been offered to your sovereign, are assured of my imperial gratitude."

This declaration was not without effect, and murmurs of applause rose from the "friends" and favorites, though less enthusiastic than Caracalla was accustomed to hear. But the feebleness of this demonstration made him all, the prouder of his own undaunted resolve.

Macrinus was one of those who had most loudly approved him, and Caracalla rejoiced to think that this prudent counsellor should advise his drinking the cup of vengeance to the dregs. Intoxicated already before he had even sipped it, he called Macrinus and Zminis to his side, and with glowing looks impressed on them to take particular care that Melissa, with her father, Alexander, and Diodoros were brought to him alive.

"And remember," he added, "there will be many weeping mothers here by to-morrow morning; but there is one I must see again, and that not as a corpse--that bedizened thing in red whom I saw in the Circus—I mean the wife of Seleukus, of the Kanopic way."

CHAPTER X.

On the wide ascent leading to the Serapeum the prætorians stood awaiting Cæsar's commands.

They had not yet formed in rank and file, but were grouped round the centurion Martialis, who had come to tell them, sadly, of his removal to Edessa, and to take leave of his comrades. He gave his hand to each one of them in turn, and received a kindly pressure in return; for the stubborn fellow, though not of the cleverest, had proved himself a good soldier, and to many of them a trusty friend. There was not one who did not regret his going from among them. But Cæsar had spoken, and there was no gainsaying his orders. In the camp, after service, they might talk the matter over; for the present it were wise to guard their tongues.

The centurion had just said farewell to the last of his cohort, when the prefect, with the legate Quintus Flavius Nobilior, who commanded the legion, and several other higher officers, appeared among them. Macrinus greeted them briefly, and, instead of having the tuba blown as usual and letting them fall into their ranks, he told them to gather close round him, the centurions in front. He then disclosed to them the emperor's secret orders.

Cæsar, he began, had long exercised patience and mercy, but the insolence and malice of the Alexandrians knew no bounds; therefore, in virtue of his power over life and death, he had pronounced judgment upon them. To them, as being nearest to his person, he handed over the most remunerative part of the work of punishment. Whomsoever they found on the Kanopic way, the greatest and richest thoroughfare of the city, they were to cut down as they would the rebellious inhabitants of a conquered town. Only the women and children and the slaves were to be spared. If for this task, a hideous one at best, they chose to pay themselves out of the treasures of the citizens, nobody would blame them.

A loud cheer followed these orders, and many an eye gleamed brighter. Even the coolest among them seemed to see a broad, deep pool of blood into which he need only dip his hand and bring out something worth the catching. And the fish that were to be had there were not miserable carp, but heavy gold and silver vessels, and coins and magnificent ornaments. Macrinus then proceeded to inform the higher and lower officers of the course of action he had agreed upon with the emperor and Zminis. Seven trumpet-blasts from the terrace of the Serapeum would give the signal for the attack to begin. Then they were to advance, maniple on maniple;

but they were not required to keep their ranks—each man had his own work to do. The legion was to assemble again at sunset at the Gate of the Sun, at the eastern end of the road, after having swept it from end to end.

By order of the emperor, each man, however, must be particularly careful whom he cut down in any hiding-place, for Cæsar wished to give the following Alexandrians —who had sinned most flagrantly against him—the benefit of a trial, and they must therefore be taken alive. He then named the gem-cutter Heron, his son Alexander, and his daughter Melissa, the Alexandrian senator Polybius, his son Diodoros, and the wife of Seleukus.

He described them as well as he was able. For each one Cæsar promised a reward of three thousand drachmas, and for Heron's daughter twice as much, but only on condition of their being delivered up unhurt. It would therefore be to their own advantage to keep their eyes open in the houses, and to be cautious. Whoever should take the daughter of the gem-cutter—and he described Melissa once more—would render a special service to Cæsar and might reckon on promotion.

The centurion Julius Martialis stayed to hear the end of this discourse, and then hurriedly departed. He felt just as he had done in the war with the Alemanni when a red-haired German had dealt him a blow on the helmet with his club. His head whirled and swam as it did then—only to-day blood-red lights danced before his eyes instead of deep blue and gold. It was some time before he could collect his thoughts to any purpose; but when he did, he clinched his fists as he recalled Cæsar's malignant cruelty in forcing him away from his family.

Presently his large mouth widened into a satisfied smile. He was no longer in that company, and need take no part in the horrid butchery. In any other place he would no doubt have joined in it like the rest, glad of the rich booty; but here, in his own home, where his mother and wife and child dwelt, it seemed a monstrous and accursed deed. Besides the gem-cutter's family, in whom Martialis took no interest, Cæsar seemed to have a special grudge against the lady Berenike, whose husband Seleukus had been master to the centurion's father; nay, his own wife was still in the service of the merchant.

Not being skilled in any trade, he had entered the army early. As Evocatus he had married the daughter of a free gardener of Seleukus, and when he was ordered to Rome to join the prætorians his wife had obtained the post of superintendent of the merchant's villa at Kanopus. For this they had to thank the kindness of the lady Berenike and her now dead daughter Korinna; and he was honestly grateful to the wife of Seleukus, for, as his wife was established in the villa, he could leave her without anxiety and go with the army wherever it was ordered.

Having by this time reached the Kanopic street on his way to his family, he perceived the statues of Hermes and Demeter which stood on each side of the entrance to the merchant's house, and his slow mind recapitulated the long list of benefits he had received from Seleukus and his wife; a secret voice urged upon him that it was his duty to warn them.

He owed nothing to Cæsar, that crafty butcher, who out of pure malice could deprive an honest soldier of his only joy in life and cheat him of half his pay—for the prætorians had twice the wages of the other troops; and if he only knew some handicraft, he would throw away his sword to-day.

Here, at least, he could interfere with Cæsar's ruthless schemes, besides doing his benefactors a good turn. He therefore entered the house of the merchant, instead of pursuing his homeward way.

He was well known, and the mistress of the house was at once apprised of his arrival.

All the lower apartments were empty, the soldiers who had been quartered in them having joined the others at the Serapeum.

But what had happened to the exquisite garden in the impluvium? What hideous traces showed where the soldiers had camped, and, drunk with their host's costly wine, had given free play to their reckless spirits!

The velvet lawn looked like a stable-floor; the rare shrubs had been denuded of their flowers and branches. Blackened patches on the mosaic pavement showed where fires had been kindled; the colonnades were turned into drying-grounds for the soldiers' linen, and a rope on which hung some newly washed clothes was wound at one end round the neck of a Venus from the hand of Praxiteles, and at the other round the lyre of an Apollo fashioned in marble by Bryaxis. Some Indian shrubs, of which his father-in-law had been very proud, were trampled under foot; and in the great banqueting-hall, which had served as sleeping-room for a hundred prætorians, costly cushions and draperies were strewn, torn from the couches and walls to make their beds more comfortable.

Used to the sights of war as he was, the soldier ground his teeth with wrath at this scene. As long as he could remember, he had looked upon everything here with reverence and awe; and to think that his comrades had destroyed it all made his blood boil.

As he approached the women's apartments he took

fright. How was he to disclose to his mistress what threatened her?

But it must be done; so he followed the waiting-maid Johanna, who led him to her lady's living-room.

In it sat the Christian steward Johannes, with writing tablets and scrolls of papyrus, working in the service of his patroness. She herself was with the wounded Apollonaris; and Martialis, on hearing this, begged to be admitted to her.

Berenike was in the act of renewing the wounded soldier's bandages, and when the centurion saw how cruelly disfigured was the handsome, blooming face of the young tribune, to whom he was heartily attached, the tears rose to his eyes. The matron observed it, and witnessed with much surprise the affectionate greeting between the young noble and the plain soldier.

The centurion greeted her respectfully; but it was not till Nemesianus asked him how it was that the troops had been called to arms at this hour, that Martialis plucked up courage and begged the lady of the house to grant him an interview.

But Berenike had still to wash and bandage the wounds of her patient—a task which she always performed herself and with the greatest care; she therefore promised the soldier to be at his disposal in half an hour.

"Then it will be too late!" burst from the lips of the centurion; then she knew, by his voice and the terror-stricken aspect of the man whom she had known so long, that he meant to warn her, and there was but one from whom the danger could come.

"Cæsar?" she asked. "He is sending out his creatures to murder me?"

The imperious gaze of Berenike's large eyes so over-

powered the simple soldier as to render him speechless
for a while. But Cæsar had threatened his mistress's life
—he must collect himself, and thus he managed to stammer:

"No, lady, no! He will not have you killed—assuredly
not! On the contrary—they are to let you live when they
cut down the others!"

"Cut down!" cried Apollonaris, raising himself up and
staring horrified at this messenger of terror; but his brother
laid his hand upon the centurion's broad shoulder, and,
shaking him vigorously, commanded him as his tribune to
speak out.

The soldier, ever accustomed to obey, and only too
anxious that his warning should not come too late, disclosed in hurried words what he had learned from the
prefect. The brothers interrupted him from time to time
with some exclamation of horror or disgust, but Berenike
remained silent till Martialis stopped with a deep breath.

Then the lady gave a shrill laugh, and as the others
looked at her in amazement she said coolly:

"You men will wade through blood and shame with
that reprobate, if he but orders you to do so. I am only
a woman, and yet I will show him that there are limits
even to his malignity."

She remained for a few moments lost in thought, and
then ordered the centurion to go and find out where her
husband was.

Martialis obeyed at once, and no sooner was the door
closed behind him than she turned to the two brothers,
and addressing herself first to one and then to the other
with equal vehemence, she cried:

"Who is right now? Of all the villains who have
brought shame upon the throne and name of mighty
Cæsar, this is the most dastardly. He has written plainly

enough upon Apollinaris's face how much he values a brave soldier, the son of a noble house. And you, Nemesianus—are you not also an Aurelius? You say so; and yet, had he not chanced to let you care for your brother, you would at this moment be wandering through the city like a mad dog, biting all who crossed your path. Why do you not speak? Why not tell me once more, Nemesianus, that a soldier must obey his commander blindly?—And you, Apollinaris, will you dare still to assert that the hand with which Cæsar tore your face was guided only by righteous indignation at an insult offered to an innocent maiden? Have you the courage to excuse the murders by Caracalla of his own wife, and many other noble women, by his anxiety for the safety of throne and state? I, too, am a woman, and may hold up my head with the best; but what have I to do with the state or with the throne? My eye met his, and from that moment the fiend was my deadly enemy. A quick death at the hands of one of his soldiers seemed too good for the woman he hated. Wild beasts were to tear me to pieces before his eyes. Is that not sufficient for you? Put every abomination together, everything unworthy of an honorable man and abhorrent to the gods, and you have the man whom you so willingly obey. I am only the wife of a citizen. But were I the widow of a noble Aurelian and your mother—"

Here Apollinaris, whose wounds were beginning to burn again, broke in: "She would have counselled us to leave revenge to the gods. He is Cæsar!"

"He is a villain!" shrieked the matron—"the curse, the shame of humanity, a damnable destroyer of peace and honor and life, such as the world has never beheld before! To kill him would be to earn the gratitude and blessing of the universe. And you, the scions of a noble house, you, I say, prove that there still are men among so many slaves! It is Rome herself who calls you through me—like her, a woman maltreated and wounded to the heart's core—to bear arms in her service till she gives you the signal for making an end of the dastardly blood-hound!"

The brothers gazed at one another pale and speech-less, till at last Nemesianus ventured to say:

"He deserves to die, we know, a thousand deaths, but we are neither judges nor executioners. We can not do the work of the assassin."

"No, lady, we can not," added Apollinaris, and shook his wounded head energetically.

But the lady, nothing daunted, went on: "Who has ever called Brutus a murderer? You are young— Life lies before you. To plunge a sword into the heart of this monster is a deed for which you are too good. But I know a hand that understands its work and would be ready to guide the steel. Call it out at the right moment and be its guide!"

"And that hand?" Apollinaris asked in anxious ex-pectation.

"It is there," replied Berenike, pointing to Martialis, who entered the room at that moment.

Again the brothers interchanged looks of doubt, but the lady cried: "Consider for a moment! I would fain go hence with the certainty that the one burning desire shall be fulfilled, which still warms this frozen heart."

She motioned to the centurion, left the apartment with him, and preceded him to her own room. Arrived there, she ordered the astonished freedman Johannes, in his office as notary, to add a codicil to her will. In the event of her death, she left to Xanthe, the wife of the centurion Martialis, her lawful property the villa at Kanopus, with all it contained, and the gardens appertaining to it, for the free use of herself and her children.

The soldier listened speechless with astonishment. This gift was worth twenty houses in the city, and made its owner a rich man. But the testator was scarcely ten years older than his Xanthe, and, as he kissed the hem of his mistress's robe in grateful emotion, he cried: "May the gods reward you for your generosity; but we will pray and offer up sacrifices that it may be long before this comes into our hands!"

The lady shook her head with a bitter smile, and, drawing the soldier aside, she disclosed to him in rapid words her determination to quit this life before the prætorians entered the house. She then informed the horror-stricken man that she had chosen him to be her avenger. To him, too, the emperor had dealt a malicious blow. Let him remember that, when the time came to plunge the sword in the tyrant's heart. Should this deed, however, cost Martialis his life—which he had risked in many a battle for miserable pay—her will would enable his widow to bring up their children in happiness and comfort.

The centurion had thrown in a deprecatory word or two, but Berenike continued as if she had not heard him, till at last Martialis cried:

"You ask too much of me, lady. Cæsar is hateful to me, but I am no longer one of the prætorians, and am banished the country. How is it possible that I should approach him? How dare I, a common man—"

The lady came closer to him, and whispered:

"You will perform this deed to which I have appointed you in the name of all the just. We demand

16*

nothing from you but your sword. Greater men than you
—the two Aurelians—will guide it. At their word of
command you will do the deed. When they give you the
signal, brave Martialis, remember the unfortunate woman
in Alexandria whose death you swore to revenge. As
soon as the tribunes—"

But the centurion was suddenly transformed.

"If the tribunes command it," he interrupted with
decision, his dull eye flashing—"if they demand it of me,
I do it willingly. Tell them Martialis's sword is ever at
their service. It has made short work of stronger men
than that vicious stripling."

Berenike gave the soldier her hand, thanked him hurriedly, and begged him, as he could pass unharmed
through the city, to hasten to her husband's counting-
house by the water-side, to warn him and carry him her
last greetings.

With tears in his eyes Martialis did as she desired.
When he had gone, the steward began to implore his
mistress to conceal herself, and not cast away God's gift
of life so sinfully; but she turned from him resolutely
though kindly, and repaired once more to the brothers'
room.

One glance at them disclosed to her that they had
come to no definite conclusion; but their hesitation vanished
as soon as they heard that the centurion was ready to
draw his sword upon the emperor when they should give
the signal; and Berenike breathed a sigh of relief at this
resolution, and clasped their hands in gratitude.

They, too, implored her to conceal herself, but she
merely answered:

"May your youth grow into happy old age! Life can
offer me nothing more, since my child was taken from

me— But time presses— I welcome the murderers, now that I know that revenge will not sleep."

"And your husband?" interposed Nemesianus.

She answered with a bitter smile: "He? He has the gift of being easily consoled.—But what was that?"

Loud voices were audible outside the sick-room. Nemesianus stationed himself in front of the lady, sword in hand. This protection, however, proved unnecessary, for, instead of the prætorians, Johanna entered the room, supporting on her arm the half-sinking form of a young man in whom no one would have recognized the once beautifully curled and carefully dressed Alexander. A long caracalla covered his tall form; Dido the slave had cut off his hair, and he himself had disguised his features with streaks of paint. A large, broad-brimmed hat had slipped to the back of his head like a drunken man's, and covered a wound from which the red blood flowed down upon his neck. His whole aspect breathed pain and horror, and Berenike, who took him for a hired cut-throat sent by Caracalla, retreated hastily from him till Johanna revealed his name.

He nodded his head in confirmation, and then sank exhausted on his knees beside Apollinaris's couch and managed with great difficulty to stammer out: "I am searching for Philip. He went into the town—ill—out of his senses. Did he not come to you?"

"No," answered Berenike. "But what is this fresh blood? Has the slaughter begun?"

The wounded man nodded. Then he continued, with a groan: "In front of the house of your neighbor Milon— the back of my head—I fled—a lance—"

His voice failed him, and Berenike cried to the tribune: "Support him, Nemesianus! Look after him and tend him.   He is the brother of the maiden—you know— If I know you, you will do all in your power for him, and keep him hidden here till all danger is over."

"We will defend him with our lives!" cried Apollinaris, giving his hand to the lady.

But he withdrew it quickly, for from the impluvium arose the rattle of arms, and loud, confused noise.

Berenike threw up her head and lifted her hands as if in prayer.   Her bosom heaved with her deep breath, the delicate nostrils quivered, and the great eyes flashed with wrathful light.   For a moment she stood thus silent, then let her arms fall, and cried to the tribunes:

"My curse be upon you if you forget what you owe to yourselves, to the Roman Empire, and to your dying friend.   My blessing, if you hold fast to what you have promised."

She pressed their hands, and, turning to do the same to the artist, found that he had lost consciousness.   Johanna and Nemesianus had removed his hat and caracalla, to attend to his wound.

A strange smile passed over the matron's stern features. Snatching the Gallic mantle from the Christian's hand, she threw it over her own shoulders, exclaiming:

"How the ruffian will wonder when, instead of the living woman, they bring him a corpse wrapped in his barbarian's mantle!"

She then pressed the hat upon her head, and from a corner of the room where the brothers' weapons stood, selected a hunting-spear. She asked if this weapon might be recognized as belonging to them, and, on their answering in the negative, said:

"My thanks, then, for this last gift!"

At the last moment, she turned to the waiting-woman;

."Your brother will help you to burn Korinna's picture. No shameless gaze shall dishonor it again."

She tore her hand from that of the Christian, who with hot tears tried to hold her back; then, carrying her head proudly erect, she left them.

The brothers gazed shudderingly after her.

"And to know," cried Nemesianus, striking his forehead, "that our own comrades will slay her! Never were the swords of Rome so disgraced!"

"He shall pay for it!" replied the wounded man, gnashing his teeth. "Brother, we must avenge her!"

"Yes—her, and—may the gods hear me!—you too, Apollinaris," swore the other, lifting his hand as for an oath.

Loud screams, the clash of arms, and quick orders sounded from below and broke in upon the tribune's vow. He was rushing to the window to draw back the curtain and look upon the horrid deed with his own eyes, when Apollinaris called him back, reminding him of their duty toward Melissa's brother, who was lost if the others discovered him here.

Hereupon Nemesianus lifted the fainting youth in his strong arms and carried him into the adjoining room, laying him upon the mat which had served their faithful old slave as a bed. He then covered him with his own mantle, after hastily binding up the wound on his head and another on his shoulder.

By the time the tribune returned to his brother the noise outside had grown considerably less, only pitiable cries of anguish mingled with the shouts of the soldiers.

Nemesianus hastily pulled aside the curtain, letting such a flood of blinding sunshine into the room that Apollinaris covered his wounded face with his hands and groaned aloud.

"Sickening! Horrible! Unheard of!" cried his brother, beside himself at the sight that met his eyes. "A battle-field! What do I say? The peaceful house of a Roman citizen turned into shambles. Fifteen, twenty, thirty bodies on the grass! And the sunshine plays as brightly on the pools of blood and the arms of the soldiers as if it rejoiced in it all. But there— Oh, brother! our Marcipor —there lies our dear old Marci!—and beside him the basket of roses he had fetched for the lady Berenike from the flower-market. There they lie, steeped in blood, the red and white roses; and the bright sun looks down from heaven and laughs upon it!"

He broke down into sobs, and then continued, gnashing his teeth with rage: "Apollo smiles upon it, but he sees it; and wait—wait but a little longer, Tarautas! The god stretches out his hand already for the avenging bow! Has Berenike ventured among them? Near the fountain —how it flashes and glitters with the hues of Iris!—they are crowding round something on the ground— Mayhap the body of Seleukus. No—the crowd is separating. Eternal gods! It is she—it is the woman who tended you !"

"Dead?" asked the other.

"She is lying on the ground with a spear in her bosom. Now the legate—yes, it is Quintus Flavius Nobilior— bends over her and draws it out. Dead—dead! and slain by a man of our cohort!"

He clasped his hands before his face, while Apollinaris muttered curses, and the name of their faithful Marcipor, who had served their father before them, coupled with wild vows of vengeance.

Nemesianus at length composed himself sufficiently to follow the course of the horrible events going on below.

"Now," he went on, describing it to his brother, "now they are surrounding Rufus. That merciless scoundrel must have done something abominable, that even goes beyond what his fellows can put up with. There they have caught a slave with a bundle in his hand, perhaps stolen goods. They will punish him with death, and are themselves no better than he. If you could only see how they come swarming from every side with their costly plunder! The magnificent golden jug set with jewels, out of which the lady Berenike poured the Byblos wine for you, is there too!— Are we still soldiers, or robbers and murderers?"

"If we are," cried Apollinaris, "I know who has made us so."

They were startled by the approaching rattle of arms in the corridor, and then a loud knock at the chamber-door. The next moment a soldier's head appeared in the doorway, to be quickly withdrawn with the exclamation, "It is true—here lies Apollinaris!"

"One moment," said a second deep voice, and over the threshold stepped the legate of the legion, Quintus Flavius Nobilior, in all the panoply of war, and saluted the brothers.

Like them, he came of an old and honorable race, and was acting in place of the prefect Macrinus, whose office in the state prevented him from taking the military command of that mighty corps, the prætorians. Twenty years older than the twins, and a companion-in-arms of their father, he had managed their rapid promotion. He was their faithful friend and patron, and Apollinaris's misfortune had disgusted him no less than the order in the execution of which he was now obliged to take part.

Having greeted the brothers affectionately, observed

their painful emotion, and heard their complaints over the murder of their slave, he shook his manly head, and pointing to the blood that dripped from his boots and greaves,. "Forgive me for thus defiling your apartments," he said. "If we came from slaughtering men upon the field of battle, it could only do honor to the soldier; but this is the blood of defenceless citizens, and even women's gore is mixed with it."

"I saw the body of the lady of this house," said Nemesianus, gloomily. "She has tended my brother like a mother."

"But, on the other hand, she was imprudent enough to draw down Cæsar's displeasure upon her," interposed the Flavian, shrugging his shoulders. "We were to bring her to him alive, but he had anything but friendly intentions toward her; however, she spoiled his game. A wonderful woman! I have scarcely seen a man look death —and self-sought death—in the face like that! While the soldiers down there were massacring all who fell into their hands—those were the orders, and I looked on at the butchery, for, rather than—well, you can imagine that for yourselves—through one of the doors there came a tall, extraordinary figure. The wide brim of a travelling hat concealed the features, and it was wrapped in one of the emperor's fool's mantles. It hurried toward the maniple of Sempronius, brandishing a javelin, and with a sonorous voice reviling the soldiers till even my temper was roused. Here I caught sight of a flowing robe beneath the caracalla, and, the hat having fallen back, a beautiful woman's face with large and fear-inspiring eyes. Then it suddenly flashed upon me that this grim despiser of death, being a woman, was doubtless she whom we were to spare. I shouted this to my men; but—and at

that moment I was heartily ashamed of my profession—
it was too late. Tall Rufus pierced her through with his
lance. Even in falling she preserved the dignity of a
queen, and when the men surrounded her she fixed each
one separately with her wonderful eyes and spoke through
the death-rattle in her throat: 'Shame upon men and
soldiers who let themselves be hounded on like dogs to
murder and dishonor!' Rufus raised his sword to make
an end of her, but I caught his arm and knelt beside
her, begging her to let me see to her wound. With that
she seized the lance in her breast with both hands, and
with her last breath murmured, 'He desired to see the
living woman—bring him my body, and my curse with
it! Then with a last supreme effort she buried the spear
still deeper in her bosom; but it was not necessary.

"I gazed petrified at the high-bred, wrathful face, still
beautiful in death, and the mysterious, wide-open eyes
that must have flashed so proudly in life. It was enough
to drive a man mad. Even after I had closed her eyes
and spread the mantle over her—"

"What has been done with the body?" asked Apollinaris.

"I caused it to be carried into the house and the
door of the death-chamber carefully locked. But when I
returned to the men, I had to prevent them from tearing
Rufus to pieces for having lost them the large reward
which Cæsar had promised for the living prisoner."

"And you," cried Apollinaris, excitedly, "had to look
on while our men, honest soldiers, plundered the house—
which entertained many of us so hospitably—as if they
had been a band of robbers! I saw them dragging out
things which were used in our service only yesterday."

"The emperor—his permission!" sighed Flavius. "You

know how it is. The lowest instincts of every nature come out at such a time as this, and the sun shines upon it all. Many a poor wretch of yesterday will go to bed a wealthy man to-day. But, for all that, I believe much was hidden from them. In the room of the mistress of the house whence I have just come, a fire was still blazing in which a variety of objects had been burned. The flames had destroyed a picture—a small painted fragment betrayed the fact. They perhaps possessed masterpieces of Apelles or Zeuxis. This woman's hatred would lead her to destroy them rather than let them fall into the hands of her imperial enemy; and who can blame her?"

"It was her daughter's portrait," said Nemesianus, unguardedly.

The legate turned upon him in surprise.

"Then she confided in you?" he asked.

"Yes," returned the tribune, "and we are proud to have been so honored by her. Before she went to her death she took leave of us. We let her go; for we at least could not bring ourselves to lay hands upon a noble lady."

The officer looked sternly at him and exclaimed angrily:

"Do you suppose, young upstart, that it was less painful to me and many another among us? Cursed be this day, that has soiled our weapons with the blood of women and slaves, and may every drachma which I take from the plunder here bring ill-luck with it! Call the accident that has kept you out of this despicable work a stroke of good fortune, but beware how you look down upon those whose oath forces them to crush out every human feeling from their hearts! The soldier who takes part with his commander's enemy—"

He was interrupted by the entrance of Johanna, the Christian, who saluted the legate, and then stood confused and embarrassed by the side of Apollinaris's bed. The furtive glance she cast first at the side-room and then at Nemesianus did not pass unobserved by the quick eye of the commander, and with soldierly firmness he insisted on knowing what was concealed behind that door.

"An unfortunate man," was Apollinaris's answer.

"Seleukus, the master of this house?" asked Quintus Flavius, sternly.

"No," replied Nemesianus. "It is only a poor, wounded painter. And yet—the prætorians will go through fire and water for you, if you deliver up this man to them as their booty. But if you are what I hold you to be—"

"The opinion of hot-headed boys is of as little consequence to me as the favor of my subordinates," interposed the commander. "Whatever my conscience tells me is right, I shall do. Quick, now! Who is in there?"

"The brother of the maiden for whose sake Cæsar—" stammered the wounded man.

"The maiden whom you have to thank for that disfigured face?" cried the legate. "You are true Aurelians, you boys; and, though you may doubt whether I am the man you take me for, I confess with pleasure that you are exactly as I would wish to have you. The prætorians have slain your friend and servant; I give you that man's life to make amends for it."

With deep emotion Nemesianus seized his old friend's hands, and Apollinaris spoke words of gratitude to him from his couch. The officer would not listen to their thanks, and walked toward the door; but Johanna stood before him, and entreated him to allow the twins, whose servant had been killed, to take another, from whom they need have no fear of treachery. He had been captured in the impluvium by the prætorians while trying, in the face of every danger, to enter the house where the painter lay, to whose father he had belonged for many years. He would be able to tend both Apollinaris and Melissa's brother, and make it possible to keep Alexander's hiding-place a secret. The soldiery would be certain to penetrate as far as this, and other lives would be endangered if they should bear off the faithful servant, and force him on the rack to disclose where Melissa's father and relatives were hidden.

The legate promised to insure the freedom of Argutis.

A few more words of thanks and farewell, and Quintus had fulfilled his mission to the Aurelians. Shortly afterward the tuba sounded to assemble the plunderers still scattered about Seleukus's house, and Nemesianus saw the men marching in small companies into the great hall. They were followed by their armor-bearers, loaded with treasure of every kind; and three chariots drawn by fine horses, belonging to Seleukus and his murdered wife, conveyed such booty as was too heavy for men to carry. In the last of these stood the statue of Eros by Praxiteles. The glorious sunshine lighted up the smiling marble face; with the charm of bewitching beauty he seemed to gaze at the lurid crimson pools on the ground, and at the armed cohorts which marched in front to shed more blood and rouse more hatred.

As Nemesianus withdrew from the window, Argutis came into the room. The legate had released him; and when Johanna conducted the faithful fellow to Alexander's bedside, and he saw the youth lying pale and with closed eyes, as though death had claimed him for his prey, the old man dropped on kis knees, sobbing loudly.

CHAPTER XI.

While Alexander, well nursed by old Argutis and Johanna, lay in high fever, raving in his delirium of Agatha and his brother Philip, and still oftener calling for his sister, Melissa was alone in her hiding-place. It was spacious enough, indeed, for she was concealed in the rooms prepared to receive the Exoterics before the mysteries of Serapis. A whole suite of apartments, sleeping-rooms and halls, were devoted to their use, extending all across the building from east to west. Some of these were square, others round or polygonal, but most of them much longer than they were wide. Painters and sculptors had everywhere covered the walls with pictures in color and in high relief, calculated to terrify or bewilder the uninitiated. The statues, of which there were many, bore strange symbols, the mosaic flooring was covered with images intended to excite the fancy and the fears of the beholder.

When Melissa first entered her little sleeping-room, darkness had concealed all this from her gaze. She had been only too glad to obey the matron's bidding and go to rest at once. Euryale had remained with her some time, sitting on the edge of the bed to hear all that had happened to the girl during the last few hours, and she had impressed on her how she should conduct herself in case of her hiding-place being searched.

When she presently bade her good-night, Melissa repeated what the waiting-woman Johanna had told her of the life of Jesus Christ; but she expressed her interest in the person of the Redeemer in such a strange and heathen fashion that Euryale only regretted that she could not at

once enlighten the exhausted girl. With a hearty kiss
she left her to rest, and Melissa was no sooner alone than
sleep closed her weary young eyes.

It was near morning when she fell asleep; and when
she awoke, accustomed as she was to early hours, she
was startled to see how much of the day was spent. So
she rose hastily, and then perceived that the lady Euryale
must already have come to see her, for she found fresh
milk by the bedside, and some rolls of manuscript which
had not been there the day before. Her first thought
was for her imperilled relatives—her father, her brothers,
her lover—and she prayed for each, appealing first to the
Manes of her mother, and then to mighty Serapis and
kindly Isis, who would surely hear her in these precincts
dedicated to them.

The danger of those she loved made her forget her
own, and she vividly pictured to herself what might be
happening to each, what each one might be doing to
protect her and save her from the spies of the despot,
who by this time must have received her missive. Still,
the doubt whether he might not, after all, be magnanimous
and forgive her, rose again and again to her mind, though
everything led her to think it impossible.

During her prayer and in her care for the others she
had felt reasonably calm; but at the first thought of
Cæsar a painful agitation took possession of her soul, and
to overcome it she began an inspection of her spacious
hiding-place, where the lady Euryale had prepared her
to be amazed. And, indeed, it was not merely strange,
but it filled her heart and mind with astonishment and
terror. Wherever she looked, mystic figures puzzled her;
and Melissa turned from a picture in relief of beheaded
figures with their feet in the air, and a representation of

the damned stewing in great caldrons and fanning themselves with diabolical irony, only to see a painting of a
female form over whose writhing body boats were sailing,
or a four-headed ram, or birds with human heads flying
away from a mummified corpse. On the ceiling, too,
there was strange imagery; and when she looked at the
floor to rest her bewildered fancy, her eyes fell on a troop
of furies pursuing the wicked, or a pool of fire by which
horrible monsters kept guard.

And all these pictures were not stiff and formal like
Egyptian decorative art, but executed by Greek artists
with such liveliness and truth that they seemed about to
speak; and Melissa could have fancied many times that
they were moving toward her from the ceiling or the walls.

If she remained here long, she thought she must go
out of her mind; and yet she was attracted, here by a
huge furnace on whose metal floor large masses of fuel
seemed to lie, and there by a pool of water with crocodiles,
frogs, tortoises, and shells, wrought in mosaic.

Besides these and other similar objects, her curiosity
was aroused by some large chests in which book-rolls,
strange vessels, and an endless variety of raiment of every
shape and size were stored, from the simple chiton of the
common laborer to the star-embroidered talar of the adept.

Her protectress had told her that the mystics who
desired to be admitted to the highest grades here passed
through fire and water, and had to go through many
ceremonies in various costumes. She had also informed
her that the uninitiated who desired to enter these rooms
had to open three doors, each of which, as it was closed,
gave rise to a violent ringing; so that she might not venture
to get away from the room, into which, however, she could
bar herself. If the danger were pressing, there was the

door, known only to the initiated, which led to the steps and out of the building. Her sleeping-place, happily, was not far from a window looking to the west, so that she was able to refresh her brain after the bewildering impressions which had crowded on her in the inner rooms.

The paved roadway dividing the Serapeum from the stadium was at first fairly crowded; but the chariots, horsemen, and foot-passengers on whose heads she looked down from her high window, interested her as little as the wide inclosure of the stadium, part of which lay within sight.

A race, no doubt, was to be held there this morning, for slaves were raking the sand smooth, and hanging flowers about a dais, which was no doubt intended for Cæsar. Was it to be her fate to see the dreadful man from the place where she was hiding from him? Her heart began to beat faster, and at the same time questions crowded on her excited brain, each bringing with it fresh anxiety for those she loved, of whom, till now, she had been thinking with calm reassurance.

Whither had Alexander fled?

Had her father and Philip succeeded in concealing themselves in the sculptor's work-room?

Could Diodoros have escaped in time to reach the harbor with Polybius and Praxilla?

How had Argutis contrived that her letter should reach Cæsar's hands without too greatly imperilling himself?

She was quite unconscious of any guilt toward Caracalla. There had been, indeed, a strong and strange attraction which had drawn her to him; even now she was glad to have been of service to him, and to have helped him to endure the sufferings laid upon him by a cruel fate. But she could never be his. Her heart belonged to another, and this she had confessed in a letter—perhaps, indeed, too late. If he had a heart really capable of love, and had set it on her, he would no doubt think it hard that he should have bestowed his affections on a girl who was already plighted to another, even when she first appeared before him as a suppliant, though deeply moved by pity; still, he had certainly no right to condemn her conduct. And this was her firm conviction.

If her refusal roused his ire—if her father's prophecy and Philostratus's fears must be verified, that his rage would involve many others besides herself in ruin, then— But here her thought broke off with a shudder.

Then she recalled the hour when she had been ready and willing to be his, to sacrifice love and happiness only to soften his wild mood and protect others from his unbridled rage. Yes, she might have been his wife by this time, if he himself had not proved to her that she could never gain such power over him as would control his sudden fits of fury, or obtain mercy for any victim of his cruelty. The murder of Vindex and his nephew had been the death-blow of this hope. She best knew how seriously she had come to the determination to give up every selfish claim to future happiness in order that she might avert from others the horrors which threatened them; and now, when she knew the history of the Divine Lord of the Christians, she told herself that she had acted at that moment in a manner well-pleasing to that sublime Teacher. Still, her strong common sense assured her that to sacrifice the dearest and fondest wish of her heart in vain would not have been right and good, but foolish.

The evil deeds which Caracalla was now preparing to commit he would have done even if she were at his side. Of what small worth would she have seemed to him, and to herself!—When this tyranny should be overpast, when he should be gone to some other part of his immense empire, if those she loved were spared she could be happy —ah! so happy with the man to whom she had given her heart—as happy as she would have been miserable if she had become the victim to unceasing terrors as Cæsar's wife.

Euryale was right, and Fate, to which she had appealed, had decided well for her. That, the greatest conceivable sacrifice, would have been in vain; for the sake of a ruthless tyrant's foul desire she would have been guilty of the basest breach of faith, have poisoned her lover's heart and soul, and have wrecked his whole future life as well as her own. Away, then, with foolish doubts! Pythagoras was wise in warning her against torturing her heart. The die was cast. She and Caracalla must go on divergent roads. Her duty now was to fight for her own happiness against any who threatened it, and, above all, against the tyrant who had compelled her, innocent as she was, to hide like a criminal.

She was full of righteous wrath against the sanguinary persecutor, and holding her head high she went back into her sleeping-room to finish dressing. She moved more quickly than usual, for the book-rolls which Euryale had laid by her bed while she was still asleep attracted her eye with a suggestion of promise. Eager to know what their contents were, she took them up, drew a stool to the window, and tried to read.

But many voices came up to her from outside, and when she looked down into the road she saw troops of youths crowding into the stadium. What fine fellows they were, as they marched on, talking and singing; and she said to herself that Diodoros and Alexander were taller even than most of these, and would have been handsome among the handsomest! She amused herself for some time with watching them; but when the last man had entered the stadium, and they had formed in companies, she again took up the rolls.

One contained the gospel of Matthew and the other that of Luke.

The first, beginning with the genealogy, gave her a string of strange, barbarous names which did not attract her; so she took up the roll of Luke, and his simple narrative style at once charmed her. There were difficulties in it, no doubt, and she skipped sundry unintelligible passages, but the second chapter captivated her attention. It spoke of the birth of the great Teacher whom the Christians worshipped as their God. Angels had announced to the shepherds in the field that great joy should come on the whole world, because the Saviour was born; and this Saviour and Redeemer was no hero, no sage, but a child wrapped in swaddling-clothes and lying in a manger.

At this she smiled, for she loved little children, and had long known no greater pleasure than to play with them and help them. How many delightful hours did she owe to the grandchildren of their neighbor Skopas!

And this child, hailed at its birth by a choir of angels, had become a God in whom many believed! and the words of the angels' chant were: "Glory to God on high, and on earth peace, good-will toward men!"

How great and good it sounded! With eager excitement she fastened the rolls together, and on her features was depicted impatient longing to put an end to an intolerable state of things, as she exclaimed, though there was no one but herself to hear: "Ay, peace, salvation, good-will! Not this hatred, this thirst for revenge, this blood, this persecution, and, as their hideous fruit, this terror, these horrible, cruel fears—"

Here she was interrupted by the clatter of arms and rapping of hammers which came up from below. Cæsar's Macedonian guard and other infantry troops were silently coming up in companies and vanishing into the side-doors which led to the upper tiers of the stadium. What could this mean? Meanwhile carpenters were busy fastening up the chief entrance with wooden beams. It looked like closing up sluice-gates to hinder the invasion of a high tide. But the stadium was already full of men. She had seen thousands of youths march in, and there they stood in close ranks in the arena below her. Besides these, there were now an immense number of soldiers. They must all get out again presently, and what a crush there would be in the side exits if the vomitorium were closed! She longed to call down, to warn the carpenters of the folly of their act. Or was it that the youth of the town were to be pent into the stadium to hear some new and more severe decree, while some of the more refractory were secured?

It must be so. What a shame!

Then came a few vexilla of Numidian troopers at a slow pace. At their head, on a particularly high horse, rode the legate, a very tall man. He glanced up to the side where she was, and Melissa recognized the Egyptian Zminis. At this her hand sought the place of her heart, for she felt as though it had ceased to beat. What! This wretch, the deadly foe of her father and brother, here, at the head of the Roman troops? Something horrible, impossible, must be about to happen!

The sun was mirrored in the shining coat of his horse, and in the lictor's axe he bore, carrying it like a commander's staff. He raised it once, twice, and, high as she was above him, she could see how sharp the contrast was between the yellow whites of his eyes and the swarthy color of his face.

Now, for the third time, the bright steel of the axe flashed in the sunshine, and immediately after trumpet-calls sounded and were repeated at short intervals, which still, to her, seemed intolerably long.

How Melissa had presence of mind enough to count them she knew not, but she did. At the seventh all was still, and soon after a short blast on the tuba rang out from above, below, and from all sides of the stadium. Each went like an arrow to the heart of the anxious, breathless girl. From the moment when she had seen Zminis she had expected the worst, but the cry of rage and despair from a thousand voices which now split her ear told her how far the incredible reality outdid her most horrible imaginings.

Breathless, and with a throbbing brain, she leaned out as far as she could, and neither felt the burning sun —which was now beginning to fall on the western face of the temple—nor heeded the risk of being seen and involving herself and her protectress in ruin. Trembling like a gazelle in a frosty winter's night, she would gladly have withdrawn from the window, but she felt as if some spell held her there. She longed to shut her ears and eyes, but she could not help looking on. Her every instinct prompted her to shriek for help, but she could not utter a sound.

There she stood, seeing and hearing, and her low moaning changed to that laughter which anguish borrows from gladness when it has exhausted all forms of expression. At last she sank on her knees on the floor, and while she shed tears of pain still laughed shrilly, till she understood with sudden horror what was happening. She started violently; a sob convulsed her bosom; she wept, and these tears did her good.

When, at one in the afternoon, the sun fell full on her window, she had not yet found strength to move. A flood of bright light, in which whirled millions of motes, danced before her eyes; and as her breath sent the atoms flying, it passed through her mind that at this very moment the reprobate utterance of a madman's lips was blowing happiness, joy, peace, and hope out of the lives of many thousands—blowing them into nothingness, like the blast of a storm.

Then she commanded herself, for the horrible scene before her threatened to stamp itself on her eye like the image her father could engrave on an onyx; and she must avoid that, or give up all hope of ever being light-hearted again. Hardly an hour since she had seen the arena looking like a basket of fresh flowers, full of splendid, youthful men. Then the warriors of the Macedonian phalanx had taken their places on the long ranks of seats on which she looked down, with several cohorts of archers, brown Numidians and black Ethiopians, like inquisitive spectators of the expected show—but all in full armor. At first the youths and men had formed in companies, with singing, talk, and laughter, and here and there a satirical chant; but presently there had been squabbles with the town-watch, and while the younger and more careless still were gay enough, whole companies on the other hand had looked up indignantly at the Romans; some had anxiously questioned each other's eyes, or stared down in sullen dismay at the sand.

The hot, seething blood of these men—the sons of a

free city, and accustomed to a life of rapid action in hard work and frenzied enjoyment—took the delay very much amiss; and when it was rumored that the doors were being locked, impatience and distrust found emphatic utterance.   Timid whistling and other expressions of disapproval had been followed by louder demonstrations, for to be locked up was intolerable.   But the lictors and guards took no notice, after removing the member of the Museum who had perpetrated the epigram on Cæsar's mother.   This one, who had certainly gone too far, was to pay for all, it would seem.

Then the trumpets sounded, and the most heedless of the troop of youths began to feel acute anxiety and alarm.   From her high post of observation Melissa could see that, although the appearance of Zminis on the scene had caused a fever of agitation, they now broke their serried squares, wandered about as if undecided what to do, but prepared for the worst, and turned their curly heads now to this side and now to that, till the trumpet-blast from the seats attracted every eye upward, and the butchery began.

Did the cry, "Stop, wretches!" really break from Melissa's lips, or had she only intended to shout it down to the people in the stadium?   She did not know; but as she recollected the long rank of Numidians who, quick as lightning, lifted their curved bows and sent a shower of arrows down on the defenceless lads in the arena, she felt as though she had again shrieked out: "Stop!"   Then it seemed as though a storm of wind had torn thousands of straight boughs with metallic leaves that flashed in the sunshine from some huge invisible tree, and flung them into the arena; and, as her eye followed their fall, she could have fancied that she looked on a corn-field beaten down by a terrific hail-storm; but the boughs and leaves were lances and arrows, and each ear of corn cut down was a young and promising human being.

Zminis's preposterous suggestion had been acted on. Caracalla was avenged on the youth of Alexandria.

Not a tongue could wag now in abuse; every pair of young lips which had dared utter a scornful cry or purse up to whistle at the sight of Cæsar, was silenced forever—and, with the few guilty, a hundred times more who were innocent. She knew now why the great gate had been barred with beams, and why the troop had entered by the side-doors. The scene of the brilliant display had become a lake of blood, full of the dead and dying. Death had invaded the rows of seats; instead of laurel wreaths and prizes, deadly weapons were showered down into the arena. It seemed now as though the sun, with its blinding radiance, were mercifully fain to hinder the human eye from looking down on the horrible picture. To avoid the sickening sight, Melissa closed her eyes and dragged herself to her feet with an effort, to hide herself she knew not where.

But again there was a flourish of trumpets and loud acclamations, and again an irresistible power dragged her to the window.

A splendid quadriga had stopped at the gate of the stadium, surrounded by courtiers and guards. It was Caracalla's, for Pandion held the reins. Could Caracalla approve of this most horrible crime, organized by the wretch Zminis, by appearing on the scene; or might it not be that, in his wrath at the bloodthirsty zeal of his vile tool, he had come to dismiss him?

She hoped it was this; and, at any cost, she must know the truth as to this question, which was not based on mere curiosity. Holding one hand to her wildly beating heart, she looked across the blood-stained arena to the rows of seats and the dais decorated for Cæsar. There stood Caracalla, with the Egyptian at his side, pointing down at the arena with his finger. And what was to be seen on the spot he indicated was so horrible that she again shut her eyes, and this time she even covered them with her hands. But she would and must see, and once more she looked across; and the man whose assurances she had once believed, that it was only his care for the throne and state, and the compulsion of cruel fate which had ever made him shed blood—that man was standing side by side with the vile, ruthless spy whose tall figure towered far above his master's. His hand lay on the villain's arm, his eye rested on the corpse-strewn arena beneath; and now he raised his head, he turned his face, whose look of suffering had once moved her soul, toward her—and he laughed—she could see every feature—laughed so loud, so heartily, so gleefully, as she had never before seen him laugh. He laughed till his whole body and shoulders shook. Now he took his hand from the Egyptian's arm and pointed to the dead lying at his feet.

As she saw that laugh, of which she could not hear a sound, Melissa felt as though a hyena had yelled in her ear, and, yielding to an irresistible impulse, she looked down once more at the destruction of youthful life and happiness which had been wrought in one short hour—at the stream of blood after which so many bitter tears must flow. The sight indeed cut her to the heart, and yet she was thankful for it; for the first time the reckless cruelty of that laughing monster was evident in all its naked atrocity. Horror, aversion, loathing for that man to whom everything but power, cruelty, and cunning was as nothing, left no room for fear or pity, or even the least shade of self-reproach for having aroused in him a desire which she could not gratify.

She clinched her little fists, and, without vouchsafing another glance at the detestable butcher who had dared to cast his eyes on her, she withdrew from the window and cried out aloud, though startled at the sound of her own voice: "The time, the time! It is fulfilled for him this day!"

And how her eyes flashed and her bosom heaved and fell! With what a firm step did she pace the long suite of rooms, while the conviction was borne in on her that this deed of the vile assassin in the purple must bring the day of salvation and peace nearer—that day of which Andreas dreamed! As in her silent walk she passed the book-rolls which the lady Euryale had so quietly laid by her bedside, she took up the glad message of Luke with enthusiastic excitement, held it on high and shouted the angels' greeting which had impressed itself on her memory out of the window, as though she longed that Caracalla should hear it—"Peace on earth and good-will toward men!"

Then she resumed her walk through the rooms of the heathen mystics, repeating to herself all the comfortable words she had ever heard from Euryale and the freedman Andreas. The image of the divine Lord, who had come to bestow love on the world, and seal his sublime doctrine by sacrificing his life, rose up before her soul, and all that the Christian Johanna had told her of him made the picture clear, till he stood plainly before her, beautiful and gentle, in a halo of love and kindness, and yet strong and noble, for the crucified One was a heroic Saviour.

At this she remembered with satisfaction the struggle

she herself had fought, and her comfort when she had decided to sacrifice her own happiness to save others from sorrow. She now resolutely grasped the lady Euryale's book-rolls, for they contained the key to the inner chambers of the wondrous structure into whose fore-court life itself and her own intimate experience had led her. She was soon sitting with her back to the window, and unrolled the gospel of Matthew till she came to the first sentence which Euryale had marked for her with a red line.

Melissa was too restless to read straight on; as impatient as a child who finds itself for the first time in a garden which its parents have bought, she rushed from one tempting passage to another, applying each to herself, to those whom she loved, or in another sense to the disturber of her peace. With a joyful heart she now believed the promise which at first had staggered her, that the Kingdom of Heaven was at hand.

But her eye ran swiftly over the open roll, and was attracted by a mark drawing her attention to a whole chapter. She there read how Jesus Christ had gone up on to a mountain to address the vast multitude who followed him. He spoke of the kingdom of heaven, and of who those were that should be suffered to enter there. First, they were the poor in spirit—and she no doubt was one of those. Among those who were rich in spirit her brother Philip was certainly one of the richest, and whither had an acute understanding and restless brain led him that they so seldom gave his feelings time to make themselves heard?

Then the mourners were to be comforted. Oh, that she could have called the lady Berenike to her side and bid her participate in this promise!—And the meek—well, they might come to power perhaps after the downfall of the wretch who had flooded the world with blood, and who, of all men on earth, was the farthest removed from the spirit which gazed at her from this scripture, so mild and genial. Of those who hungered and thirsted after righteousness she again was one: they should be filled, and the lady Euryale and Andreas had already loaded the board for her.

The merciful, she read, should obtain mercy; and she, if any one, had a right to regard herself as a peace-maker: thus to her was the promise that she should be called one of the children of God.

But at the next verse she drew herself up, and her face was radiant with joy, for it seemed to have been written expressly for her; nay, to find it here struck her as a marvel of good fortune, for there stood the words: "Blessed are they which are persecuted for righteousness' sake: for theirs is the kingdom of heaven. Blessed are ye when men shall revile you, and persecute you, and shall say all manner of evil against you."

All these things had come upon her in these last days—though not, indeed, for the sake of Jesus Christ and righteousness, but only for the sake of those she loved; yet she would have been ready to endure the worst.

And the hapless victims in the arena! Might not the promised bliss await them too? Oh, how gladly would she have bestowed on them the fairest reward! And if this should indeed be their lot after death, where was the revenge of their bloodthirsty murderer?

Oh, that her mother were still alive—that she, Melissa, had been permitted to share this great consolation with her! In a brief aspiration she uplifted her soul to the beloved dead, and as she further unrolled the manuscript her eye fell on the words: "Love your enemies; bless them that curse you, and do good to them that hate you." No, she could not do this; this seemed to her to be too much to ask; even Andreas had not attained to this; and yet it must be good and lovely, if only because it helped to cement the peace for which she longed more fervently than for any other blessing.

Next she read: "For with what judgment ye judge, ye shall be judged," and she shuddered as she thought of the future fate of the man who had by treachery brought murder and death on an industrious and flourishing city as a punishment for the light words and jests of a few mockers, and the disappointment he had suffered from an insignificant girl.

But then, again, she breathed more freely, for she read: "Ask, and it shall be given unto you; seek, and ye shall find; knock, and it shall be opened." Could there be a more precious promise? And to her, she felt, it was already fulfilled; for her trembling finger had, as it were, but just touched the door, and lo! it stood open before her, and that which she had so long sought she had now found. But it was quite natural that it should be so, for the God of the Christians loved those who turned to him as His own children. Here it was written why those who asked should receive, and those who sought should find: "For what man is there of you whom if his son ask bread, will he give him a stone?"

If it were only as a peacemaker, she was already a child of Him who had asked this, and she might look for none but good gifts from Him. And what was commanded immediately after seemed to her so simple, so easy to obey, and yet so wise. She thought it over a little, and saw that in this precept—of which it was said that it was all the law and the prophets—there was in fact a rule which, if it were obeyed, must keep all mankind guiltless, and make every one happy. These words, she thought, should be written over every door and on every heart, as the winged sun was placed over every Egyptian temple gate, so that no one should ever forget them for an instant. She herself would bear them in mind and she repeated them to herself in an undertone. "Whatsoever ye would that men should do unto you, even so do unto them." Her eye wandered to the window and out to the stadium. How happy might the world be under a sovereign who should obey that law! And Caracalla?—No, she would not allow the contentment which filled her to be troubled by a thought of him.

With a hasty gesture she placed the ivory rod which she had found in the middle of the roll so as to flatten it out, and her eye fell on the words, "Come unto me, all ye that are weary and heavy-laden, and I will give you rest." To her, if to any one, was this glorious bidding addressed, for few had a heavier burden to bear. But indeed she already felt it lighter, after the terrors she had gone through on the very verge of despair; and now, even though she was still surrounded by dangers, she was far from feeling oppressed or terrified. Now her heart beat higher with hopeful gladness, and she was full of fervent gratitude as she told herself with lively and confident assurance that she had found a new guide, and, holding His loving and powerful hand, could walk in the way in safety. She felt as though some beloved hand had given her a vial of precious medicine that would cure every disease, when she had learned this verse, too, by heart. She would never forget the friendly promise and invitation that lay in those words. And to Alexander, at least—

poor, conscience-stricken Alexander—they might bring
some comfort, if not to her father and Philip, since
the call of the Son of God had gone forth to him too.
And she looked as happy as though she had heard something to rejoice her heart and soul. Her red lips parted
once more, showing the two white teeth which were never
to be seen but when she smiled and some real happiness
stirred her soul.

She fancied she was alone, but, even while she was
reading the words in which the Saviour called to him the
weary and heavy-laden, the lady Euryale had noiselessly
opened a secret door leading to Melissa's hiding-place,
known only to herself and her husband, and had come
close to her. She now stood watching the girl with
surprise and astonishment, for she had expected to find
her bedside herself, desperate, and more than ever need-
ing comfort and soothing. The unhappy girl must have
been drawn to the window by the cries of the massacred,
and at least have glanced at the revolting scene in the
stadium. She would have thought it more natural if she
had found Melissa overcome by the horrors she had
witnessed, half distraught or paralyzed by distress and
rage. And there sat the young creature, whom she
knew to be soft-hearted and gentle, smiling and with
beaming eyes—though those eyes must have rested on
the most hideous spectacle—looking as though the roll
in her lap were the first enchanting raptures of a lover.
The book lying on Melissa's knees was the gospel of
Matthew, which she herself early this morning, while the
girl was still sleeping, had laid by her side to comfort her
and give her some insight into the blessings of Christianity.
But these scriptures, so sacred to Euryale, had seemed

to count for less than nothing to this heathen girl, the sister of Philip the skeptic.

Euryale loved Melissa, but far dearer to her was the book to whose all-important contents the maiden seemed to have closed her heart in coldness.

It was for Melissa's sake that, when the high-priest's dwelling was searched by the new magistrate's spies from cellar to garret, she had patiently submitted to her husband's hard words. She had liked to think that she might bring this girl as a pure white lamb into the fold of the Good Shepherd, who to herself was so dear, and through whom her saddened life had found new charm, her broken heart new joys. A few hours since she had assured her friend Origen that she had found a young Greek who would prove to him that a heathen who had gone through the school of suffering with a pure and compassionate heart needed but a sign, a word of flame, to recognize at once the beatitude of Christianity and long to be baptized. And here she discovered the maiden of whom she had such fair hopes, with a smile on her lips and beaming looks, while so many innocent men were being slaughtered, as though this were a joy to her!

What had become of the girl's soft, tender heart, which but yesterday had been ready for self-sacrifice if only she might secure the well-being of those she loved? Was she, Euryale, in her dotage, that she could be so deceived by a child?

Her heart beat faster with disappointment; and yet she would not condemn the sinner unheard. So, with a swift impulse she took the roll up from Melissa's lap, and her voice was sorrowful rather than severe as she exclaimed:

"I had hoped, my child, that these scriptures might

prove to you, as to so many before you, a key to open the gates of eternal truth. I thought that they would comfort you, and teach you to love the sublime Being whose exemplary life and pathetic death are no longer unknown to you, since Johanna told you the tale. Nay, I believed that they might presently arouse in you the desire to join us who—"

But here she stopped, for Melissa had fallen on her neck, and while Euryale, much amazed, tried to release herself from her embrace, the girl cried out, half laughing and half in tears:

"It has all come about as you expected! I will live and die faithful to that sublime Saviour, whom I love. I am one of you—yes, mother, now—even before the baptism I long for. For I was weary and heavy-laden above any, and the word of the Lord hath refreshed me. This book has taught me that there is but one path to true happiness, and it is that which is shown us by Jesus Christ. O lady, how much fairer would our life on earth be if what is written here concerning blessedness were stamped on every heart! I feel as though in this hour I had been born again. I do not know myself; and how is it possible that a poor child of man, in such fearful straits and peril as I, and after such a scene of horror, should feel so thankful and so full of the purest gladness?"

The matron clasped her closely in her arms, and her tears bedewed the girl's face while she kissed her again and again; and the cheerfulness which had just now hurt her so deeply she now regarded as a beautiful miracle.

Her time was limited, for she was watched, and she had seized the half-hour during which the town-guard had been mustered in the square to report progress. So Melissa had to be brief, and in a few hasty words she told her friend all that she had seen and heard from her high window, and how the gospel of Matthew had been to her glad tidings; how it had given her comfort and filled her soul with infinite happiness in this the most terrible hour of her life. At this, Euryale also forgot the horrors which surrounded them, till Melissa called her back to the dreadful present; for, with bowed head and in deep anxiety, she desired to know whether her friend knew anything of her relations and Diodoros.

The matron had a painful struggle with herself. It grieved her to inflict anxiety on Melissa's heart, as she stood before her eyes like one of the maidens robed in white and going to be baptized, to whom presents were given on the festive occasion, and who were carefully sheltered from all that could disturb them and destroy the silent, holy joy of their souls. And yet the question must be answered: so she said that of the other two she knew nothing, any more than of Berenike and Diodoros, but that of Philip she had bad news. He was a noble man, and, notwithstanding his errors in the search after truth, well worthy of pity. At this, Melissa in great alarm begged to be told what had happened to her brother, and the lady Euryale confessed that he no longer walked among the living, but she did not relate the manner of his death; and she bade the weeping girl to seek for comfort from the Friend of all who grieve and whom she now knew; but to keep herself prepared for the worst, in full assurance that none are tried beyond what they are able to bear, for that the fury of the bloodthirsty tyrant hung like a black cloud over Alexandria and its inhabitants.

She herself, merely by coming to Melissa, exposed herself to great danger, and she could not see her again till the morrow. To Melissa's inquiry as to whether it was her refusal to be his which had brought such a fearful fate on the innocent youth of Alexandria, Euryale could reply in the negative; for she had heard from her husband that it was a foul epigram written by a pupil of the Museum which had led to Cæsar's outbreak of rage.

With a few soothing words she pointed to a basket of food which she had brought with her, showed the girl once more the secret door, and embraced her at parting as fondly as though Heaven had restored to her in Melissa the daughter she had lost.

CHAPTER XII.

MELISSA was once more alone.

She now knew that Philip walked no longer among the living. He must have fallen a victim to the fury of the monster, but the thought that he might have been slain for her sake left her mind no peace.

She felt that with the death of the youth—so gifted, and so dear to her—a corner-stone had been torn from the paternal house.

In the loving circle that surrounded her, death had made another gap which yawned before her, dismal and void.

One storm more, and what was left standing would fall with the rest.

Her tears flowed fast, and the torturing thought that the emperor had slain her brother as a punishment for his sister's flight pierced her to the heart.

Now, indeed, she belonged to the afflicted and oppressed; and as yesterday, in the trouble of her soul, she had called upon Jesus Christ, though she scarcely knew of Him then, so now she lifted up her heart to Him who had become her friend, praying to Him to remember His

promise of comfort when she came to Him weary and
heavy-laden.

And while she tried to realize the nature of the Saviour
who had laid down his life for others, she remembered all
she had dared for her father and brothers, and what fate
had been hers during the time since; and she felt she
might acknowledge to herself that even if Philip had met
his death because of Caracalla's anger toward her, at any
rate she would never have approached Cæsar had she
not wanted to save her father and brothers. She had
never glossed over any wrong-doing of her own; but her
open and truthful nature was just as little inclined to the
torment of self-reproach when she was not absolutely
certain of having committed a fault.

In this case she was not quite sure of herself; but she
now remembered a saying of Euryale and Andreas which
she had not understood before. Jesus Christ, it said, had
taken upon Himself the sins of the world. If she understood its meaning aright, the merciful Lord would surely
forgive her a sin which she had committed unwittingly
and in no wise for her own advantage. Her prayer grew
more and more to be a discourse with her new-found
friend; and, as she finished, she felt absolutely sure that
He at least understood her and was not angry with her.
This reassured her, but her cheerfulness had fled, and she
could read no more.

Deeply troubled, and more and more distressed as
time went on by new disturbing thoughts, she hurriedly
-paced from side to side of the long, narrow chamber in
the gathering darkness. The revolting images around her
began to affect her unbearably once more. Near her
chamber, to the west, lay the race-course with its horrible
scenes; so she turned to the eastern end that looked out

upon the street of Hermes, where the sight could scarcely
be so terrible as from the windows at the opposite end.
But she was mistaken; for, looking down upon the pavement, she perceived that this, too, swam with blood, and
that the ground was covered with corpses.

Seized with a sudden horror, she flew back into the
middle of the long room. There she remained standing,
for the scene of slaughter in the west was still more ap-
palling than that from which she had just fled. She could
not help wondering who could here have fallen a victim
to the tyrant after he had swept all the youth of the
city off the face of the earth.

The evening sun cast long shafts of golden light
across the race-course and in at the western window, and
Melissa knew how quickly the night fell in Alexandria. If
she wished to find out who they were who had been sacrificed to the fury of the tyrant, it must be done at once,
for the immense building of the temple already cast long
shadows. Determined to force herself to look out, she
walked quickly to the eastern window and gazed below.
But it was some moments before she had the fortitude to
distinguish one form from another; they melted before her
reluctant eyes into one repulsive mass.

At last she succeeded in looking more calmly and
critically.

Not heaped on one another as on the race-course,
hundreds of Caracalla's victims lay scattered separately
over the open square as far as the entrance to the street
of Hermes. Here lay an old man with a thick beard,
probably a Syrian or a Jew; there, his dress betraying
him, a seaman; and farther on—no, she could not be
mistaken—the youthful corpse that lay so motionless just

beneath the window was that of Myrtilos, a friend of Philip, and, like him, a member of the Museum.

In a fresh fit of terror she was going to flee again into her dreadful hiding-place, when she caught sight of a figure leaning against the basin of the beautiful marble fountain just in front of the eastern side-door of the Serapeum, and immediately below her. The figure moved, and could therefore only be wounded, not dead; and round the head was bound a white cloth, reminding her of her beloved, and thereby attracting her attention. The youth moved again, turning his face upward, and with a low cry she leaned farther forward and gazed and gazed, unmindful of the danger of being seen and falling a victim to the tyrant's fury. The wounded, living man—there, he had moved again—was no other than Diodoros, her lover!

Till the last glimmer of light disappeared she stood at the window with bated breath, and eyes fixed upon him. No faintest movement of his escaped her, and at each one, trembling with awakening hope, she thanked Heaven and prayed for his rescue. At length the growing darkness hid him from her sight. With every instant the night deepened, and without thinking, without stopping to reflect—driven on by one absorbing thought—she felt her way back to her couch, beside which stood the lamp and fire-stick, and lighted the wick; then, inspired with new courage at the thought of rescuing her lover from death, she considered for a moment what had best be done.

It was easy for her to get out. She had a little money with her; on her peplos she wore a clasp that had once belonged to her mother, with two gems in it from her father's hand, and on her rounded arm a golden circlet.

With these she could buy help. The only thing now was to disguise herself.

On the great, smoke-blackened metal plate over which those mystics passed who had to walk through fire, there lay plenty of charcoal, and yonder hung robes of every description. The next moment she had thrown off her own, in order to blacken her glistening white limbs and her face with soot. Among the sewing materials which the lady Euryale had laid beside the scrolls was a pair of scissors. These the girl seized, and with quick, remorseless hand cut off the long, thick locks that were her brother's and her lover's delight. Then she chose out a chiton, which, reaching only to her knees, gave her the appearance of a boy. Her breath came fast and her hands trembled, but she was already on her way to the secret door through which she should flee from this place of horror, when she came to a standstill, shaking her head gently. She had looked around her, and the wild disorder she was leaving behind her in the little room went against her womanly feelings. But though this feeling would not in itself have kept her back, it warned her to steady her mind before leaving the refuge her friend had accorded to her. Thoughtful, and accustomed to have regard for others, she realized at once how dangerous it might prove to Euryale if these unmistakable traces of her presence there should be discovered by an enemy. The kindness of her motherly friend should not bring misfortune upon her. With active presence of mind she gathered up her garments from the floor, swept the long locks of hair together, and threw them all, with the sewing and the basket that had contained the food, into the stove on the hearth and set them alight. The scissors she took with her as a weapon in case of need.

Then, laying the books of the gospels beside the other manuscripts, and casting a last look round to assure herself that every sign of her presence had been destroyed, she addressed one more prayer to the tender Comforter of the afflicted, who has promised to save those that are in danger.

She then opened the secret door.

With a beating heart, and yet far more conscious of the desire to save her lover while there was yet time than of the danger into which she was rushing headlong, she flitted down the hidden staircase as lightly as a child at play. So much time had been lost in clearing the room —and yet she could not have left it so!

She had not forgotten where to press, so that the heavy stone which closed the entrance should move aside; but as she sprang from the last step her lamp had blown out, and blackest darkness concealed the surface of the smooth granite wall which lay between her and the street.

What if, when she got outside, she should be seen by the lictors or spies?

At this thought fear overcame her for the first time. As she felt about the door her hands trembled and beads of perspiration stood upon her brow. But she must go to her wounded lover! When any one was bleeding to death every moment might bring the terrible "too late." It meant Diodoros's death if she did not succeed in opening the granite slab.

She took her hands from the stone and forced herself, with the whole strength of her will, to be calm.

Where had been the place by pressing which the granite might be moved?

It must have been high up on the right side. She carefully followed with her fingers the groove in which the stone lay, and having recalled its shape by her sense of touch, she began her search anew. Suddenly she felt something beneath her finger-tips that was colder than the stone. She had found the metal bolt! With a deep breath, and without stopping to think of what might be before her, she pressed the spring; the slab turned—one step—and she was in the street between the race-course and the Serapeum.

All was still around her. Not a sound was to be heard except from the square to the north of the temple, where all who carried arms had gathered together to enjoy the wine which flowed in streams as a mark of the emperor's approbation, and from the inner circle of the race-course voices were audible. Of the citizens not one dared show himself in the streets, although the butchery had ceased at sundown. All who did not carry the imperial arms had shut themselves up in their houses, and the streets and squares were deserted since the soldiers had assembled in front of the Serapeum.

No one noticed Melissa. The dangers that threatened her from afar troubled her but little. She only knew that she must go on—go on as fast as her feet would carry her, if she were to reach her loved one in time.

Skirting the south side of the temple, in order to get to the fountain, her chief thought was to keep in its shadow. The moon had not yet risen, and they had forgotten to light either the pitch-pans or the torches which usually burned in front of the south façade of the temple. They had been too busy with other matters to-day, and now they needed all hands in heaping the bodies together. The men whose voices sounded across to her from the race-course had already begun the work. On—she must hurry on!

But it was not so easy as last night. Her light sandals were wet through, and there was ever a fresh impediment in her way. She knew what it was that had wetted her foot—blood—noble, human blood—and every obstacle against which she stumbled was a human body. But she would not let herself dwell upon it, and hurried on as though they were but water and stones, ever seeing before her the image of the wounded youth who leaned against the basin.

Thus she reached the east side of the temple. Already she could hear the splashing of the fountain, she saw the marble gleaming through the darkness, and began seeking for the spot where she had seen her lover. She suddenly stopped short; at the same time as herself, lights faint and bright were coming along from the south, from the entrance of the street that led to Rhakotis, and down to the water. She was in the middle of the street, without a possibility of concealing herself except in one of the niches of the Serapeum.

Should she abandon him? She must go on, and to seek protection in the outer wall of the temple meant turning back. So she stood still and held her breath as she watched the advancing lights.

Now they stopped. She heard the rattle of arms and men's voices. The lantern-bearers were being detained by the watch. They were the first soldiers she had seen, the others being engaged in drinking, or in the work on the race-course. Would the soldiers find her, too? But, no! They moved on, the torch-bearers in front, toward the street of Hermes.

Who were those people who went wandering about among the slain, turning first to this side and then to that, as if searching for something? They could not be robbing the dead, or the watch would have seized them.

Now they came quite close to her, and she trembled with fright, for one of them was a soldier. The light of the lantern shone upon his armor. He went before a man and two lads who were following a laden ass, and in one of them Melissa recognized with beating heart a garden slave of Polybius, who had often done her a service.

And now she took courage to look more closely at the man—and it was—yes, even in the peasant's clothes he wore he could not deceive her quick eyes—it was Andreas!

She felt that every breath that came from her young bosom must be a prayer of thanksgiving; nor was it long before the freedman recognized Melissa in the light-footed black boy who seemed to have sprung from the earth and was pointing the way; and he, too, felt as if a miracle had been wrought.

Like fair flowers that spring up round a scaffold over which the hungry ravens croak and hover, so here, in the midst of death and horror, joy and hope began to blossom in thankful hearts. Diodoros lived! No word—only a fleeting pressure of the hand and a quick look passed between the elderly man and the maiden—who looked like a boy scarcely passed his school-days—to show what they felt as they knelt beside the wounded youth and bound up the deep gash in his shoulder dealt by the sword that had felled him.

A little while afterward, Andreas drew from the pannier which the ass carried, and from which he had already taken bandages and medicine, a light litter of matting. He then lifted Melissa on to the back of the beast of burden, and they all moved onward.

The sights that surrounded them as long as they were near the Serapeum forced her to close her eyes, especially when the ass had to walk round some obstruction, or when it and its guide waded through slimy pools. She could not forget that they were red, nor whence they came; and this ride brought her moments in which she thought to expire of shuddering horror and sorrow and wrath.

Not till they reached a quiet lane in Rhakotis, where they could advance without let or hindrance, did she open her eyes. But a strange, heavy pain oppressed her that she had never felt before, and her head burned so that she could scarcely see Andreas and the two slaves, who, strong in the joy of knowing that their young lord was alive, carried Diodoros steadily along in the litter. The soldier—it was the centurion Martialis, who had been banished to the Pontus—still accompanied them, but Melissa's aching head pained her so much that she did not think of asking who he was or why he was with them.

Once or twice she felt impelled to ask whither they were taking her, but she had not the power to raise her voice. When Andreas came to her side and pointed to the centurion, saying that without him he would never have succeeded in saving her beloved, she heard it only as a hollow murmur, without any consciousness of its meaning. Indeed, she wished rather that the freedman would keep silent when he began explaining his opportune arrival at the fountain, which must seem such a miracle to her.

The slave-brand on his arm had enabled him to penetrate into the house of Seleukus, where he hoped to obtain news of her. There Johanna had led him to Alexander, and with the Aurelians he had found the centurion and the slave Argutis. Argutis had just returned from the lady Euryale, and swore that he had seen the wounded Diodoros. Andreas had then declared his intention of bringing the son of his former master to a place of safety, and the centurion had been prevailed upon by the young tribunes to open a way for the freedman through the sentinels. The gardeners of Polybius, with their ass, had been detained in an inn on this side of Lake Mareotis by the closing of the harbor, and Andreas had taken the precaution of making use of them. Had it not been for the centurion, who was known to the other soldiers, the watch would never have allowed the freedman to get so far as the fountain; Andreas therefore begged Melissa to thank their preserver. But his words fell upon her ear unnoticed, and when the strange soldier left her to devote himself again to Diodoros she breathed more freely, for his rapidly spoken words hurt her.

If he would only not come again—only not speak to her!

She had even ceased to look for her lover. Her one desire was to see and hear nothing. When she did force herself to raise her heavy, throbbing lids, she noticed that they were passing poor-looking houses which she never remembered seeing before. She fancied, however, from the damp wind that blew in her face and relieved her burning head, that they must be nearing the lake or the sea. Surely that was a fishing-net hanging yonder on the fence round a hut on which the light of the lantern fell. But perhaps it was something quite different, for the images that passed before her heavy eyes began to mingle confusedly, to repeat themselves, and be surrounded by a ring of rainbow colors. Her head had grown so heavy that her mind had lost all sense of hope or fear; only her thoughts stirred faintly as the procession moved on and on through the darkness, without a pause for rest.

When they had passed the last of the huts she managed to look upward.

The evening star stood out clear against the sky, and she seemed to see the other stars revolving quickly round it.

Her mouth was painful and parched, and more than once she had been seized with giddiness, which forced her to hold tightly to the saddle.

Now they stopped beside a large piece of water, and she felt strangely well and light of heart. That must be the dear, familiar lake. And there stood Agatha waving to her, and at her side the lady Euryale under the spreading shade of a mighty palm. Bright sunshine flooded them both, and yet it was the night; for there was the evening star beaming down upon her.

How could that be?

Yet, when she tried to understand the mystery, her head pained her so, and she turned so giddy, that she clutched the neck of the ass to save herself from falling.

When she raised herself again she saw a large boat, out of which several people came to meet them, the foremost of them a tall man in a long, white garment. That was no dream, she was quite certain. And yet—why did the lantern which one of them held aloft burn her face so much and not his? Oh, how it burned!

Everything turned in a circle round her, and grew dark before her eyes.

But not for long; suddenly it became light as day, and she heard a deep and friendly voice calling her by name. She answered without fear, "Here am I," and saw before her a stranger in a long, white robe, of lofty yet gentle aspect, just as she had imagined the crucified Saviour of the Christians, and in her ear sounded the loving message with which he bids the weary and heavy-laden come to him that he may give them rest.

How gentle, how consoling, and how full of gracious promise were the words, and how gladly would she do his bidding! "Here am I!" she cried again, and saw the arms of the white-robed man stretched out to receive her. She staggered toward him, and felt a firm and manly hand clasp hers, and then rest in blessing on her throbbing brow. All grew dark again before her, and she saw and heard no more.

Andreas had lifted her from the ass and supported her, while the two Christians thanked the soldier for his timely aid.

Having assured them that he had had no thought of helping them, but only of obeying his superior officers, he disappeared into the night, and the freedman lifted Melissa in his strong arms and carried her down to Zeno's boat, which was waiting for them.

"Her mind wanders," said the freedman, with a loving look at the precious burden in his arms. "Her spirit is strong, but the shocks she has sustained this day have been too much for her. 'Thou wilt give me rest,' were her last words before losing consciousness. Can she have been thinking of the promise of the Saviour?"

"If not," answered the deep, musical voice of Zeno, "we will show her Him who called the little children to Him, and the weary and heavy-laden. She belongs to them, and she will see that the Lord fulfills what He so lovingly promises."

"One of Christ's sayings, and repeated by Paul in his letter to the Galatians, has taken great hold upon her," added Andreas, "and I think that in these days of terror, for her, too, the fullness of time has come."

As he spoke he stepped on to the plank which led to the boat from the shore: Diodoros had already been placed on board. When Andreas laid the girl on the cushioned seat in the little cabin, he exclaimed, with a sigh of relief, "Now we are safe!"

CHAPTER XIII.

CARACALLA'S evening meal was ended, and for years past his friends had never seen the gloomy monarch in so mad a mood. The high-priest of Serapis, with Dio Cassius the senator, and a few others of his suite, had not indeed appeared at table; but the priest of Alexander, the prefect Macrinus, his favorites Theocritus, Pandion, Antigonus, and others of their kidney, had crowded round him, had drunk to his health, and wished him joy of his glorious revenge.

Everything which legend or history had recorded of similar deeds was compared with this day's work, and it was agreed that it transcended them all. This delighted the half-drunken monarch. To-day, he declared with flashing eyes, and not till to-day, he had dared to be entirely what Fate had called him to be—at once the judge and the executioner of an accursed and degenerate race. As Titus had been named "the Good," so he would be called "the Terrible." And this day had secured him that grand name, so pleasing to his inmost heart.

"Hail to the benevolent sovereign who would fain be terrible!" cried Theocritus, raising his cup; and the rest of the guests echoed him.

Then the number of the slain was discussed. No one could estimate it exactly. Zminis, the only man who could have seen everything, had not appeared. Fifty,

sixty, seventy thousand Alexandrians were supposed to
have suffered death; Macrinus, however, asserted that
there must have been more than a hundred thousand,
and Caracalla rewarded him for his statement by exclaiming loudly: "Splendid! grand! Hardly comprehensible
by the vulgar mind! But, even so, it is not the end of
what I mean to give them. To-day I have racked their
limbs; but I have yet to strike them to the heart, as they
have stricken me!"

He ceased, and after a short pause repeated unhesitatingly, and as though by a sudden impulse, the lines with
which Euripides ends several of his tragedies:

> "Jove in high heaven dispenses various fates;
> And now the gods shower blessings which our hope
> Dared not aspire to, now control the ills
> We deemed inevitable. Thus the god
> To these hath given an end we never thought." *

And this was the end of the revolting scene, for, as
he spoke, Cæsar pushed away his cup and sat staring
into vacancy, so pale that his physician, foreseeing a fresh
attack, brought out his medicine vial.

The prætorian prefect gave a signal to the rest that
they should not notice the change in their imperial host,
and he did his best to keep the conversation going, till
Caracalla, after a long pause, wiped his brow and exclaimed hoarsely: "What has become of the Egyptian?
He was to bring in the living prisoners—the living, I say!
Let him bring me them."

He struck the table by his couch violently with his
fist; and then, as if the clatter of the metal vessels on it
had brought him to himself, he added, meditatively: "A

* Potter's translation.

hundred thousand! If they burned their dead here, it would take a forest to reduce them to ashes."

"This day will cost him dear enough as it is," the high-priest of Alexander whispered; he, as idiologos, having to deposit the tribute from the temples and their estates in the imperial treasury. He addressed his neighbor, old Julius Paulinus, who replied:

"Charon is doing the best business to-day. A hundred thousand obolus in a few hours. If Tarautas reigns over us much longer, I will farm his ferry!"

During this whispered dialogue Theocritus the favorite was assuring Cæsar in a loud voice that the possessions of the victims would suffice for any form of interment, and an ample number of thank-offerings into the bargain.

"An offering!" echoed Caracalla, and he pointed to a short sword which lay beside him on the couch. "That helped in the work. My father wielded it in many a fight, and I have not let it rust. Still, I doubt whether in my hands and his together it has ever before yesterday slaughtered a hundred thousand."

He looked round for the high-priest of Serapis, and after seeking him in vain among the guests, he exclaimed:

"The revered Timotheus withdraws his countenance from us to-day. Yet it was to his god that I dedicated the work of vengeance. He laments the loss of worshippers to great Serapis, as you, Vertinus"—and he turned to the idiologos—"regret the slain tax-payers. Well, you are thinking of my loss or gain, and that I can not but praise. Your colleague in the Service of Serapis has nothing to care for but the honor of his god; but he does not succeed in rising to the occasion. Poor wretch! I will give him a lesson. Here Epagathos, and you, Claudius

—go at once to Timotheus; carry him this sword. I devote it to his god. It is to be preserved in his holy of holies, in memory of the greatest act of vengeance ever known. If Timotheus should refuse the gift— But no, he has sense—he knows me!"

He paused, and turned to look at Macrinus, who had risen to speak to some officials and soldiers who had entered the room. They brought the news that the Parthian envoys had broken off all negotiations, and had left the city in the afternoon. They would enter into no alliance, and were prepared to meet the Roman army.

Macrinus repeated this to Cæsar with a shrug of his shoulders, but he withheld the remark added by the venerable elder of the ambassadors, that they did not fear a foe who by so vile a deed had incurred the wrath of the gods.

"Then it is war with the Parthians!" cried Caracalla, and his eyes flashed. "My breast-plated favorites will rejoice."

But then he looked grave, and inquired: "They are leaving the town, you say? But are they birds? The gates and harbor are closed."

"A small Phœnician vessel stole out just before sundown between our guard-ships," was the reply.

"Curse it!" broke from Cæsar's lips in a loud voice, and, after a brief dialogue in an undertone with the prefect, he desired to have papyrus and writing materials brought to him. He himself must inform the senate of what had occurred, and he did so in a few words.

He did not know the number of the slain, and he did not think it worth while to make a rough estimate. All the Alexandrians, he said, had in fact merited death.

A swift trireme was to carry the letter to Ostia at day-break.

He did not, indeed, ask the opinion of the senate, and yet he felt that it would be better that news of the day's events should reach the curia under his own hand than through the distorting medium of rumor.

Nor did Macrinus impress on him, as usual, that he should give his dispatch a respectful form. This crime, if anything, might help him to the fulfillment of the Magian's prophecy.

As Cæsar was rolling up his missive, the long-expected Zminis came into the room. He had attired himself splendidly, and bore the insignia of his new office. He humbly begged to be pardoned for his long delay. He had had to make his outer man fit to appear among Cæsar's guests, for—as he boastfully explained—he himself had waded in blood, and in the court-yard of the Museum the red life-juice of the Alexandrians had reached above his horse's knees. The number of the dead, he declared with sickening pride, was above a hundred thousand, as estimated by the prefect.

"Then we will call it eleven myriad," Caracalla broke in. "Now, we have had enough of the dead. Bring in the living."

"Whom?" asked the Egyptian, in surprise.

Hereupon Cæsar's eyelids began to quiver, and in a threatening tone he reminded his bloody-handed tool of those whom he had ordered him to take alive. Still Zminis was silent, and Cæsar furiously shrieked his demand as to whether by his blundering Heron's daughter had escaped; whether he could not produce the gem-cutter and his son.

The blood-stained butcher then perceived that Cæsar's

murderous sword might be turned against him also. Still, he was prepared to defend himself by every means in his power. His brain was inventive, and, seeing that the fault for which he would least easily be forgiven was the failure to capture Melissa, he tried to screen himself by a lie. Relying on an incident which he himself had witnessed, he began: "I felt certain of securing the gem-cutter's pretty daughter, for my men had surrounded his house. But it had come to the ears of these Alexandrian scoundrels that a son of Heron's, a painter, and his sister, had betrayed their fellow-citizens and excited your wrath. It was to them that they ascribed the punishment which I executed upon them in your name. This rabble have no notion of reflection; before we could hinder them they had rushed on the innocent dwelling. They flung fire-brands into it, burned it, and tore it down. Any one who was within perished, and thus the daughter of Heron died. That is, unfortunately, proved. I can take the old man and his son to-morrow. To-day I have had so much to do that there has not been time to bind the sheaves. It is said that they had escaped before the mob rushed on the house."

"And the gem-cutter's daughter?" asked Caracalla, in a trembling voice. "You are sure she was burned in the building?"

"As sure as that I have zealously endeavored to let the Alexandrians feel your avenging hand," replied the Egyptian resolutely, and with a bold face he confirmed his lie. "I have here the jewel she wore on her arm. It was found on the charred body in the cellar. Adventus, your chamberlain, says that Melissa received it yesterday as a gift from you. Here it is."

And he handed Caracalla the serpent-shaped bracelet

which Cæsar had sent to his sweetheart before setting out for the Circus. The fire had damaged it, but there was no mistaking it. It had been found beneath the ruins on a human arm, and Zminis had only learned from the chamberlain, to whom he had shown it, that it had belonged to the daughter of Heron.

"Even the features of the corpse," Zminis added, "were still recognizable."

"The corpse!" Cæsar echoed gloomily. "And it was the Alexandrians, you say, who destroyed the house?"

"Yes, my lord; a raging mob, and mingled with them men of every race—Jews, Greeks, Syrians, what not. Most of them had lost a father, a son, or a brother, sent to Hades by your vengeance. Their wildest curses were for Alexander, the painter, who in fact had played the spy for you. But the Macedonian phalanx arrived at the right moment. They killed most of them and took some prisoners. You can see them yourself in the morning. As regards the wife of Seleukus—"

"Well," exclaimed Cæsar, and his eye brightened again.

"She fell a victim to the clumsiness of the prætorians."

"Indeed!" interrupted the legate Quintus Flavius Nobilior, who had granted Alexander's life to the prayer of the twins Aurelius; and Macrinus also forbade any insulting observations as to the blameless troops whom he had the honor to command.

But the Egyptian was not to be checked; he went on eagerly: "Pardon, my lords. It is perfectly certain, nevertheless, that it was a prætorian—his name is Rufus, and he belongs to the second cohort—who pierced the lady Berenike with his spear."

Flavius here begged to be allowed to speak, and reported how Berenike had sought and found her end. And he did so as though he were narrating the death of a heroine, but he added, in a tone of disapproval: "Unhappily, the misguided woman died with a curse on you, great Cæsar, on her treasonable lips."

"And this female hero finds her Homer in you!" cried Cæsar. "We will speak together again, my Quintus."

He raised a brimming cup to his lips and emptied it at a draught; then, setting it on the table with such violence that it rang, he exclaimed: "Then you have brought me none of those whom I commanded you to capture? Even the feeble girl who had not quitted her father's house you allowed to be murdered by those coarse monsters! And you think I shall look on you with favor? By this time to-morrow the gem-cutter and his son Alexander are here before me, or by the head of my divine father you go to the wild beasts in the Circus."

"They will not eat such as he," observed old Julius Paulinus, and Cæsar nodded approvingly. The Egyptian shuddered, for this imperial nod showed him by how slender a thread his life hung.

In a flash he reflected whither he might fly if he should fail to find this hated couple. If, after all, he should discover Melissa alive, so much the better. Then, he might have been mistaken in identifying the body; some slave girl might have stolen the bracelet and put it on before the house was burned down. He knew for a fact that the charred corpse of which he had spoken was that of a street wench who had rushed among the foremost into the house of the much-envied imperial favorite —the traitress—and had met her death in the spreading flames.

Zminis had but a moment to rack his inventive and prudent brain, but he already had thought of something which might perhaps influence Cæsar in his favor. Of all the Alexandrians, the members of the Museum were those whom Caracalla hated most. He had been particularly enjoined not to spare one of them; and in the course of the ride which Cæsar, attended by the armed troopers of Arsinoë, had taken through the streets streaming with blood, he had stayed longest gazing at the heap of corpses in the court-yard of the Museum. In the portico, a colonnade copied from the Stoa at Athens, whither a dozen or so of the philosophers had fled when attacked, he had even stabbed several with his own hand. The blood on the sword which Caracalla had dedicated to Serapis had been shed at the Museum.

The Egyptian had himself led the massacre here, and had seen that it was thoroughly effectual. The mention of those slaughtered hair-splitters must, if anything, be likely to mitigate Cæsar's wrath; so no sooner had the applause died away with which the proconsul's jest at his expense had been received, than Zminis began to give his report of the great massacre in the Museum. He could boast of having spared scarcely one of the empty word-pickers with whom the epigrams against Cæsar and his mother had originated. Teachers and pupils, even the domestic officials, had been overtaken by the insulted sovereign's vengeance. Nothing was left but the stones of that great institution, which had indeed long outlived its fame. The Numidians who had helped in the work had been drunk with blood, and had forced their way even into the physicians' lecture-rooms and the hospital adjoining. There, too, they had given no quarter; and among the sufferers who had been carried thither to be healed they had found Tarautas, the wounded gladiator. A Numidian, the youngest of the legion, a beardless youth, had pinned the terrible conqueror of lions and men to the bed with his spear, and then, with the same weapon, had released at least a dozen of his fellow-sufferers from their pain.

As he told his story the Egyptian stood staring into vacancy, as though he saw it all, and the whites of his eyeballs gleamed more hideously than ever out of his swarthy face. The lean, sallow wretch stood before Cæsar like a talking corpse, and did not observe the effect his narrative of the gladiator's death was producing. But he soon found out. While he was yet speaking, Caracalla, leaning on the table by his couch with both hands, fixed his eyes on his face, without a word.

Then he suddenly sprang up, and, beside himself with rage, he interrupted the terrified Egyptian and railed at him furiously:

"My Tarautas, who had so narrowly escaped death! The bravest hero of his kind basely murdered on his sick-bed, by a barbarian, a beardless boy! And you, you loathsome jackal, could allow it? This deed—and you know it, villain—will be set down to my score. It will be brought up against me to the end of my days in Rome, in the provinces, everywhere. I shall be cursed for your crime wherever there is a human heart to throb and feel and a human tongue to speak. And I—when did I ever order you to slake your thirst for blood in that of the sick and suffering! Never! I could never have done such a thing! I even told you to spare the women and help-less slaves. You are all witnesses. But I—you all hear me—I will punish the murderer of the wretched sick! I will avenge you, foully murdered, brave, noble Tarautas!

—Here, lictors! Bind him—away with him to the Circus with the criminals thrown to the wild beasts! He allowed the girl whose life I bade him spare to be burned to death before his eyes, and the hapless sick were slain at his command by a beardless boy!—And Tarautas! I valued him as I do all who are superior to their kind; I cared for him. He was wounded for our entertainment, my friends. Poor fellow—poor, brave Tarautas!"

He here broke into loud sobs, and it was so unheard-of, so incomprehensible a thing that this man should weep who, even at his father's death had not shed a tear, that Julius Paulinus himself held his mocking tongue.

The rest of the spectators also kept anxious and uneasy silence while the lictors bound Zminis's hands, and, in spite of his attempts to raise his voice once more in self-defence, dragged him away and thrust him out across the threshold of the dining-hall. The door closed behind him, and no applause followed, though every one approved of the Egyptian's condemnation, for Caracalla was still weeping.

Was it possible that these tears could be shed for sick people whom he did not know, and for the coarse gladiator, the butcher of men and beasts, who had had nothing to give Cæsar but a few hours of excitement at the intoxicating performances in the arena? So it must be; for from time to time Caracalla moaned softly, "Those unhappy sick!" or "Poor Tarautas!"

And, indeed, at this moment Caracalla himself could not have said whom he was lamenting. He had in the Circus staked his life on that of Tarautas, and when he shed tears over his memory it was certainly less for the gladiator's sake than over the approaching end of his own existence, to which he looked forward in consequence of

Tarautas's death. But he had often been near the gates of Hades in the battle-field with calm indifference; and now, while he thus bewailed the sick and Tarautas with bitter lamentations, in his mind he saw no sick-bed, nor, indeed, the stunted form of the braggart hero of the arena, but the slender, graceful figure of a sweet girl, and a blackened, charred arm on which glittered a golden armlet.

That woman! Treacherous, shameless, but how lovely and beloved! That woman, under his eyes, as it were, was swept out of the land of the living; and with her, with Melissa, the only maid for whom his heart had ever throbbed faster, the miracle-worker who had possessed the unique power of exorcising his torments, whose love —for so he still chose to believe, though he had always refused her petitions that he would show mercy—whose love would have given him strength to become a bene-factor to all mankind, a second Trajan or Titus. He had quite forgotten that he had intended her to meet a dis-graceful end in the arena under fearful torments, if she had been brought to him a prisoner. He felt as though the fate of Roxana, with whom his most cherished dream had perished, had quite broken his heart; and it was Melissa whom he really bewailed, with the gladiator's name on his lips and the jewel before his eyes which had been his gift, and which she had worn on her arm even in death. But he ere long controlled this display of feeling, ashamed to shed tears for her who had cheated him and who had fled from his love. Only once more did he sob aloud. Then he raised himself, and while holding his handkerchief to his eyes he addressed the company with theatrical pathos:

"Yes, my friends, tell whom you will that you have

seen Bassianus weep; but add that his tears flowed from grief at the necessity for punishing so many of his subjects with such rigor. Say, too, that Cæsar wept with pity and indignation. For what good man would not be moved to sorrow at seeing the sick and wounded thus maltreated? What humane heart could refrain from loud lamentations at the sight of barbarity which is not withheld from laying a murderous hand even on the sacred anguish of the sick and wounded? Defend me, then, against those Romans who may shrug their shoulders over the weakness of a weeping Cæsar—the Terrible. My office demands severity; and yet, my friends, I am not ashamed of these tears."

With this he took leave of his guests and retired to rest, and those who remained were soon agreed that every word of this speech, as well as Cæsar's tears, were rank hypocrisy. The mime Theocritus admired his sovereign in all sincerity, for how rarely could even the greatest actors succeed in forcing from their eyes, by sheer determination, a flood of real, warm tears—he had seen them flow. As Cæsar quitted the room, his hand on the lion's mane, the prætor Priscillianus whispered to Cilo:

"Your disciple has been taking lessons here of the weeping crocodile."

Out on the great square the soldiers were resting after the day's bloody work. They had lighted large fires in front of the most sacred sanctuary of a great city, as though they were in the open field. Round each of these, foot and horse soldiers lay or squatted on the ground, according to their companies; and over the wine allowed them by Cæsar they told each other the hideous experiences of the day, which even those who had grown rich by it could not think of without disgust.   Gold and silver cups, the plunder of the city, circulated round those campfires, and the juice of the vine was poured into them out of jugs of precious metal.   Tongues were wagging fast, for, though there was indeed but one opinion as to what had been done, there were mercenaries enough and ambitious pretenders who could dare to defend it.   Every word might reach the sovereign's ears, and the day might bring promotion as well as gold and booty.   Even the calmest were still in some excitement over the massacre they had helped in, the plunder was discussed, and barter and exchange were eagerly carried on.

As Caracalla passed the balcony he stepped out for a moment, followed by the lamp-bearers, to thank his faithful warriors for the valor and obedience they had shown this day.   The traitorous Alexandrians had now met their deserts. The greater the plunder his dear brethren in arms could win the better he would be pleased.   This speech was hailed with a shout of glee drowning his words; but Caracalla had heard his dearly bought troops cheer him with greater zeal and vigor. There were here whole groups of men who did not join at all, or hardly opened their mouths.   And his ear was sharp.

What cause could they have for dissatisfaction after such splendid booty, although they did not yet know that a war with the Parthians was in prospect?

He must know; but not to-day.   They were to be depended on, he felt sure, for they were those to whom he was most liberal, and he had taken care that there should be no one in the empire whose means equalled his own. But that they should be so lukewarm annoyed him. To-day, of all days, an enthusiastic roar of acclamations would have been peculiarly gratifying. They ought to have known it; and he went to his bedroom in silent anger.

There his freedman Epagathos was waiting for him, with Adventus and his learned Indian body slave Arjuna. The Indian never spoke unless he was spoken to, and the two others took good care not to address their lord. So silence reigned in the spacious room while the Indian undressed Caracalla. Cæsar was wont to say that this man's hands were matchless for lightness and delicacy of touch, but to-day they trembled as he lifted the laurel wreath from Cæsar's head and unbuckled the padded breast-plate. The events of the day had shaken this man's soul to the foundations. In his Eastern home he had been taught from infancy to respect life even in beasts, living exclusively on vegetables, and holding all blood in abhorrence. He now felt the deepest loathing of all about him, and a passionate longing for the peaceful and pure home among sages, from which he had been snatched as a boy, came over him with increasing vehemence. There was nothing here but what it defiled him to handle, and his fingers shrank involuntarily from their task, as duty compelled him to touch the limbs of a man who, to his fancy, was dripping with human blood, and who was as much accursed by gods and men as though he were a leper.

Arjuna made haste that he might escape from the presence of the horrible man, and Cæsar took no heed either of the pallor of his handsome brown face or the trembling of his slender fingers, for a crowd of thoughts made him blind and deaf to all that was going on around him. They reverted first to the events of the day; but as the Indian removed the warm surcoat, the night breeze blew coldly into the room, and he shivered. Was it the spirit of the slain Tarautas which had floated in at the open window? The cold breath which fanned his cheek was certainly no mere draught. It was exactly like a human sigh, only it was cold instead of warm. If it proceeded from the ghost of the dead gladiator he must be quite close to him. And the fancy gained reality in his mind; he saw a floating human form which beckoned him and softly laid a cold hand on his shoulder.

He, Cæsar, had linked his fate to that of the gladiator, and now Tarautas had come to warn him. But Caracalla had no mind to follow him; he forbade the apparition with a loud cry of "Away!"

At this the Indian started, and though he could scarcely utter the words, he besought Cæsar to be seated that he might take off his laced shoes; and then Caracalla perceived that it was an illusion that had terrified him, and he shrugged his shoulders, somewhat ashamed. While the slave was busy he wiped his damp brow, saying to himself with a proud smile that of course spirits never appeared in broad light and when others were present.

At last he dismissed the Indian and lay down. His head was burning, and his heart beat too violently for sleep. At his bidding Epagathos and Adventus followed the Indian into the adjoining room after extinguishing the lamp.

Caracalla was alone in the dark. Awaiting sleep, he stretched himself at full length, but he remained as wide awake as by day. And still he could not help thinking of the immediate past. Even his enemies could not deny that it was his duty as a man and an emperor to inflict

the severest punishment on this town, and to make it feel
his avenging hand; and yet he was beginning to be aware
of the ruthlessness of his commands. He would have been
glad to talk it all over with some one else. But Philostratus,
the only man who understood him, was out of reach; he
had sent him to his mother. And for what purpose? To
tell her that he, Cæsar, had found a wife after his own
heart, and to win her favor and consent. At this thought
the blood surged up in him with rage and shame. Even
before they were wed his chosen bride had been false to
him; she had fled from his embraces, as he now knew,
to death, never to return.

He would gladly have sent a galley in pursuit to bring
Philostratus back again; but the vessel in which the philosopher had embarked was one of the swiftest in the imperial fleet, and it had already so long a start that to overtake it would be almost impossible. So within a few
days Philostratus would meet his mother; he, if any one,
could describe Melissa's beauty in the most glowing colors,
and that he would do so to the empress, his great friend,
was beyond a doubt. But the haughty Julia would scarcely
be inclined to accept the gem-cutter's child for a daughter;
indeed, she did not wish that he should ever marry again?

But what was he to her? Her heart was given to the
infant son of her niece Mammæa*; in him she discovered
every gift and virtue. What joy there would be among the
women of Julia's train when it was known that Cæsar's
chosen bride had disdained him, and, in him, the very
purple. But that joy would not be of long duration, for
the news of the punishment by death of a hundred thou-

* The third Cæsar after Caracalla, Alexander Severus.

sand Alexandrians would, he knew, fall like a lash on the women. He fancied he could hear their howls and wailing, and see the horror of Philostratus, and how he would join the women in bemoaning the horrible deed! He, the philosopher, would perhaps be really grieved; aye, and if he had been at his side this morning everything might perhaps have been different. But the deed was done, and now he must take the consequences.

That the better sort would avoid him after such an act was self-evident—they had already refused to eat with him. On the other hand, it had brought nearer to him the favorites whom he had attracted to his person. Theocritus and Pandion, Antigonus and Epagathos, the priest of Alexander, who at Rome was overwhelmed with debt, and who in Egypt had become a rich man again, would cling to him more closely.

"Base wretches!" he muttered to himself.

If only Philostratus would come back to him! But he scarcely dared hope it. The evil took so much more care for their own well-being and multiplication than the good. If one of the righteous fell away, all the others forthwith turned their backs on him; and when the penitent desired to return to the fold, the immaculate repelled or avoided him. But the wicked could always find the fallen man at once, and would cling to him and hinder him from returning. Their ranks were always open to him, however closely he might formerly have been attached to the virtuous. To live in exclusive intercourse with these reprobates was an odious thought. He could compel whom he chose to live with him; but of what use were silent and reluctant companions? And whose fault was it that he had sent away Philostratus, the best of them all? Hers

—-the faithless traitress from whom he had looked for peace and joy, who had declared that she felt herself bound to him, the trickster in whom he had believed he saw Roxana —But she was no more. On the table by his bed, among his own jewels, lay the golden serpent he had given her—he fancied he could see it in the dark—and she had worn it even in death. He shuddered; he felt as though a woman's arm, all black and charred, was stretched out to him in the night, and the golden snake uncurled from it and reached forth as though to bite him.

He shivered, and hid his head under the coverlet; but, ashamed and vexed at his own foolish weakness, he soon emerged from the stifling darkness, and an inward voice scornfully asked him whether he still believed that the soul of the great Macedonian inhabited his body. There was an end of this proud conviction. He had no more connection with Alexander than Melissa had with Roxana, whom she resembled.

The blood seethed hotly in his veins; to live on these terms seemed to him impossible.

As soon as it was day it must surely be seen that he was very seriously ill. The spirit of Tarautas would again appear to him—and not merely as a vaporous illusion— and put an end to his utter misery.

But he felt his own pulse; it beat no more quickly than usual. He had no fever, and yet he must be ill, very ill. And again he flushed so hotly that he felt as if he should choke. Breathing hard, he sat up to call his physician. Then he observed a light through the half-closed door of the adjoining room. He heard voices— those of Adventus and the Indian.

Arjuna was generally so silent that Philostratus had vainly endeavored to discover from him any particulars as to the doctrine of the Brahmans, among whom Apollonius of Tyana declared that he had found the highest wisdom, or concerning the manners of his people. And yet the Indian was a man of learning, and could even read the manuscripts of his country. The Parthian ambassador had expressly dwelt on this when he delivered Arjuna to Cæsar as a gift from his king. But Arjuna had never favored any of these strangers with his confidence. Only with old Adventus did he ever hold conversation, for the chamberlain took care that he should be supplied with the vegetables and fruit on which he was accustomed to live for meat never passed his lips; and now he was talking with the old man, and Caracalla sat up and laid his hand to his ear.

The Indian was absorbed in the study of a bookroll in his own tongue, which he carried about him.

"What are you reading?" asked Adventus.

"A book," replied Arjuna, "from which a man may learn what will become of you and me, and all these slaughtered victims, after death."

"Who can know that?" said the old man with a sigh; and Arjuna replied very positively:

"It is written here, and there is no doubt about it. Will you hear it?"

"Certainly," said Adventus eagerly, and the Indian began translating out of his book:

"When a man dies his various parts go whither they belong. His voice goes to the fire, his breath to the winds, his eyes to the sun, his spirit to the moon, his hearing becomes one with space, his body goes to the

earth, his soul is absorbed into ether, his hairs become
plants, the hair of his head goes to crown the trees, his
blood returns to water. Thus, every portion of a man is
restored to that portion of the universe to which it belongs;
and of himself, his own essence, nothing remains but one
part: what that is called is a great secret."

Caracalla was listening intently. This discourse attracted him.

He, like the other Cæsars, must after his death be
deified by the senate; but he felt convinced for his part,
that the Olympians would never count him as one of
themselves. At the same time he was philosopher enough
to understand that no existing thing could ever cease to
exist. The restoration of each part of his body to that
portion of the universe to which it was akin, pleased his
fancy. There was no place in the Indian's creed for the
responsibility of the soul at the judgment of the dead.
Cæsar was already on the point of asking the slave to
reveal his secret, when Adventus prevented him by exclaiming:

"You may confide to me what will be left of me—
unless, indeed, you mean the worms which shall eat me
and so proceed from me. It can not be good for much,
at any rate, and I will tell no one."

To this Arjuna solemnly replied: "There is one thing
which persists to all eternity and can never be lost in all
the ages of the universe, and that is—the deed."

"I know that," replied the old man with an indifferent shrug; but the word struck Cæsar like a thunder-
bolt. He listened breathlessly to hear what more the
Indian might say; but Arjuna, who regarded it as sacri-
lege to waste the highest lore on one unworthy of it,

went on reading to himself, and Adventus stretched himself out to sleep.

All was silent in and about the sleeping-room, and the fearful words, "the deed," still rang in the ears of the man who had just committed the most monstrous of all atrocities. He could not get rid of the haunting words: all the ill he had done from his childhood returned to him in fancy, and seemed heaped up to form a mountain which weighed on him like an incubus.

The deed!

His, too, must live on, and with it his name, cursed and hated to the latest generations of men. The souls of the slain would have carried the news of the deeds he had done even to Hades; and if Tarautas were to come and fetch him away, he would be met below by legions of indignant shades—a hundred thousand! And at their head his stern father, and the other worthy men who had ruled Rome with wisdom and honor, would shout in his face: "A hundred thousand times a murderer! robber of the state! destroyer of the army!" and drag him before the judgment-seat; and before judgment could be pronounced the hundred thousand, led by the noblest of all his victims, the good Papinian, would rush upon him and tear him limb from limb.

Dozing as he lay, he felt cold, ghostly hands on his shoulder, on his head, wherever the cold breath of the waning night could fan him through the open window; and with a loud cry he sprang out of bed as he fancied he felt a touch of the shadowy hand of Vindex. On hearing his voice, Adventus and the Indian hurried in, with Epagathos, who had even heard his shriek in the farther room. They found him bathed in a sweat of horror and struggling for breath, his eyes fixed on vacancy, and the freedman flew off to fetch the physician. When he came Cæsar angrily dismissed him, for he felt no physical disorder. Without dressing, he went to the window. It was about three hours before sunrise.

However, he gave orders that his bath should be prepared, and desired to be dressed; then Macrinus and others were to be sent for. Sooner would he step into boiling water than return to that bed of terror. Day, life, business must banish his terrors. But then, after the evening would come another night; and if the sufferings he had just gone through should repeat themselves then, and in those to follow, he should lose his wits, and he would bless the spirit of Tarautas if it would but come to lead him away to death.

But "the deed!" The Indian was right—that would survive him on earth, and mankind would unite in cursing him.

Was there yet time—was he yet capable of atoning for what was done by some great and splendid deed? But the hundred thousand!

The number rose before him like a mountain, blotting out every scheme he tried to form as he went to his bath,—taking his lion with him; he revelled in the warm water, and finally lay down to rest in clean linen wrappers. No one had dared to speak to him. His aspect was too threatening.

In a room adjoining the bath-room he had breakfast served him. It was, as usual, a simple meal, and yet he could only swallow a few mouthfuls, for everything had a bitter taste. The prætorian prefect was roused, and Cæsar was glad to see him, for it was in attending to affairs that he most easily forgot what weighed upon him. The more serious they were, the better, and Macrinus looked as if there was something of grave importance to be settled.

Caracalla's first question was with reference to the Parthian ambassadors. They had, in fact, departed; now he must prepare for war. Cæsar was eager to decide at once on the destination of each legion, and to call the legates together to a council of war; but Macrinus was not so prompt and ready as usual on such occasions. He had that to communicate which, as he knew, would to Cæsar take the lead of all else. If it should prove true, it must withdraw him altogether from the affairs of government; and this was what Macrinus aimed at when, before summoning the legates, he observed with a show of reluctance that Cæsar would be wroth with him if, for the sake of a council of war, he were to defer a report which had just reached his ears.

"Business first!" cried Caracalla, with decisive prohibition.

"As you will. I thought only of what I was told by an official of this temple, that the gem-cutter's daughter —you knew the girl—is still alive—"

But he got no further, for Cæsar sprang to his feet, and desired to hear more of this.

Macrinus proceeded to relate that a slaughterer in the court of sacrifice had told him that Melissa had been seen last evening, and was somewhere in the Serapeum. More than this the prefect knew not, and Cæsar forthwith dismissed him to make further inquiry before he himself should take steps to prove the truth of the report.

Then he paced the room with revived energy. His

eye sparkled, and, breathing fast, he strove to reduce the storm of schemes, plans, and hopes which surged up within him to some sort of order. He must punish the fugitive—but yet more surely he would never again let her out of his sight. But if only he could first have her cast to the wild beasts, and then bring her to life again, crown her with the imperial diadem, and load her with every gift that power and wealth could procure! He would read every wish in her eyes, if only she would once more lay her hand on his forehead, charm away his pain, and bring sleep to his horror-stricken bed. He had done nothing to vex her; nay, every petition she had urged— But suddenly the image rose before him of old Vindex and his nephew, whom he had sent to execution in spite of her intercession; and again the awful word, "the deed," rang in his inward ear. Were these hideous thoughts to haunt him even by day?

No, no! In his waking hours there was much to be done which might give him the strength to dissipate them.

The kitchen-steward was by this time in attendance; but what did Caracalla care for dainties to tickle his palate now that he had a hope of seeing Melissa once more? With perfect indifference he left the catering to the skilful and inventive cook; and hardly had he retired when Macrinus returned.

The slaughterer had acquired his information through a comrade, who said that he had twice caught sight of Melissa at the window of the chambers of mystery in the upper story of the Serapeum, yesterday afternoon. He had hoped to win the reward which was offered for the recovery of the fugitive, and had promised his colleague

half the money if he would help him to capture the
maiden. But just at sunset, hearing that the massacre
was ended, the man had incautiously gone out into the
town, where he had been slain by a drunken soldier of
the Scythian legion. The hapless man's body had been
found, but Macrinus's informant had assured him that he
could entirely rely on the report of his unfortunate colleague, who was a sober and truthful man, as the chief
augur would testify.

This was enough for Caracalla. Macrinus was at
once to go for the high-priest, and to take care that he
took no further steps to conceal Melissa. The slaughterer
had ever since daybreak kept secret watch on all the
doors of the Serapeum, aided by his comrades, who
were to share in the reward, and especially on the stair-
way leading from the ground floor up to the mystic
galleries.

The prefect at once obeyed the despot's command.
On the threshold he met the kitchen-steward returning to
submit his list of dishes for Cæsar's approval.

He found Caracalla in an altered mood, rejuvenescent
and in the highest spirits. After hastily agreeing to the
day's bill of fare, he asked the steward in what part of
the building the chambers of mystery were; and when he
learned that the stairs leading up to them began close
to the kitchens, which had been arranged for Cæsar's
convenience under the temple laboratory, Caracalla declared in a condescending tone that he would go to look
round the scene of the cook's labors. And the lion
should come too, to return thanks for the good meat
which was brought to him so regularly.

The head cook, rejoiced at the unwonted gracious-

ness of a master whose wrath had often fallen on him,
led the way to his kitchen hearth. This had been constructed in a large hall, originally the largest of the
laboratories, where incense was prepared for the sanctuary
and medicines concocted for the sick in the temple
hospital. There were smaller halls and rooms adjoining,
where at this moment some priests were busy preparing
kyphi and mixing drugs.

The steward, proud of Cæsar's promised visit, announced to his subordinates the honor they might expect,
and he then went to the door of the small laboratory to
tell the old pastophoros who was employed there, and
who had done him many a good turn, that if he wished
to see the emperor he had only to open the door leading
to the staircase. He was about to visit the mystic chambers
with his much-talked-of lion. No one need be afraid of
the beast; it was quite tame, and Cæsar loved it as a son.

At this the old drug-pounder muttered some reply,
which sounded more like a curse than the expected
thanks, and the steward regretted having compared the
lion to a son in this man's presence, for the pastophoros
wore a mourning garment, and two promising sons had
been snatched from him, slain yesterday with the other
youths in the stadium.

But the cook soon forgot the old man's ill-humor; he
had to clear his subordinates out of the way as quickly
as possible and prepare for his illustrious visitor. As he
bustled around, here, there, and everywhere, the pastophoros entered the kitchen and begged for a piece of
mutton. This was granted him by a hasty sign toward
a freshly slaughtered sheep, and the old man busied himself for some time behind the steward's back. At last he

had cut off what he wanted, and gazed with singular tenderness at the piece of red, veinless meat. On returning to his laboratory, he hastily bolted himself in, and when he came out again a few minutes later his calm, wrinkled old face had a malignant and evil look. He stood at the bottom of the stairs, looking about him cautiously; then he flew up the steps with the agility of youth, and at a turn in the stairs he stuck the piece of meat close to the foot of the balustrade.

He returned as nimbly as he had gone, cast a sorrowful glance through the open laboratory window at the arena where all that had graced his life lay dead, and passed his hand over his tearful face. At last he returned to his task, but he was less able to do it than before. It was with a trembling hand that he weighed out the juniper berries and cedar resin, and he listened all the time with bated breath.

Presently there was a stir on the stairs, and the kitchen slaves shouted that Cæsar was coming. So he went out of the laboratory, which was behind the stairs, to see what was going forward, and a turn-spit at once made way for the old man so as not to hinder his view.

Was that little young man, mounting the steps so gayly, with the high-priest at his side and his suite at his heels, the dreadful monster who had murdered his noble sons? He had pictured the dreadful tyrant quite differently. Now Cæsar was laughing, and the tall man next him made some light and ready reply—the head cook said it was the Roman priest of Alexander, who was not on good terms with Timotheus. Could they be laughing at the high-priest? Never, in all the years he had known him, had he seen Timotheus so pale and dejected.

The high-priest had indeed good cause for anxiety, for he suspected who it was that Cæsar hoped to find in the mystic rooms, and feared that his wife might, in fact, have Melissa in hiding in that part of the building to which he was now leading the way. After Macrinus had come to fetch him he had had no opportunity of enquiring, for the prefect had not quitted him for a moment, and Euryale was in the town busy with other women in seeking out and nursing such of the wounded as had been found alive among the dead.

Cæsar triumphed in the changed, gloomy, and depressed demeanor of a man usually so self-possessed; for he fancied that it betrayed some knowledge on the part of Timotheus of Melissa's hiding-place; and he could jest with the priest of Alexander and his favorite Theocritus and the other friends who attended him, while he ignored the high-priest's presence and never even alluded to Melissa.

Hardly had they gone past the old man when, just as the kitchen slaves were shouting "Hail, Cæsar!" the lady Euryale, as pale as death, hurried in, and with a trembling voice inquired whither her husband was conducting the emperor.

She had turned back when half way on her road, in obedience to the impulse of her heart, which prompted her, before she went on her Samaritan's errand, to visit Melissa in her hiding-place, and let her see the face of a friend at the beginning of a new, lonely, and anxious day. On hearing the reply which was readily given, her knees trembled beneath her, and the steward, who saw her totter, supported her and led her into the laboratory, where essences and strong waters soon restored her to consciousness. Euryale had known the old pastophoros a long time, and, noticing his mourning garb, she asked sympathetically: "And you, too, are bereft?"

"Of both," was the answer. "You were always so good to them— Slaughtered like beasts for sacrifice— down there in the stadium," and tears flowed fast down the old man's furrowed cheeks. The lady uplifted her hands as though calling on Heaven to avenge this outrageous crime; at the same instant a loud howl of pain was heard from above, and a great confusion of men's voices.

Euryale was beside herself with fear. If they had found Melissa in her room her husband's fate was sealed, and she was guilty of his doom. But they could scarcely yet have opened the chambers, and the girl was clever and nimble, and might perhaps escape in time if she heard the men approaching. She eagerly flew to the window. She could see below her the stone which Melissa must move to get out; but between the wall and the stadium the street was crowded, and at every door of the Serapeum lictors were posted, even at that stone door known only to the initiated, with the temple slaughterers and other servants who seemed all to be on guard. If Melissa were to come out now she would be seized, and it must become known who had shown her the way into the hiding-place that had sheltered her.

At this moment Theocritus came leaping down the stairs, crying out to her: "The lion—a physician—where shall I find a leech?".

The matron pointed to the old man, who was one of the medical students of the sanctuary, and the favorite shouted out to him, "Come up!" and then rushed on, paying no heed to Euryale's inquiry for Melissa; but the old man laughed scornfully and shouted after him, "I am no beast-healer."

Then, turning to the lady, he added:

"I am sorry for the lion. You know me, lady. I could never till yesterday bear to see a fly hurt. But this brute! It was as a son to that bloodhound, and he shall feel for once something to grieve him. The lion has had his portion. No physician in the world can bring him to life again."

He bent his head and returned to his laboratory; but the matron understood that this kind, peaceable man, in spite of his white hair, had become a poisoner, and that the splendid, guiltless beast owed its death to him. She shuddered. Wherever this unblest man went, good turned to evil; terror, suffering, and death took the place of peace, happiness, and life. He had forced her even into the sin of disobedience to her husband and master. But now her secret hiding of Melissa against his will would be avenged. He and she alike would probably pay for the deed with their life; for the murder of his lion would inevitably rouse Cæsar's wildest passions.

Still, she knew that Caracalla respected her; for her sake, perhaps, he would spare her husband.

But Melissa! What would her fate be if she were dragged out of her hiding-place?—and she must be discovered! He had threatened to cast her to the beasts; and ought she not to prefer even that fearful fate to forgiveness and a fresh outburst of Cæsar's passion?

Pale and tearless, but shaken with alarms, she bent over the balustrade of the stairs and murmured a prayer commending herself, her husband, and Melissa to God.

Then she hastened up the steps. The great doors leading to the chambers of mystery stood wide open, and the first person she met was her husband.

"You here?" said he in an undertone. "You may thank the gods that your kind heart did not betray you into hiding the girl here. I trembled for her and for ourselves. But there is not a sign of her; neither here nor on the secret stair. What a morning—and what a day must follow! There lies Cæsar's lion. If his suspicion that it has been poisoned should be proved true, woe to this luckless city, woe to us all!"

And Cæsar's aspect justified the worst anticipations. He had thrown himself on the floor by the side of his dead favorite, hiding his face in the lion's noble mane, with strange, quavering wailing. Then he raised the brute's heavy head and kissed his dead eyes, and as it slipped from his hand and fell on the floor, he started to his feet, shaking his fist, and exclaiming:

"Yes, you have poisoned him! Bring the miscreant here, or you shall follow him!"

Macrinus assured him that if indeed some basest of base wretches had dared to destroy the life of this splendid and faithful king of beasts, the murderer should infallibly be found. But Caracalla screamed in his face:

"Found? Dare you speak of finding? Have you even brought me the girl who was hidden here? Have you found her? Where is she? She was seen here and she must be here!"

And he hurried from room to room in undignified haste, like a slave hunting for some lost treasure of his master's, tearing open closets, peeping behind curtains and up chimneys, and snatching the clothes, behind which she might have hidden, from the pegs on which they hung. He insisted on seeing every secret door, and ran first down and then up the hidden stairs by which Melissa had in fact escaped.

In the great hall, where by this time physicians and courtiers had gathered round the carcass of the lion, Cæsar sank on to a seat, his brow damp with heat, and stared at the floor; while the leeches, who, as Alexandrians for the most part, were anxious not to rouse the despot's rage, assured him that to all appearance the lion, who had been highly fed and getting little exercise, had died of a fit. The poison had indeed worked more rapidly than any the imperial body physician was acquainted with; and he, not less anxious to mollify the sovereign, bore them out in this opinion. But their diagnosis, though well meant, had the contrary effect to that they had intended. The prosecution and punishment of a murderer would have given occupation to his revengeful spirit and have diverted his thoughts, and the capture of the criminal would have pacified him; as it was, he could only regard the death of the lion as a fresh stroke of fate directed against himself. He sat absorbed in sullen gloom, muttering frantic curses, and haughtily desired the high-priest to restore the offering he had wasted on a god who was so malignant, and as hostile to him as all else in this city of abomination.

He then rose, desired every one to stand back from where the lion lay, and gazed down at the beast for many minutes. And as he looked, his excited imagination showed him Melissa stroking the noble brute, and the lion lashing the ground with his tail when he heard the light step of her little feet. He could hear the music of her voice when she spoke coaxingly to the lion; and then again he started off to search the rooms once more, shouting her name, heedless of the bystanders, till Macrinus made so bold as to assure him that the slaughterer's report must have been false. He must have mistaken some one else for Melissa, for it was proved beyond a doubt that Melissa had been burned in her father's house.

At this Cæsar looked the prefect in the face with glazed and wandering eyes, and Macrinus started in horror as he suddenly shrieked, "The deed, the deed!" and struck his brow with his fist.

From that hour Caracalla had lost forever the power of distinguishing the illusions which pursued him from reality.

CHAPTER XIV.

A week later Caracalla quitted Alexandria to make war on the Parthians. What finally drove the unhappy man to hurry from the hated place was the torturing fear of sharing his lion's fate, and of being sent after the murdered Tarautas by the friends who had heard his appeal to fate.

Quite mad he was not, for the illusions which haunted him were often absent for several hours, when he spoke with perfect lucidity, received reports, and gave orders. It was with peculiar terror that his soul avoided every recollection of his mother, of Theocritus, and all those whose opinion he had formerly valued and whose judgment was not indifferent to him.

In constant terror of the dagger of an avenger—a dread which, with many other peculiarities, the leech could hardly ascribe to the diseased phenomena of his mental state—he only showed himself to his soldiers, and he might often be seen making a meal off a pottage he himself had cooked to escape the poison which had been fatal to his lion. He was never for an instant free from the horrible sense of being hated, shunned, and persecuted by the whole world.

Sometimes he would remember that once a fair girl had prayed for him; but when he tried to recall her features he could only see the charred arm with the golden snake held up before him as he had pictured it that night

after the most hideous of his massacres; and every time,
at the sight of it, that word came back to him which still
tortured his soul above all else—"The deed." But his
attendants, who heard him repeating it day and night,
never knew what he meant by it.

When Zminis met his end by the wild beasts in the
arena, it was before half-empty seats, though several
legions had been ordered into the amphitheatre to fill
them. The larger number of the citizens were slain, and
the remainder were in mourning for relatives more or less
near; and they also kept away from the scene to avoid
the hated despot.

Macrinus now governed the empire almost as a
sovereign, for Cæsar, formerly a laborious and autocratic
ruler, shrank from all business. Even before they left
Alexandria the plebeian prefect could see that Serapion's
prophecy was fulfilling itself. He remained in close intimacy with the soothsayer; but only once more, and just
before Cæsar's departure, could the Magian be induced
to raise the spirit of the dead, for his clever accomplice,
Castor, had fallen a victim in the massacre because,
prompted by the high price set on Alexander's head, and
his own fierce hatred of the young painter, he would go
out to discover where he and his sister had concealed
themselves.

When at last the unhappy monarch quitted Alexandria
one rainy morning, followed by the curses of innumerable
mourners—fathers, mothers, widows, and orphans—as
well as of ruined artisans and craftsmen, the ill-used city,
once so proudly gay, felt itself relieved of a crushing
nightmare. This time it was not to Cæsar that the cloudy
sky promised welfare; his life was wrapped in gloom; but
to the people he had so bitterly hated. Thousands looked

forward hopefully to life once more, in spite of their mourning robes and widows' veils, and notwithstanding the serious hindrances which the malice of their "afflicted" sovereign had placed in the way of the resuscitation of their town, for Caracalla had commanded that a wall should be built to divide the great merchant city into two parts.

Nay, he had intended to strike a death-blow even at the learning to which Alexandria owed a part of her greatness, by decreeing that the Museum and schools should be removed and the theatres closed.

Maddening alike to heart and brain was the memory that he left behind him, and the citizens would shake their fists if only his name were spoken. But their biting tongues had ceased to mock or jest. Most of the epi-grammatists were silenced forever, and the nimble wit of the survivors was quelled for many a month by bitter curses or tears of sorrow.

But now—it was a fortnight since the dreadful man had left—the shops and stores, which had been closed against the plunderers, were being reopened. Life was astir again in the deserted and silent baths and taverns, for there was no further fear of rapine from insolent soldiers, or the treacherous ears of spies and delators. Women and girls could once more venture into the high-ways, the market was filled with dealers, and many an one who was conscious of a heedless speech or suspected of whistling in the circus, or of some other crime, now came out of his well-watched hiding-place.

Glaukias, the sculptor, among others, reopened his work-rooms in Heron's garden-plot. In the cellar beneath the floor the gem-cutter had remained hidden with Polybius and his sister Praxilla, for the easy-going old man could

not be induced to embark in the vessel which Argutis
had hired for them. Sooner would he die than leave
Alexandria. He was too much petted and too infirm to
face the discomforts of a sea voyage. And his obstinacy
had served him well, for the ship in which they were to
have sailed, though it got out before the harbor was
closed, was overtaken and brought back by an imperial
galley.

Polybius was, however, quite willing to accept Heron's
invitation to share his hiding-place.

Now they could both come out again; but these few
weeks had affected them very differently. The gem-cutter
looked like the shadow of himself, and had lost his upright carriage. He knew, indeed, that Melissa was alive,
and that Alexander, after being wounded, had been carried by Andreas to the house of Zeno, and was on the
way to recovery; but the death of his favorite son preyed
on his mind, and it was a great grievance that his house
should have been wrecked and burned. His hidden
gold, which was safe with him, would have allowed of his
building a far finer one in its stead, but the fact that it
should be his fellow-citizens who had destroyed it was
worst of all. It weighed on his spirits, and made him
morose and silent.

Old Dido, who had risked her life more than once,
looked at him with mournful eyes, and besought all the
gods she worshiped to restore her good master's former
vigor, that she might once more hear him curse and storm;
for his subdued mood seemed to her unnatural and alarming—a portent of his approaching end.

Praxilla, too, the comfortable widow, had grown pale
and thin, but old Dido had learned a great deal from
her teaching. Polybius only was more cheerful than

ever. He knew that his son and Melissa had escaped the most imminent dangers. This made him glad; and then his sister had done wonders that he might not too greatly miss his cook. His meals had nevertheless been often scanty enough, and this compulsory temperance had relieved him of his gout and done him so much good that, when Andreas led him out into daylight once more, the burly old man exclaimed: "I feel as light as a bird. If I had but wings I could fly across the lake to see the boy. It is you, my brother, who have helped to make me so much lighter."

He laid his arm on the freedman's shoulder and kissed him on the cheeks. It was for the first time; and never before had he called him brother. But that his lips had obeyed the impulse of his heart might be seen in the tearful glitter of his eyes, which met those of Andreas, and they, too, were moist.

Polybius knew all that the Christian had done for his son and for Melissa, for him and his, and his jest in saying that Andreas had helped to make him lighter referred to his latest achievement. Julianus, the new governor of the city, who now occupied the residence of the prefect Titianus, had taken advantage of the oppressed people to extract money, and Andreas, by the payment of a large sum, had succeeded in persuading him to sign a document which exonerated Polybius and his son from all criminality, and protected their person and property against soldiers and town guards alike. This safe conduct secured a peaceful future to the genial old man, and filled the measure of what he owed to the freedman, even to overflowing. Andreas on his part felt that his former owner's kiss and brotherly greeting had sealed his acceptance as a free man. He asked no greater reward than this he had just received; and there was another thing which made his heart leap with gladness. He knew now that the fullness of time had come in the best sense for the daughter of the only woman he had ever loved, and that the Good Shepherd had called her to be one of His flock. He could rejoice over this without a pang, for he had learned that Diodoros, too, had entered on the path which hitherto he had pointed out to him in vain.

A calm cheerfulness, which surprised all who knew him, brightened the grave man; for him the essence of Christian love lay in the Resurrection, and he saw with astonishment that a wonderful new vitality was rising out of death. For Alexandria, too, the time was fulfilled. Men and women crowded to the rite of baptism. Mothers brought their daughters, and fathers their sons. These days of horror had multiplied the little Christian congregation to a church of ten thousand members. Caracalla turned hundreds from heathenism by his bloody sacrifices, his love of fighting, his passion for revenge, and the blindness which made him cast away all care for his eternal soul to secure the enjoyment of a brief existence. That the sword which had slain thousands of their sons should have been dedicated to Serapis, and accepted by the god, alienated many of the citizens from the patron divinity of the town. Then the news that Timotheus the high-priest had abdicated his office soon after Cæsar's departure, and, with his revered wife Euryale, had been baptized by their friend the learned Clemens, confirmed many in their desire to be admitted into the Christian community.

After these horrors of bloodshed, these orgies of hatred and vengeance, every heart longed for love and peace and brotherly communion. Who of all those that had looked death in the face in these days was not anxious to know more of the creed which taught that the life beyond the grave was of greater importance than that on earth?—while those who already held it went forth to meet, as it were, a bridegroom. They had seen men trodden down and all their rights trampled on; and now every ear was open when a doctrine was preached which recognized the supreme value of humanity, by ascribing, even to the humblest, the dignity of a child of God. They were accustomed to pray to immortal beings who lived in privileged supremacy and wild revelry at the golden tables of the Olympian banquet; and now they were told that the church of the Christians meant the communion of the faithful with their fatherly God, and, with His Son who had mingled with other mortals in the form of man and who had done more for them than a brother, inasmuch as He had taken upon Himself to die on the cross for love of them.

To a highly cultured race like the Alexandrians it had long seemed an absurdity to try to purchase the favor of the gods by blood-offerings. Many philosophical sects, and especially the Pythagoreans, had forbidden such sacrifices, and had enjoined the bringing of offerings not to purchase good fortune, but only to honor the gods; and now they saw the Christians not making any offerings at all, but sharing a love-feast. This, as they declared, was to keep them in remembrance of their brotherhood and of their crucified Lord, whose blood, once shed, His heavenly Father had accepted instead of every other sacrifice. The voluntary and agonizing death of the Redeemer had saved the soul of every Christian from sin and damnation; and many who in the late scenes of horror had been inconsolable in anticipation of the grave, felt moved to share in this divine gift of grace.

Beautiful, wise, and convincing sentences from the Bible went from lip to lip; and a saying of Clemens, whose immense learning was well known, was especially effective and popular. He had said that "faith was knowledge of divine things through revelation, but that learning must give the proof thereof"; and this speech led many men of high attainments to study the new doctrines.

The lower classes were no doubt those most strongly attracted, the poor and the slaves; and with them the sorrowing and oppressed. There were many of these now in the town; ten thousand had seen those dearest to them perish, and others, being wounded, had within a few days been ruined both in health and estate.

As to Melissa in her peril, so to all these the Saviour's call to the heavy-laden that He would give them rest had come as a promise of new hope to ear and heart. At the sound of these words they saw the buds of a new spring-time for the soul before their eyes; any one who knew a Christian improved his intimacy that he might hear more about the tender-hearted Comforter, the Friend of children, the kind and helpful Patron of the poor, the sorrowful, and the oppressed.

Assemblies of any kind were prohibited by the new governor; but the law of Aelius Marcianus allowed gatherings for religious purposes, and the learned lawyer, Johannes, directed his fellow-Christians to rely on that. All Alexandria was bidden to these meetings, and the text with which Andreas opened the first, "Now the fullness of time is come," passed from mouth to mouth.

Apart from that period which had preceded the birth of Christ, these words applied to none better than to the days of death and terror which they had just gone through.

Had a plainer boundary-stone ever been erected between a past and a future time? Out of the old vain and careless life, which had ended with such fearful horrors, a new life would now proceed of peace and love and pious cares.

The greater number of the citizens, and at their head the wealthy and proud, still crowded the heathen temples to serve the old gods and purchase their favor with offerings; still, the Christian churches were too small and few to hold the faithful, and these had risen to higher consideration, for the community no longer consisted exclusively of the lower rank of people and slaves. No, men and women of the best families came streaming in, and this creed—as was proclaimed by Demetrius, the eloquent bishop; by Origen, who in power and learning was the superior of any heathen philosopher; by the zealous Andreas, and many another chosen spirit—this creed was the religion of the future.

The freedman had never yet lived in such a happy and elevated frame of mind; as he looked back on his past existence he often remembered with thankful joy the promise that the last should be first, and that the lowly should be exalted. If the dead had risen from their graves before his eyes it would scarcely have surprised him, for in these latter days he had seen wonder follow on wonder. The utmost his soul had so fervently desired, for which he had prayed and longed, had found fulfillment in a way which far surpassed his hopes; and through what blood and fear had the Lord led His own, to let them reach the highest goal! He knew from the lady Euryale that his desire to win Melissa's soul to the true faith had been granted, and that she craved to be baptized. This had not been confirmed by the girl herself, for, attacked by a violent fever, she had during nine days hovered between life and death; and since then Andreas had for more than a week been detained in the town arranging affairs for Polybius.

The task was now ended which he had set himself to carry through. He could leave the city and see once more the young people he loved. He parted from Polybius and his sister at the garden gate, and led Heron and old Dido to a small cottage which his former master had given him to live in.

The gem-cutter was not to be allowed to see his children till the leech should give leave, and the unfortunate man could not get over his surprise and emotion at finding in his new home not only a work-table, with tools, wax, and stones, but several cages full of birds, and among these feathered friends a starling. His faithful and now freed slave, Argutis, had, by Polybius's orders, supplied everything needful; but the birds were a thought of the Christian girl Agatha. All this was a consolation in his grief, and when the gem-cutter was alone with old Dido he burst into sobs. The slave woman followed his example, but he stopped her with loud, harsh scolding. At first she was frightened; but then she exclaimed with delight from the very bottom of her faithful heart, "The gods be praised!" and from the moment when he could storm, she always declared, Heron's recovery began.

The sun was setting when Andreas made his way to Zeno's house—a long, white-washed building. The road led through a palm-grove on the Christian's estate. His anxiety to see the beloved sufferers, urged him forward so quickly that he presently overtook another man who was walking in the same direction in the cool of the evening. This was Ptolemæus, the physician.

He greeted Andreas with cheerful kindness, and the freedman knew what he meant when, without waiting to be asked, he said:

"We are out of the wood now; the fever has passed away. The delirious fancies have left her, and since noon she has slept. When I quitted her an hour ago she was sleeping soundly and quietly. Till now the shaken soul has been living in a dream; but now that the fever has passed away, she will soon be herself again. As yet she has recognized no one; neither Agatha nor the lady Euryale; not even Diodoros, whom I allowed to look at her yesterday for a moment. We have taken her away from the large house in the garden, on account of the children, to the little villa opposite the place of worship. It is quiet there, and the air blows in on her through the open veranda. The Empress herself could not wish for a better sick-room. And the care Agatha takes of her! You are right to hasten. The last glimmer of sunshine is extinct, and divine service will soon begin. I am satisfied with Diodoros too; youth is a soil on which the physician reaps easy laurels. What will it not heal and strengthen! Only when the soul is so deeply shaken, as with Melissa and her brother, matters go more slowly, even with the young. However, as I said, we are past the crisis."

"God be praised!" said Andreas. "Such news makes me young again. I could run like a boy."

They now entered the well-kept gardens which lay behind Zeno's house. Noble clumps of tall old trees rose above the green grass plots and splendid shrubs. Round a dancing fountain were carefully kept beds of beautiful flowers. The garden ended at a palm-grove, which cast its shade on Zeno's little private place of worship—an open plot inclosed by tamarisk hedges like walls. The little villa in which Melissa lay was in a bower of verdure, and the veranda with the wide door through which the bed of the sufferer had been carried in, stood open in the cool evening to the garden, the palm-grove, and the place of worship with its garland, as it were, of fragile tamarisk boughs.

Agatha was keeping watch by Melissa; but as the last of the figures, great and small, who could be seen moving across the garden, all in the same direction, disappeared behind the tamarisk screen, the young Christian looked lovingly down at her friend's pale and all too delicate face, touched her forehead lightly with her lips, and whispered to the sleeper, as though she could hear her voice:

"I am only going to pray for you and your brother."

And she went out.

A few moments later the brazen gong was heard—muffled out of regard for the sick—which announced the hour of prayer to the little congregation. It had sounded every evening without disturbing the sufferer, but to-night it roused her from her slumbers.

She looked about her in bewilderment and tried to rise, but she was too weak to lift herself. Terror, blood, Diodoros wounded, Andreas, the ass on which she had ridden that night, were the images which first crowded on her awakening spirit in bewildering confusion. She had heard that piercing ring of smitten brass in the Serapeum. Was she still there? Had she only dreamed of that night-ride with her wounded lover? Perhaps she had lost consciousness in the mystic chambers, and the clang of the gong had roused her.

And she shuddered. In her terror she dared not open her eyes for fear of seeing on all hands the hideous images on the walls and ceiling. Merciful gods! If her flight from the Serapeum and the rescue of Diodoros by Andreas had really been but a dream, then the door might open at any moment, and the Egyptian Zminis or his men might come in to drag her before that dreadful Cæsar.

She had half recovered consciousness several times, and as these thoughts had come over her, her returning lucidity had vanished and a fresh attack of fever had shaken her. But this time her head seemed clearer; the cloud and humming had left her which had impeded the use of her ears and eyes. Her brain too had recovered its faculties. As soon as she tried to think, her restored intelligence told her that if she were indeed still in the Serapeum and the door should open, the lady Euryale might come in to speak courage to her and take her in her motherly arms, and—

And she suddenly recollected the promise which had come to her from the Scriptures of the Christians. It stood before her soul in perfect clearness that she had found a loving comforter in the Saviour; she remembered how gladly she had declared to the lady Euryale that the fullness of time had now indeed come to her, and that she had no more fervent wish than to become a fellow-believer with her kind friend—a baptized Christian. And all the while she felt as though light were spreading in her and around her, and the vision she had last seen when she lost consciousness rose again before her inward eye. Again she saw the Redeemer as He had stood before her at the end of her ride, stretching out his arms to her in the darkness, inviting her, who was weary and heavy laden, to be refreshed by him. A glow of thankfulness warmed her heart, and she closed her eyes once more.

But she did not sleep; and while she lay fully conscious, with her hands on her bosom as it rose and fell regularly with her deep breathing, thinking of the loving Teacher of the Christians, and of all the glorious promises she had read in the Sermon on the Mount, and which were addressed to her too, she could fancy that her head rested on Euryale's shoulder, while she saw the form of the Saviour robed in light and beckoning to her.

Her whole frame was wrapped in pleasant languor. Just so had she felt once before—she remembered it well —and she remembered when it was. She had felt just as she did now after her lover had for the first time clasped her to his heart, when, as night came on, she had sat by his side on the marble bench, while the Christian procession passed. She had taken the chanting train for the wandering souls of the dead and—how strange! No—she was not mistaken. She heard at this moment the selfsame strain which they had then sung so joyfully, in spite of its solemn mode. She did not know when it had begun, but again it filled her with a bitter-sweet sense of pity. Only it struck deeper now than before, for she knew now that it applied to all human beings, since they were all the children of the same kind Father, and her own brethren and sisters.

But whence did the wonderful music proceed? Was she—and a shock of alarm thrilled her at the thought— was she numbered with the dead? Had her heart ceased to beat when the Saviour had taken her in His arms after her ride through blood and darkness, when all had grown dim to her senses? Was she now in the abode of the blest?

Andreas had painted it as a glorious place; and yet she shuddered at the thought. But was not that foolish? If she were really dead, all terror and pain were at an end. She would see her mother once more; and whatever might happen to those she loved, she might perhaps be suffered to linger near them, as she had done on earth, and hope with assurance to meet them again here sooner or later.

But no! Her heart was beating still; she could feel how strongly it throbbed. Then where was she?

There certainly had not been any such coverlet as this on her bed in the Serapeum, and the room there was much lower. She looked about her and succeeded in turning on her side toward the evening breeze which blew in on her, so pure and soft and sweet. She raised her delicate emaciated hand to her head and found that her thick hair was gone. Then she must have cut it off to disguise herself.

But where was she? Whither had she fled?

It mattered not. The Serapeum was far away, and she need no longer fear Zminis and his spies.

Now for the first time she raised her eyes thankfully to Heaven, and next she looked about her; and while she gazed and let her eyes feed themselves full, a faint cry of delight escaped her lips. Before her, in the silvery light of the bright disk of the young moon, lay a splendid blooming garden, and over the palms which towered above all else in the distance, in shadowy masses, the evening star was rising. Just in front, the moonlight twinkled and flashed in the rising and falling drops of the fountain;

and as she lay, stirred to the depths of her soul by this silent splendor, thinking of kindly Selene moving on her peaceful path above, of Artemis hunting in the moonlight, of the nymphs of the waters, and the dryads just now perhaps stealing out of the great trees to dance with sportive fauns, the chant suddenly broke out again in solemn measure, and she heard, in deep manly voices, the beginning of the Psalm:

"Give thanks unto the Lord, and declare his name: proclaim his wonders among the nations.

"Sing of him and praise him; tell of all his wonders; glorify his holy name; their hearts rejoice that seek the Lord."

Here the men ceased and the women began as though to confirm their praise of the most High, singing the ninetieth Psalm with enthusiastic joy:

"O Lord, thou hast been our dwelling-place in all generations.

"Before the mountains were brought forth, or, ever thou hadst formed the earth and the world, even from everlasting to everlasting, thou art God.

"For a thousand years in thy sight are but as yesterday when it is passed, and as a watch in the night."

Then the men's voices broke in again:

"The heavens declare the glory of God and the firmament showeth his handiwork.

"Day unto day uttereth speech and night unto night showeth knowledge."

And the women in their turn took up the chant, and from their grateful breasts rose clear and strong the Psalm of David:

"Bless the Lord, O my soul, and all that is within me, bless his holy name.

"Bless the Lord, O my soul, and forget not all his benefits.

"Who forgiveth all thine iniquities; who healeth all thy diseases.

"Who redeemeth thy life from destruction; who crowneth thee with loving-kindness and tender mercies." *

Melissa listened breathlessly to the singing, of which she could hear every word; and how gladly would she have mingled her voice with theirs in thanksgiving to the kind Father in heaven who was hers as well as theirs! There lay his wondrous works before her, and her heart echoed the verse!

"Who redeemeth thy life from destruction; who crowneth thee with loving-kindness and mercies," as though it were addressed especially to her and sung for her by the choir of women.

The gods of whom she had but just been thinking with pious remembrance appeared to her now as beautiful, merry, sportive children, as graceful creatures of her own kind, in comparison with the Almighty Creator and Ruler of the universe, whose works among the nations, whose holy name, whose wonders, greatness, and loving-kindness these songs of praise celebrated. The breath of His mouth dispersed the whole world of gods to whom she had been wont to pray, as the autumn wind scatters the many-tinted leaves of faded trees. She felt as though He embraced the garden before her with mighty and yet loving arms, and with it the whole world. She had loved the Olympian gods; but in this hour, for the first time, she felt true reverence for one God, and it made her proud to think that she might love this mighty Lord, this

* From the Bible version.

tender Father, and know that she was beloved by Him. Her heart beat faster and faster, and she felt as though, under the protection of this God, she need never more fear any danger.

As she looked out again at the palm-trees beyond the tamarisk, above whose plumy heads the evening star now rode in the azure blue of the night sky, the singing was taken up again after a pause; she heard once more the angelic greeting which had before struck her soul as so comforting and full of promise when she read it in the Gospel:

"Glory to God on high, on earth peace, good-will toward men."

That which she had then so fervently longed for had, she thought, come to pass. The peace, the rest for which she had yearned so miserably in the midst of terror and bloodshed, now filled her heart—all that surrounded her was so still and peaceful! A wonderful sense of home came over her, and with it the conviction that here she would certainly find those for whom she was longing.

Again she looked up to survey the scene, and she was now aware of a white figure coming toward her from the tamarisk hedge. This was Euryale. She had seen Agatha among the worshippers, and had quitted the congregation, fearing that the sick girl might wake and find no one near her who cared for her or loved her. She crossed the grass plot with a swift step. She had passed the fountain; her head came into the moonlight, and Melissa could see the dear, kind face. With glad excitement she called her by name, and as the matron entered the veranda she heard the convalescent's weak voice and hastened to her side. Lightly, as if joy had made her young again, she sank on her knees by the bed of the resuscitated girl to kiss her with motherly tenderness and press her head gently to her bosom. While Melissa asked a hundred questions the lady had to warn her to remain quiet, and at last to bid her to keep silence.

First of all Melissa wanted to know where she was. Then her lips overflowed with thankfulness and joy, and declarations that she felt as she was sure the souls in bliss must feel when Euryale had told her in subdued tones that her father was living, that Diodoros and her brother had found a refuge in the house of Zeno, and that Andreas, Polybius, and all dear to them were quite recovered after those evil days. The town had long been rid of Cæsar, and Zeno had consented to allow his daughter Agatha to marry Alexander.

In obedience to her motherly adviser, the convalescent remained quiet for a while; but joy seemed to have doubled her strength, for she desired to see Agatha, Alexander, and Andreas, and—she colored, and a beseeching glance met Euryale's eyes—and Diodoros.

But meanwhile the physician Ptolemæus had come into the room, and he would allow no one to come near her this evening but Zeno's daughter. His grave eyes were dim with tears as, when taking leave, he whispered to the Lady Euryale:

"All is well. Even her mind is saved."

He was right. From day to day and from hour to hour her recovery progressed and her strength improved. And there was much for her to see and hear, which did her more good than medicine, even though she had been moved to fresh grief by the death of her brother and many friends.

Like Melissa, her lover and Alexander had been led by thorny paths to the stars which shine on happy souls and shed their light in the hearts of those to whom the higher truth is revealed. It was as Christians that Diodoros and Alexander both came to visit the convalescent. That which had won so many Alexandrians to the blessings of the new faith had attracted them too, and the certainty of finding their beloved among the Christians had been an added inducement to crave instruction from Zeno. And it had been given them in so zealous and captivating a manner that, in their impressionable hearts, the desire for learning had soon been turned to firm conviction and inspired ardor.

Agatha was betrothed to Alexander.

The scorn of his fellow-citizens, which had fallen on the innocent youth and which he had supposed would prevent his ever winning her love, had in fact secured it to him, for Agatha's father was very ready to trust his child to the man who had rescued her, whom she loved, and in whom he saw one of the lowly who should be exalted.

Alexander was not told of Philip's death till his own wounds were healed; but he had meanwhile confided to Andreas that he had made up his mind to fly to a distant land that he might never again see Agatha, and thus not rob the brother on whom he had brought such disaster of the woman he loved. The freedman had heard him with deep emotion, and within a few hours after Andreas had reported to Zeno the self-sacrificing youth's purpose, Zeno had gone to Alexander and greeted him as his son.

Melissa found in Agatha the sister she had so long pined for; and how happy it made her to see her brother's eyes once more sparkle with gladness! Alexander, even as a Christian and as Agatha's husband, remained an artist.

The fortune accumulated by Andreas—the solidi with which he had formerly paid the scapegrace painter's debts included—was applied to the erection of a new and beautiful house of God on the spot where Heron's house had stood. Alexander decorated it with noble pictures, and as this church was soon too small to accommodate the rapidly increasing congregation, he painted the walls of yet another, with figures whose extreme beauty was famous throughout Christendom, and which were preserved and admired till gloomy zealots prohibited the arts in churches and destroyed their works.

Melissa could not be safe in Alexandria. After being quietly married in the house of Polybius, she, with her young husband and Andreas, moved to Carthage, where an uncle of Diodoros dwelt. Love went with them, and, with love, happiness. They were not long compelled to remain in exile; a few months after their marriage news was brought to Carthage that Cæsar had been murdered by the centurion Martialis, prompted by the tribunes Apollinaris and Nemesianus Aurelius. Immediately on this, Macrinus, the prætorian prefect, was proclaimed emperor by the troops.

The ambitious man's sovereignty lasted less than a year; still, the prophecy of Serapion was fulfilled. It cost the Magian his life indeed; for a letter written by him to the prefect, in which he reminded him of what he had foretold, fell into the hands of Caracalla's mother, who opened the letters addressed to her ill-fated son at Antioch, where she was then residing. The warning it contained did not arrive, however, till after Cæsar's death, and before the new sovereign could effectually protect the soothsayer. As soon as Macrinus had mounted the throne the persecution of those who had roused the ire of the unhappy Caracalla was at an end. Diodoros and Melissa, Heron and Polybius, could mingle once more with their fellow-citizens secure from all pursuit.

Diodoros and other friends took care that the suspicion of treachery which had been cast on Heron's household should be abundantly disproved. Nay, the death of Philip, and Melissa's and Alexander's evil fortunes, placed them in the ranks of the foremost foes of tyranny.

Within ten months of his accession Macrinus was overthrown, after his defeat at Immae, where, though the prætorians still fought for him bravely, he took ignominious flight; Julia Domna's grand-nephew was then proclaimed Cæsar by the troops, under the name of Heliogabalus, and the young emperor of fourteen had a statue and a cenotaph erected at Alexandria to Caracalla, whose son he was falsely reputed to be. These two works of art suffered severely at the hands of those on whom the hated and luckless emperor had inflicted such fearful evils. Still, on certain memorial days they were decked with beautiful flowers; and when the new prefect, by order of Caracalla's mother, made inquiry as to who it was that laid them there, he was informed that they came from the finest garden in Alexandria, and that it was Melissa, the wife of the owner, who offered them. This comforted the heart of Julia Domna, and she would have blessed the donor still more warmly if she could have known that Melissa included the name of her crazed son in her prayers to her dying day.

Old Heron, who had settled on the estate of Diodoros and lived there among his birds, less surly than of old, still produced his miniature works of art; he would shake his head over those strange offerings, and once when he found himself alone with old Dido, now a freed-woman, he said, irritably:

"If that little fool had done as I told her she would be empress now, and as good as Julia Domna. But all has turned out well—only that Argutis, whom every one treats as if our old Macedonian blood ran in his veins, was sent yesterday by Melissa with finer flowers for Caracalla's cenotaph than for her own mother's tomb— May her new-fangled god forgive her! There is some Christian nonsense at the bottom of it, no doubt. I stick to the old gods whom my Olympias served, and she always did the best in everything."

Old Polybius, too, remained a heathen; but he allowed the children to please themselves. He and Heron saw their grandchildren brought up as Christians without a remonstrance, for they both understood that Christianity was the faith of the future.

Andreas to his latest day was ever the faithful adviser of old and young alike. In the sunshine of love which smiled upon him his austere zeal turned to considerate tenderness. When at last he lay on his death-bed, and shortly before the end, Melissa asked him what was his favorite verse of the Scriptures, he replied firmly and decidedly:

"Now the fullness of time is come."

"So be it," replied Melissa with tears in her eyes. He smiled and nodded, signed to Diodoros to draw off his signet ring—the only thing his father had saved from the days of his wealth and freedom—and desired Melissa to keep it for his sake. Deeply moved, she put it on her finger; but Andreas pointed to the motto, and said with failing utterance:

"That is your road—and mine—my father's motto:

Per aspera ad astra.   It has guided me to my goal, and
you—all of you.   But the words are in Latin; you understand them?   By rough ways to the stars—   Nay, what
they say ·to me is: Upward, under the burden of the
cross, to bliss here and hereafter—   And you too," he
added, looking in his darling's face.   "You too, both of
you; I know it."

He sighed deeply, and, laying his hand on Melissa's
head as she knelt by his bed, he closed his faithful eyes
in the supporting arms of Diodoros.

THE END.

PRINTING OFFICE OF THE PUBLISHER.